INCREDIBLE BODIES

INCREDIBLE BODIES

Ian McGuire

BLOOMSBURY

First published 2006

Copyright © 2006 by Ian McGuire

The moral right of the author has been asserted

No part of this book may be used or reproduced in any manner
whatsoever without written permission from the Publisher except
in the case of brief quotations embodied in critical articles or reviews.

Bloomsbury Publishing Plc
36 Soho Square
London W1D 3QY

www.bloomsbury.com

Bloomsbury Publishing, London, New York and Berlin

A CIP catalogue record for this book is available from the British Library

ISBN 0 7475 7847 8
ISBN 13 97807475 78475

1 2 3 4 5 6 7 8 9 10

Typeset by Hewer Text UK Ltd, Edinburgh
Printed in Great Britain
by Clays Ltd, St Ives plc

The paper this book is printed on is certified by the © Forest Stewardship
Council 1996 A.C. (FSC). It is ancient-forest friendly. The printer holds FSC
chain of custody SGS-COC-2061

FSC
Mixed Sources
Product group from well-managed
forests and other controlled sources

Cert no. SGS-COC-2061
www.fsc.org
© 1996 Forest Stewardship Council

For Abigail, Grace and Eve

Acknowledgements

I have been helped in any number of ways by the following people (in order of appearance): Francine Prose, Denise Shannon, Deborah Eisenberg, Priyavadita, Su Carroll, Richard Kirkland, Gail Ashton, Arabella Stein, Caleb Thompson, Adisa Lokmic, Rosemary Davidson, Arzu Tahsin. Thanks to all of you.

Part One

Chapter 1

Morris Gutman was woken from a series of astonishing dreams by the unharmonious yelp of his neighbour's car alarm. It was 5.30 a.m. His wife, E, rolled over, relieving him of half the bed clothes.

'It's that bloody Land Rover again,' she whispered.

The air invading Morris's pyjamas was damp, and, he felt, inhumanly chilly. He retrieved the blanket and in doing so caught a gust of E. She smelt as hot and fragrant as a haystack. Their neighbour's car alarm, he suspected, had been designed not only to scare off intruders, but to aurally disable them. It was treating their double glazing with disdain. He put his fingers in his ears. Better, but would it really be possible to sleep in that position, he wondered. Would it be safe? What if he rolled over? Might he pierce an eardrum?

When the alarm finished, Morris experienced a moment of joy so intense it brought tears to his sleep-crusted eyes. Oh, thank God for that, he thought. He closed his eyes and fell back asleep.

Ten minutes later there was a sudden and appalling scream from the next room, a blast of raw noise of the kind you might normally associate with shrapnel wounds or industrial injury. It was Molly, their daughter. Morris sat straight up: his heart was clattering around inside him, he didn't recognise the bedroom, his eyes felt useless and he was gripped by despair. E touched his arm.

'Just leave her,' she said. 'It's just a dream.'

That was right of course, a dream.

He lay down again and realised disconsolately that he needed to pee. Perhaps if he stopped thinking about it . . . No, he definitely needed to go. He crept across the landing. He paused at Molly's door and listened for her breath cutting back and forth like a tiny hacksaw. Once finished, he pondered over whether to flush. Oh well. He flushed. The roar seemed Niagaran; he was certain Molly would wake up. As the tank refilled with a hiss, he stood in pained anticipation. His toes ached with cold, he could hear gusts of rain on the window; downstairs the fridge was humming.

Joy! He tiptoed back past Molly's door. (There was a blue gorilla holding a 'Molly' sign. There were stickers.) He lay down again feeling supremely happy. His newly lightened bladder floated righteously inside his abdomen like a lily on a pond. He checked the alarm clock: 5.50 a.m. Another hour, God willing.

He closed his eyes. E snuffled. He thought he heard something else too. A whimper?

No.

Yes.

Yes, definitely a whimper. Another. Then there was a noise of nasal complaint, followed by a strangulated scream which might in other circumstances have presaged the fall of some mighty oak. Molly was awake for good.

Cursing, Morris Gutman fumbled for his slippers and stomped from the room. Molly was sitting upright, crying. Her open mouth, a small black square cut into the felty greyness of the unlit room, seemed to Morris like the entrance to a secret world of pain and calamity.

'Mol, Mol,' he cooed against the outrageous din. 'What's the matter, sweetheart?'

'Maa, Maa, Maa, Maa,' she cried, 'MaaMaa.'

It was like the plaint of a wounded mastodon, like the moan of some strange and vitriolic football crowd.

'No need for that,' he said, more in hope than in expectation. 'No need for all that, is there? It's just a dream, a *dream*.'

Morris worried as he always did that she would wake the neighbours and that they would start, as they had once or twice before, banging on the walls. That would be more than he could bear.

'Shush,' he said, 'Shush.' Then finally, 'I'll give you a treat, a *treat.*'

She stopped crying.

'Treat, treat, treat, treat,' she sang.

Morris dashed into his study and retrieved a Jammy Dodger from the secret stash unknown even to E. As he gave it to Molly and she lapsed into a contented, crumby silence he experienced a momentary but familiar feeling of failure.

Five minutes later, after an interlude of snorts and tear-wiping, he curled up beside his daughter on the little bed and covered them both with her novelty duvet. She smelt of raspberry jam and sour milk. She was mumbling to herself a word that sounded like 'falafel'. Half asleep, Morris's mind veered, as it always did, towards work. He remembered with dismay the classes he had scheduled that day. In the morning 'Aspects of the Ode', followed by 'Misogyny and the Novel'. Then in the afternoon, what was it again? He was sure something particularly bad. Oh, Christ, yes, 'The History of Critique' – two MA seminars in a row.

Morris held a ten-month post in the Department of English and Cultural Studies at the University of Coketown. He had been hired at the lowest legal salary to replace two professors: one was drying out and the other was touring China on a fat British Academy grant. The advertisement had sought someone with a strong interest in the history of punctuation, queer theory and *ideologikritik* with secondary strengths in diasporic literature, Chaucer and the age of Spenser. The way to get such jobs, Morris had discovered, was to maintain a façade of scholarly endeavour while strongly hinting at one's willingness to cheerfully accept untold amounts of work. There was a certain element of skill involved in this process of placating the consciences of the interviewing panel, who always liked to believe that by offloading their own work they were assisting a young person on to the path of scholarship and wisdom. It was a skill, yes, and one that Morris had, in the five years since he had received his Ph.D., honed, sharpened, even perhaps perfected. But he knew very well that his time was now running out. As in the case of the unmarried debutante (he thought, for example, of Dorothy Portugal in Arthur Alderley's criminally neglected *The Hour of Lead*), there came a time in the career of an academic when 'undrunk the milk of youth curdled in its pot'. After six or seven years the trick would be impossible to pull off. It would be obvious to any panel, however unethical, that his career was going nowhere and that, instead of assisting a young man of promise, they would be merely encouraging someone who probably should not be encouraged any longer.

Molly rolled over sharply and kicked him in the groin. Morris, swallowing a shriek, felt the tingling numbness volley from his stomach to his knees and then back again. She turned back over and whistled briefly like a pressure cooker. Morris reclosed his eyes.

He needed a permanent job. Without one, he wondered, what did the future hold? He would be on the shelf, scrambling each semester for hourly work: proof-reading for Japanese postgrads, Continuing Education – the children of Osaka, the housewives of Alderley Edge. He would be the academic equivalent of hired help. Oh yes, he knew the type too well. There were one or two at every institution he had been to – harried and badly shaven men, their briefcases bristling with dog-eared anthologies and un-marked essays, their bitterness concealed behind thick hedges of outdated literary chit-chat. It was, all in all, a desperate scene. That was why Friday's interview was so important for Morris. A permanent post on offer and he was the inside candidate. *The inside man.* Even though he had been there less than a year. That was how Declan 'The Mad' Monk, Hubert Professor of Anglo-Irish literature had referred to him last week when they had passed in the corridor.

'Oh Morris,' he had called, without breaking stride. 'We're asking for twenty-minute presentations next week. There'll be a letter. Good shortlist I hear, but you're the inside man!'

He had winked and given the thumbs up. Morris never knew how to read the casualness of the Mad Monk – was it a sign of intimacy or disdain? Certainly the Mad Monk was like that with everyone, Morris knew. He wore a fisherman's sweater and jeans and was perpetually ruddy; informality was his *thing*. But as a temporary employee, Morris was unnaturally sensitive to signs from above. He knew how these things worked; he had seen others nip in ahead of him too many times before. It was the small things that counted – the pithy interjections in a departmental meeting, the right riposte over coffee and KitKats, the knowing reference to the latest *TLS*. Oh God, God, God, Morris wondered vehemently, would things *ever* fall his way? He had tried so hard this time. He had even taken up smoking in the face of E's vehement protests, so as to be able to stand shivering outside the south entrance with the department's sickly gang of nicotine addicts: Roy Forecastle, Nigel Qwerty, Pedma Roshi. Not big players any of them, but all senior lecturers who might perhaps bend an ear. He had paid a price of course – two chest infections and his teeth were turning yellow. E didn't like that one bit, but it would all be worth it if only . . . if only . . . But now he had the presentation to consider. That had come out of the blue. All he had to hand was his old stuff on Alderley – 'Alderley in America', 'Alderley and Phrenology'. What did they expect? Over the last five years he had taught twenty-eight different courses at four separate institutions. They had ranged in content from *Beowulf* to *Police Academy II*. He had had no time to read or write or research. He had no sense of what his interests were; he had no interests left, not really. Oh, occasionally he caught a glimpse of an idea, something which might make an article or con-ference paper; once or twice he snatched an afternoon in the library, but it never went anywhere. During the year he was too exhausted, and the summers he seemed to spend mainly at the hospital: his father's cancer, E's complex pregnancy, Molly's ever-evolving allergies.

That was one reason he needed this job, to give his brain a chance to breathe. Perhaps he could tart up the phrenology essay. Wasn't the body still big? Of course he would be the only person in the room ever to have read Alderley. He may indeed have been the only person north of Birmingham ever to have read Alderley – not of course counting the bastard Conrad Underseel at Bangor. That was always a disadvantage, but it was too late to be helped. If he actually got a job he could branch out, Kipling perhaps. Then there was the panel to consider, of course. Declan was OK, but then there was the Dean, 'Crocodile' McWurter – even professors were frightened of him. Darian Cavendish (*The Catholic Sensibility of Coventry Patmore*, Oxford, 1972), was just weird. There would be someone from Middle Eastern Studies – another loose cannon – and most troubling of all, Zoe Cable, the new research fellow.

Zoe Cable was younger than Morris and already had a book and some monster grant under her belt. But it wasn't that, or it wasn't only that, which bothered him. There was something else, much more disturbing: on the brief occasions Morris had met and talked to Zoe, she had seemed to be genuinely happy. He had never encountered that in an academic before and it bothered him a lot; indeed, it threw everything he had learnt into question. Academics were not happy. Not English academics with no travel funds and lecture rooms packed with truculent and underachieving students. Granted, they were occasionally smug if they had put one over on a colleague, or gleeful when they were first hired, or uproarious if they were drunk, but no one was ever happy, never really happy. He had the troubling sense that Zoe Cable was playing by different rules. He had heard her refer to the Crocodile as a sweetie; he had heard her bandy sexual innuendos with Mabel in the office. This was not normal, this was not right. It was clear that Zoe Cable knew something he didn't. She made him feel stupid, and for Morris, as for any academic on a temporary contract, that was definitely the worst feeling in the world.

It was not yet 6 a.m. but he was already horribly wide awake. His head was dense with unpleasantness and his stomach felt like a grease-clogged drain. How would he survive the day? Without waking up, Molly rolled over again, kicked him in the stomach and stuck her fist into his mouth. Her hand tasted soft and salty.

8

He opened his eyes and there she was, her face big and blurry pushed right up against his. He reached under her pyjama top and felt the vertebrae of her back like a row of pebbles under the skin. Her hair smelt musty and rancorous; it hadn't been washed for weeks. She had a small rosette of eczema on her chin.

Before her arrival, Morris had not expected to love her in the way he did. He had expected pride and pleasure and sentiment of various kinds, but not yearning or desire, not this craving to smell and touch. He wondered sometimes whether he should be ashamed of it, whether he had stepped over some line. Morris gently bit her forearm; it was soft and damp as unrisen dough. She pushed him off.

'Move along,' she shouted drowsily. 'Go to Rotherham.'

E was in the bathroom, groaning. That was something they shared. They had run out of dried prunes two days ago and now look (or listen) where they were. His turn would come, no doubt after coffee. Such things creep up on you, he thought: constipation, nasal hair, tooth decay. He hadn't danced for years, not that he was ever any good at it, but it was the principle he was thinking of.

He dressed Molly in slippers and a robe and carried her downstairs. Several slugs were stuck to the outside of the kitchen window like slick globs of chewing gum. The perpetual dampness of Coketown formed an ideal climate for gastropods. Birds found it hard to survive the pollution, but their garden in particular seemed to serve as a Club Med for snails and other molluscs. Molly could gather them by the bucket load.

'Toast or cereal?' he asked.

'Egg.'

'Egg *what*?'

'Egg now.'

As he boiled the water, the kitchen fogged up like a sauna. Molly was running around pretending to be a goat. Morris felt suddenly drawn out and wretched. His eyes ached from behind, and his insides felt as though they had recently been sandpapered. The thought of Declan Monk popped into his head for no

9

reason. He wanted to cry. Molly collided with a chair, spilled her cup of milk across the floor and started howling.

'Oh for *Godsake*, Molly.'

Morris picked her up too abruptly and dropped her into the booster seat. As he mopped the floor, the howling became louder and more deliberate. Morris felt anger, red and hollow, ballooning inside him. For a second he didn't care about anything at all.

'Will you please BE QUIET!'

The roar of his voice filled and sharpened the room like a flashbulb. There was a blissful second of silent backwash before Molly's face turned red, her mouth reopened and the scream whirred and wowed above them like an air-raid warning.

E arrived, shot a glance at Morris and picked Molly up for a cuddle. Her face paled from plum to peach.

Morris sat down in the corner and began to read the *South Coketown Advertiser*.

'They're putting double yellow lines on Oswald Road,' he said. 'There's been another cock-up at the Coketown Royal Infirmary.'

'What now?'

'Corpse in the laundry. They're reviewing procedures.' He read a little more. 'It's a cost benefit sort of thing apparently.'

'It usually is.' She was feeding Molly half a satsuma.

He paused. 'Are you implying something by that?'

'Implying?'

'By that remark. It just seems to me that that remark is freighted with implications. Of various kinds.' Now he was reading the small ads.

'Does your mother still want a bread maker? There's one in here for twenty pounds, *need a quick sale*.'

'No, that was just a phase. You know how she is with labour-saving devices.'

'She has the roving eye.'

'Now it's high-pressure washers.'

'That follows.'

'I wasn't implying anything. There was no implication at all. I can't imagine what you are thinking of.'

'More satsuma,' demanded Molly. She seemed to be developing a nasty eye infection.

'Are you worried about Friday?'

Morris put down the paper.

'Now there's a presentation,' he said. 'Did I mention that?'

'That's late in the day, isn't it? Don't they have rules?'

'What can I do? I'm powerless. My hands are tied.'

There was a pause.

'Alderley?' she asked.

He nodded.

'America or phrenology?'

'Phrenology I think.'

'It's worked before.'

'The Eccles Institute, yes. But it was my enthusiasm for marking that really swung it there.'

'That was the feedback you got?'

'That was it. This time it's the panel which concerns me most.'

'But you know them. You're the inside candidate.'

'The inside man. Yes, but that's it – I lack the element of surprise, of mystery. I'm an open book. What you see is what you get.'

'That's good.'

'No, it's not good. It's bad. Panels don't want certainty. They don't want knowledge. They want hope, possibility. They want someone to mirror their desires, however perverse and varied they may be.'

'And do their marking for them.'

'That too. But don't you see? The perfect candidate, should he or she exist, will be contentless. Just a shiny, fractured surface with no depth – glints and flashes, pure expectation.'

'Very postmodern.'

'I'm practising. How do I sound?'

'Like the inside man.'

*　　*　　*

11

Their car squirted erratically down Sheffield Road. Morris needed to have the clutch looked at again. The MOT was due soon. He feared the garage. Whenever he went there he felt his manliness was on trial. The frequent and incomprehensible payments he made to Derek the mechanic served only, he felt, as a kind of bail whose term he was sure would eventually, inevitably expire. Last time, Derek had implied that the effort of getting the car through its MOT was above and beyond the call of duty, and that Morris should really consider upgrading his vehicle. The thought of doing so filled Morris with horror: the money, the decision – which he would almost certainly get wrong. He hoped vaguely that Derek, whose mental processes were as much a mystery to Morris as the machinery he worked on, would forget or forgive his previous prophecy.

'Funny game!' cried Molly as they kangarooed away from a zebra crossing. E was reading her work diary.

'My boss really is a bitch on wheels,' she said.

'Yes you've mentioned that before.'

'Oh have I? Well I'm sorry to bore you. I'm sorry to make your life so fucking dull!'

Morris held up his hands.

She yelled: 'Idiot! What are you doing? You'll crash!'

He put his hands back on the wheel.

There were several minutes of silence.

'Sorry to be an arsehole,' she said. 'My diary is a real horror story.'

Morris nodded. In the back, Molly was beginning to voice her feelings about going to nursery. The rain blew hard and horizontal.

'Is it all worth it?' Morris asked.

'You're not thinking of Majorca again?'

'Majorca is just a symbol, just a metaphor.'

'Then it doesn't exist.'

'You should read Coleridge.'

'Are you still practising?'

'No.' He looked sullen. 'When are we ever happy?'

'Is that a real question?'

12

He nodded.

'You arsehole.'

'I want an answer.'

'All the time, that's when we're happy, Morris. All the bloody time.'

Chapter 2

Zoe Cable was woken at 7 a.m. by the monotonal trills of her Nokia. She reached over blurrily.

'Who on earth is it?' she shouted. 'And have you even the merest conception of the fucking time?'

'Gaston, no, we're eight hours *ahead* you twat. You're having drinks with who? Well tell him *From Dusk Till Dawn* was unwatchable. Love you too. Buy another watch. Taarah.'

Zoe Cable stood up and stretched. She blinked twice and shook her head. The purple parabolas of her bedroom partition shuddered then settled. She had been up late working on a funding proposal, then a swift nightcap at the Pooh Bar had turned into three or four, as it usually did. At least, she thought, in her own defence, she had fended off Berthold the web designer. Sunday-night shagging, for all its charms, played hell with one's schedule. Talking of which, she picked up her Palm Pilot. Before lunch she had her serial killer seminar, then in the afternoon a meeting with Jocelyn and Darren, her research assistants; her regular weekly cabal with Donald; Faculty RPC at four; workout with Rumi at five; then, in the evening, noodles and dancing with Melvin, her editor, up from London for the night. She was trusting that if she got Melvin sufficiently pissed and showed him the delights of the ladyboys of Coketown he would stop dragging his high heels on that series proposal. She went into the kitchen, switched on the coffee maker, got a bottle of seaweed smoothie from the fridge and lit a cigarette.

She looked out of the circular kitchen window: Corporation Square was already clogged by traffic; sad-looking commuters were traipsing like a beaten army over the new teak and steel footbridge linking Peterloo station with the Metro tram depot. It was raining torrentially, of course, but that barely registered: in the six months Zoe had been in Coketown she had already become acclimatised – here, as someone had mentioned at the interview, soddenness quickly became a way of life. But at least it was only for three years. After that, London; then, when her contacts panned out, America. Coketown was just a stepping stone, albeit a particularly wet and slippery one.

After finishing her cigarette, Zoe Cable lay down on the kitchen floor and imagined a warm golden light was sweeping over her body from head to toe. As the light passed over, her muscles relaxed one by one. After a few minutes her flesh felt sodden and imprecise. She breathed deeply in and out five times and began to visualise *the scene*. *The scene* in essence had not changed for three years. She had allowed herself certain updates – mainly dictated by changes in circumstances and developments in technology or fashion – but at heart it was the same. Indeed, with every step she took forwards (and over the last three years she had taken very many steps – some small; some, even to her, astonishingly large) the more *the scene* solidified and the less possible it was to imagine it as anything other than it always was.

Zoe is sitting by a pool in Beverley Hills with cult movie director Hoyt Dashell. She is wearing a black T-shirt and sunglasses. Her hair is cut short and dyed bright red. Hoyt Dashell, who has aged poorly, is wearing a red cheesecloth shirt and matching sweatband. He has a grey beard and bright green contacts. It is early evening. She is smoking. You can hear cicadas in the background. Hoyt Dashell occasionally brushes away a fly. They are discussing his next film project, which is to be based on her last book, *Again, Again – serialcomputersexcrime*.

'This'll be the first feature based on an academic work,' Hoyt Dashell explains. 'I'm *real* excited.'

'Oh, Hoyt, you old curmudgeon, those labels are all out

15

of date. The publishers boggle when they see my books. Look how it's listed.' She picks up a copy of *Again, Again* from the mosaic coffee table next to her. 'Fiction, Faction, Autobiography, Travel, New Age, Theology, Economics, History, Technology, Erotica . . . Young Adults.'

Hoyt Dashell jumps.

'I'm just being facetious, but really, academic *schmacademic*. Now, who have you got lined up to play me?'

Hoyt passes her a sheaf of headshots. Zoe rifles though them rapidly.

'This one,' she finally announces. (It is a woman of astonishing, alien beauty.) 'This is the one.'

Hoyt Dashell looks at it.

'This *is* the one,' he says. He makes a series of rapid phone calls. Zoe Cable lights a humungous joint. The kidney-shaped pool is lit from below; next to it the hot tub steams. There is a whiff of mesquite and swordfish from the outside grill.

'Let's talk money,' Zoe says. 'What's my cut?'

'Oh, millions and millions, I guess. But really, Zoe, man,' Hoyt Dashell gestures around. 'You're not hurting.'

The coffee machine pinged and Zoe Cable slowly opened her eyes. She smiled gently and began her daily affirmations.

'You zig,' she stated, 'and I zag.'

She drank her coffee, took two vitamin tablets, ran a bath and opened her laptop. She had seventeen emails. She discarded five of them and opened one from Declan Monk. Subject: Interviews on Friday.

Hey Zoe, I attach all the guff for Friday. It'll be piss easy (fingers crossed). There's you, me, the Crocodile, nutty Darian, and Mohammad from Middle Eastern Studies. Crocodile wants anyone willing and cheap, I play squash with Mohammed so he'll do what we say, Darian probably wants a Jesuit or at least a Catholic, but since there's none on the shortlist (as far as I can tell) I'm assuming she'll sulk.

16

Have a gander anyway. We'll meet @ 12. You're a champ.
Luv Declan.

Zoe Cable printed the attachment (CVs and cover letters) and read it in the bath. There were five people on the shortlist. She had slept with only one of them. Having swiftly read each application, she arranged them in order of preference, placed the pile on the toilet seat and got out of the bath. The person she had slept with was second. Morris Gutman was fourth. Her decisions were not tainted by emotion or guesswork. There was no one in the country with a subtler sense of the academic job market than Zoe Cable. She had tracked its patterns for years, she had observed and absorbed its quirks and trends, its aberrations. She understood it, she trusted it, perhaps in some odd way she even loved it – it was after all her chosen vehicle. So when she rated Morris Gutman fourth in a field of five, it was not a sign of peevishness, prejudice, ideological disagreement, ignorance, or even (hardly!) jealousy. It was a clear-headed assessment of his candidature, which was – to put it frankly and in layman's terms – piss-poor. She knew Morris, of course, from corridors and staff meetings and recognised that his position as inside candidate offered certain advantages, but these advantages were outweighed, far outweighed by the horrors of his CV. Reading it prompted within her sensations of compassion, disdain and mild nausea. Compassion: well with better guidance, with *any* guidance, some of the worst things might at least have been avoided. Disdain: *Alderley* for Christsake. Nausea: the Eccles Institute – was that a cry for help?

Zoe Cable got dressed, messed up her hair and put on her waterproofs. She walked through the usual downpour to the tram stop. As she waited amidst a gaggle of gloomy temps, gay businessmen and sodden students, she closed her eyes and imagined that there was a silver cord linking the crown of her head to the dark blanket of clouds above her and another linking the soles of her feet to the centre of the earth. This provoked, as usual, a sense of immense certainty and inner spaciousness. She smiled. The tram arrived, the doors slid open directly in front of her and Zoe got on, taking the last available seat.

The tram started with a hum. Zoe looked up: one of the temps wearing a goatee beard and a sou'wester smiled at her lasciviously. She winked back at him and bared her teeth.

You zig, she silently reminded herself, and I zag.

Chapter 3

Morris Gutman's 11–1 class, 'Misogyny and the Novel', was not going well. It was not going terribly badly, he thought to himself as he waited for an answer to what he considered a rather good question about vaginal symbolism, but it was certainly not going well. The group had never really re-bounded, he felt, from learning in week two that this semester's course would be taught not by Professor Deirdre Pluck – author of the bestselling *The End of Sex*, well-known 70s feminist and occasional contributor to *Going Critical* on BBC2 – but instead by Morris Gutman, author of 'Arthur Alderley in America', published to vast uninterest in the *Hong Kong Journal of English Studies*, as well as numerous (unpaid) book reviews in the same organ. Yes, ever since then he felt there had been an atmosphere of languid belligerence about them. A tendency to clam up was not, in itself, unusual among Coketown students, but on this occasion it was combined with sporadic outbursts, either individual or communal, which seemed to Morris to express a belief that they had been somehow duped – though whether they considered themselves victims of Morris, Professor Pluck, the University of Coketown or life in general, he found it impossible to say.

'Let's put it this way then,' Morris said after three and a half minutes of silence. 'Has anyone here been potholing?'

Rather surprisingly, a feeble-looking youth with bleached hair raised his hand.

'Urr, yeh,' he said. 'When I was a Venture Scout, we went to Derbyshire a lot.' He blushed.

'Ah, Derbyshire, the High Peak, prime potholing country.'

Morris felt enlivened by this unusual level of cooperation. 'So what was it like?'

'Sorry?'

'The caves, the potholing . . . If you had to choose the word to describe it, what would it be?'

The youth thought for a moment.

'Life-threatening,' he finally said.

'That's two words,' someone objected.

'It could be hyphenated,' Morris said. 'We'll let it pass. Let's not get entangled in minutiae. Life-threatening is good. Anything else?'

The youth thought again.

'Dark,' he said, 'wet, smelly. Er, it were quite exciting though.'

'Great.' Morris wrote a list of the youth's words on the whiteboard.

'All right, anyone else? You don't have to have had personal contact with caves – just whatever springs to mind. Free association.'

'Pardon?'

'Just whatever you think of.'

'Hermits,' someone said. Morris wrote that in small letters.

'Safety,' someone else said. Morris wrote that in rather larger letters.

'Holes.'

'Hiding.'

'Smugglers.'

'Plato,' (a foreign student).

After a few minutes, the whiteboard was quite full.

'OK,' Morris stepped to one side. 'Ring any bells?'

Morris felt he had them, for once. They seemed, if not interested, at least alert.

After a few minutes, Peter – twenty-seven, keen, idiosyncratic, disorganised hair, Oxfam poncho, new tongue stud – raised his hand.

'I'm a bit confused,' he said. 'I read the whole thing. OK, I may have skimmed some bits, but I don't remember any potholing in it at all.'

'Me neither,' said someone else.

'Not potholing *per se*. But the Marabar Caves – remember them?' Several people nodded. There was life in them yet. 'So what do you think?' he pointed at the board.

Peter squinted. 'Those words are misogynist words. This must be another of them misogynist novels.'

'Well, *yes*, but hold on a second.' But before he could intervene, they had all written it down (except of course those that never wrote anything down): 'Misogynist novel.'

Peter was shaking his head. 'I read the whole thing,' he said, 'and I never realised.'

'Are there any novels which *aren't* misogynist?' someone clever shouted out belligerently from the back.

'Well that's a good question,' said Morris, whose enthusiasm was not entirely dampened. 'If you look, for example, at the oeuvre of Arthur Alderley, a self-proclaimed feminist, albeit to modern eyes of a rather Victorian kind . . .'

They were looking at their watches: it was already one. The corridors were filling with hordes of hungry students; a chattering, grumbling mass in quest of food. Baked potatoes, chunky soup, meat pies, pasties, curry – they were omnivorous as lava.

'*To the Lighthouse* next week,' he shouted above the noises of departure.

Morris yawned and aimlessly scanned the smelly and denuded seminar room. He had an hour. If he ate quickly, that would give him forty minutes to at least half-prepare for the very dreadful 'History of Critique'. What was it this week? He found a syllabus near the bottom of his briefcase: Kant and Foucault. Shit. He would have to skim even more aggressively than normal.

On the way to the Staff House, Morris ran into Bernard Littlejohn, romanticist and notorious malcontent.

'Morris,' he called, 'will you join me in a mess of pottage before the swine descend once more?'

'How are you Bernard?'

'What? Oh, don't ask. They're banging on my door asking for essays already. I tell them to fuck off. I send them to the Mad Monk – go and ask him why I haven't marked your bloody essays. Ask him about the whereabouts of Professors Greenspot and Dawlish while you're there. One's in the Priory sipping non-alcoholic cocktails, and the other's sitting on his fat arse in Ho Chi Minh City; they're both pulling down three times my salary. How are you, anyway?'

Morris grimaced. ' "History of Critique" after lunch.'

' "History of Critique", bloody hell. That's one of Greenspot's, isn't it? No offence Morris, but really, what's the bloody point? This lot can't read a poem. Their ignorance astounds me; they're so ignorant they're not even ashamed of it. I tell them to bugger off and read the Bible. They think I'm joking. They think the Passion is some kind of fruit. Ecclesiastical history is a completely closed book. They ring me up at home to complain about their marks. They ask for *pointers* on how to *improve*. I tell them: switch off your mobile phone, take out your nose ring and read a bloody book or two. They don't like that one bit – they want handouts, websites. They ring me *at home*! In my day . . . What have we got here then? The usual array of insults.'

Bernard was surveying the sandwiches on offer in the Staff House chiller cabinet. He selected one with a look of revulsion and they joined the rag-tag queue of bearded men in patterned sweaters. 'Coronation chicken,' Bernard read from his sandwich box, 'but which coronation, I'd like to know – George the bloody V I bet. It's all frozen and microwaved – two pounds ten. What's wrong with a nice hot lunch? Bit of beef, few veg, sets you up nicely for the afternoon. With this stuff, I'm farting till five o'clock. It's no wonder the peasants are revolting.'

Morris ordered a baked potato and a cup of tea. They sat down at a wobbly table beside a dusty cheese plant.

'I've got my interview on Friday. There's a presentation.'

'Oh Jesus,' Bernard looked suddenly alarmed. 'Who's on the panel?'

Morris told him. Bernard grimaced. 'If they had one slightest shred of common decency between them, you wouldn't even have to interview. What's your presentation?'

'Alderley.'

'Oh yes, I've always meant to read him. Who was it who wrote the biography? Bloke from Bangor?'

'Conrad Underseel.'

'That's right. Solid stuff, real scholarship. Won't go down too well with Zoe Cable, I'm afraid. She's all hegemony and decentring. Perhaps you could spice it up a bit.'

Morris looked blank and fearful.

'No, of course not, why should you? Stick to your guns.'

Bernard bit into his sandwich; the pale yellow filling oozed from its seams. Morris poured his tea. Half of it dribbled down the spout and on to his jeans.

'Those teapots are made in Taiwan,' Bernard said. The Vice-Chancellor has Wedgwood apparently. Oh yes, at his official residence. Declan was there the other day. Did you hear? Official luncheon for some bigwig from the Ministry. So much for left-wing politics – don't suppose Declan sold too many copies of *Socialist Worker* over the canapés.'

'Is Declan political?'

'Used to be. But I think he was mainly in it for the shagging. "Up the Revolution" and all that. Now he's got his sights on Zoe Cable apparently.'

'Really?'

Bernard shrugged. Then his eyes widened with alarm.

'Oh bugger it. It's her and the Crocodile. They've seen us.'

Morris turned round. Zoe Cable and the Dean were heading for their table. Oh God, no, why was this happening? Morris's stomach clenched and his mouth turned suddenly arid.

'Aren't there any other tables?' he hissed.

Without looking at Morris, Bernard shook his head and then grinned hugely.

'Donald,' he said, 'do join us.'

The Crocodile, who was best known for his terrifying unpredictability, smiled weakly.

'Thanks Bernard, don't mind if I do. Hello Morris.'

Morris smiled. Zoe Cable sat down next to him. She smelled of fruit and swimming pools.

'All right Bernard? Hiya Morris,' she touched him lightly on the shoulder.

Morris sustained his smile a little longer.

'Anyway Donald,' she said, 'as I was saying, this student Dirck van Camper in "Serial Killers". He's just so terrific and wonderful we have to keep him. I insist.'

The Crocodile smiled. 'He's from the Netherlands?'

'Amsterdam, yes. He's worked with Serge Rubicon and Tatyana Balti. I'd have him as a research assistant, but I'm full up with Jocelyn and Darren. He'll definitely stay if we put together the right package. Can you talk to Hildegaard for me? After RPC I'm in her bad books.'

'Oh, are you really?' The Crocodile licked the cappuccino foam from his moustache and looked interested.

'Oh yes, you know. There was that row about bursary disembursement and I backed Geraldine. I owed her one after that UPP cock-up, but Hildegaard didn't see it like that.'

The Crocodile chuckled. 'Oh no, she wouldn't,' he said.

Morris was tucking into his baked potato, searching urgently for something clever, witty or at least grammatical to say. He was having lunch with forty per cent of the interview panel. He was their inside man. It was crunch time.

'Honestly Donald, we should do what it takes. Dirck van Camper is simply brilliant, isn't he Morris? You must know him from "History of Critique." You can back me up.'

'After last semester's shortfall, and with the projected recruitment numbers, you'll get nothing from Hildegaard. We could use the claw-back overheads, but it would have to be a very special case.'

They all looked at Morris.

'Ummm.' Morris knew Dirck van Camper very well. He was a spindly six-foot five with a shaved head and little rectangular glasses. He wore a vintage three-piece suit to class. It was brown and the trousers were flared; it made him look like a disco Nazi. He was the only person Morris had ever met whose speech seemed footnoted. The term that sprang to Morris's mind was 'smartarse'.

24

'Oh yes. He's certainly very . . . very adept.'

'*Adept!*'

The Crocodile had pounced. He leaned forward and looked straight into Morris's eyes. Bernard cringed. Morris shuddered and turned red. Panicking, he tried to reassure himself that 'adept' was a real word, an English word.

'He's always struck me,' Morris croaked, 'as extremely fluid, flu*ent*. His English.'

'Oh well, they always are aren't they?' Bernard chipped in helplessly. 'Put our lot to shame. You'll get more sense from one foreign student than a room full of English. I feel sorry for them sometimes, coming here. They've been sold a pig in a poke.'

The Crocodile looked surprised.

'Some of them have,' Bernard backtracked. 'Not talking about the Japanese of course. I have a Japanese postgrad. Yuka something. Bird imagery in Wordsworth, a lovely person, but it's like getting blood out of a stone. It really is . . .' Bernard faded away. He took another, rather desperate, bite of coronation chicken.

'So Morris,' the Crocodile continued as if Bernard had never spoken, 'you're backing Zoe on this. You think he's worth a studentship.' He looked over at Zoe. 'Well, it would have to be three years.'

Zoe nodded.

Morris swallowed. 'Yes I do. Absolutely.'

The Crocodile sat back. 'Very well, I'll get Sam to do the paperwork. Could you ask him to come and see me, Morris? I have to go through FBC, of course, but I don't see a problem.'

'That's smashing,' said Zoe.

Was the Crocodile taking the piss? Morris wondered. As if Morris's opinion meant anything.

'Aren't you going to eat the skin, Morris?' Zoe asked.

'What?'

'The potato. It's the best bit.'

'Oh yes, all the vitamin C is in there,' agreed the Crocodile.

After a moment Morris started eating the skin.

25

'Talking of the Orient,' the Crocodile said, 'has anyone met Professor Yin? He's exchanging with Dawlish. A very unusual chap.'

'Oh he's a total wanker,' Zoe said. 'I asked him about Manga, but all he wants to talk about is Malory.'

They all laughed.

'He's a real man of letters,' said the Crocodile.

'Don't you mean pictograms?' joked Bernard.

As they bantered, Morris pondered the earlier exchange. Was there any way back? *Adept*, what could he have meant by that? Perhaps he should have told them what he really thought of Dirck van Camper. No, that would only have antagonised Zoe Cable, and the Crocodile wouldn't have believed him. Maybe Dirck van Camper *was* some kind of genius; how would Morris know? God, 'The History of Critique', a nightmare. He looked at his watch: 1.25 p.m. He should go and cram for half an hour. But he couldn't just leave – they would think that was odd. They would talk about him after he left. Bernard wouldn't save him. He turned to Play-Doh whenever the Crocodile was on the scene.

'Donald, can I bring you another cappuccino?' asked Bernard, rising. The Crocodile shook his head.

'Zoe?'

'Double espresso thanks.'

'Morris?'

'Same for me.' He had already drunk too much coffee, he was supposed to be leaving and he hated espresso. But it seemed the easiest thing to say. He immediately hated himself for it. He thought about calling Bernard back but didn't dare.

Zoe Cable reached into her bag (an Italian construction of fibreglass and suede) and took out her cigarettes and mobile phone.

'You can't smoke in here,' Morris blurted before he knew what he was saying.

Zoe was unfazed. 'Oh Christ, I know. But I just like to look at them. It's a comfort thing.' Then, to the Crocodile, 'You know I'm down to eight a day?'

Cigarettes, Morris thought, might be a topic he could engage with.

'I just started,' he said. 'Smoking.'

'Really?' They both looked at him with interest.

'Splendid,' said the Crocodile, who had a well-known penchant for cheroots. 'Nothing like bucking the trend.'

'Bloody hell Morris, you're a renegade. What's next? Fox hunting, whaleburgers, paedophilia, unsafe sex?'

The Crocodile roared with laughter.

'That's right,' joked Morris, getting into the swing, feeling rather encouraged. 'I only eat genetically modified food. And my hobbies include tree felling and vivisection.'

Zoe laughed. Bernard came back.

'It's political correctness gone mad,' he said, half-hearing Morris's last remark. 'I get it all the time. They don't know a sonnet from a hole in the ground, but they call me a sexist for not teaching Dorothy Wordsworth. I tell them if we had world enough and time, I'd do it all, but I've only got eleven weeks and you lot think that Ozymandias is in Black Sabbath.'

'The sonnet is an inherently phallocentric form,' Zoe said. 'Ten lines and a climax – wham bam thank you ma'am. Where's the fun in that? No wonder they're not interested.'

'Wham bam!' Bernard momentarily forgot the company he was in. 'What about Elizabeth Barrett Browning, Christina Rossetti, Emily Dickinson, even bloody Sylvia Plath? That's theoretical fascism!'

'Are you joking?' Morris asked Zoe.

'Yes I am, but I like to wind Bernard up. It gives him something to live for.'

The Crocodile roared again.

Bernard went pink. 'Oh bloody hell,' he said.

Morris drank his double espresso and looked at his watch. He felt the situation had improved, if only mildly. If he could engineer a quick and reasonably successful exit, then perhaps the lunch would not have damaged his chances too grievously. They had seemed to like the smoking thing.

The conversation had moved on to classical music. Bernard

27

was denouncing the conductor of the Coketown Philharmonic as a talentless fraud; the Crocodile was offering outside information on his probable successor; Zoe was explaining that she once shared a flat in Berlin with Yo Yo Ma.

'Well, I have to go,' Morris said, ostentatiously rechecking his watch. No one responded. He wasn't sure what to do next. Should he just get up and leave, or should he say it again more loudly? He felt suddenly overheated and in need of the toilet – probably the double espresso. He stood up. 'Well I'm off,' he said.

'Cheers Morris,' said Bernard vaguely.

Morris stared at the other two – were they deliberately snubbing him? Or was this normal in these circles? Perhaps goodbyes were no longer de rigueur – if so his hesitation was only more humiliating. They were talking as if he were no longer there. After a few seconds he caught the Crocodile's eye and saw, he thought, the tiniest of nods. Zoe? He couldn't stand there any longer waiting for her to respond, it was ludicrous. He walked away flushed and breathless. It had been a disaster after all. He passed the chiller cabinet and pushed through the double doors. He wished, madly, that he had an axe with him. He couldn't imagine what he would do with such an instrument, but it would at least serve as a focus for the sensations of rage and shame which rocked him at times like this. It could certainly be a small axe if necessary – a hatchet – and it wouldn't even have to be particularly sharp. He just needed something, a symbol.

Oh Christ, it was 1.55, 'The History of Critique.'

Chapter 4

Zoe Cable's enthusiasm for Dirck van Camper had begun two weeks before, when they had run into each other at a party. It was then that she had learned not only that he had worked with Rubicon and Balti, but also, amazingly, that he was the stepson of über-theorist Firenze Beach, author of *Incredible Bodies: Flesh Without Form* and latterly the magisterial three-volume *History of Dismay*. Firenze Beach was hot, painfully, pulsatingly hot. She still rather quirkily based herself in Belgium, but after her last two books she could really have taken her pick. There were already several adulatory websites and one actual journal devoted to her work. Zoe Cable had seen her at conferences – Copenhagen, San Diego, Venice – but she had never managed to snatch more than a few words with her before Beach was swept off to a dinner or prize-giving. Now Firenze Beach's stepson was her student. Zoe Cable was not terribly surprised – she accepted extraordinary strokes of luck as a normal effect of her visualisation regime – but all the same she was never fully prepared for the form they would take. Firenze Beach's stepson. Bloody hell!

The party took place in the penthouse apartment of the Cottonopolis – a new warehouse conversion on the edge of the Coketown ship canal. After chatting for a while, Zoe and Dirck van Camper wandered out onto the terrace to share a joint. Although the terrace was sensibly roofed with glass, gusts of lukewarm drizzle still occasionally reached them. Zoe was wearing red, wet-look waders. Dirck, clad only in a brown corduroy catsuit and desert boots, shivered theatrically.

As Dirck fired it up, Zoe Cable looked eastwards along the

canal towards central Coketown. There it all was, snug under a crust of drizzle and light pollution: the soot-smirched brutalism of Corporation Square, the pillowy yellow floodlights of the all-seater Postlethwaite Stadium, the velodrome, the skateboard park and, crouched like a giant armadillo among the huddled terraces of Rawpool, the lottery-funded Museum of Artificial Fabrics. Far to the west she could see the vainglorious minarets of the Beigewater shopping complex, while closer by a mile or so shone the newly completed five-star Orpington Hotel, a confection of concrete and stainless steel whose shape recalled, depending on whom you spoke to, either the subtle action of light on water or a giant silver lasagne. Dirck van Camper was rather a long way from home, Zoe thought. Much further, surely, than he himself could realise. She wondered to herself how exactly this would play out. What precise form her advantage would take. She took another huge hit and waited. She had learned long ago not to press such things.

The lights of Coketown glowed momentarily brighter.

'Great weed,' she said at last.

'Yeh, my mother grows it.'

'Does she really?!' (She was smoking Firenze Beach's pot!)

'I like your boots,' he said.

'Indeed.' She swiveled slightly to show them off. 'Fetishistic yet practical – nowhere else but Coketown.'

Dirck chortled. 'My bicycle has moss growing on it. It's just incredible.'

'Oh that's par for the course. Wait for the mushrooms. So Dirck,' she stood back and looked him up and down, 'what brings you to the plughole of England?'

'My lover.' He grinned rather lasciviously and pointed back through the plate-glass double doors to a tall lymphatic woman with big earrings and extreme make-up.

'Dorothy. She's a grad student in anthropology. We met in Uttar Pradesh.'

'She's terrifically beautiful.'

Dorothy, Zoe noticed, was wearing paratrooper boots beneath her sleeveless ivory silk sheath. She was as tall, white and ropey as he was. Zoe imagined their copulation would resemble the tying of a large fleshy knot.

'Of course.'

'Will you marry her?'

Dirck van Camper, who was twenty-five, seemed rather taken aback by this suggestion. Zoe Cable had guessed he might be.

'I have only one semester here. And then I must return to the Netherlands for my exams.'

'Why don't you stay?'

'No, it is not possible. I had discussions with Barbara at Student Exchange. She said only if I pay, what, five grand?' He shrugged at the absurdity of the idea.

'Anthropology?' Zoe said speculatively. 'She must know Ross Goater.' Ross Goater was a young, handsome and notoriously oversexed anthropology lecturer – he worked on patterns of promiscuity in tribal cultures and in the right light resembled Antonio Banderas.

Dirck nodded sullenly. 'He is her advisor.'

So that was how it would work. Sex. What else really was there? All the energies of the universe coalesced in that one thing. If mass was energy, Zoe thought, (she really was quite stoned) what was energy but lust? Lust in action. Those worlds upon worlds, those swooping, wild-haired galaxies were just gatherings of cosmic lewdness: expansion, attraction, arousal, collapse. The pulsar. The black hole. The big bang! God, how obvious did it need to be?

'I hear he's terribly good.'

Dirck swallowed without wishing to. 'Do you know him?'

'Only by reputation. I hear he's very hands-on.' Dirck's eyes widened. This was easier than she expected.

'Did I tell you how much I enjoyed your neo-cannibalism presentation?' Zoe Cable had no plan, but she knew she didn't need one. She was tuned in, swimming with the tide.

'Ah, for me it was easy of course. I studied Theoretical Gastronomy with Rubicon at the Sorbonne. We covered expectoration in great detail.'

'I bet you did.' She smiled hugely. She found his polyglot Euro-arrogance rather charming given what was about to occur.

31

'Isn't that Ross Goater over there, now talking to Dorothy?'

He turned. It was him, Ross 'the goat' Goater – all stubble and turquoise jewelry. He had a bottle of Peroni in one hand and half a garlic ciabatta in the other. He was gesturing furiously with the ciabatta. Dorothy was laughing uproariously.

Looking from the silent patio through the plate-glass doors, it appeared, Zoe Cable had to admit, quite appalling. Dirck was clearly dismayed. He started biting his fingernails and spitting the pieces over the balcony into the Coketown Ship canal.

'Could you help me stay?' he asked. He sounded momentarily pathetic.

Zoe felt a warm wave of disingenuousness break over her.

'But you have already spoken to Barbara right?'

'She was useless.'

'I do admire your mother's work.'

Dirck frowned. It took him a minute or two to realize that Zoe Cable wasn't changing the subject.

'A lecture?' he asked

'A seminar series.'

'That's impossible, she's over-committed as it is. Her schedule is berserk.'

They looked again. The Goat had stopped gesturing with the ciabatta, but now seemed to be miming what Zoe Cable could only assume was a tribal initiation ritual. Dorothy glanced back at them. Dirck was about to wave but, before he could do so, Zoe Cable pulled his head down and kissed him fully on his thin-lipped Dutch mouth.

It was not by any means an amateurish kiss, it was not the kind of kiss, for instance, which relies for its impact either on previous stores of goodwill or the expectation of further delights to come. No, this was a free-standing, self-sustaining kiss, a kiss which rose and fell on its own merits. And its own merits, Zoe Cable knew, were considerable. She had been developing the kiss for two decades and her field testing had been extensive. There had been several failed prototypes before she had arrived at what she now considered this final, unsurpassable version. The kiss, which had been described by one concussed boyfriend as not so much a kiss but more a total mouth-fuck, involved a combination of twirling, probing, nibbling, blowing and sucking, of such complex beauty that to do it justice would have required a page or two of quadrilateral equations or a half-decent sonnet sequence. It was not, in short, a kiss to be described. Not even, some had argued, to be enjoyed, but only to be experienced, to be marvelled at, to be lived through whenever possible.

Afterwards, Dirck van Camper looked (they always did) like the victim of an extraordinary erotic mugging. His eyeballs, already dilated, bobbed like ping-pong balls on the colourless puddle of his face. His mouth had the bruised looseness of a dental patient enjoying a temporary respite from the drill. In the meantime Dorothy, who had for the duration of the kiss remained pressed, goggle-eyed, against the plate-glass like a desperate but penniless shopaholic, now freed herself from the door, from 'the goat', from the kiss, and was walking, no, running (as best she could given the density of the partygoers and the unsuitability of her paratrooper boots) away from Dirck and Zoe towards the private escalator.

Dirck van Camper gurgled and blinked. Zoe squeezed his corduroy buttock and giggled.

'You'd better be off, sweetheart,' she said. 'And remember, it's Charles Manson next week.'

33

Chapter 5

Walking back from the Staff House to the Arts Faculty, Zoe and the Crocodile shared a golf umbrella.

'So what's your angle,' the Crocodile asked, 'with Dirck Van Camper?'

'He's Firenze Beach's stepson.'

The Crocodile whistled. 'So what's the play? Small grant, seminar series, sign her up for the editorial board of *Vagina Dentata*?'

'Oh there's more.'

'How much more?'

'Day conference, plenary address, published proceedings. Plus she has a finger in the EU gravy train.'

'The Goethe Fellowship?'

'Precisely.'

The Crocodile purred. Zoe Cable had been his big idea. Her purpose (for with the Crocodile there was always a purpose) was to suck prestige from Mordred Evans, Arthur Andersen Professor of Anglo-Saxon Studies. Donald McWurter and Mordred Evans were the bitterest of enemies. Thirty years before, when they had been junior lecturers under the tyrannical regime of Professor Ronald Doppet, they had been the closest of friends. In those days, they would huddle together after lectures in the snug of the University Arms (long since demolished) to smoke their pipes, pore over the *TLS*, swap anecdotes about the hideous Doppet and console themselves for the disappointments of all of the above with dreams of eventual promotion. They lived two streets apart in the academic garden suburb of Gooseberry Hill; their children played together after school; their wives met for

34

coffee; their families gathered every week or two for fondue and Liebfraumilch.

Doppet's death changed all that. He keeled over one Tuesday morning during a lecture on 'Samson Agonistes'. When they met that Thursday in the University Arms their conversation was guarded, hesitant, brief. The death of Doppet was like the death of a pope; it implied not merely a change of leadership but a change of epoch. Nothing could be the same. Mordred and Donald were both forty-eight but they were still the youngest members of the department. The future belonged to them, but which one of them?

Perhaps neither one was a natural schemer, but they both had scheming thrust upon them and they rose to the challenge. There was to be an election for head of department and it was understood that the winner would inherit Doppet's Chair. There may never have been an election before: no one was certain, no one could remember life before Doppet. There were certainly election rules – there were indeed three sets of them which, a minute from the late forties indicated, should be read concurrently. When this was done, the rules seemed to undermine themselves, to suggest that no election was necessary, or possibly that any election would be itself against the rules. Mordred campaigned for a change of rules – he took it to the University Council, Donald opposed him. Mordred won. This, however, was part of Donald's plan. He wished to portray Mordred as a schemer, a Jesuit, a vile politician. His victory over the election rules was prima facie evidence of this. Donald, on the other hand, wished to present himself, oxymoronically, as concerned yet indifferent, interested and disinterested, above it all yet willing to get his hands dirty. He calculated that this impossible persona, if accepted, would see him to victory. He was right; it did. It was his subsequent decade as head of department which earned Donald his nickname, the Crocodile.

His accession (for that was what it seemed like) coincided with an onslaught of government initiatives to do with expansion, cost-cutting and quality management. The Crocodile, who had by then lost interest in his research on Ben Jonson and was

35

seeking some other outlet for his executive energies, took to the new regime with unguarded enthusiasm. When looked at from the top rather than the bottom, he saw that the department was not the intricate intellectual topiary Doppet had always claimed, but just a tangled thicket of dead wood. There were people who had taught the same courses for twenty-five years and who refused to read books written after the Great War. He decided to hack away. Since it was impossible to fire people, even the worst, he set about undermining them, eroding their confidence, making their lives intolerable. Since most of the people he targeted lived entirely in worlds of their own devising this was not easy to do. He waged, of necessity, a dirty war of infiltration, interception and psychic betrayal. Graduate students were his weapon of choice – he would befriend them, wine them, dine them and turn them against their mentors. He would show them that what they had taken for academic eccentricity was actually professional incompetence, that what they had written off as clumsiness was sexual harassment. He would surprise them, he would support them, he would suggest they file formal complaints.

The Crocodile scored some notable early successes – people were pushed over the edge. Magnus Walhalla, a specialist in Old Norse who had hardly spoken to or seen an undergraduate for twenty years, was taken before two disciplinary tribunals and, quite hysterical, ended his career by attempting to assault the Crocodile in the Department Office with a replica Iron Age rake. Landry Valentine, a specialist in the poetry of Edna St Vincent Millay and a functioning alcoholic, was, following a three-month external audit of his teaching practices, discovered unconscious in the University Arms, lying in a vomit-spattered pile of final exam scripts. The following day the Dean accepted his resignation. And there were others, several others: early retirements, constructive dismissals, resignations made in the heat which could not be recanted, sandaled feet which didn't even touch the floor. The Crocodile had no doubt of the ethical probity of his actions. Coketown, England, the world had moved on and the University must move with them – modernisation, professionalism, quality. But at the same time, of course, he enjoyed himself. The Crocodile had always relished a fight.

The Crocodile had grown up in a large and raucous family. His father, who worked as a postman, was a ferocious auto-didact; his mother was a school teacher; he had three brothers and two sisters. Over dinner they would argue about Zionism, the Suez crisis, Elvis Presley, transubstantiation; they would howl and bark, they would gesture and denounce. In the evening they would retire to their crowded, book-crammed parlour to read and listen to the wireless, and then over breakfast they would begin it all again. Their vehemence was a form of love, displaced a little, but no less real for that. And at nineteen, as a scholarship student choosing to pursue the life of the mind, that was what the Crocodile had been seeking – another family, more of the same. He had never found it, of course – English uni-versities, he soon learned, were places of deference and probity. If you shouted, people got upset. He learned to adjust, to curb himself, but as a new Chair and Head of Department he remembered finally who he was. He attacked without retreating, he slashed and he burned, he crunched and he most certainly chewed. If there was pleasure in this, it was the natural pleasure of the intellectual carnivore, the Crocodile, and if there was a measure of revenge, it was revenge for the twenty years of captivity and muzzling. As colleagues, deferential and incompe-tent every one of them, had strokes, lapsed into addiction, disappeared into premature and inglorious old age, the Croco-dile lost no sleep. There was only one thing that still bothered him: Mordred Evans.

Since his defeat in the election, Mordred Evans had pursued the quite brilliant strategy of applying for and winning every major grant, first in Great Britain, then in Europe. Barricaded behind these piles of money and research assistants, he was untouchable. He had his own fiefdom. Without teaching a single student he earned the faculty more money than many mid-sized departments. And from this fastness in the east wing, he waged a subtle yet concerted campaign against the Crocodile and all he stood for. He had the ear, the Crocodile knew, of more than one

Pro-Vice-Chancellor. And when it came to new appointments, computer upgrades, debates about the recurrent grant he was always there in the background, like a kind of noxious gas, a silent force of reaction and restraint.

He had not, however, managed to stop the Crocodile from becoming Dean, and from these new heights the Crocodile launched what he confidently believed would be his final assault in their ten-year war. He hired Zoe Cable. He hired Zoe Cable as a Faculty Research Fellow, a position which had not existed before and the like of which did not exist anywhere else in the university. The Faculty Research Fellow was paid entirely out of faculty funds, but her renumeration and her job description were both closely guarded secrets. She was reportable only to the Dean. Zoe Cable was *his*. The purpose of Zoe Cable was to win more in outside grants than Mordred Evans and thus to cut the ground from beneath his well-polished Anglo-Welsh brogues. If Mordred could be toppled from his position as champion grant winner he would become vulnerable. He would begin to lose the confidence of the Centre, research assistants would gradually decamp, the edifice would crumble and the Crocodile would come down from the north like the Huns of old and with the mighty flamethrower of modernisation he would destroy. The Crocodile was convinced that Mordred's days were numbered. If he had any sense he would already be canvassing for positions elsewhere.

'Remind me again of the totals,' he said as they slalomed through a crowd of damp undergraduates.

'It's like fiscal pornography for you, isn't it Donald? Do you have a pile of stinky old *Economists* under your bed?'

'Allow an old man his pleasures.'

'350k. Mordred's on 175.'

'178.'

'Bloody hell. Why don't you two just get your wodgers out? I've got a ruler you can borrow.'

The Crocodile waved it off with a grin.

'What about the appointment on Friday? Anything in it for you?'

Zoe shook her head. 'They're just touting for another tutorial whore.'

'Morris then?'

'Christ no, there are standards. Morris'll take it up the jacksie and say thank you. We want someone with a *bit* more class.'

The Crocodile nodded.

'Is Dirck van Camper really any good by the way?'

'Oh he's terrific, like I said, a real Eurogeek. He thinks Morris is a complete lightweight because he doesn't read Russian.'

'What does Morris do again? It's Arthur Alderley isn't it? That's someone I always meant to read.'

Zoe rolled her eyes. '*The Hour of Lead* is sentimental twaddle. *The House at Hough End* is probably his best, but even that's hit and miss, and the late stuff, *A Flag for Veronica*, *The Scent of Horseradish*, is just execrable – of course he was syphilitic by then.'

'You've actually read him?'

Zoe grinned. 'Well, what do you think Donald?'

Chapter 6

When Morris reached the seminar room the students were already there, arranged in a threatening semi-circle with Dirck van Camper in the middle as always. Their keenness dismayed him. Whatever they were expecting, he thought, they were certain to be disappointed. He was utterly unprepared and after that lunch with Zoe Cable and the Crocodile, well, whatever the opposite of adrenalin was, his veins were coursing with it. His axe-wielding anger had lasted only a minute or two and in its wake came only maudlin enervation.

He put down his bag and stretched his features into a smile. One or two of the nicer ones smiled back – Dirck van Camper did not raise his eyes from his German edition of *The Phenomenology of Spirit*. Morris opened his course reader, 'Immanuel Kant – An Answer to the Question: What is Enlightenment?' He read the first paragraph.

> *Enlightenment is man's release from his self-incurred tutelage. Tutelage [Unmundigkeit] is man's inability to make use of his understanding [Verstand] without direction from another. It is self-incurred when its cause lies not in lack of understanding but in lack of resolution and courage to use it without direction from another.* Sapere Aude! *'Have courage to exercise your own understanding!' – that is the motto of enlightenment.*

'*Sapere Aude!*'. That assumed, of course, that one had some understanding to exercise. Morris's brain felt like a soft-boiled egg. The double espresso was giving him hot flushes. Perhaps he should throw himself on their mercy, explain what had happened and suggest that they just have a drink.

He glanced up. They looked even less merciful than usual, and besides, they had paid fees for this – he would have to rearrange class and it might get back to the Director of Graduate Studies. On the other hand, given the lunchtime debacle he had no chance of the permanent job so sod it. Then again, maybe the lunchtime thing hadn't been so bad after all, perhaps he was over-reacting; he tended to do that sometimes, didn't he? And if there was still a chance of the permanent job, even a slim one, wasn't it better to push on and try to salvage something? He glanced again at the essay. Oh, why hadn't he read it over the weekend? OK, there had been Molly's stomach bug, the birthday party, shopping for kitchen tiles, but still, half an hour would have been better than nothing and he'd spent most of Sunday afternoon watching a Stewart Grainger film on Channel 5. Morris felt like punching himself hard in the head. He imagined picking up a house brick and smashing it into his own face. Flattening his nose, breaking some teeth. There would be blood and mucus – lots of it. That would be one way of escaping all this.

'So,' he said, 'does anyone have any preliminary thoughts or questions before we get into the essay itself?'

They looked entirely blank. There was nothing to indicate they had understood or even heard the question. Morris felt woozy from lack of sleep and was developing a headache. Was it possible, he wondered, that he hadn't actually spoken the question out loud? Had he just thought about it? No, that was insane. He remembered his lips moving, there had definitely been sound.

'Anyone?'

Dirck van Camper slowly and unnecessarily raised a hand.

'May I hand in my essay today?'

'Well, the essays aren't due for,' Morris checked the syllabus, 'three weeks. Three weeks on Friday.'

'Yes, but I wrote mine last week. I was reading Schopenhauer and I got a little carried away.' He smiled mischievously.

Morris tried to smile back. A couple of other students rolled their eyes and made vomiting motions.

41

'Terrific. Just give it to me at the end of the class.'

Dirck nodded.

'Any other questions?' Morris glanced at his watch. Five past two. OK then, it was a two-hour class, he could end twenty-five minutes early if it looked like he had something pressing to go to, fifteen minutes' break in the middle – that still left him over an hour to fill. Fuck.

'An Answer to the Question: "What is Enlightenment?"' Morris read. 'Well,' he paused. The silence seemed painfully empty – vacuous. 'Why don't we just grasp the nettle? What *is* Enlightenment?'

They all looked down intently at their course readers except Dirck, who looked quizzically at Morris.

'Is it something to do with like wisdom?' someone said. (At least Morris wasn't the only one who was unprepared.)

'Generally yes. But I would guess,' (he wasn't being euphemistic), 'that Kant is using it in a more specialised sense.'

Morris expected Dirck to jump in here; he usually did. But this time he remained silent. Morris had an uneasy feeling that Dirck was biding his time. He looked oddly silent, smug. Could Zoe Cable already have told him about the fellowship?

'Enlightenment is man's release from his self-incurred tutelage,' someone quoted facetiously.

'Right, but what does that mean? Tutelage? And why self-incurred?' The student frowned. Morris thought that perhaps this wasn't going to be so bad after all. There were things in here he could get his teeth into.

They talked fitfully for ten minutes about science, especially gravity, personal liberty, the Catholic Church, Divine Right of Kings and Reason with a capital R. When another silence descended, Morris went to the board and wrote down a list of names in order to buy some time: Descartes, Rousseau, Locke, Hobbes, Voltaire, Newton, Pope. The eighteenth was his least favourite century – really it was neither one thing nor the other. And those bloody novels – why couldn't they just stay in one place? He looked at his list, thought about it for a moment and then rubbed out Hobbes.

He was struggling to keep his mind on the class. He kept remembering Zoe Cable's fulsome endorsement of Dirck – 'terrific', 'wonderful', 'simply brilliant'. He felt, as he added, rather uncertainly, Thomas Jefferson to the list, a hot cummerbund of jealousy tightening around his middle. He considered her fulsomeness in retrospect to be a terribly bad sign – a person can only have a finite store of enthusiasm, he reasoned, and if so much of Zoe Cable's was carelessly spent on the frankly undeserving Dirck van Camper, could any at all be left over for him when it mattered most? Fruit and swimming pools – that's what she had smelt of, and she had been wearing strange matt purple lipstick which had made her mouth look out of kilter with her face.

He turned around to look at them again.

'So let's review.' It was only two fifteen and he was already reviewing! What on earth could he do next?

'Enlightenment: eighteenth-century intellectual movement, emphasised individual reason as opposed to faith. Faith in what exactly? It's a rhetorical question, Martin. God, King, that sort of thing. Errm, in Science – Newton, gravity, the billiard-ball theory. In politics – the French Revolution, all men are created equal, life, liberty and so on. And what else?'

Dirck raised his hand. Morris flinched.

'Yes Dirck.'

'If you are talking about Kant, that's all wrong.'

'Sorry?'

'If you're talking about Kant, then everything you have said is wrong I think. Kant's whole problematic involves saving faith from the onslaughts of dogmatic rationalism as exemplified by Liebnitz and Wolff. The second critique makes that quite clear, I believe. Incidentally, you may be using 'reason' as term a little sloppily. Kant is quite precise.'

'I see.' Morris ground his teeth. He was in a tight spot. Kant's religious views were a complete mystery to him. 'Yes, perhaps I was painting with rather a broad brush,' he said, attempting a tactical retreat. 'There are exceptions to every rule of course.'

Dirck pointed to the list of names.

'Every one of them believed in God.'

Morris swallowed. He began to experience a strangely dis-passionate curiosity as to how he would get out of this situation. In an hour or so it would be over, of course, but how exactly would he get from here to there? What would fill the intervening time? He noticed with equal detachment a gathering feeling of panic in his bowels and brain and the beginning of perspiration on his brow. He swallowed again and waited for something to happen. Nothing did. Perhaps if he opened his mouth.

'Uuuummmmmm . . . Errrr.' He was touched by the curious, anticipatory way they were looking at him now (all except Dirck of course). They still believed in him, he could tell. They still thought he knew what he was talking about.

'Well, I expect that's a matter of opinion.'

'Not really, I think it's a matter of fact. Kant took communion every Sunday.'

The looks of curiosity and anticipation were beginning to turn to frowns.

'They all believed in God?' The question was directed not to Morris but to Dirck.

Dirck turned to face the questioner and smiled. 'Yes, yes, of course. The task of Enlightenment is not to kill off God – that is Nietzche's little job,' he smirked, 'but to reconcile his existence with Reason.'

'Isn't that impossible?'

'Oh not at all, although it is a little tricky, ha, ha.'

'But religious belief is irrational.'

'Not exactly. Kant argues that we cannot *know* God – that's the dogmatic position – but we can deduce his existence from the fact of our moral consciousness.'

The other students looked blank and rather scared.

'Moral consciousness?' someone asked.

'Yes,' Dirck said. "Allow me to explain." He walked over to the board and started writing. So this is how the hour would be passed, Morris thought: Dirck van Camper holding forth, the other students asking him questions, and Morris Gutman sitting silently at the front like a red-faced pillock. There probably were

44

more degrading scenarios for a temporary lecturer, but he couldn't immediately bring one to mind. While Dirck diagrammed the Kantian theory of knowledge, Morris imagined stabbing himself in the gut with a bread knife, deliberately impaling himself on a pitchfork, jumping on to iron railings from a first floor balcony.

'You've misspelled cogitative,' he shouted pathetically. Dirck was explaining the categorical imperative – we should act as if we wished everyone else to act the same way. What an appalling rule, Morris thought, what a grotesque burden to imagine yourself somehow responsible for the universe, but then again, that's what parenthood was like. Every action becomes an example, every fart and blasphemy something to be copied and repeated back. Your life was no longer your own. Molly was building herself up out of bits of both of them – bits, often, that they had forgotten about or did not care to notice. He remembered her in bed that morning. 'Go to Rotherham' – it was what E said when their rows reached a certain point: 'Go back to Rotherham, to your mother. Leave us both alone if you hate it so much.' As he remembered such things, sadness enfolded Morris like a warm woolly blanket. He felt terribly tired.

Some of the students were looking over at him – they looked concerned, sympathetic, confused. They knew that something wasn't quite right and they wanted him, he realised, to retake control, to restore order and decorum, to put Dirck van Camper firmly back in his place. It was the same with Molly – if you rearranged the furniture or had your hair cut, she became upset. Conservatism in a way, but then again, there was safety in routine. He winked at them as if to suggest that he knew what he was doing, that it was all going to be OK.

Then Morris looked at Dirck banging on about the difference between noumena and phenomena. He was wearing his trademark three-piece suit. Thin white lines of fluorescent light reflected off his shaven skull like minimalist horns, his rectangular lenses were tinted blue and looked like tiny Post-it notes attached to his eyebrows. *He* would be OK, Morris thought, whatever happened. That was the kind of person Dirck van

45

Camper was. His self-belief was planetary, it drew things to him – the fellowship, Zoe Cable, the Crocodile, the ideas of Immanuel Kant, God knows what else – with the force of gravity. At that moment Morris felt for him a deep and complete loathing, a sense of hatred unmitigated for once by involuntary doubt, sympathy or moral qualm. If he could have pressed a button – he imagined a large, red button like an old person's panic alarm – to eliminate Dirck van Camper from the earth, he would happily have done so.

'Of course,' Dirck said, 'Kant makes the mistake of repeating (albeit in a very sophisticated way) that old Platonic distinction between the real and the apparent. Whereas Nietzsche, Oscar Wilde and,' he gestured vaguely, 'many others remind us rightly that the apparent *is* the real.'

'Oh, let's have a bloody break,' Morris announced rather more loudly than he meant to. It was only two thirty. 'Twenty minutes.'

Dirck looked offended. The others laughed. On the way out, they checked their text messages and asked each other for cigarettes or change. When they had gone, Morris rested his head on the formica desk. The double espresso had left him and he felt like his blood sugar had jumped off a cliff. As he closed his eyes the room began slowly to revolve.

His mind slid down a coal-black chute into a paddling pool of anxious imagery. While his students sucked frappuccino in the refectory Morris, as he did almost every night, sat exams he had never revised for, performed plays he had never heard of, gave public lectures without notes. When he woke up it was five-thirty. His neck felt like it had been broken and badly reset, his shirt sleeve was soaked with drool and there were three notes by his elbow. One was from the class as a whole explaining that they had thought it better, under the circumstances, not to wake him but had gone instead to the Coal Bar to continue 'discussions' (Ha-Ha). The second was from Dirck van Camper, requesting a private meeting to discuss his concerns about the class, which so far he was finding, he found himself forced to admit, an acute disappointment. And the third, from Declan

Monk, pointed out that he had been scheduled to teach in that room at five and reminded Morris that he was contractually obliged to inform the Head of Department of any medical or psychological ailments which might impair his professional performance.

Chapter 7

So that was that.

E closed her eyes and sighed. The smell of the ladies' was getting to her – apricot disinfectant, cigarette smoke, hairspray, poopoo (Molly's vocabulary was infectious) and a cacophony of perfumes. She had always been sensitive to smell but this seemed worse than usual – was there a hint of onion in there? Someone's lunch? She unspooled some toilet paper. What a day.

Alison, the education curator, had overbooked the morning session. Two freelancers had cancelled, leaving a hundred soggy kids loose in Coketown Art Gallery (home of the country's finest collection of mid-Victorian pottery) with only her and two lackadaisical teachers to corral them. There had been something like a riot in the North Mezzanine. Someone had overturned the art cart. Misspelled obscenities had been pastelled onto the East Gallery walls. The attendants were understandably up in arms, and when Alison had deigned to appear after one of her pointless bloody meetings, instead of apologising for the mess she had had a stand-up row with the modern art curator then instructed E (it was beyond, far beyond annoying) that she should really be firmer with the attendants since it was their job to help not whinge.

Then after lunch (the Bistro's rather gruelling minestrone) Professor Urquhart from the Eccles Institute had phoned and requested a talk on surrealism for next Monday evening. The fact that Coketown Art Gallery housed no surrealist works and was closed on Monday evenings had not dissuaded him. After E had said no, he'd called Alison directly. Alison agreed to have the gallery opened specially, and suggested that E herself might give the talk – she had a degree in modern art after all, Alison explained, and seemed quite keen on all that. When E had pointed out that as an administrative assistant in the education department her job involved taking bookings, arranging workshops and endlessly faffing with brochures and publicity, but definitely *not* giving ad hoc lectures on surrealism, Alison had become very red in the face and started wobbling with anger.

That was when E left. She couldn't stand to be close to Alison when she started wobbling. It was unattractive and, since their office was the size of a telephone box, potentially dangerous. Soon though, she would have to go back and patch things up.

E looked again at the thin blue line and checked the instructions. Positive. Her stomach rumbled. The first signs of intelligent (you hoped) life. A germ-sized blob making itself known. So thin. It struck her already as plaintive and yearning, like the miniaturised wail, a tiny bruise on the blotting paper. She wanted to look after it, fatten it up a bit. She could still smell her own urine, dark and tannic. Someone went into the next stall – Opium and Right Guard. That was that then. She was always faintly surprised when plans worked out – her plans anyway. The future was such a vast, howling darkness and making plans was like throwing yourself into it and expecting to be caught. Not that it never happened, but well, it was always a little disconcerting to be noticed like that, to be singled out.

And Morris would have to be told.

Why did she say it like that? Morris knew what they were doing after all. He was a full participant, at least after a drink or two. It was because she knew how his mind worked: another baby, another bloody ball to keep up in the air. It was arse backwards, but that was how he was at the moment – gloomy and rebarbative. He roared and sulked, and on the few occasions when he lapsed back into happiness he seemed afterwards to be actually ashamed of his recidivism. OK, there were reasons, a trail that could be followed: the Coketown job, his father's death, the Bangor humiliation. But they were both nearly forty years old for Christsake, everyone was the same. Everyone had their list of woes and might-have-beens, their personal spaghetti junction of roads not taken. Wasn't it a kind of arrogance to take one's own sufferings quite so seriously? To imagine (as Morris with that look of grumpy, button-lipped hauteur surely did) that his were so much bigger and better than other people's? She sighed at the uncharitable path her thoughts were taking. Perhaps it wasn't as bad as all that. Perhaps Morris's character just needed a good yank and a twist and it would click back into place like a dislocated shoulder: he would become once again the intense and sexually enthusiastic man she had fallen in love with.

Morris, of course, did not understand the secret of his own attractiveness. He imagined it had something to do with his being clever, whereas actually it was the opposite of that. Not that she would have wished him stupid, but Morris was most loveable in those rare moments when his brain failed him – she thought of Molly's birth, his father's death, certain exceptional hours of their honeymoon – moments when he seemed simply and charmingly flummoxed.

A good yank and a twist, she thought again, perhaps that's what he needs. Well that was what he was going to get whether he needed it or not.

The woman next to her left the stall. E smelled soap. She looked again at the plastic stick, the blue line. It was out of their hands now anyway. There were other parties involved. When she stood up her head swam for a moment. She pulled up her knickers and smoothed her skirt. Leaving the stall felt like revisiting somewhere she had been to as a child. It was all – sinks, mirrors, soap dispensers, tampon machines – smaller, more fragile than it had seemed only twenty minutes before.

Chapter 8

Back in his office, Morris felt strangely alert – he had not had a nap for years. His professional future was of course a high price to pay for a few good hours, but there was no denying the splendid effects. It was as though the floral wallpaper of his mind had been stripped and replaced by something subtle, airy, off-white. He felt half-drunk with energy. He checked the time and then rang E to ask her to take Molly home on the bus. He wanted to stay for a while to work on his presentation. Then he sent two emails – a long, apologetic one to Declan Monk assuring him that his unexpected drowsiness was the result of the punishing research schedule which kept him awake regularly until dawn, rather than any mental or physical ailment, and a shorter one to his class hinting jovially that the incident had been the result of an excess of 'larging' the night before. He would, he thought, leave that arsehole Dirck van Camper for later. He got his dissertation manuscript out of a filing cabinet and began to skim it for anything useable.

The dissertation entitled 'Jam Tomorrow: Conserving Guilt in Arthur Alderley' was based on Morris's theory that Alderley's notorious misanthropy and self-loathing, most notable perhaps in *The City of Rats* (1905), was a consequence not, as had been previously assumed, of his conviction and subsequent three-year imprisonment for shoplifting in 1902, but emerged instead from an incident some twelve years earlier at the family home in Whitstable, when the young Arthur accidentally upset a boiling pot of his mother's gooseberry jam on to his younger brother Causley, causing such severe burns that Causley's right leg was eventually amputated below the knee, blighting his hopes of a naval career and leading him eventually to a sad and inebriate death at thirty-two. It had been Morris's contention that this incident, with its powerful associations of fruit and fratricide, had haunted Alderley throughout his life and was endlessly replayed in his novels.

When he was working on the dissertation under Conrad Underseel's supervision he had felt his ideas to be rather brilliant. He had anticipated that they would become known far beyond the admittedly fairly small and eccentric community of Alderley scholars; they might indeed, if he allowed himself to think that far ahead, serve as a model for a general revival of psycho-biographical criticism. Nowadays when he reread it, however, they struck him more often than not as forced and sophomoric. All that pedantic image spotting – every penknife, a scalpel, every bite of breakfast, a pot of gooseberry jam. Hopeless. Why had he wasted his time like that? It had been Underseel's fault. He had flattered him and egged him on, persuaded him to work on Alderley when he hadn't much wanted to; lured him with unpublished letters (little more than laundry lists) and offers of teaching (they came to nothing). Then, when Morris had completed on time, when Underseel had extracted the last drop of kudos from him (there was not much to extract but Underseel had supervised only one postgraduate in twelve years, he needed something) he dropped him.

Underseel had refused him a reference. It had happened the day after Morris's viva. Morris's mood that morning had been understandably buoyant. As he made his way across the un-dulant and mismatched campus, he felt absurdly fond of it. The dank institutional odour of the Arts Building and the dark clatter of the corridor leading to Underseel's office did not, for once, dishearten him but inspired instead a sense of warm nostalgia. As Morris entered, Underseel had his back to the door. He was eating a chocolate biscuit and staring out of the window at the to and fro of the short-stay car park.

'Ah, Morris, I've been expecting you,' he said, without turning round. Morris could see the ragged 'w' where the back of Conrad's toupee met his badly hennaed hair. Conrad Underseel

52

was something of a drama queen but this was unusual even for him.

'It's about the Banbury job,' said Morris.

'Yes, yes, I saw it in the *Guardian* of course.'

'I'm going to apply.'

'I thought you might.'

There was a pause. Morris could hear the beep-beep of a lorry reversing and the chomp of Conrad's dentures as he worked through his chocolate digestive.

'I'm afraid I can't help you with that, Morris.'

'I'm sorry?'

Conrad Underseel sighed and swivelled back round to face Morris.

'Morris,' he said, 'you may think of me as a rather easygoing person, lackadaisical sometimes, devil-may-care.' (Morris had never thought of him in this way.) 'But actually,' he pursed his lips and swallowed as though rather moved by what he was about to say, 'I am a man of some principle. I believe in scholarship. *Scholarship*.' When he said the word he made a gesture with his fingers and thumbs as though stretching a long piece of elastic.

'Scholarship I define as the slow and methodical accumulation of knowledge.' Morris nodded nervously. There was fear growing at the back of his mind which he dared not name.

'These days, we have made speed our god, Morris – fast food, Kwik Save, rush hour, speed dial, express delivery, nought to sixty. Need I go on? But scholarship cannot be rushed. I trained, as you know, with Gaston Stichey at Cambridge. Stichey wrote only one book. It was a great book. It took him fifty years. He had no pride. May I explain why?'

Morris nodded. Underseel was aggressively sweeping the biscuit crumbs off his blotting pad. He was in no mood for interruption.

'Because the work of scholarship, Morris, is silent. You may read for thirty, forty, fifty years. You may gather, you may clarify, you may annotate and rearrange. No one need know

53

what you are up to – indeed, it may be better if they don't. That is scholarship Morris. The writing,' he actually stuck out his tongue, 'is nothing.'

'The teaching?'

Underseed gave a look of pale dismay. 'A disease. An allergy. You must beware of it Morris. It can destroy you. It can deceive you into believing you know something when really you know nothing.'

'*Nothing?*'

'Allow me to explain. You aspire, as I do myself, to be scholar of the work of Arthur Alderley.' Morris nodded once more. 'In order to pursue this path one must first, of course, acquire detailed and comprehensive knowledge of the writings of Alderley himself, both published and unpublished, and an understanding, as far as is possible, of his life, his contacts, his milieu. This is really only stage one (it may be less than that, but let us for now call it stage one) because to properly understand Alderley you must first understand the writings, the lives, the milieu of (to mention just the most obvious names): Hardy, Shaw, Housman, Dickens, Kipling, Meredith, Eliot, Gissing, Disraeli, Carlyle, Huxley, Browning and Clough. In order to fully understand Alderley's immediate predecessors, however, you must already have a comprehensive knowledge of the eighteenth century: Fielding, Austen, Pope, Johnson, Defoe, Addison and Swift; and before you can gain that knowledge, before indeed ground can be broken in any meaningful way at all, you must master, not merely understand you see but *master*, the greats: Milton and Shakespeare; Spenser and Sidney; Malory and Chaucer. I will pass over the classical authors at this time, but I hope my point is adequately made, Morris. There is a tradition, an alphabet you must learn. You are currently at A. Are you ready to proceed to B?'

'Yes I am.'

'No you are not. That is the painful news I am passing on. Do you know Victor Morley-Brown?'

Victor Morley-Brown was Conrad Underseel's previous postgraduate. They had met only once, but Morris knew the name well. He had always wondered what had become of him but never dared to ask. There had been rumours of glamorous overseas appointments, British Council grants.

'Do you know where he is now?'

'Prague?'

'Safeway.'

'He gave up?'

'On the contrary. He has reached stage two. At night he stacks shelves; in the day he reads. We are in regular contact. I can give you his number.'

Morris looked at Conrad Underseel. His hair was dappled and strangely terraced. He had a nose like a pomegranate. His clothes were twenty years old but looked brand new, as though he had access to a secret 70s fashion bunker. His face had a menacing blankness. He was clearly brutal and unhinged, yet Morris had placed his future in this man's hands. What did that tell you about Morris Gutman, he wondered, about his judgement and perspicuity? Perhaps he deserved what he got.

As he left Underseel's office and started walking back down the hill towards Deiniol Road and the Garth Street bus station, Morris felt like a child who had been violently orphaned. Seagulls barked and wheeled above his head. To the west, sandwiched between asphalt slabs of sea and sky, the edge of Anglesey lay hazed by margarine light. It was all over with Banbury.

Rereading his dissertation now in the gathering gloom of his shared office at the University of Coketown, that mood of anguished loneliness gradually seeped back. How flimsy his words seemed, how gauche his arguments. Jam and amputation – it wasn't interesting, just weird. Underseel's reactionary madness was, in retrospect, written all over it. Going up against Zoe Cable, the Crocodile and Declan Monk he would normally have needed something at least solid – phrenology might have qualified – but after the events of that afternoon and lunchtime it would have to be better than that; it would have to be remarkable. Was he still capable of that? He didn't know. After the Bangor catastrophe he had lost not only his confidence but also his bearings. That and two years' sleep deprivation had left him essentially clueless. But he had to try. He would never get a better chance. He was their inside man. He switched on his computer, opened his dissertation file and began ferociously cutting. The dissertation was three hundred pages long, and after forty-five minutes all he had left was twenty-three pages and a footnote. It was the footnote he was most interested in. It was an offhand remark about sexual dismay in the late stories but he thought something might be made of it. Wasn't there a new book about dismay by Firenze Beach? He had read a review and could remember the main idea. What was it – dismay as a feminised anguish and something about the beautiful and the sublime, fancy and imagination?

He recalled the late stories, *Two Masts over Hastings*, *The Mountebank* – great works in many ways although a little peculiar because of the syphilis – and if you thought about it, they were really packed with dismay. It was everywhere you looked. He made some preliminary notes and became rather excited. He drew some arrows, a few circles and did some underlining. He got out a highlighter. This might just work, he thought. If dismay was gendered then you could make a contrast here, maybe throw in some Kierkegaard for the men-folk, and look, if you trace it out Alderley becomes a post-feminist *avant la lettre*. Great stuff. He imagined Zoe Cable nodding in agreement, Declan Monk giving him a grinning thumbs-up. Morris started typing like a fiend. He was really on to something, it all fell into place. He wrote seven pages without stopping (too much! he needed five) then went to the toilet.

When he came back, he reread what he had done and felt a little less certain. Hadn't he said essentially the same thing twice or even three times, and didn't he contradict himself a little on page six? Never mind, a little trimming and tightening would do the trick. He cut out some of the more florid prose and then moved a couple of paragraphs from the end to the middle, to consolidate and avoid repetition. A little better, but now it seemed unbalanced – the climax came at the beginning not the end. Perhaps, he thought boldly, if he reversed it completely and began with the ending then worked back . . . It took him half an hour or so to make the change. On rereading it was stylistically successful but the logic seemed patchy. Perhaps he needed to bolster the discussion of *Two Masts over Hastings* with a reference to the implicit treatment of dismay in *City of Rats*. He did it, but that raised the tricky question of allegory, since *City of Rats* was narrated in part (in Alderley's boldest stylistic gambit) by rodents, and the gender of the rodents was far from clear (should he go into that?). It was difficult to know where to end. Ten minutes was no time at all. What did they expect?

He rewrote it again, adding and deleting considerable amounts. The more he worked on it however, the less clear he was about just what he was trying to say. The idea of dismay became more and more puzzling to him. He wondered what it really meant. Perhaps he should have read Firenze Beach's book, but it was too late for that now. He had another run at it. The sentences seemed to be fading into pablum, losing colour and sense. Morris began to feel panicky. It was Monday. Tuesday night he would need to prepare for Wednesday's classes. Wednesday night was E's yoga, he would have Molly. There was Thursday, but he was usually knackered by then. He really needed to do something *now*. It was nine-thirty, he was hungry and once again tired. He went over it once more and it just fell apart – it made no sense at all. The paragraphs were just half-baked fragments shimmering facetiously on the screen – mocking him. He imagined Zoe Cable suppressing a laugh, the Crocodile looking up at the ceiling and sucking his teeth, Declan saying they would let him know. He felt like smashing his head through the computer monitor, setting his hair on fire. He was fucked. Exhausted and fucked. Underseel was right after all.

The phone rang on his desk. It was E.

'It's nine-thirty, Morris, what's gone wrong?'

'Why do you always assume the worst? Why do you always leap to the most damaging conclusion?'

'You said you'd be an hour or so.'

'You're such a literalist. I'm constantly amazed by that aspect of your character.'

'Molly's in bed. There's something important I want to say.'

'My *presentation*,' Morris hissed. 'I'm working on my presentation.'

'Is it going well?'

Morris was stunned by the idiocy of the question. It took him a moment to regather his forces.

'It is not going well, no. In fact, I cannot imagine a situation in regard to my piece-of-shit presentation when the phrase "going well" would be appropriate.'

'Sorry Morris.'

'Indeed, even,' he went on, 'if we accept the popular theory that our universe is only one of an infinite number of parallel universes, I think it unlikely that you would find even one of that infinite number of universes in which my presentation could be accurately described as *going well*.'

'I take your point. Don't get frantic Morris, have a cigarette.'

Morris was momentarily touched by this suggestion. Since E's attitude to smoking was generally vitriolic, it indicated that she at least understood the gravity of his situation.

'I will. Thank you.' He lit a cigarette and inhaled. His eyes smarted. It tasted like car exhaust.

'We're pregnant, Morris.'

Morris inhaled again.

'You mean you're pregnant.'

There was a pause.

'I'll let that one go. Try again.'

Morris was thinking of computers. Computers on TV, the green and black screens, the big spinning reels – you could ask them anything. Those lines of 0s and 1s would go frantic for a while, and then you'd have your answer, bang. That struck him as deeply plausible – appropriate, right. He exhaled. His face looked like the back of a bus. Would he ever get used to the way things weren't?

58

'That's great news,' he said.

'Perhaps it's not the best time.'

'I'm coming home.'

He glanced at the garbled document once more before deleting it. Phrenology after all then.

Walking back to the car park, Morris felt as though each one of his internal organs was under extreme pressure and might at any moment sheer off or implode. The air seemed full of animosity, and he felt like he was walking though fudge. How big would it be now, his child – a grain of rice, a nail clipping, a piece of fluff? The future was a vast vacuum cleaner sucking him in.

The Dalton Street car park was large and empty. The halogen security lights were, as usual, not working. After starting the engine, he waited a few minutes for the car to warm up, for its heart beat to regularise. The interior still smelt faintly of Molly's vomit; it was amazing, he thought, the crannies she could reach. With this memory of his daughter's last regurgitation – an avocado-coloured heave en route to Rotherham two weeks before – came, for Morris, a sudden and unexpected spasm of joy. There was something about Molly's guttural roar, her unapologetic arm-waving puke which, despite its revoltingness, touched him deeply. 'Here I am,' it seemed to say, 'and why not?' Why not indeed? Morris thought. Now another one in the pipeline. Nine months' time, one more person, one less job. Morris laughed manically and reversed at speed without looking.

There was a loud, gut-felt thump and also some kind of high-pitched noise. A squeal? A tear? Had he really hit something? What could he possibly have hit? An unexpected bollard? A dog? The car park was entirely bloody empty. And what about his no-claims bonus? Without switching off the engine, he got out and ran angrily round the back. Dirck van Camper was lying beneath the rear axle. His bald head was split and bleeding, his little rectangular glasses were cracked and disarrayed, part of his overcoat was pinned beneath the off-side tyre. His eyes were rolled back to the whites and there was something strange about one arm. Beside him, his copy of *The Phenomenology of Spirit* was flapping in the wet wind like an injured owl. Morris dropped to his knees, astonished. What, he wondered, could have prompted such an onslaught of calamity? What could have brought it on?

'Dirck,' he shouted. 'Are you there mate?'

Dirck van Camper moved a little; the blood was dripping off his forehead on to the tarmac. It looked black like an oil leak. Morris thought of touching it but decided not to. He shook Dirck's shoulder – cold gaberdine. Dirck did not respond. Morris covered his eyes with his hands and groaned. This was a true disaster. He needed to act. The longer he waited, the worse it would seem. It might come up in court.

'So Mr Gutman, how long *were* you kneeling by the deceased?'

'I see, and are you trained in first aid?'

Deceased. Why was he thinking like that? It was only a knock, a few bruises. Dirck would shake it off. He groaned. His arm had too many joints, he must have broken it as he fell. Morris needed a phone. Why had he never bought a mobile? Because they were youthful and appalling.

He looked around the car park. A Mondeo was leaving on the far side. Had they seen? Could they help? He waved and shouted, but nobody responded. There was a phone box on Leach Street. It was half a mile. Should he run or drive? Run – but wasn't it bad taste to leave Dirck entirely alone? The car was company of a kind, and if anyone else came it would serve as a form of explanation. But then they, this other person, would assume Morris had fled the scene. It would look suspicious; he would have to explain himself. Wasn't the car quicker anyway, more logical? He got back in and put it in gear. It struck him that Dirck might be somehow attached to the underside, caught up in the suspension. He didn't want to risk dragging him along. That would be grotesque. He got out to check.

'I'm getting help Dirck,' he shouted at the lifeless heap.

As he squealed away through the automatic barrier, he could

see Dirck in the wing mirror – a bundle of black and a blob of white. Morris was panting and shuddering, his head felt over-inflated by a long, internal scream. He'd known appalling coincidence before, but *this* . . . He reached the phone box and dashed out. It smelt mildly of chow mein and was peppered with ads for perverse and inexplicable practices. He had no change. He remembered he didn't need any. The phone was dead anyway. What next? On Monday nights the campus was deserted. The Arts Faculty was locked by now, and as a temporary lecturer he had no key. The chances of finding a working phone box on the nearby Galsworthy Estate were, he estimated, significantly less than his chances of being mugged in the attempt. Rawpool Station, two miles away at least, was his best bet. He set off at speed, but ran almost immediately into a sluggish jam of cars coming from a death-metal concert at the velodrome. The creeping vehicles that surrounded him were full of sweaty Do It To Julia fans wearing rubber fright masks and ski goggles. When Morris glanced at them they mouthed obscenities and gave him the finger.

Morris thought for a moment: once he had called the ambulance he would have to go back and wait for them. Then the police would come and ask questions. They would arrest him. Why wouldn't they? What could he claim? That Dirck had thrown himself under the car? Hardly likely. Careless driving? Manslaughter? It would take forever; he would be embroiled in legal niceties, paperwork. And by the end? Sometimes the sentence bore no relation to the crime. He knew that, he read the *South Coketown Advertiser* – it was a lottery. His interview would be nullified, his job would disappear. His life was being peeled away from him. He was being raped by circumstance. Tonight, he realised, was the beginning of something (the vacuum-cleaner future was sucking him in), but the beginning of what exactly?

Morris thought of Dirck van Camper, disabled, dying, alone in the middle of the huge empty car park, and then he thought of E at home watching the ten o'clock news, Molly snoozing above her head, the germinating proto-child bubbling inside her. How could both these things be real, he thought, amazed, how could they possibly coexist? The bleeding Dirck, the fertile E?

Any impartial review of Morris's life, up to this point, would have revealed that his behaviour had never been characterised by clarity or decisiveness. The major turning points – Alderley, marriage, Molly – had not been proceeded by a judicious weighing of options, a sensible listing of pros and cons, but rather by prolonged periods of vagueness, uncertainty and denial followed by bouts of (often drunken) impetuosity. That night, however, as he sat sweating and fitful at the wheel of his eroding Fiesta, Morris knew an immediate decision had to be made. The stream of clashing panic that had filled his mind since seeing Dirck protrude from beneath his car like a comatose mechanic froze at that moment into a fixed, unignorable form. It was either – or. He saw that with a stark sobriety. E or Dirck? Love or death? There was no time for nuance or muddle. Not to act was to act. Rawpool Station was straight on; home was to the right down Cemetery Road.

He lit a cigarette. His car started coughing and gulping beneath him. It began to rain heavily. That made it worse of course – Dirck would be cold and soaking. Had anyone found him yet? Was he still alive? He thought of E and Molly. They were the precipitate of his life. If you boiled it dry they were what would be left at the bottom, a yellow rubble of love. Dirck van Camper? He was nothing; a fiction, just words, mouthings, gratuitous patterns of sound and sense whirling around an empty core. He had left the car park only ten minutes before, but already it seemed to Morris like a year or more. The whole scene felt like something he had read about once in an in-flight magazine. He looked up through his squeaky windscreen wipers at the rain-soaked sky. It was blurred black and starless. Every moment, he thought, people are dying and being born. Every moment there is killing and coming, lying and prayer – a frenzy of 0s and 1s. There were billions of people on the earth and Dirck van Camper was just one of them.

There was really no choice at all. Morris indicated right and pulled out of the stationary line, risking collision for a moment before he found the safety of Cemetery Road. Before he got home, he stopped at a remote phone box and made an anonymous call to the Coketown police. No one saw him.

Chapter 9

Zoe Cable heard about the accident while undergoing routine acupuncture at the Coketown Wellness Clinic. It was the next afternoon. The Crocodile sent her a text message. *Dirck Van Camper in hit and run. 'Serious' in CRI. Please advise, Don.* (The Crocodile was of a generation that assumed the text message was merely a more developed form of telegram.) When she read it, Zoe Cable sat straight up.

'Well, that's buggered up my yin and yang,' she said. 'Best call it a day, Chan.'

As Chan silently but a little resentfully began removing needles, Zoe rang the Coketown Royal Infirmary to enquire about Dirck's injuries. She pretended to be his stepsister, Saskia. The nurse recited them like a shopping list:

'Spinal contusions, whiplash, fractures. His legs aren't moving.'

'Vill he ever valk again?'

'Maybe, maybe not.'

Maybe, maybe not? Zoe thought. Do you have to pay extra for a bedside manner these days?

'Zankyou very much,' she said.

Zoe switched off the phone and pondered her options. Although she put her faith in the generative forces of the universe, she was not above a little scheming at times. Perhaps if she hung around the ward, she could manufacture a meeting with Firenze Beach – surely she was on her way (and if not the Crocodile's secretary should call her). The timing was improbable, she thought, and the whole thing was a little ghoulish, but Zoe decided to go anyway – her morning was open and she loved hospitals. She texted the Crocodile: *Gone to CRI. CU L8R Z.*

Yes, Zoe Cable loved hospitals. They were so entertaining, so true to life, so *pagan*. And in her experience, NHS hospitals were the best by far. You never knew just what you would stumble upon: bottled organs, dead bodies, rusting iron lungs, the demented and distraught. And the smells! You couldn't make them up.

She had not always loved hospitals, however. As a child, she had feared them. As a child, indeed, Zoe Cable had feared almost everything. Tall, timid, awkward and charmless, even her parents had at times found Zoe Cable hard to love. Her sensitivities had been so ubiquitous as to make normal domestic life all but impossible for them: she hated sunlight, she thought water was dangerous, music of any kind made her cry. She lived on Weetabix and Lucozade and refused shampoo. Then, when she was almost fourteen, she was knocked from her bicycle by a mobile fruiterer. Her unhelmeted and odorous head clashed with the trunk of a nearby elm. Her skull fractured, her brain received a severe jolting and Zoe Cable lay in a coma in Kingston General for three days. Her parents worried that she would not wake or that, if she did, she would be so upset by what had happened that she would never speak to them again.

Zoe Cable was conscious for some time before she decided to try to move an eyelid or raise a finger. She lay in the darkness of her own body, listening and thinking. She wondered why she was not afraid. She was nearly dead after all – a machine was breathing for her, she had tubes up her nose, she could feel vague flurries of pain across her thighs and torso. So why was she not afraid? She considered this as she listened to her parents talking. They were discussing whether to bring in her mole collection; they thought it might cheer her up, but were worried about the risk of losing a mole in transit (there were 228 of them after all) or even worse, perhaps, misarranging them in the hospital room. The thought of Zoe waking to the sight of a disordered or incomplete mole collection filled them both with dread.

She heard relations, nurses, auxiliary staff. They talked about her in frightened whispers; they touched her, if at all, with the wary gentleness of bomb disposal experts. Her accident, she realised, had invested her with an obscure kind of power – the power of autism and haemorrhage, the power of blood. She was living in a world they dared not enter. Even the doctors were scared, she could tell. You could hear it in their voices, the special tenor of their rudeness. There was something within her they couldn't control. Death was scampering around inside her like a dark hamster, blind, random; she could keep it or she could let it go. When she opened an eye, her mother started howling. She closed it again before anyone else noticed. She could bring them to their knees with her little finger.

Everything that happened afterwards – the surgeries, the rehab, the occasional epileptic fits – was a price worth paying. Once released from hospital, she started wearing black and backcombing her hair. Her make-up became thick and cadaverous. She liked, whenever possible, to describe the metal plate screwed into her skull, her tendency to foam at the mouth. Most people were disturbed by this, a few were excited – she made new friends. They would spend Saturdays together in Epsom town centre, smoking and walking around the shops. People looked askance, children pointed, store detectives asked them to leave. They were cleverer than the people around them and less squeamish – they pierced their own ears, did their own tattoos. They picked magic mushrooms and did controlled experiments with nutmeg and morning glory; they wasted no time on Rick Astley or Kajagoogoo. Zoe was the cleverest and the least squeamish of them all. She lived off lentils and Cup-a-Soup and treated her A-levels with disdain. Her teachers loved her. She could have gone to Cambridge but opted, for reasons no one could understand, for Barnstaple College.

She chose Barnstaple College because she wished to escape her friends and parents. Barnstaple had some of the worst rail connections in the country, making it almost impossible to reach at weekends. She needed to move on. She gave her old clothes to Oxfam and started wearing spandex leggings and strategically torn sweatshirts. She got highlights, drank voluminously and had a lot of sex. Zoe Cable was never beautiful. Her body was awkward and ungainly – when she danced, she seemed like a person removed from their authentic element, like a creature that had evolved beyond its means. That was her attraction. Silently, with her unabashed clumsiness and lack of symmetry, she spoke of other places, other media, more primitive and truer than our own. And in Barnstaple that was quite a draw. Men ran to her like lemmings to a cliff.

It was all very well, but after three years she decided to do a Ph.D. She finally went to Cambridge. She became older, and wore trouser suits. She became aware of her brain as a sexual organ, the power of blood transmuted into words, sense. Cambridge taught her that the border between the actual and the imagined was frail and osmotic: what she wanted she could have; what she willed could be real. She fantasised about her notoriously prim advisor Wilmot Herringham: during their first meeting he developed an unruly erection; by Easter he was offering to leave his wife. She argued violently with her flatmate, Crispin; two days later his Dr Who scarf caught on his bicycle derailleur while crossing Bridge Street. He blacked out and woke up an hour later in Addenbrookes with wool burns and a broken arm. It made sense, she realised, to try to control this power, to shape it to her own ends. She visualised publication: Routledge accepted her dissertation. She visualised success: she was made a junior fellow. She visualised more success: she was headhunted by the Crocodile.

She never visualised Coketown, of course; that came as a surprise. Its provincialism appalled her, but it had, nonetheless, a kind of gothic charm. There was something swampish, uncooked about it, which she felt she could work with. Ever since her arrival she had been making notes, sketching proposals. On Saturday nights she would don her body suit and transparent raincoat and blend with the hordes of vertical drinkers who had come down in fragrant and barely clad busloads from the brutal *banlieus* of Porksby and Wetterton. She was never disappointed – on the dancefloor of the Kum Bar, in the chill-out rooms of Stiffy McGees, lived strange, mutated forms of desire unknown to sociology or cultural studies. There were couplings and animosities which she had witnessed with her own eyes but which she was still trying to decipher. There were elaborate dialects of finger and tooth which she had to admit were quite beyond her, but to which she responded nonetheless. They touched her, they moved her, these boundary failures, these moments of pure anality. Public defecation, somnophilia, GBH – it was all freely available when the pubs kicked out, when the unlicensed cabs began to swarm; it was run-of-the-mill. Raw data, untheorised, uncharted, but for how much longer? Zoe Cable was working something up. She had a talk arranged at the ICA – it had a crossover appeal, she could pull in money from all angles.

CRI, as she had suspected, was a treasure trove of ghoulish misfortune. She paused in A&E, she made brief side trips to Oncology and the Renal Unit. Everywhere she saw people brutalised by time – their hair turned yellow, their eyes evacuated. They were propped on pillows, ga-ga in wheelchairs. They inched shambolically down the corridor with their arses hanging out. They seemed to Zoe Cable like the crude icons of an ancient pagan religion. The force of death was in them, as it had once been in her, that black hamster death. She could hear it in their scratchy breathing, see it in their tremulous hands, the oscillating wobble of their Rich Tea biscuits. These people, she thought, deserve our veneration, not pity. They require animal sacrifice, not our lukewarm shepherd's pie.

Zoe Cable was wearing a full-length white Italian mac; she looked vaguely, if stylishly, medical. Someone asked her for directions to Gastroenterology.

'I'm a doctor of philosophy,' she said. 'Read the signs and trust your instincts.'

When Zoe reached the ICU, Dorothy was just leaving. She was wearing jeans and a man's coat. Without her extreme make-up, she looked surprisingly young. Zoe embraced her (the kiss was long since behind them).

'What a terrible shock,' she said.

Dorothy gulped.

'I can't believe he didn't stop. What a coward.'

'Any forensics?'

'There were tyre tracks on the overcoat. But the police don't seem optimistic.'

'GCP? They need a map to find their own arseholes.'

Dorothy smiled. One or two of the other visitors looked round. There were six beds in the ward, three on either side. High on the far wall was a television silently showing racing from Lingfield. Zoe felt strangely at home.

'Is that Dirck in the corner?'

'Yes, he's dozing, but he'll wake up soon. Actually, there's already someone else here from the University.'

There was a man sitting by the head of the bed, three-quarters concealed by the floral curtains. Zoe could see a shoulder and the back of an orange plastic chair. She assumed it was the Crocodile or one of his minions.

Stripped of his three-piece suit and little glasses, stitched, plastered and badly bruised, Dirck van Camper resembled a tortoise that had been violently prised from its shell. He had a tube up his nose. He was snoring. Reaching the foot of the bed, Zoe Cable turned to greet the Crocodile but saw instead, to her great surprise, Morris Gutman. Morris was leaning forward with his head in his hands, his hair was tussled and dusty, he smelled like a rough pub.

'Morris. It's you.'

Morris looked up with a start.

'Zoe.'

He stood up and rather solemnly shook her hand. They both looked down at Dirck. Spots of blood had oozed through the dressing on his head. Morris lifted his arm as if in a dream and touched the bandage with his finger tip.

'Terrible,' Zoe said.

Morris didn't say anything.

'I didn't know you two were close.'

Morris looked amazed at the suggestion.

'Well . . . not in an orthodox way,' he said after a moment. And then, as if realising it was an odd thing to say, 'I mean an incident like this, a terrible incident such as this one, brings things to the surface which might otherwise remain concealed.'

'Oh absolutely.' Zoe glanced again at the snoring Dirck. She wondered what on earth was going on here. Could Morris actually have an angle? Was he making some kind of play?

'Morris, do you know if any of Dirck's relatives are coming over? Parents? Mother?'

It seemed to take Morris a moment or two to understand the question.

'I don't think so. They're in Thailand I believe, the parents. They want to bring him home in an air ambulance.'

'Fair enough.' (It had been a long shot.) 'How long have you been here?'

'An hour or so. I'll stay until he wakes up.'

'That could be ages. You look knackered already.'

'I'm fine. I couldn't sleep last night – it bothers me.'

'Bothers you?'

'This.'

'Oh, when did you hear about it anyway?'

Morris looked suddenly sick.

'Morris?'

'Umm, I was in my office late. I saw the police and so on.'

Zoe nodded, she was remembering the odd way Morris had touched Dirck's bandages. What was that about?

Dirck groaned and twisted. Morris jumped.

'Morris,' Zoe said. 'You seem really upset. Can I help?'

It was a shameless fishing expedition. She put her hand on his forearm. He looked down at it. She left it another second then took it away. Morris squinted at her like a driver looking into the sun. Around them, the smell of antiseptic fought the odour of bed pans and hospital food. The racing was over; *Countdown* had just started.

'What is the worst thing you have ever done?' he said.

Zoe thought. She had top tens for most things. Top ten most venal acts? They almost all involved sexual betrayal. Morris was married. Was that it? Good Lord. Morris and Dirck van

Camper, lovers? Why not? Why else would he be in his office late? He was waiting for Dirck. It would also explain how tongue-tied he had been when Dirck came up at lunch that time. And Dirck's rudeness about Morris was obviously just a smokescreen.

'How did you get over it?' Morris continued.

There was a pause, Zoe Cable was temporarily speechless.

'I favour confession,' he said.

'Morris,' Zoe said slowly in reply. 'Could you be a little more specific?'

Morris's skin was blotchy and damp, his face was two-toned.

'This is all my fault,' he said.

'God no, Morris. It's bonkers to blame yourself. I mean really, what could you have done?'

She imagined Morris high up in his shared office hotly waiting for Dirck. Probably he had rearranged the furniture already, closed the blinds, prepared himself. How long before he heard the sirens and realised what had befallen them? For a man like Morris (a man with a wife, a family and several God-awful articles on Arthur Alderley) it must have seemed, she imagined, crushingly literal: a swift and targeted riposte to his libidinal waywardness. Hence, she supposed, the guilt. Hence, she supposed again, the quite irrational claim of personal responsibility.

'I should have looked in the mirror,' he said.

The mirror, Zoe thought, what an astonishing suggestion. The *mirror*? As though self-examination would have cooled his lust.

'*Riiight*.' She paused. 'And what do you think you would have seen in the mirror, Morris?' OK, it was facile, but honestly she was floundering. Dirck and Morris! Normally she could scent adultery from a hundred yards.

'Dirck of course.'

Morris looked at her quizzically, as though this deeply peculiar answer would have been obvious to anyone at all.

Christ, Zoe thought, he must really have been besotted. How else to explain this extraordinary suggestion? *Dirck*. To look in the mirror and see not your own face but the face of your lover –

71

Zoe was glad to say she had never been that far gone. There had been that time with José in Guadalajara, when she had looked at her own reflection in the fish tank and seen some kind of dog-lady, but that had been the peyote. This was drug-free. It was also truly fascinating and – although she couldn't yet see all the angles – potentially usable.

'What are you going to do next?' She was genuinely curious.

'I'm going to confess,' he said. 'I'm going to the police.'

'The *police*?' Zoe squealed. 'This is the twenty-first century, Morris. You were consenting adults.'

Morris looked shocked.

'You think he consented?'

This, Zoe thought, is getting weirder all the time. Had there been some kind of role-play involved? Was this an S&M thing?

'Are you saying you forced yourself on him, Morris?'

'God no! It wasn't deliberate. It just happened. It was beyond my control.'

'Of course it was. So what is there to confess?'

'You don't think I'm culpable at all?'

'Absolutely not. You can't legislate desire.'

'Desire?'

Morris looked suddenly offended. Zoe wondered whether she had gone too far. She reached out and touched his forearm again. It felt as thin and shaky as a dowsing rod.

'You think,' Morris continued, 'that I really wanted . . .' His words trailed off but his glance drifted on, past the nurses' station and the roll-top drug trolley, to Dirck's bent and bandaged body.

Morris had buggered Dirck van Camper, and Dirck van Camper was now quite plainly buggered. The link between these two events was metaphorical at best, but Morris, being a literary critic, took metaphors rather more seriously than he should have. It was ludicrous, of course, but also, Zoe thought, sort of charming when looked at the right way.

'I understand how you feel, Morris,' she said, 'but these lines are there to be crossed. I've done similar things myself.'

Morris stared. His red-rimmed eyes were a ruckus of hope and disbelief.

'You have?' he said. 'You've done similar things?'

'Of course.' Zoe smiled. His naivety was sweet if, in a man of his age, a little alarming. 'Did you really think you were breaking new ground?'

'Well I suppose not,' Morris hesitated, 'but still.'

'You'd be amazed what people get up to in their free time.'

'I've got a child,' he blurted suddenly, as though in answer to an unspoken question.

'Oscar Wilde had two.'

'Is that relevant?'

'Let's just say, Morris, that I'm good with secrets.' Zoe smiled again. 'By the way, have you had much contact with Dirck's family?'

Morris, who had not stopped staring at Dirck, shook his head absent-mindedly. 'Not much,' he said.

Zoe nodded. They fell into a minute or two of reverential silence. The air carried faint scents of stool and sticking plaster, and beneath the TV chatter there was the low hum of complex, life-saving machinery. Dirck, she realised, looking closely at him for the first time, looked distinctly ill. He was pale as a root, and his face had the desolate, sunken quality of a beach at low-tide. Assuming he survived the initial ministrations of the NHS, he would be airlifted to the Netherlands for further treatment, she was sure of that. Afterwards the likelihood of him continuing his studies at Coketown were tiny. The path to Firenze Beach was proving to be rather more twisty and rugged than she had imagined. OK, there were still possibilities with Dirck – the cards, the flowers, the condoling and supportive emails – but with him gone from Coketown, what did she really have left? She looked up. Morris was sniffing. His eyes were damp and baggy; he looked like he had slept in his clothes. She had, she realised, Morris Gutman: Dirck's clandestine and guilt-racked lover. Who would have thunk it? Morris, who an hour before she would have dismissed as mere academic boilerplate – lank, sexless and stained by failure – was now an object of interest, at least, if not a

73

site of possibility. Zoe swallowed. She found such evidence of her own blindness strangely exciting – there were twists and crannies it seemed that even she had yet to explore. She stretched her arm around Morris's hunched and fleece-wrapped shoulders.

'Fancy a really bad cup of cocoa?' she cooed.

Chapter 10

When Morris arrived home after making the anonymous phone call, E was, as he had imagined she would be, seated on the sofa with her legs tucked up, watching the news. She was surrounded by a chaos of bright plastic items. The violence of Molly's playtime was clearly increasing.

'Another train crash in toy town,' E said. 'Sorry, I just couldn't be bothered to tidy.'

'You're not sick already, are you?'

'Do I look sick?'

'It was just a question.'

Morris went into the kitchen, opened the ice-choked fridge and retrieved a king-sized bottle of Brewmeister from the back. He went back into the living room. E looked at him.

'Are you OK?'

Morris felt close to tears. The normality of his house was overwhelming him. Outside, the frigid darkness clashed and whirred like a frenzied death machine, but here inside was life, light, love, happiness. These were not empty platitudes as he had often feared. They were real: solid as the Artex ceiling, the combi-boiler, the dual-action microwave. Why had it taken the darkness and the blood to make him realise that? He looked at E. She smiled. Her face seemed like something that had slipped his mind but that now at the very last moment he had remembered. This life had been waiting on the tip of his tongue. Delayed, rolled over, but not lost, and it had taken Dirck van Camper – dead, dying, Dirck van Camper – to remind him of it.

He sat down on the tartan sofa. He took of sip of Brewmeister – he had never noticed the sour, ferric taste before or the ferocity of the carbonation. He squeezed E's foot – hard, soft, curved, straight. It felt like a strange antique device whose purpose had long been forgotten.

'We must change the way we live our lives,' he said.

E looked at him again. 'Are you announcing a mid-life crisis? Are you planning to buy a motorbike?'

'Actually it's Rilke, but there may be a continuum.'

'There usually is.'

'I was thinking of the baby – we need real nappies, a new high chair, names. We need books and catalogues; we need advice, confidential counselling, support. We have a myriad needs.'

'But we're second-timers.'

'Exactly. We've never been that before, this is a first for us.'

They watched the beginning of *North-West Tonight*.

'Do you like Magnus?'

'No, absolutely not. Scandinavia is out. I exercise my veto on anything Nordic.'

E shuffled across the tartan sofa and leaned her head on Morris's shoulder. She touched his knee. There was a weight to her which surprised him, which he hadn't noticed before, as though she had become denser with age. He put his hand on her shoulder; it felt seasoned, smooth. What were they becoming? What were they growing into?

'Molly was a compromise,' she said.

'She was. We found it hard to agree. Your parents suggested we try arbitration.'

'Arbitration Gutman.'

'That was the joke.'

'What about Dirck?'

Morris stood up and circumnavigated the sofa twice before speaking. It felt like a rabbit punch, like a wedge of darkness had come through the curtains and whacked him on the back of the head. He needed to reorient, gather himself. Perhaps he should tell E what had happened. Perhaps he should explain. It was as though he had something inside him, some living creature he needed to expunge. If he let it loose in here, in his house, would it shrivel and die, or would it live, flourish, grow, like a hellish

76

illegal pet they could neither kill nor give away? He swallowed. He couldn't take the risk.

'Dirck, berk, dork – he'd never survive junior school. It's the nominal equivalent of "kick me".'

'It might be a girl – Dorca?'

'Now you're being facetious. Listen, I'm thinking of giving up my job, down-sizing.'

'Is that feasible?'

'I can't bear it anymore. I'm throwing good money after bad.'

'It rarely brings a smile to your face, I must admit.'

'It's been downhill since the Bangor incident. We both know it. There must be other avenues. Our needs are modest. I'll go to the Job Centre.'

Morris was surprising himself. It was as though he were stepping into negative space, as though he had become suddenly and profoundly aware of everything that wasn't his job, the university, his career, Dirck.

E snuggled up. Her face was the colour of cork. Her hair was tied with a spangly red elastic band. She smelt of mashed potato. He kissed her cheek. It felt at first vast and foreign, like kissing a wall or an official building. She shifted slightly and touched his hair. Morris felt like an animal – an ape or a cow. His consciousness was seeping down from his brain into his body. Thoughts were being back-engineered into sensations, impulses. They went upstairs. Their sex was like a reckless swimming – formless, amniotic, unchlorinated. Afterwards, E admitted that she was already craving parsley, that she could smell things at a distance. Morris had not slept unclothed for years, there were parts of his person he had forgotten about, allowed to lapse. He was fatter, in all honesty, than he had ever expected to be. There were lumps, nodules he had not been aware of before. As he fell asleep he thought lazily of gathering himself in, trawling for his pieces like an old Greek fisherman.

Sometime before dawn, the thought of Dirck van Camper distended, angry, haloed with black blood, wielding his water-damaged copy of *The Phenomenology of Spirit*, visited Morris. But it did not come alone – it was accompanied by unbidden memories of the Kant debacle, of his lunchtime humiliation, of Conrad Underseel and the Bangor calamity. What breathless anxieties these shades conjured up – what thoughts of bitter failure, of humiliation and wastage, of the urge, the *need*, to do better. Flummoxed and half asleep, he pledged himself, as if by rote, to work harder, to do more. Then he remembered that he had reversed over Dirck van Camper, that his chances on Friday were all but shot, that the police would already be making their enquiries. He had failed already, he had already lost. Clodding waves of anger and shame beat and bruised him. He would be exposed for what he was, stripped bare. He opened his eyes; the room was the colour of prunes. Sitting up he felt ashamed of his nakedness. He found a T-shirt and trousers. It was five-thirty. He went downstairs in a crushing vortex of gloom – Molly, E, the house were nowhere. How could he fail so badly when he had started off so well? He sat in the kitchen. It was bitterly cold, but he could not remember how to work the heating. He went to the cupboard and found a duffle coat that had belonged to his father. The room was dark; unwashed pans and plates gathered like storm clouds at its edges.

It *had* started well, he remembered. Six o'clock on an autumn afternoon in Rotherham, 1972; the visit from Miss Baxter, his form teacher. His father had assumed she was the pools lady. When Morris saw it was Miss Baxter he felt suddenly sick. Her presence on his doorstep terrified him. Two things which should never be connected had been. It was like a mix-and-match book – the Hipporaffe, the Pengotamus. She was wearing a green woollen coat with black zip-up boots, and she was carrying a handbag. After explaining who she was she smiled at Morris and assured him that he was not in any trouble; he turned purple and grunted. His parents became immediately and unnaturally cheerful: they made tea, found biscuits, bustled Miss Baxter into the lounge. Morris could hear his father asking questions, *making conversation*. For the seven-year-old Morris, this was the equivalent of graves giving up their dead, horses eating themselves. He sensed that something had gone terribly wrong. She stayed for half an hour. (His father dashed into the kitchen to retrieve a cut-glass ashtray, which Morris had never seen before, from the very top cupboard). There was the unprecedented smell of cigarette smoke. When she had gone, his parents came back in smiling and looking smug. They seemed possessed of a strange, secret knowledge. Miss Baxter had told them that Morris was unusually bright, that he should be encouraged to read more widely and that, if they liked, she would give him coaching once a week for the Rotherham Grammar School scholarship exam.

The exam was easy. Morris took the bus out every day – fifteen miles or so through council estates, past the municipal cemetery and sewage farm. He liked to sit downstairs, next to a window with his hood up and his face in a book. There were many dangers in attending Rotherham Grammar, the finest (the only) independent boys school in the Rother Valley. For pupils of other less selective institutions the isolated Grammar School boy was fair game. There was taunting, theft, assault and battery. Morris lost biology text books and shoes; he collected black eyes, dead legs and brutal Chinese burns. Summer was the worst. There was a special uniform: a purple and cream boating blazer with matching bow-tie. It dated from the Edwardian period; Morris's mother got one cheap at the Easter bring-and-buy. On the twenty-nine circular it was suicidal. They wrote on him in felt-tip pen – *poof, homo, bum boy* – they extorted his dinner money and daubed him in Tipp-Ex. Adults turned a blind eye. Their children did CSEs. They voted Labour. Morris got what he deserved.

Once at school, through the Palladian iron gates, down the pebbled driveway, there were other, subtler risks to endure: his ignorance, for example, of holidays in France, his failure to own a bike, a cassette radio, a record player, his loathing of games. He talked like the dinner ladies; he wore nylon shirts. All these things marked him as vulnerable, open to abuse. His weakness was a temptation to others, an incitement; he drew violence to him – corporal punishment, kneeings, water bombs. He had no comeback, no recourse. He didn't tell his parents – even at ten he knew it would only sadden and confuse them. All Morris had was his own cleverness. He hoarded it, he built it up like

79

breastworks. He was small and bony, his father owned a hot-dog van, but he understood quadrilateral equations, he was the master of the irregular verb. It was his cleverness which saved him, as always. There were tricks he could perform: naming every UK number one, translating Plastic Bertrand – it was like being double jointed or having pubic hair. It was a *thing*. It earned him respect and safety. Playing rugby one freezing Wednesday afternoon, he accidentally poked Rory Chaplin, captain of the under-fourteens, in the eye. They were both trapped beneath a collapsed scrummage. Rory had a chest like Tom Selleck; he was already shaving. His fist, as big as a Melton pie, moved back, ready to punch his unlucky assailant. Morris awaited the sensation of flayed lip – the not unfamiliar taste of blood. Then Rory recognised who it was. It was that Morris Gutman, the Mekon, the one who knew the lyrics to every song on *Goodbye Yellow Brick Road*. He stopped, rubbed his ox-like eye and blinked. His fist reversed itself and he shot off like a laser-guided bullock in search of the ball. It had only taken a second, half a glance, but Morris knew what he meant. He was immune.

They called him the Mekon, even the teachers (Meek for short). Dan Dare's sworn enemy, all brain and no body. It was meant affectionately; he liked it, he took it on board. He was not the cleverest boy at Rotherham Grammar – that was Derek Spencer, whose father was a judge; there was also Lester Krauthammer, who had been born in Austria and was naturally trilingual – but Morris used his cleverness, he made it work for him.

'You'll make a fearsome bookie one day,' Mr Callas his maths teacher had joked. That was what it was like. Even in his pomp there was a tinge of commonness, something vocational about Morris; he could never entirely shake it off. Derek and Lester went to Oxford, Morris went to Sheffield. He got three As at A Level but his Oxbridge interview was a catastrophe – high in his corduroy eyrie the don, who assumed Rotherham Grammar was somewhere in Cumbria, seemed unimpressed by Morris's ability to memorise and skim. When Morris confessed his ignorance of

80

eighteenth-century French poetry, he seemed faintly alarmed; when Morris admitted a fondness for the sea novels of Hammond Innes, he hastily relit his pipe to cover his amusement.

At Sheffield, he had had to retune his cleverness so as to appeal to women. This was not easy: there was an initial period of disorientation and rebuff. Women, he quickly realised, were not impressed by his ability to recall verbatim the albums of Jasper Carrott or to argue the toss on nuclear disarmament. They were unmoved (one or two seemed actually repulsed) by his narrative poem on the Falkands Conflict, which had won him prizes at Rotherham Grammar. He would need, he realised, new tactics, a whole new approach. The clothes – peg trousers, cavalry shirts, winkle pickers – were no problem. Likewise the hair, shaved at the back and sides, moussed vertical on top. It was the attitude he needed, the repartee. He set to work to transmute his cleverness into wit. It took him about a year. After that he began sleeping with women far above his station: women with double-barrelled names, women who studied Art History. They found him charming, quirky, Woody Allenish. They would never really go out with him, they would never invite him to their homes (which they returned to frequently), but he was tremendous fun, a terrific experience.

If there was a sadness in Morris at this time, it was prompted by his parents. He wanted them to be impressed by his achievements, but when they visited on the train they seemed bemused and at cross purposes. They thought his dissertation very nice, but they reserved their greatest enthusiasm for the spotlessness of the refectory toilets, the reliability of Morris's new deep-fat fryer. He wanted something they could recognise – perhaps that was why he chose to do a Ph.D. (he would be a doctor!), perhaps (as E had asserted angrily more than once) that was why he had married. If so, his tactics were quite wrong. As his parents grew older they retreated, their vocabulary shrank and their willingness to acknowledge new experiences disappeared entirely. They wished Morris well, but it felt to all three of them like he was disappearing over the horizon.

The Bangor calamity followed his father's death by three

months. It was from those events that he dated his current woe.

'I'm like a piece of wood,' his father had said from his hospital bed. 'A useless pork chop.'

The tumour was just above his left eye. When he first went in for radiation they marked him up with a black felt pen: little arrows and dots like a treasure map. When they brought him back from the hospital, he had lost the use of his remote control. He fell down in the toilet; he wept and asked for tripe and pictures of his granddad. It was hard to say whether he was becoming more himself or less. Morris felt he should do *something*, as if cancer was a problem he could solve. He had come to think of his brain as infinitely flexible, up to any challenge. While his mother responded with food – extraordinary puddings, jelly laced with protein powder – Morris went on the Internet and yelled at the consultants. None of it worked. His father chewed and chewed but had forgotten how to swallow. Brown, masticated goo dribbled out of his mouth and back on to his barely-touched plate. As she scraped another Tesco ready-meal into the bin his mother shed silent tears of defeat. At the hospital, Morris explained carefully how his father's life might still be saved; he mentioned the names of radical treatments, invasive possibilities. They offered him leaflets and freephone numbers, they suggested addresses he could write to, groups he might join. But Morris had never been a joiner.

As his father's coffin disappeared behind the electric curtains of the crematorium, he felt the clay of his brain hardening in his head. Death was like a furnace: firing, fixing. When Underseel gave him the scholarship speech three months later, Morris had no elasticity left, no give. All he could think of was to lower his sights – Eccles not Banbury – and return to his work.

After that came marriage, then Molly, and through it all the interminable quest for employment, the endless interviews and self-promotion like a mirror image of celebrity. Perhaps he was fighting on too many fronts; perhaps he needed to rationalise. What was he talking about? He was already fucked. He had just made the biggest mistake of his life, bigger even than choosing to write his dissertation under the supervision of Underseel. He had left Dirck van Camper, stepson of Firenze Beach, for dead on the tarmac waste of the Dalton Street car park. Even if he was never caught, even if Dirck van Camper lived, how could he bear the knowledge of what he had done? Not just the reversing but the running away? He would break under the strain; he could already feel it inside him, taking him over like a virus, like an unlicensed drug.

When E came downstairs with Molly it was too late; Morris was consumed by the unspeakableness of his dilemma. All he could do was glare.

'I had this dream about my mother,' E said. She was heating Molly's milk. Molly was playing with the fridge magnets. 'We were bungee jumping, but she wanted me to stop because of the baby, she said it might fly out on its own. The bungee cords were sort of umbilical. What do you think it means?'

She was putting Marmite on toast. Molly was climbing into her chair.

Morris shook his head.

'What did Molly dream about?' E asked.

Molly thought.

'Balloons,' she said.

'What did Daddy dream about?'

Morris looked up. What should he say? Dead bodies, manslaughter, the unravelling of their lives?

'Balloons,' he said emptily.

E tutted and smiled. She was still feeling cheerful from the night before.

'Liar.'

E was frying an egg, Molly was eating her toast. Morris remembered their lovemaking. In his memory it seemed ghastly: a clashing of gross, untended flesh; a futile, pathetic denial of the doom that surrounded them. Then he remembered the pregnancy, his foetal child, a whole hive of new difficulties waiting to be born – just add time. It was all too much. He needed to extend his brain to house all this stuff, add another room, build a conservatory, a shed. He couldn't cope. He thought of biting off his own fingers, sticking a ballpoint pen in his eye.

'Are you OK?' E asked. She waited several seconds for a reply.

'I couldn't sleep at all. I'm utterly exhausted.' It was as though the words had to be hauled from a tremendous depth, and the effort of hauling was almost too much for him.

'You were up late last night.' E winked and pushed her tongue into her cheek.

Morris scowled. 'What?'

E reddened. She turned abruptly back to her egg.

Morris closed his eyes. He noticed he had a headache. At some point, the central heating had clicked on; that, plus the boiling and frying, left the atmosphere inside his duffle coat damp and fetid. He could hear the crinkling of the oil in the pan, the insistent banging of Molly's teddy-bear spoon on the table: *bang, bang, bang, bang*.

'Please don't bang, Molly, sweetheart.' E's voice was gruffer than before, constrained by her awareness of Morris's mood. There was silence for a few seconds then: *bang, bang, bang, bang*.

Morris's whole body felt tense, tight as though he had recently undergone comprehensive cosmetic surgery. His throat was raw, his eyes were outlined with pain. Was he going down with something? He had six hours of teaching on Tuesday and hadn't prepared a thing. He was weeks behind with marking.

'Molly, *please* stop.'

He hated that tone of pleading in E's voice. They were being bullied by a bloody two-year-old.

There was another pause then: *BANG, BANG, BANG*.

Morris stood up and violently threw off his hood like a disguised nobleman revealing himself at the end of a melodrama.

'Shut the fuck up!' he yelled. His voice felt awkward and high-pitched. 'Shut up NOW!'

There was half a second of silence during which they both looked at him with open mouths, then Molly's head turned purple and she began to scream like a jet engine. E plucked her out of the booster seat and hugged her.

'Oh, oh, oh, oh, oh, sweetheart,' she said. 'Oh, oh, oh, oh.' She stared at Morris. 'That was unforgivable,' she hissed at him above the screams. 'I hope your interview's a bloody calamity. You're such an arsehole.'

Morris stamped up the stairs like a pantomime giant. He put yesterday's clothes on; he didn't wash or brush his teeth. In three minutes he was back in the car. The death car! It took him a few moments to readjust. The steering wheel was cold and clammy to the touch, the interior smelled as usual of mildew, sourness and burning. Had he checked his bumper for damage? Might there be bloodstains, fibres, fluids, *tell-tale signs*? He dashed round the back, but as far as he could tell there was no difference, just the usual bowing plastic and rust blisters. It was a cold, windless morning; the cloud cover was solid grey and seamless, like a high ceiling. What could he do? He ran his hand over the crude fibreglass patch which constituted his rear offside wheel arch. Nothing. It was obviously best to do nothing at all: lay low, keep your head down, do your work – the time-honoured academic tactics. They would not think of him; he would be overlooked. He had always been overlooked before, so why not now, when it mattered most? Temporary lecturers were all but invisible anyway. Yes, nothing was obviously the thing to do, but could he do it?

He started the car with some difficulty, then reversed with minute attention to detail into the empty road. He already felt an itchy, irrational urge to return to the Dalton Street car park. Wasn't that the normal thing to do? Not at six-thirty in the morning. He needed to kill some time. What would he see there anyway? The blood would have washed away. Perhaps the police had taped the area off or put up one of those signs: 'Accident Here. Can U Help?' Morris gulped and missed a gear – he had just had an image of cheap floral tributes taped to the lamp standard, laser-printed farewells covered in cling film, cards, cuddly toys. Surely it would be too soon for that? But still, he should use the Apollo Avenue car park instead, and he should certainly not seek information about the incident, even if such information took days or weeks to reach him or never came at all. He must remain quite firmly, as he always had been, out of the loop.

Morris drove around Coketown for two hours. He tried to daze himself with driving, to lose himself in the dull mechanics of it. He checked his mirror frequently, he used the handbrake at traffic lights, he assiduously obeyed the speed limit. He drifted into parts of Coketown – Brotdean, Sanctum, Boilswitch Moor – that he had never seen before. He was surprised by their ugliness and lack of vim. They reminded him of Rotherham twenty years before: concrete shopping precincts and Mecca bingo halls. There were no coffee bars he could see, no chain stores worthy of the name. The people, as they stood by their shattered bus stops or drove their ancient British cars, seemed grainy and pre-Thatcherite. The buildings were dark and moist. There was a general smell of soot and gas, a palpable air of public ownership. Had Morris simply forgotten such people and places still existed, he wondered to himself, or had his crime actually conjured them into being like ghosts of the future, images of what he might yet become?

He drove on past Victorian swimming pools, free-standing pubs and cinder car parks until he crossed the border into the strange, unpeopled landscape of the East Coketown redevelopment zone. Wide new roads wound past empty office developments and hangar-like supermarkets. Most of the zone still lay fallow – there were prairies of hard core and high, rough grass where slums had disappeared and where, according to the frequent hoardings, there would soon be high-class housing and retail opportunities. The centrepiece of the zone was to be The Matterhorn – the world's largest indoor ski-slope: artificial snow, hotels, restaurants, go-karting. Already half-built, it struck Morris as hubristic and Babylonian. The thought of its vast and inevitable success, conjuring as it did thoughts of his equally vast and inevitable failure, made him furious. Now he was jealous of a leisure complex! He felt an urge to beat himself with his car lock, tear at his nostrils with pliers.

An hour or so later, Morris sat in his swivel chair, hugging himself and dreading the arrival of the ten o'clock students – 'Aspects of the Augustan Age', Level One. Alone, if he tensed all his muscles and allowed himself only one small thought at a time, he could manage, but with other people around there were too many dangerous variables. He would have to loosen his grip, unclench his jaw, exhale. And once that happened, the deluge. Even the thought was disturbing. He needed to read something bland and cakey to settle his mind. He went to check his pigeon-hole. There were bound to be some committee minutes in there or a lengthy memo or two, mental wadding.

The departmental office was down the corridor on the right. It housed three vicious secretaries: Mabel, Heather and Joan. Mabel and Joan had both been there thirty-five years. They were tall and grey with gaunt, rather hungry faces. Joan was married to a librarian. Mabel was unmarried, although it was well-known that in the 70s she had had several affairs with faculty members. Neither had children. Heather, who was nineteen but wore kilts, was new, a sort of apprentice. Bernard had long since advised Morris not to ask for anything or even speak to the 'Furies' (as he called them) before elevenses: 'They can turn nasty when they haven't been fed.'

When Morris entered, Heather was glumly filing and Mabel and Joan were laying into an unfortunate student who had enquired about his exam marks.

'What's the exam code? What was your seat number? No seat number? Look at this.' Mabel waved an armful of box files which may or may not have had anything to do with exams. 'Do you expect me to go through this for your benefit? Do you imagine I have nothing better to do with my time?'

'I think he does think that,' Joan chipped in. 'They all do. They think we're all here to serve them, to bow and scrape.'

'You have no idea,' Mabel said, 'of the pressures we're under. No conception of the workload we're required to do.'

'And yet we do it gladly,' Joan said.

'Yes, we do it gladly. But there's always a percentage.' They glared at the unfortunate student. 'A small percentage who make things difficult.'

'Impossible.'

'For the rest of us.'

87

'I thought the results might be posted on the notice-board,' ventured the student.

'No, they *will not* be posted,' said Mabel. 'Do you think we're here to spoonfeed you? Do you imagine our role in life is to wipe your bottom? Do you think that's what we aspire to? Botty-wiping? Hand-holding? Spoonfeeding? Cleaning up your vomit? Changing your nappy? Waking up in the middle of the night to cuddle you and make sure the bogeyman isn't hiding under your bed?'

The student looked entirely beaten.

'So what should I do?'

'See your personal tutor.'

'Who's he?'

'It's on the notice-board.' Both Mabel and Joan had turned their backs on the student and resumed their laborious typing.

'Which notice-board?'

'*Which notice-board!*'

The student fled.

Morris crouched behind the counter, partly for cover and partly because the temporary lecturers' pigeon-holes consisted of three cardboard shoeboxes on the floor. There were, surprisingly, no memos or minutes in his, only an essay. He looked at the cover sheet: 'Total Mindfuck: A Study in Ethics and Embodiment' by Dirck van Camper. Morris stumbled slightly and knocked over a box of student questionnaires.

'Is someone there?' called Mabel.

Morris stood up.

'Just me.' He smiled weakly. They looked alarmed, astonished, superior, as though Morris had just committed the most appalling faux pas.

'Just picking up an essay,' Morris said. 'From,' he looked again at the cover sheet, 'Dirck van Camper – do you know him?' Morris couldn't help himself: this was just what he had feared, that, shorn of his solitude, shaken from his traffic-induced reverie, he would lose control, begin blurting. 'He's Dutch,' he offered, hoping to prod their memories.

88

Mabel and Joan looked at each other as if wondering where to begin their attack.

'I know him,' said Heather. 'Lanky sod.' (She still had certain edges, which Mabel and Joan were endeavouring to smooth off). 'He was in here yesterday wanting paper-clips.'

'For the essay,' Morris suggested.

'Paper-clips!' said Joan. 'Do they think we're stationery suppliers? Do they imagine that's our business? I'm sorry, but is there a sign saying WH Smith above that door?'

'We need to do something about those foreign students,' Mabel said. 'They know nothing.'

'Oh really, I've found them quite bright,' said Morris.

'About departmental rules and procedures, I mean,' Mabel went on. 'They haven't even read the handbook.'

'Do we send them handbooks?' Morris asked, unwisely.

'Of course we don't.' Her expression seemed to add, 'you idiot'. 'We can't waste handbooks on every Franz, Dirck and Heinrich. Printing costs are astronomical.'

Mabel began briskly rearranging the fluffy parrots on her desk as a sign that their exchange was at an end. The Furies clearly knew nothing about the incident, Morris thought. The opportunities to moralise on such an event were too great for them to have remained silent if they had.

Through the window behind Heather, Morris could see the Dalton Street car park. It was half-full. The administrators had, as usual, got there first and put their BMWs and Range Rovers in the finest spots. Now the lecturers were coming in – pre-owned hatchbacks and antique Volvos with roof-racks and 'Baby on Board' stickers. There was no sign of police activity, no obvious tape. The landlady of The Revolving Door, which edged onto the car park, was sweeping the pavement in her slippers. Might she have seen something, Morris wondered? What about her customers? The Revolving Door was a deeply unpopular pub; its financial survival was a constant cause of wonder on campus. But still, there must have been one or two people in there and the crumbling bay windows looked right across the car park. Morris dashed from the office like an addict in search of his next fix.

The interior of The Revolving Door was murky and water-stained, as though it had been flooded some time after the war and never properly redecorated. There were curling posters of the 1973 Coketown United squad and advertisements for drinks whose manufacture had ceased some years before. The bar was plywood stained with creosote and the beer towels seemed capable of sustaining a variety of wetland fauna. It was ten o'clock in the morning.

'Could I have a cup of tea?' Morris asked. The landlady had followed him in.

'This is a pub, love.'

'Right. A pint then.' She checked her watch, raised her eyebrows and walked round the bar. It took her a surprisingly long time to find a glass. Morris wondered how to broach the subject of hit-and-run.

'That's one pound seventy.' Whilst she was getting his change, it seemed to occur to the landlady that it was usual to chat with the customers.

'Hear about that accident last night?' she said.

'What?'

'Bald student. They carted him off in an ambulance.' She spoke as if all this was common knowledge, as though the morning papers had been full of it.

'Was he OK?'

'I should think not. His head was cracked open like a cantaloupe.' She lit another cigarette and wrapped herself more tightly in her lengthy mohair cardigan.

'Mind you,' she said speculatively, 'it's amazing what they can do.'

'But he wasn't dead?'

'Not as such, no.'

The beer had an unusual taste which Morris couldn't immediately identify. That was it: formaldehyde. He took several more compulsive gulps then ordered another one. The landlady disappeared to make sausage rolls for the evening's darts match. Morris stared at the grim effluvia that topped his pint. He thought about the students waiting outside his office door.

At first they would be irritated that he was late, then, when they realised he wasn't showing up at all, they would be pleased. What did they think about him anyway, those eighteen-year-olds? What did they imagine his life was like? To the extent that they thought about him at all, Morris assumed they considered him to be a giant swot, someone who read books all the time and possessed a bizarre, unbroken knowledge of Augustan Literature and its environs. As they sat in his office he could sense their careless laconic faith; when he said things they wrote them down and quoted them back to him with embarrassing accuracy in exams. When he admitted he didn't know something they assumed it wasn't worth knowing. They had no idea that his knowledge was a loose crochet-work of platitudes and cramming, that he was drifting helplessly away from the things that mattered most. They were like children. They believed in him.

He was at the bottom of his second pint and the thought brought tears to his eyes. The beer, for all its ghastliness, was having an effect. Morris began to imagine that he had a real rapport with his students; he began to think that teaching was his passion. It was the teaching that was important after all, he said to himself, the lives he touched. *That* would survive him, not the writing which no one ever read, not the grubby politics of promotion. He was sitting on his own in a side room that smelt of Dettol and was painted entirely brown. He saw the way forward quite clearly. He would go to the hospital, find Dirck van Camper, assess the extent of his injuries, then confess. He would accept the consequences of his actions. If he had to spend a year or two in an open prison, so be it – it would give him time for reading, lesson plans, correspondence.

That was the impulse that brought Morris to Dirck van Camper's hospital bed. His enthusiasm for confession was dulled a little, however, when he realised that Dirck's injuries, although serious, were not life-threatening. Moreover, Dirck had no memory at all of the incident.

Then Zoe Cable appeared, like a visitor from another dimension. She was wearing a long white overcoat, her lips were purple, her hair was asymmetrical; she smelled of grapefruit and plasticine. Had they found him out already?

'Morris, it's you,' she said.

Morris was filled with terror. Dirck van Camper *and* Zoe Cable. What could he do? Running away was an obvious option, so was bursting into tears, but instead he stood up slowly and shook her hand. At some deep and entirely irrational level, he realised, he was still hoping to get the permanent job.

'I didn't know you two were close,' she said.

Morris realised with a sudden start how peculiar this must look to her – him standing by Dirck van Camper's hospital bed when he should, by rights, have been in room N2B of the Mick McManus Building teaching 'Aspects of the Augustan Age' for the third time that day.

'Well,' he mumbled, 'not in an orthodox way. I mean an incident like this, a terrible incident such as this one, brings things to the surface which might otherwise remain concealed.'

Zoe looked unconvinced.

'Oh absolutely,' she said. 'By the way Morris, do you know if any of Dirck's relatives are coming over? Parents? Mother?'

He repeated something that Dirck's extraordinarily tall girl-friend had told him about Thailand. Zoe continued to make small talk.

'When did you hear about it anyway?' she asked.

Morris gulped.

'I was in my office late,' he said. 'I saw the police and so on.'

Zoe nodded.

Morris began anxiously mapping the logical *cul de sac* into which he had just wandered. If I *was* in my office late, he thought, then why haven't I told anyone else? Why didn't I talk to the police? And *where*, most awkwardly, did I park my bloody car? It was no good. He was snookered.

'What is the worst thing you have ever done?' He asked suddenly, 'and how did you get over it? I favour confession.'

Zoe's eyes widened. Her forehead was corrugated with concern.

'Morris,' she replied, 'could you be a little more specific?'

'This is all my fault.'

'God no,' she said. 'It's bonkers to blame yourself. I mean really what could you have done?'

'I should have looked in the mirror.'

Zoe seemed non-plussed. Her mouth moved but for a moment no words came out.

'*Riiight*,' she said eventually. 'And what do you think you would have seen in the mirror Morris?'

Was she an idiot, he wondered, or was this some special interrogation technique?

'Dirck of course.'

At that Zoe actually took a step backwards. The dividing curtain behind her wafted slightly. If she had suspected something, Morris realised, she had certainly not suspected that. He felt momentarily proud to have taken Zoe Cable so clearly by surprise.

'What are you going to do next?' she asked.

'I'm going to confess,' he said. 'I'm going to the police.'

'The *police*?' Zoe squealed.

There was a brief commotion, heads turned. Morris reddened.

'This is the twenty-first century Morris,' she hissed. 'You were consenting adults.'

Now Morris took a step backwards. Consenting? He was aware that Zoe's research encouraged a certain ethical murkiness, but hit-and-run? And what did consent have to do with it? Was she really suggesting that on some unconscious, non-verbal level, Dirck, because he was there, because he was dressed entirely in black, because he was directly behind the car, *wanted* to be run over?

'You think he consented?'

'Are you saying you forced yourself on him Morris?'

'God no! It wasn't deliberate. It just happened. It was beyond my control.'

'Of course it was. So what is there to confess?'

'You don't think I'm culpable at all?'

'Absolutely not. You can't legislate desire.'

This, Morris thought, is getting weirder all the time. He could see the appeal, if not the logical basis, of the idea that Dirck van Camper had really wanted to be run down, but was she now suggesting that he, Morris, may really have wanted to do it, that it hadn't been accidental at all?

'You think I really wanted . . .' He couldn't finish. The thought was too strange and too illegal.

'I understand how you feel, Morris,' she said. 'But these lines are there to be crossed. I've done similar things myself.'

'You have?' he said. 'You've done similar things?'

'Of course. Did you really think you were breaking new ground?'

'Well I suppose not.' Morris hesitated. 'But still.'

'You'd be amazed what people get up to in their free time.'

Morris *was* amazed. Was it possible that, rather than confirming his personal and professional isolation, his assault on Dirck might become a way of making new friends? Was there really, as Zoe Cable seemed to be suggesting (was that a *wink*?) a community of like-minded people who enjoyed that kind of thing?

'I've got a child,' he blurted nonsensically.

'Oscar Wilde had two.'

Did he? *Oscar Wilde*? What on earth was she talking about?

'Let's just say,' Zoe continued, 'that I'm good with secrets, Morris.'

She was smiling at him now. Between the wide white lapels of her Italian mac her breastbone glimmered hard and knobby, like the ridgepole of a tiny suntanned tent. She took a step forward and placed an arm round his shoulder. She was inviting him in, he realised, into the guiltless zone. She was assuring him that it was safe there, that he was welcome. He smelled the plasticine. He smelled the grapefruit. A tear came to Morris's eye. Hitherto he had never considered Zoe Cable to be remotely motherly, but at that moment he had the urge to lay his care-bruised head on the taut yellow zigzags of her Eley Kishimoto skirt and bawl like a child.

94

Chapter 11

E had arranged to have lunch with her friend Stella. They were sitting in a booth in Totally Tarquin, one of the new restaurants on Grundy Street.

'Morris flounced out again this morning,' she said.

'Flounced?'

'Flounced, stormed, whatever.'

'Is he still obsessed with that job?'

'It's an addiction – which in itself is OK with me, but it brings him no pleasure at all.'

'I believe there is a name for that.'

The starters arrived: garlic mushrooms, deep-fried Brie. E attacked hers with gusto.

'I am hungry and angry at the same time,' she said. 'Those two emotions are vying for control.'

'Is hunger an emotion?'

'Yes, it bloody well is.' She squeegeed the empty mushroom plate with her forefinger then sucked. 'I worry that Morris is becoming bipolar,' she continued. 'It's hard to find grounds for optimism.'

'Is there a family history at all?'

E paused and frowned as though trying to recall an unusual name.

'His mother sends us monthly food parcels – canned goods, crab paste, macaroons.'

'So there are boundary issues.'

E nodded.

'If it weren't for the macaroons I'd say something myself, but Morris won't go there at all. He still feels guilty that they have nothing in common. You should hear them on the phone – weather, cat food, it's truly painful. Then there's the death.'

'His dad's?'

'Right. His father owned a hot-dog van. Football matches, greyhound races, he would park up near the town hall on Saturday nights to catch them after closing time. Twenty years of boiled onions and brown sauce.'

'That would take its toll I imagine.'

'Of *course*. Of course it would. Morris had to help. His Dad would cook and Morris would serve. They wore long white coats, the van was spotless, but you can never quite erase that smell of onion. His mother still mentions it.

'Morris went to Rotherham Grammar School. He was a scholarship boy. There were encounters involving the hot-dog van. Boys would stop (often with their fathers), there would be a cheerful exchange, smiles, introductions, but the repercussions still haunt him. Mockery, looks – it's the little things. His father had no idea; he was proud of the hot-dog van. When people asked for his occupation, he said businessman. There was a certain amount of anger. Morris felt abandoned. And then the guilt of course.'

'What happened to the van?'

'Crushed after the funeral. Recycled I imagine. But part of him is still in it.'

They were eating heated ciabattas: ham and gruyère, roasted pepper salad. The smells were orchestral: layered, swelling counterpoints of mellowness and tang.

'Sometimes I fear we married in haste.'

'North Devon,' Stella remembered. 'It was a lovely weekend.'

'Yes, but did we really need to attach a wedding to it? It was rather *literal*.'

'How does Molly fit in?'

'Molly never fits in. That's her charm. She's the original refusenik.'

'I think she is gorgeous. That little pudding face.' Stella made a squeezing motion as though testing an invisible grapefruit.

'That's her image. Cute kid, on the quiet side. She cultivates it. She practises in the mirror. The truth is more horrible.'

'But now you're having another.'

'That's a strategic move. We'll play them off against each other. They'll cancel themselves out. It was Morris's idea.'

'Really?'

'No. Not at all. I'm joking. I fear I bullied him into it. I'm not loud, but I am constant – I have a drip-drip quality at times.'

'So how does Morris feel about kids?'

'Deep down I think he fears them. They make him nervous. He looks at Molly sometimes as though he thinks she might suddenly go off like a bomb.'

'I thought they were close.'

'That's his image: cheerful father, chuckle-headed academic. It's served him well but now . . .'

'Thirty-seven's a tricky one.'

They looked at each other, then down at the empty plates. E sniffed.

'Someone's eating key lime pie. Do they serve that here?'

They called for a dessert menu.

'How's work?' E asked. Stella was assistant producer for *Camcorder Calamity*, a Friday evening blooper show hosted by ex-footballer Dave Piston and made on a budget by Ringroad Productions of Coketown.

Stella rolled her eyes.

'You know, calamity's like porn,' she said. 'There are only so many variations.'

'But people watch it.'

'Our share is up. We'll run forever so long as people keep toppling into swimming pools and sitting on birthday cakes. Misfortune is a cash cow.'

'It's a strange business.'

'It's a twisted world we live in. You should see some of the things they send in: bloodshed, sex. We've had to involve the police more than once. I've seen an actual amputation – chainsaw up a stepladder. Bestiality is commonplace. These people are exhibitionists. The posting is part of the pleasure.'

'Is this how you imagined your career path?'

'Now you're mocking me. It's steady money. I'm writing links.

"This next lot are animal crackers", that sort of thing. I still dream of radio drama, but we'd have to move back south. Did I tell you we're looking at flats in Tintagel Forest?'

'Tintagel Forest?' E puffed at her herbal tea. 'Didn't that used to be Bogdean?'

'That's right. The estate agents changed the name. They chopped down some woods, put up a John Lewis and a stack of yuppie prefabs. Environmentally it's not so great, but you can't argue with the commute.'

On their way out E waved and flashed a smile to a dark-jowled man in the corner who seemed to be speed-reading the *Times Higher Education Supplement*.

'Who's that?' asked Stella.

'They call him the Crocodile,' she said. 'I could strangle the bastard with my bare hands.'

Chapter 12

The tragedy of Arthur Alderley is, therefore, the tragedy of western modernity itself. For Rufus Clerkenwell, protagonist of A Scent of Horseradish, *as for the honourable but finally unhinged Maddy Puberly of* The House at Hough End, *the drive for personal liberty cannot ultimately be unentangled from the centrifugal experience of subjective decentring. The ironic finale of* A Scent of Horseradish, *in which the manic Clerkenwell is asphyxiated in a hopperload of the very root vegetables which have brought him his fortune, only serves to italicise this overdetermined yet critically underprivileged linkage. For Alderley himself (if I may risk a concluding deviation into the theoretically prickly forest of the biographical), the compulsive ritornello of his late novels may be back-allegorised to the adolescent Alderley's own 'primal scene', in which the Promethean and the Oedipal remarkably cross-refer. The scorching of Causley is the symbolic origin, the always absent cause, of Alderley's subsequent literary expulsions. His work is, for all its extraordinary lubricity, a Janus-faced pushme-pullyou, pointing both forwards and backwards, up and down, towards the very meaning he would like to expunge; away, in a liberating gesture, from the very murky material trauma which gives him his identity.*

Back allegorise? It stank of desperation. Morris was sitting in the death car going over his presentation one more time before the interview. The windows were fogged up; hail was beating on the

99

roof and gathering in the moss-grown gutters. It was April. Morris could smell his own aftershave, feel the cold sweat dripping from his armpits on to his love handles. He must have gone over the presentation thirty times since Wednesday – Zoe Cable had lent him Jocelyn and Darren so he had done no teaching – and once or twice it had actually seemed quite good. Now it read like a suicide note, a farewell to his career.

His nascent friendship with Zoe Cable, which at one point he had thought might save him in the interview, had actually only added (if that was possible) more pressure. She had unexpectedly come into his office half an hour before. She was wearing dark glasses and stylised camouflage gear; she smelt of airports and olive oil.

'Morris, one word of advice,' she hissed.

Morris nodded eagerly. Zoe lifted up her sunglasses. She was wearing camouflaged contacts.

'Attack!'

'Attack?'

'I think the military metaphor is appropriate in these circumstances. No blood will be shed, but there is booty. We have it, you want it. You must wrest it from us.'

'I've never thought of an interview in those terms before.'

Zoe nodded and glanced over the sparse office he shared with three other temporary lecturers, as if that proved her point.

'There are elemental forces at work here, Morris. I know what you're capable of.' Morris blushed a little. 'But do the others? I doubt it. They look at you, they look at your CV and, forgive my harshness, they smell your fear. And fear is annoying, no one hires fear. Remember that, Morris. You need to show us something.'

Morris winced. 'I was going to photocopy my teaching evaluations.'

Zoe rolled her eyes.

'Let me put it this way, Morris. We have a shortlist of five. There is an order of preference and you're at the bottom. Student evaluations won't do it, you need to go nuclear. We've just seen someone with large tits from Wolverhampton who's already

100

pulled in 15k from the ESRC. Declan's mind is all but made up. Listen, I'm on a bathroom break, this conversation is completely off the record. See you at two.'

It was one forty-five. The hail was easing slightly. From Recreation Road there was a roar of deregulated buses, and from the student union steps the sound of someone with a megaphone shouting about Third World debt. What had Morris expected? That on the basis of his shared hit-and-run secret Zoe Cable would get him the job? Probably. Their conversation on Tuesday afternoon had so affected his thinking that it had been hard ever since for Morris to know what was real or possible. If reversing into Dirck van Camper was a) OK and b) what he had really wanted to happen, what was the new status of his other fears and desires? If he wanted a permanent job intensely enough wouldn't he get it? He had hoped, a trifle desperately perhaps, that it might work like that. But now Zoe Cable was saying he had to act, he had to 'wrest it from them'. Hopeless. Of course they could smell his fear; fear was all he consisted of. He was the insubstantial sum of all his errors and anxieties, all his failures to act or speak. He was a large jelly in a bad suit.

He was so tired of this: this job search, this whole process emptying him out like a vast, brutal enema again and again. How many interviews had he had over the last five years? He added them up – Eccles, Peterborough, Gwent . . . twenty-two. Twenty-two interviews. He needed to bring it to an end one way or another. It had to stop.

Morris opened the glove compartment and removed a clear plastic folder that had been in there since Tuesday. He walked carefully across the hail-slickened car park towards the Arts Faculty. As he walked, the sun blinked brightly on then off as though its bulb had just blown. Morris puffed out his chest; he got ready to attack.

The seat they offered him was warm and smelt of CK One. It was at the head of a rectangular conference table. The panel had arranged themselves around the remaining edges in, as far as Morris could tell, no particular order: the Crocodile, Declan Monk, Darian Cavendish, Mohammed Ganguly, Zoe Cable.

101

Mohammed Ganguly was the only one smiling. The others, including Zoe, were either staring grumpily into space or, more disturbingly, reviewing his CV. The residue of their coffee break – broken biscuits, unused crockery – formed an untidy centre-piece. As he looked out at them, Morris felt a moment of intense loneliness, a mixture of terror and exhilaration which reminded him most vividly of the dizzying confusions he had experienced as a child on trying to imagine the death of his parents.

'We'd like to begin with the presentation,' the Crocodile said. 'Whenever you're ready.'

Morris retrieved the plastic folder from his bag and placed it in front of him. He took from it a sheaf of typewritten sheets. He cleared his throat and made direct, unyielding eye contact with each of the interviewers in turn. Then he began.

'The title of my paper today is "Total Mindfuck: A Study in Ethics and Embodiment."'

He read Dirck van Camper's words slowly and carefully, partly to increase their impact and partly because he had never read them before and wasn't exactly sure what some of them meant. The argument, as far as he could understand it, was that the Body was a terribly good thing, especially in compar-ison to the Mind, and that most philosophers, novelists and literary critics, in fact almost everyone prior to Dirck van Camper himself, had neglected this fact. It struck him as overblown and self-evident, but he could tell that the panel were eating it up. Several were actually nodding, making notes. Twenty-two interviews and he had never known anyone nod before.

'This tendency in Western ethics towards decorporalisation, which I have been tentatively mapping,' Morris read, 'must be met not with a reactionary return to the body as *logos*, but rather with an expansion of the category body to include, to incorpo-rate as it were, the non-physical and non-human – the animal, the machine, the network. We must seek a body not only *sans* organs, as Delueze argues, but also *sans frontières*.'

The first question came from Darian Cavendish.

'What about the incarnation?' she said. 'Christ – the spirit made flesh. Some might say that since Western philosophy comes through Aquinas of Hippo that's rather important.'

Morris had not known how he would handle the questions. He had not thought that far ahead. He looked at Darian. She was wearing an Arran-knit cardigan buttoned up to her neck. Her hair, rough cut below the ear, had the brittle frizziness of middle-age. She looked intense and vulnerable. He weighed his options. He knew that Darian, a fierce Anglo-Catholic, was not well-liked. She was seen as an eccentric obstructionist saved from the axe only by her reputation as a first-class textual editor and her personal links to the Vice-Chancellor. The Crocodile undoubt-edly hated her since she had been there longer than him and regarded his new regime as a passing fad. Zoe Cable, he knew, didn't take her seriously. Declan Monk, probably the least godly of them all, had rolled his eyes at the question, and Mohammad (leaving aside his natural religious differences) would go along with Declan (Morris knew they played squash together). Darian was friendless. Morris would take her down.

'I regard the myth of the incarnation,' he said, 'as merely an idealist response to the scandal of subjectivity, a response which unfortunately reinforces rather than deconstructs the opposition of body and spirit. I recommend that you read a little Nietzsche.'

Zoe snorted, Darian turned pink.

'Oh it's always Nietzsche with you people,' she said. 'When will you learn?'

'Thank you Darian,' said the Crocodile, as though nothing had happened. 'I believe Mohammad is next.'

Mohammad had not stopped smiling since Morris had come in. Morris was beginning to wonder whether it was a permanent facial peculiarity.

'Morris,' he said. 'Have you ever considered teaching the novels of C.S. Forrester? I think they're terribly good.'

'I'm afraid I'm not familiar with his work. Does the library carry it?'

'Our holdings are surprisingly patchy, but I have my own copies. I'd be happy to lend them to you.'

'That would be fascinating.'

There was a puzzled pause before the Crocodile called on Declan. Declan coughed, tugged his beard and shimmied sideways in his seat. He offered Morris his conventional chummy smile. Morris smiled back and readied himself. He was like a savage that had eaten the heart of his vanquished enemy. The spirit of Dirck van Camper was in him now, spreading, blending. Morris felt a visceral surge of self-belief.

'Morris,' Declan said, 'I was a little surprised by the subject of your presentation. Since all your previous work has been on . . .' He lowered his half-moon glasses and rifled uneasily through the documentation. 'Arthur Alderley. Can you explain the relationship between Alderley and your current interests?' Declan pulled a long face, leaned back in his seat and squinted at him like a high-court judge.

'There is no connection,' Morris said. 'I believe in *dis*continuity, *dis*junction, the incommensurate. The urge to coherence is, as your own masterful work on the poetry of William Butler Yeats attests, proto-fascist. How can we expect to respond,' he glanced at the Crocodile, 'to the recent revolutions in learning delivery except by a constant process of self-reinvention? Yesterday I was a scholar of Arthur Alderley; today I am a theorist of the body; tomorrow, who knows? The commodification of knowledge is over, now the flow of information is unstoppable, it moves like the weather. The idea that we can specialise, corner the market, is absurd. All we can do is tap its flow, surf its waves. Alderley was a phase, a moment, but knowledge is a process.'

'How does this relate to teaching?' the Crocodile broke in.

'I regard my classes as learning delivery systems. I teach technique – content is a side issue.'

'You mean you are prepared to teach anything?'

'Yes, absolutely anything. Without warning.'

The Crocodile nodded eagerly and wrote something in his notebook.

'You're something of a chameleon,' said Declan.

'I'll pass on the reptile image,' he glanced surreptitiously at the Crocodile, who smiled. 'I am reprogrammable, capable of infinite upgrades.'

'The brain is a machine,' Declan offered.

'No, or only in the sense that a computer is a machine, which is no sense at all – it's a locus of possibility.'

'Truly fascinating,' said Mohammad Ganguly out of the blue. Everyone looked at him for a second.

'Sheer verbiage,' grumbled Darian.

'Morris,' Zoe said without being asked, 'are you aware that the AHRB recently announced an open competition for a Research Hub in Body Studies? They're seeking a single institution to act as the centrally-funded fulcrum for Body Studies in the UK.'

Zoe's khaki-and-brown eyes were egging him on, urging him to finish what he had started. Morris had never heard of the Research Hub in Body Studies.

'I certainly am,' he said. 'Indeed, my initial informal soundings suggest that a Coketown bid would be warmly welcomed. Its ultimate success, of course, would depend on a convincing display of intra-institutional synergies.'

'Of course,' Zoe replied, absent-mindedly. She scribbled something on a Post-it note and passed it over to the Crocodile. The Crocodile's eyes widened noticeably.

'Your own projects on urban sex-crime, for instance,' Morris went on, 'offer an interesting potential linkage with my recent work on the post-ethical.' Morris had long passed the tipping point. The world seemed for that dizzying moment entirely downhill.

'There are obvious bolt-on possibilities,' agreed Zoe.

'A Research Hub's two hundred grand per annum,' exclaimed Declan, almost in protest.

'Two hundred and fifty actually,' said Zoe, 'with overheads.'

'That's simply obscene,' Darian scowled.

'It would be a new record,' said the Crocodile.

Two hundred and fifty grand! The figure hung in the air like an ectoplasm before Mohammad Ganguly, still smiling, emitted a loud – and, in Morris's experience of twenty-three separate job interviews, entirely unprecedented – wolf-whistle.

Part Two

Chapter 13

Morris's slide from sleep to wakefulness was gradual and frictionless. His mind drifted gently from a strange dream about Daphne DuMaurier to an awareness of light (bright, white sunshine filtered through a double layer of walnut curtains), texture (the soft stiffness of white sheets) and temperature (sixty-eight degrees precisely). He rolled over and then, astonished by the lack of obstructions, did it again. Where was the edge of his bed? He reached out fruitlessly. Where was E? He opened one eye: the bedspread was the size of a football pitch. He opened the other eye: there was an expanse of purple carpet then, far off in the distance, a brown leather armchair with his crumpled clothes on it. The spackled ceiling was the height and texture of the Coketown sky in August.

He remembered where he was – the Malibu Hilton. The LA Body Conference. After several more rolls he reached the edge of the bed and stood up. He checked his symptoms: his head was clear and unaching and his vision was sharp and painless, his stomach felt settled but just pleasantly empty. He was actually looking forward to breakfast. Scanning his torso and legs, he was taken aback by the lack of knotting or stiffness. He checked his watch. It was six-thirty; he had gone to bed just after ten. Good God, he had slept for eight hours! No wonder he felt so odd. He walked over to the window and pulled back the curtain. He could feel heat radiate off the glass for an inch or two before being crushed by the air conditioning. Outside there were palm trees, billboards, large, silent cars. Sunlight glared off mirrored office buildings and concrete roofs. The only people he could see were black. He stepped back into the room. Something else was strange. Yes, he was unusually well-rested and felt bizarrely alert, but what else? He listened. There was the faintest hum of top-class air conditioning, but apart from that, nothing. Silence. The more he listened, the less he heard. It was dizzying. He sat down in the leather armchair. It was the first time he had been away from Molly. He remembered how she smelt in the mornings – cheesy, slightly burned. He remembered the machine-gun jabber of the first good cry of the day. It was strange to think of her for once as detachable, an option, to realise there were places where she wasn't.

He was having breakfast with Zoe Cable at seven. Her paper was at eight. The bathroom shower had a force of a sandblaster. It felt like mild plastic surgery. Descending on the escalator, Morris felt cleaner, newer than ever before.

Zoe was wearing mirrored goggles and a patchwork denim kaftan. She was eating watermelon and waving an unlit cigarette.

'8 a.m.,' she said. 'It's idiocy. Who do they think I am? Ben-fucking-Franklin?'

'There won't be much of an audience I suppose.'

'You're kidding. They'll all be there. Look around.'

Morris scanned the dining room. She was right. It was clogged with conferencees – power breakfasts and grim post-coital chit-chat. Over by the waffle irons some of the body art contingent were comparing tattoos.

'The American middle classes,' Zoe Cable went on, 'God love 'em, are notoriously bad at laziness. They don't do it well at all.'

'They have other people to do it for them.'

'Exactly, that's where we come in. We're a bit of rough. We drink, we smoke, we stay up late. We no longer believe in the healing power of education. British academics – we're a walk on the wild side. Unfortunately,' she waved the conference pro-gramme, 'someone seems to have forgotten that.'

'Were you up late last night?'

'Yes, but it was all research. I have the receipts. Look.' She fished a damp ball of paper from her pocket. She sniffed it.

110

'Oops, it might not be wise to take that through customs. How about you?'

'I slept for eight hours. It's a personal best.'

'Insomnia?'

'Children.'

Zoe nodded. 'Yo Bernice. You look radiant.' She waved at a broad-beamed, bald-headed woman who laughed back and gave her the finger. 'Bernice Plummer,' Zoe whispered. 'I've asked her for a letter for the Hub.'

'I've never seen a bed that size,' said Morris, still thinking of his sleep. 'It's really not necessary.'

'Well, that all depends.' Zoe lifted up her goggles and gave Morris a wobbly, red-eyed stare. Morris realised she was still a little drunk. 'On what you're planning to use it for.' She winked.

'What *would* you use it for – refugee camps, nuclear dumping? It's a trackless waste half the size of Wales.'

'Let's just say, Morris, there are certain team activities for which such an arena might be suitable.'

'Netball? Grand Prix racing?'

Zoe stuck out her tongue, there was a shiny silver stud through the middle of it.

'Bloody hell, is that new?'

'Last night. I fell in with the neo-primitive crowd. You don't want to know the details, Morris, but let's just say I'm no longer sitting comfortably.'

Zoe Cable yawned and ate a large chunk of watermelon. She smelt of baked potato and iodine. Morris couldn't remember the last time he had had breakfast with someone he was not attached to by blood or marriage. Zoe waved to a tall, thin man with a green goatee and a ring through his nose. Morris excused himself and went over to the smorgasbord. Ranged before him were golden-brown foothills of muffins, doughnuts and Danish pastries, steaming stainless-steel troughs of brittle bacon, sausage and scrambled eggs. Further along came pink banks of cold cuts, a gallimaufry of sliced and shredded fruits, tubs of cold cereals, warm cereals, pancakes, a half-hacked ham, raw steaks, sushi.

At home, Morris usually settled for a boiled egg, occasionally toast.

Other conferencees milled and grazed around him. They picked and frowned and picked again. Their plates, which were as big as dartboards, gradually and unrelentingly filled. They dipped maple syrup and hollandaise sauce; they taste-tested the blackened shrimps; they changed their minds about the bruschetta; they conferred at length about the saltiness of the anchovies and the arterial implications of the Eggs Benedict. Such plenitude took Morris aback. After several uncomfortable minutes he selected a hard-boiled egg and a bowl of All Bran. He walked carefully back to the table, worried that he was already out of his depth.

Someone touched him on the elbow. It was the man with the green goatee. 'Morris Gutman!' he exclaimed, as though they had known each other for years. 'Hank Bernebau. Listen, I read "Mindfuck." Outstanding, just outstanding. Zoe pointed you out.'

Morris glanced over at Zoe, who blew him a kiss. Hank was still shaking his hand.

'She says you're the next big thing.' He chuckled conspiratorially. His voice had the low breathlessness of a late night DJ. Despite the piercings and dyed facial hair, he must have been close to fifty. 'Listen, I'm doing a collection for UCP – the body-machine nexus. We've got the usual guys: Franz Poppenheim on race and machinery, Celie Humm on reconstructive surgery. But an ethics piece would be a terrific addition, if you've got anything along those lines?'

He stopped talking and looked at Morris. Women with long floral scarves manoeuvred around them.

'The post-Nietzschean stuff is just outstanding,' Hank added. There was another pause.

'Are you offering to publish something I've written?' asked Morris.

'It could be short,' he said, 'or indeed long. The longness or shortness would be entirely up to you.' He smiled.

Morris looked down at his hard-boiled egg, his bowl of

112

crumbling All Bran. The austerity of his choices seemed suddenly absurd.

'I accept,' he said. 'I mean, yes, I will.'

'Fantastic,' Hank seemed overjoyed, his nose ring wobbled. He gave Morris his card. 'Let me buy you dinner. I know an outstanding Polynesian place, the breadfruit . . . Ah!' Someone had started beckoning him from the other side of the room. He was retreating as he spoke, waving, winking, making gestures of friendship and excitement.

Morris sat back down. He mouth was slightly open.

'Hank loved "Total Mindfuck",' he said after a moment. 'He wants me to write something for his new edited collection.'

Zoe was sending a text message.

'That's a result,' she said without looking at him. 'Mention that in your book proposal. Hank's a name, they'll gobble it up.' She pressed 'send' then looked up at him. 'You know, ethics is an excellent angle Morris. It has that slightly ponderous, corduroy quality which in the context of Body Studies is actually very sexy. It's sly. And with something like "Total Mindfuck" – with that swerve from Aristotle to Internet porn – it feels much denser than it actually is. It gives the requisite sense of seriousness without that annoying philosophical complexity. It's heavy but light. Heavy-light. I like it a lot. It works.'

Morris smiled. Since its publication in *Vagina Dentata* he had begun to feel oddly proud of 'Total Mindfuck', even though not a word of it was his. It seemed somehow to reflect his character, to express, in a glancing way perhaps, who he really was. He shelled his egg and gobbled it in two bites. He sucked down his All Bran as though suffering from a deadly form of constipation.

He checked his watch: seven thirty-five.

'You'd better go and get changed,' he said.

'I beg your bloody pardon! What's wrong with this?'

'Isn't Firenze Beach on the panel? You look like a road protester.'

Zoe frowned and looked down at the denim kaftan.

'Wear the gold suit,' said Morris.

'The ABC suit? The "Look of Love" suit?'

'With the velvet corset.'

'The velvet corset, with the gold suit – it's a double whammy. I love it. Morris, when did you become a girl?'

'I like to keep my eyes open.'

They took the express elevator to the fifteenth floor. Zoe Cable dashed away to change. Morris telephoned E at work to tell her the good news.

'Hank Bernebau wants to publish an essay of mine,' he said. He was lying horizontally on the unmade bed. A silent slab of CNN was twitching and changing in the corner of the room.

'Hank who?' She sounded weary. He wondered what time Molly had woken up.

'Bernebau. It doesn't matter. It's an edited collection.'

'A collection of essays about Alderley? That's great.'

'No, not Alderley, the body-machine nexus.'

'Your essay is about this body-machine thing and Alderley?'

'No, it's nothing to do with Alderley. It's a new essay. I haven't written it yet.' Was it a bad line, Morris wondered, or was she being deliberately obtuse?

'You haven't written it yet? Isn't that a problem?' He heard E yawn and then answer someone.

'Why should it be a problem? It's standard practice. Do you expect me to write essays just for the sake of it? On the off chance?'

'Yes, I mean sorry to be obtuse Morris, but I thought that's what you did.'

'It's what I *used* to do.'

There was an extensive pause. In the background, Morris could hear the chitter of keyboards. Alison's shrieky laugh.

'Well I'm glad you've been having a good time, Morris.'

'I didn't say I was having a good time.'

'I just assumed you would be. On holiday in California.'

'I'm not on *holiday*. Why do you use that term? I find it quite maddening.'

'Vacation then?'

'Not funny E. This is work. I'm here on business.'

'Isn't it sunny?'

114

'Yes, it's sunny.'

'That must be nice. We had sleet last night. Molly's got glue ear.'

'The sunniness is beside the point. We went over this at length. I'm here to consolidate the impact of "Total Mindfuck".'

'I really hate that title.'

'You've made that absolutely clear,' he said, 'on more than one occasion. I've been left in no doubt as to your opinion on that matter.'

'Don't get bureaucratic on me, Morris. You're sounding like a press release.'

'With respect, you're driving me to it. I'd envisaged a brief and happy chat.'

'That's what we're having.'

Morris sighed. He had the urge to drop the phone in boiling water.

'Don't sigh, Morris, it makes you sound so defeated. Oooo, I think junior's just woken up. I just felt a big kick.'

Defeated? And Morris hated the way she always brought the foetus into it. Whenever things got heated these days, she always played the foetus card. It was so infuriating.

'Leave the foetus out of this,' he said

'The *foetus?*'

'Listen, I have to go. Zoe's paper is in five minutes and the rates here are a sick joke.'

'Aren't you on expenses?'

'There's always a deductible.'

'OK, then. We miss you Morris. Don't drink the mineral water.'

Chapter 14

Zoe Cable's paper, 'Radical Puke', was a tremendous success. She had known it would be. She had planned it that way. Nothing had been left to chance, or rather, once chance had tossed her the opportunity of sitting on a panel with Firenze Beach at the LA Body Conference she had nudged chance to one side and taken over herself. The primary purpose of her paper was to ingratiate herself with Firenze Beach, whose recommendation, could she secure it, would all but guarantee them the Research Hub. She was the leading figure in Body Studies, yet she was notoriously reticent at back-scratching. No one else had her yet, of that Zoe Cable was sure.

Months ago, when the panel had first been mooted (not long, funnily enough, after the Dirck van Camper incident), she had set Darren and Jocelyn to work. They had rooted up everything on Beach, not only the books and articles and interviews, but unpublished conference contributions, lecture notes, seminar series. They had photographs, videos and bootleg tapes. And once the information had been gathered they processed it, they boiled it down. Jocelyn wrote a special programme. They traced the recurrence of ideas, the growing and waning popularity of certain turns of phrase. You could diagram it all: the break-throughs, the failures and cul-de-sacs. If you look hard enough into anything, Zoe thought, you will find the throb. There is always a throb. They got it down to one side of A4 – everything she had ever written or said. Then they carefully inserted it, like a strand of alien DNA, into Zoe Cable's work on urban inebriation. At first the combination seemed gawky and unnatural. The rococo theorising of Firenze Beach seemed to clash, to grate with

116

Zoe Cable's sinewy cyber-argot. Certain adjustments needed to be made: sentences were clipped and joined, vocabulary was subtly altered. It began to come together. What had seemed merely awkward become dialogic, incoherence slid into multiplicity and 'Radical Puke' was born.

The drink-addled bodies of the youth of Greater Coketown (of which Zoe Cable had a small library of digital images) gave damp and stinky form to Firenze Beach's seminal notion of the unbody, the body without bounds. French feminism meets the Bacardi Breezer. It was a perfect instrument of intellectual seduction – flattering but cheeky, sexy yet censorious, serious and scatological at the same time. It could not fail. It did not fail.

After the question period, Zoe stayed in her seat. She pretended to adjust her Palm Pilot. She waved absent-mindedly to friends. She waited for Firenze Beach to approach. Zoe Cable believed in patterns, webs, indefinite chains of causality and chance. It was not a question of law or fate – since law and fate were just constructs designed to head off the multiplicities of desire – but of patterns of energy, intensities ebbing and flowing across space-time: jealousy, need, anger, love. She didn't *know* Firenze Beach would approach, but she knew it. It was not *true* but it would certainly happen.

Firenze Beach came from the left out of a ruck of admirers and hangers-on. She was wearing a knee-length linen tunic embroidered with images from ancient Greek pornography; she had a heavy bosom, the thighs of a footballer, her hair was hennaed and lengthy. Her glasses spoke of Paris in June.

'Zoe Cable,' she declared. 'I am astonished.'

They embraced. Zoe had imagined it would be like this – the astonishment, the embrace.

Firenze Beach sniffed.

'You smell of mulled wine and coconuts.'

'It's new.'

'Delightful.'

A semicircle formed. People were actually watching, trying to take notes. Firenze Beach was whispering in Zoe's ear.

117

'Tell me about these practices of vertical drinking. I am fascinated. What is their disciplinary context? How are they policed? Is there really a club called the Vomitorium? What is the genealogy of the kebab?'

'It all comes back to bursts, Firenze. If I may borrow your own terrific metaphor. The burst is crucial in this context. The burst of ketchup, urine, hot sauce, vomit, blood vessels – the shattering of containment and decorum. You should see the pavements afterwards.'

'I can only imagine.' She squeezed Zoe Cable's elbow. 'Those pictures – truly astonishing.'

After several more congratulatory minutes, Zoe beckoned to Morris. He ascended the platform and was introduced. 'Morris taught your stepson, Dirck,' she said, 'before the unfortunate collision.'

'Oh Dirck!' Firenze Beach opened her arms to Morris as though Zoe had just introduced him as a long-lost grandchild. Morris, who had turned greyish white, descended into the embrace. Zoe watched them carefully.

'How *is* Dirck?' he asked upon release.

Firenze Beach's eyes moistened, her jaw stiffened. She seemed in an instant both softer and more virile. Zoe felt these to be good signs. Even if Dirck hadn't told his mother the whole thrilling truth about his relationship with Morris, perhaps he had at least hinted at its unusualness.

'He has a new wheelchair. He is learning the harpsichord. He and Dorothy are living with us for a while, *en famille*. It's terribly nice. Dorothy's ratatouille is remarkable.

'We were in Thailand of course, Bertrand and I, at the time of the collision. But our gratitude to all of you is boundless. I must buy you dinner. Dirck will be angry if I don't. Here.'

Firenze Beach scribbled her room number on the back of a business card. As she did so, there was the tiniest of pauses into which a conference organiser inserted herself with urgent demands for Firenze Beach's presence. Firenze Beach bent a heavily jewelled ear then threw up her arms in disgust.

'I must leave. The transgender caucus have organised a balloon ride. Why do we do this to ourselves?' She laughed. 'Please call me about dinner. I know a fabulous Polynesian place. The breadfruit . . . Ah!'

At 8 p.m. Zoe Cable and Morris were seated at a thatched corner table in the Kon Tiki Restaurant. They were sucking large, volcano-shaped cocktails called Krakatoas.

'This tastes like kerosene,' Morris said.

A waiter approached them.

'Not more breadfruit, *please*,' said Zoe.

He handed her a message from Firenze Beach. Zoe read it.

'Let's see,' she summarised. 'Meteorological cock-up. Balloons blown off course. Trannies crash land in an avocado grove in Orange County. All hell breaks loose as you can imagine. In short, Firenze Beach is a no-show, but she's given the maître d' her credit card number so all is not lost.'

Zoe called for more Krakatoas.

'Will this impact the Hub?'

Zoe shook her head without ceasing to suck.

'I've already sunk my teeth in on that one. It's non-negotiable – not that she realises it yet.'

After the second Krakatoa, Morris started fumbling his cutlery. At one point he had three cigarettes alight at once.

'Are you OK, Morris?'

'I'm a little drunk.'

His hair had become ruffled; his tie was askew. He looked at that moment, Zoe thought, crumpled and charming, as if drink had naturalised his awkwardness.

'Can I ask you something?' he said.

They were eating pineapple fritters and boar burgers. Zoe had rather lost track of which course was which.

'Is this goat or wild pig?'

'Is that the question?'

'No. My question concerns Firenze Beach.'

'The wondrous Ms Beach.'

'Her. My question is . . .' He leaned forward. Zoe could see tiny pimples of sweat on the slopes of his nose. Up from his unbuttoned shirt collar poked two tufts of hair, one grey and one black. 'Do you *really* believe any of that?'

'Absolutely, yes. Although believe is not quite the right word.'

Morris had his elbow halfway across the table. He was leaning his head on one hand and moving his jaw from side to side. His lips looked red and ponderous.

'May I say something, Zoe?'

'You may.'

'I have read *Incredible Bodies* quite recently and in some detail. My conclusion? It is a melange of verbosity and half-truth.'

'A melange?'

'A melange I say!' He waved his arms about like Kenneth Branagh. 'Should we have another Krakatoa?'

'Why not?'

'The body is not a verbal construct. Only an academic would believe that.'

'You're an academic, Morris.'

'Quite, so I see the attraction. But you have to remember I'm an unsuccessful academic, or at least I have been for some time, so I can see around the edges.'

'You've glimpsed the other side?'

'Yes.'

The Krakatoas arrived and with them something pink which may have been dessert. Morris's appetite seemed to be increasing as the meal went on. He finished the pink thing and called, incredibly, for more breadfruit.

'Why do men persist in believing in reality?' Zoe asked. 'It's touching, but really.'

'You're being deliberately aphoristic. May I direct your attention to this table?'

'Oh it's always the bloody table.' Zoe plucked Morris's cigarette from his lips to light her own. 'Who cares about tables? Do you ever fall in love with a table? Did you ever fuck a table? Don't answer that.'

'People are real.'

'Power is real.'

'That's an appalling statement. Simply appalling.' His anger spiked for just a moment.

Zoe raised her eyebrows, leaned forward and whispered. 'Perhaps, but what if it's true?'

'Firenze Beach doesn't believe in truth.'

Morris had sat back and folded his arms. His shirt sleeves were rolled: he had the forearms of a gardener, sinewy, freckled, sparsely haired. His skin was just beginning to lose its elasticity.

'No, but like me she believes in *truths* – multiple, contingent, contestory, always at odds.'

'You can't make a philosophy out of squabbling.'

'Squabbling? Is that what we're doing now?'

He flashed her an uncertain look which Zoe held on to a second or two longer than was really necessary. Had Dirck van Camper been Morris's first lover, she wondered, or was Morris one of those Harold Nicholson, cottaging types, for whom being regularly rogered was a kind of marital safety-valve, a way of expunging his beastliness before returning to wifey? Was Morris really one of those? Did he loiter in the late-night toilets in Palmerston Square? Did he lurk amidst the unkempt rhododendrons of Macaroni Park? Did Morris, for Christsake, actually cruise? She gave him a hard, if drunken, stare. If he did, then his powers of disguise were truly impressive. Zoe had known, in both a professional and personal capacity, any number of closeted, semi-closeted, questioning, confused or downright clueless homosexuals, but hitherto she had always recognised what they were and what they wanted, quite often before they recognised it themselves. When it came to desire Zoe's sensitivities were seismographic. But Morris Gutman? There was nothing to work with. Perhaps Dirck really was the first. But if so, how on earth had it happened? She was, she realised, as she blinked back a wave of inebriation and sucked down some more Krakatoa, deeply intrigued by Morris Gutman. He was, she thought with a nigh-on zoological thrill, a brand new species, something beyond even her vast and liquid experience.

'So Morris,' she ventured, 'how did you and Dirck first, you know, meet?'

Morris looked at her strangely for a moment.

'Um,' he said. 'Well . . .' He shook his head as though the answer was both blazingly obvious and quite difficult to remember. '"The History of Critique". God!' He snuffled and loosened his tie. 'And what a fucking disaster that was. Did I ever tell you about the time he completely took over the class? Started banging on about Kant. I could have killed him, honestly. If I'd have had a weapon, God help me, I would have used it.'

Zoe chuckled conspiratorially.

'Love n' Hate,' she said, executing a one-two punch over the empty breadfruit basket. 'So that was how it started, eh? And one thing led to another.'

'Well . . .' Morris had finished all the available food – his tie was lightly breaded and his hair was streaked with avocado and cigarette ash. He tilted unsteadily backwards in his chair. 'Maybe it did. Maybe unconsciously at least, you know . . .'

'*Right.*' Zoe was feeling peculiarly excited by all this. Was it the Krakatoas, she wondered; was it her successful courting of Firenze Beach; or was it this odd, even surreal idea of Dirck van Camper and Morris Gutman *getting it on*? The deep, transfixing, wondrous absurdity of that idea brought tears to her eyes. She wanted more.

'Unconsciously at least . . .' she repeated, letting the ellipses float out over the table like soap bubbles.

'Maybe that led to the car park,' said Morris.

'The car park?' said Zoe.

Morris nodded.

'The rear-ending,' he said. His eyes dropped for a moment and then picked themselves up.

Wow! thought Zoe. Jesus Christ! Rear-ending in the Dalton Street car park. Why had she not heard of this before?

'The car park,' she gurgled. 'Is that common?'

'Common?'

'Is there a scene?'

'How could there be a scene?'

'Oh God, Morris, I just realised!' Zoe had her hands in the air and was shouting like an evangelist. 'The terrible irony of it. That

122

was where you two first, you know, got together. And that was where someone almost killed Dirck. It's horrible, and *really* weird.'

'Horrible?' Morris's long face, blurred and blotched by alcohol, looked first blank, then angry, then terribly sad. 'You said it was all right,' he said. 'You told me it was common. OK, I ran him down, strictly speaking, yes. But we agreed that it was consensual, that despite the apparent randomness he wanted to be there. It was his fault. Or at least it wasn't mine. That's what we agreed.'

Zoe tried to remember how many Krakatoas she had had. Five? Six? Seven? She was having trouble making sense of this, which normally would have been OK – she was quite comfortable with alcohol-induced confusion – but Morris appeared genuinely upset.

'We agreed that?'

'At the hospital.'

Zoe's drink-fuddled brain ratcheted back to the scene two months before: CRI, Dirck van Camper's bedside. What she thought they had agreed – implicitly, knowingly, and with a level of unspoken sophistication which did them both proud – was that Morris was Dirck's secret lover, not (and was this really what he was suggesting?) that Morris had run Dirck down. That was absurd.

Morris lit a cigarette, stubbed it out, then immediately retrieved it from the Captain Cook ashtray and began incompetently trying to straighten it again.

'Have one of mine,' Zoe said. 'Really.'

Around her, the restaurant's pink interior was beginning to undulate like a colon. She gripped the edge of the bamboo table. Was it possible, she wondered, that she had entirely missed the point? That Morris, rather than being a fascinating pan-sexual Bloomsbury throwback, was actually a hit-and-run driver?

'So let's get this straight, Morris.' Her voice was slow and overpunctuated. '*You* ran Dirck down? Was this, like, a lovers' tiff?'

'Are you taking the piss?' yelled Morris. 'A lovers' tiff! Is that a cheap attempt at surrealism?'

123

'Right,' announced Zoe, standing up with an inadvisable suddenness. 'OK. I am now going to the ladies' to regroup.'

In the relative sanctuary of the coconut-lined lavatories, Zoe looked at herself in the mirror. Her three-tone hair was chaotic, but in a good way. Her make-up seemed en masse to have shifted a little to the left.

'Wow.'

Her evening with the urban primitives had been wild enough, but *this*. Morris Gutman was a murderer, or if not a murderer a manslaughterer, a grievous-bodily-harmer, a fully-fledged criminal. She blinked, sniffed and began woozily to plot the implications of this new alignment. If Morris was not Dirck's secret lover then her plan of cultivating him as an alternative route to Firenze Beach was completely crocked, of course, but then again, since the triumph of 'Radical Puke' Firenze was on board anyway, so that hardly mattered. *Qué sera*, *sera*.

What else?

If Morris was not Dirck's secret lover then he was probably not gay at all, not even a little bit, which explained the almost total lack of gay indicators. And if Morris was not gay at all then she was currently enjoying breadfruit and Tahitian cocktails with a straight man who was six thousand miles from his wife and children. The dots, she realised, were not difficult to join: by all the unwritten conventions of academic conferences they were practically betrothed. Zoe did not need to check her Palm Pilot to know that shagging Morris Gutman had not been on her 'to do list' for the day, but blindfolded by her own enthusiasms she had, it seemed, stumbled so far in that direction that backing out now might pose practical problems, besides being crucially uncool. To admit her deep misreading of Morris's motives was unthinkable – what if it ever got out? – whereas having sex with him would furnish an excellent alibi. Besides the pleasures it might offer – she thought of his inelastic skin, of his salt-and-pepper chest tufts – it would be an ironclad explanation for all that faghaggy flirtiness.

And why not? OK, Morris was straight (in every sense) – but he was also guilty of a serious crime. He was both less than she had imagined and quite a lot more. She thought of him sitting outside at their food-spattered table, his eyes half-closed, his sleeves rolled up, his gardener's forearms exposed to the world. He had almost killed someone, she thought, and no one else knew it but her. Not even, she was sure, his own dear wife.

The mirror gave back a look Zoe knew well. It was the one she always tried to capture on her book jackets – gaunt, windblown, black-and-white – a look that spoke equally of intellectual vehemence and vast erotic hunger. She began to reapply her purple lipstick and disarrange her tri-tone hair. Morris Gutman, she thought, for all his hidden depths, did not have a clue what he was in for.

Chapter 15

Morris reclined his seat. There was a squeal of pain from the African lady behind him but he was determined to ignore it. It was a detail, and one thing he had learned during the three days in LA was that certain details, especially ones relating to other people, deserved to be carefully ignored. It was a question of boundaries. He pulled a notebook and pen out of his carry-on. *Note to self – A paradox – the dissolution of false boundaries/ difference (physical, sexual, emotional) allows the discovery of true boundaries/difference.* He read it over to himself several times, changed 'discovery' to 'ecstatic discovery' and smiled. A week before, the African lady's squeal would have filled him with guilt. He would have returned his seat to the upright position, apologised and suffered for the remainder of the flight under a mixture of fury, resentment and lower back pain. No longer. He felt a new sense of surety and power. His needs (in this admittedly trivial case, the need to recline) were real, he 'owned' them. More than that, he actually rather liked them. His needs, so he had discovered – sex, power, fun – had both a classical simplicity and a gawkish charm. He felt towards them a quasi-paternal warmth.

Morris pulled down his sleeping mask and closed his eyes. He could hear the hollow rumble of the aircraft and the continuing hisses of the African lady – he paid attention to neither. Zoe was up in business class. She had just brought back a miniscule jar of caviar. 'My seat goes completely horizontal,' she had whispered, 'the possibilities are enormous!' Then she spotted someone else and disappeared.

Zoe was always disappearing, he realised. That was her

greatest charm, her greatest skill: the way she left. Just when you were most expecting her, she wasn't there. At first Morris had found this disconcerting, even upsetting. The day after their Polynesian triste, for example, she was nowhere to be seen. He later discovered she had been holed up all day in a radical juice bar with Firenze Beach, drinking mango smoothies and plotting. She broke into his room at 3 a.m. the next morning and felt him up. She was drunk. All day he had been writing speeches in his head, explaining what he thought about the night before, laying out their options. She filled his mouth with tongue, she stuck an index finger up his bum. She came at him like a combine harvester. Afterwards, pieces of him were scattered across the mammoth bed like the aftermath of a high-speed crash. 'Now, was that so awful?' she asked. When he woke she was gone, but he had rarely felt less lonely.

It was 11 p.m. LA time, 7 a.m. in Coketown. They were due to land at nine. Morris lifted his mask and stretched. The little screen in front of him was showing a map of the North Atlantic. The small blue plane tilted imperceptibly but unstoppably forward along the dotted blue arc like the minute hand of a clock. LA to Coketown – six thousand miles, a little under ten hours. The temperature at Coketown International Airport was 9°C, with drizzle. For the first time in four days Morris felt a pinch of fear. There were children in the plane. He had not noticed them before but now he did, yawning, whining, running up and down the aisles. At LAX he had bought Molly a stuffed Goofy and E a bottle of Scotch. He remembered now that she couldn't drink while pregnant. He could give her a Queer Caucus T-shirt. Would she find that funny? Perhaps not. The thought of their house worried him like a dog worrying sheep. Molly's eczema had flared up again, E was putting her in cold wraps at night. As the plane gradually lost altitude he felt he was descending into an ocean of guilt and shame. He could hardly breathe. His heart was pounding; he looked manically for the sick bag. An attendant asked if he needed help.

'Yes, I'm having a panic attack. I need to sit in business class!' She frowned and looked suspicious.

'You think I'm angling for an undeserved upgrade?' he shouted. 'We're about to fucking land. I need to sit with my friend in business class.'

She led him forward and sat him next to Zoe. The seats were leather and absurdly large. He felt immediately better.

'Way to get an upgrade Morris,' Zoe said. 'Although this is a little late in the day.'

Morris gripped her hand.

'Are you scared of flying?'

'No, just of landing. Actually, not of landing, more of what comes after.'

She turned off her MP3 player, removed her sunglasses and looked straight at him. She smelt of linseed oil and sangria.

'Morris, sweetie,' she said. 'Everything has changed. You kicked ass at the LABC.'

'I didn't give a paper.'

'That's fine. You're a bottom-up phenomenon. You're word-of-mouth.'

'Really?'

'I'm telling you. Firenze is keen. Hank's on board.'

Morris nodded.

'And by the way, it's perfect for the Research Hub. Associate Fellow Morris Gutman. Your salary will double and you will never teach again. Ever. Give me your foot.'

'Pardon?'

'Shiatsu, Morris. Fear is just a blockage of energy. Take off your sock.'

Zoe studied the sole of his foot for several seconds then pressed with astonishing force at a point one centimetre south of his middle toe. A sudden halo of heat shot up Morris's spine and through the top of his skull.

The plane banked to the right and a tiny but exact model of Coketown slid into view. Despite the blurring veil of rain, Morris could still make out the Coketown Ship Canal, the Museum of Artificial Fabrics, the rose-hued and grandiloquent Beigewater Centre. Wrapped around them all like the grey rakings of a Zen garden were row upon row of wet slate roofs. One roof, he knew, was his roof; one out of thousands. But why should it be his, he thought? Why should it be him? There was no logic to that (he realised giddily), no necessity. One life was like one word – just an arbitrary cut into experience. It was too easy to imagine that all of it was real, *natural* – the wife and child, the house, the job, the constant aching fear – when it was just a collision of contingencies, a whimsical although far from random exercise of power. But he had learned that power was reversible, unstable, prone to crumbling, desiccation and collapse. You could tunnel beneath it or chop away at its edges. He was no longer exactly himself. The hit-and-run, the plagiarism, the adultery – these were clearly not the acts of Morris Gutman. He was becoming deframed, reimagined, remade. Morris Gutman the long running character persisted, but now he was played by a quite different actor. The change, as he saw it, was quite blatant, rather ridiculous, but that was the trick: like a truly terrible wig, it was just too big to draw comment, it had to be ignored.

They dropped down over the ruinous and crumbling Galsworthy Estate, the noxious spools of the Port Stanley sewage farm. Zoe Cable held her nose and blew. Sucking on a boiled sweet, Morris remembered involuntarily, but with the force of a revelation, the plummy purple swell of her labial piercing. They hit the Coketown runway with a scream.

Chapter 16

E gripped the sides of the toilet bowl and, with a roar and a heave, renewed acquaintance with her morning muesli. God, she thought, the smell of one's own vomit – is there anything quite so ghastly? And lately, just when her sense of smell was heightened, there had been so bloody much of it. Having to eat at all was bad enough, but then being forced to confront the nuts and bolts of the digestive process . . . If it happened to men, the drug companies would be on to it in a flash. There would be charity balls, celebrity appeals, the whole paraphernalia. Although, in fairness, Morris was being quite good: he cooked and cleaned, patted her on the back as she blurted out his fettucine and then wielded the toilet brush with rare equanimity. The new job had made a big difference. She had hardly ever seen him so happy as that week after he got the news. It was like travelling back in time. Once more he became – as he had been when they first met at Bangor – young, enthusiastic and highly sexed. He chased Molly around the house, making her squeal and scream. He held E's hand in the supermarket; they made love every night. The future, for once, seemed not a dark and violent necessity but a place of hope and humour.

E rinsed out her mouth, spat into the toilet bowl and flushed. She looked in the mirror. Her face was the colour of skimmed milk. Her hair was thinned and frizzy. She put on some lipstick which made her look vaguely clownish. Oh well. Nearly four months – the baby was six inches long. She measured six inches roughly with her thumb and forefinger, looked at it, then placed it against her bump. One thing she had never understood about Morris was the vulnerability of his happiness, its tendency to crumble and retreat at the first sign of woe. It was as if he didn't really believe in it, as if joy were some kind of fakery or fiction which might be enjoyable for a while but could never last. They were opposites in that. After that first week, for instance, she had noticed hairline cracks, tiny reversions. He snapped at Molly once or twice and sat up late reading books he didn't care to talk about. As though happiness were some great effort that he couldn't be expected to keep up.

9 a.m. in Coketown, 1 a.m. in LA. Morris would be asleep; he was flying in the morning. She hoped the trip had done him good. That's why she had agreed to it, even though it was at the worst time, what with work, vomiting and Molly's continual ailments. Surely it would perk him up again, give him another boost. The Bangor incident had been such a blow to his confidence. Now, with hindsight, E could see that more clearly than ever. She had never trusted the bastard Underseel. He had struck her from the off as creepy and abusive. Morris didn't notice anything, of course, or if he did he complicated his qualms out of existence. Literary critics were no good at judging character, that was certain. They were far too hesitant, too keen on complexity and ambivalence to see the simple things.

Nine thirty: it was time to leave. How would she prise Molly from the television? She could hear from downstairs the demented cries of *Daybreak TV*. And how, after that, would she get her into the car seat? Without Morris to play bad cop, bribery was her only option. She went downstairs and rooted in the cupboard for chocolate. As she approached the television, E held a Cadbury's Button between herself and her daughter the way a lion tamer might hold a wooden chair. Molly's eyes locked on.

'Raincoat, then chocolate,' said E, raising it at the last moment, just beyond her reach.

It was a mile or so from the nursery to the art gallery. Fifteen minutes' walk. The route passed through the university's new Nanotechnology Research Village, a pedestrianised pickle of interlinked glass domes, cubes and pyramids. Its construction – which had cost tens of millions of pounds and had involved an armada of governmental, educational, quasi-governmental, commercial and non-profit bodies – had, E knew, generated a tidal wave of furious if unheeded resentment in the Arts Faculty, where, as one of Morris's colleagues put it, the toilets didn't get cleaned from one decade to the next. There had also been a letter from Darian Cavendish in the *South Coketown Advertiser* denouncing the architectural vulgarity of the village ('footling and weak-minded') and questioning the ethics of the research ('hubristic and sinful') which would be undertaken there. E, on the other hand, felt rather taken in by the playful gaudiness of the place. The buildings were like giant children's toys scattered across the rubberised and colour-coded pavement. The transparent tunnel which linked them glowed magically green and blue in the Coketown gloom. Whatever the economics of the construction, however dubious the manipulations that would occur within, it cheered E up in the morning to see something so whimsical made real.

Just before the gallery came into view she heard the faint sound of chanting from round the corner of Rudeboy Street, a vague collective plaint which came and went amidst the aural brew of buses, trams and ancient lead-emitting student cars. She stopped for a moment to listen. Could it really be a student protest? How many years had it been since she had heard one of those? 1985? 1986? The spring of '85 she had thrown eggs at the Home Secretary; Stella had been arrested as a flying picket. It was like hearing the call of a bird you had assumed was long ago extinct. She rounded the corner and there they were, outside the gallery gates: a small, surprisingly well-dressed group holding placards and golf umbrellas. Their chant came gradually into focus: 'What do we want?' 'Proper respect!' 'When do we want it?' 'Now!' The signs were even odder: 'Stop the obscenity', 'Hands off my corpse', 'Death porn, no thanks!'

Then E remembered that tonight was the opening of 'Radical Taxidermy', the Nick Kidney retrospective. Nick Kidney had been running around all week setting up his bottled foetuses, his patchwork skin art, his paddling pool of bobbing and plasticised

132

brains. They had a new curator who was keen on controversy. This was his first and, many secretly hoped, last major show. Out with Europe's leading teapot collection, in with 'Gutta-percha' – a visual satire on colonic irrigation. Nick Kidney, who had first come to public attention with 'Big Cum', a work which involved a lawn sprinkler and ten gallons of patiently collected human sperm, was, at forty-one, the latest *enfant terrible* of British Art. Getting the retrospective for Coketown was a coup (although it helped that the curator was married to Nick Kidney's first wife, Gloria, and that Kidney had grievously offended the directors of all the major London galleries).

As she passed them, a grim-faced protestor handed E a flier. E glanced at it; it began with a passage from Genesis. The protestors smelt of mothballs and embrocation. She said hello to Godfrey, the foyer guard, who glanced at the protestors, raised his eyebrows and grinned. She avoided the galleries and walked straight to the Education Department, where Alison was already in a tizzy. As she sat at her miniscule desk, the baby flipped and jiggled inside her.

'Have you walked through it?' Alison asked.

'Not yet.' E felt a bubble of nausea rising up her oesophagus. She reached for a Rich Tea.

'It's a nightmare. Worse than my worst imaginings. There are real body parts out there. He has some kind of chemical process.'

'I read that it involves silicon.'

'You may be right, but is it legal? Are we sure of our legal footing? I doubt it. We've got Orpington Primary coming in on Friday. What am I supposed to tell them?'

E picked up the exhibition guide and read.

'"Nick Kidney's work explores the untidy edges of human corporality – the fleshy lumps, the noisome fluids, the cystic danglings that make us who we are."'

'That's bollocks.'

'It *is* bollocks.'

'Ha-bloody-ha. I tell you, we can kiss goodbye to Lottery funding after this. It's a slap in the face for the ordinary art-goer.'

E switched on her computer.

'*Ordinary art-goer?* Alison, sometimes you sound like the *Daily Mail.*'

Alison went red in the face. E realised it was going to be one of those days.

'I believe in Art,' said Alison. 'Damn it, I believe in impressionism. I'm going to talk to Tony about this now.'

At noon, E decided to walk through the galleries. If nothing else, she thought, the show would distract her from the terrible realities of her lunchtime sandwich. When it came to art, E was a hard nut to crack. Although she had never completed her dissertation, she had not spent four years boiling her head in Bangor for nothing. She knew, both literally and pragmatically, which end was up.

'Half-baked Duchamp,' she muttered to herself, gazing at the stainless steel bedpans and carefully arranged stool samples of 'Guttapercha'.

'Second-rate Fluxus,' before the paddling pool of brains.

'Yoko Ono did all this much better,' the nasty (if not Nazi) 'Skinorak'.

Although the flayed dogs were occasionally amusing, E was largely unimpressed. As a whole, Nick Kidney's work struck her as overwrought, underweight and immature.

She swallowed the last bite of her tomato sandwich and was about to return to her desk when she noticed a darkened room that she hadn't explored. With a silent hiccup and a long, subdued belch, she walked in unoptimistically. A motion detector clicked as she entered and the far wall lit up with what looked like a home video. Children were playing in a back garden. There was a climbing frame and a bouncy castle. It was a party of some kind. The image was abnormally large: it filled the entire wall and as a result the figures were life-size or even larger. E watched and waited for something clever or ghoulish to happen, but it didn't. All the faces were fuzzed out except one – a little girl, six or seven, with brown curly hair. She was wearing a swimming costume, shorts and jelly sandals. She was running and squealing. She disappeared from the frame then came back panting and rather theatrically holding her ribs. She said something to another fuzzed-out child. A plastic football flew over her head; in the background children ricocheted off the bouncy castle. She saw the camera, waved, laughed and shouted. She pushed her hair behind her ears. The dark shadow of adult fingers returning her wave passed back and forth over the bottom of the frame. There were voices but they seemed either slowed down or speeded up – long, trawling words without consonants.

The video stopped abruptly and then, a second or so later, began again. It was a loop. E watched again. Above the turrets of the leylandii hedge, the sky was pale blue with a chalky criss-cross of aircraft trails. The girl again ran round, squealed, disappeared. Her run was high-kneed, lopsided. Her hair was cut in a bob, her lips were red with artificial colouring. What was this, E wondered, where had she seen it before? On the news? *Crimewatch*? The fuzzed-out faces made it look like something released by the police, but perhaps it was just a knowing parody of that. The girl held her ribs, the adult fingers waved. Behind the bouncy castle, a man in a T-shirt was drinking bottled beer. A naked boy ate orange cake while hanging upside down from the climbing frame.

E tried to remember the names of recently missing children: Chelsea Craddock, little Joey Ogg. It was easy to lose track – they blurred into each other. The woodland searches, the parental appeals, the dredging, the combing of the family home. By now there was a routine, a pattern, a profile. Everyone knew the stages.

The screen went blank and then began again. You could see a portion of patio, half a barbecue; a mother was calling 'Jennifer, Jennifer'. Light glanced off painted metal, white flesh. The fuzzed-out heads bobbed, veered, like balls of summer insects. The figures were too big, designed to unsettle, she assumed, to discomfort the viewer. The voices were echoey and disturbed. The little girl flashed her smile at the camera. On then off. She waved and dashed away. Children can be so brisk, E thought. The adult hand waved belatedly. In the top right was a dark triangle – the eaves of the house? A fault with the camera? There were speakers in every corner of the little room – noises swirled and lassoed around her.

135

E sighed and closed her eyes. She felt tired, but she could also feel, somewhere below, the gentle slosh of emotion. She could hear a faint humming from another room and smell the soupy scent of the gallery bistro. The loop began again. Soon she would have to leave to go back to the office, but at least this was a peaceful way to end. If it was meant to be troubling (the fuzzed-out heads), it really wasn't. It achieved, in spite of itself, a kind of gentleness. The boy hung from the climbing frame, the man finished his beer, the little girl theatrically held her ribs. The same every time.

'Jesus Christ, what have they done to the sound?' Someone was standing in the doorway. E squinted. It was Nick Kidney. Tall, pompadoured, wearing a Versace shirt and multipocketed fisherman's vest. 'It sounds like they're down a fucking well.'

'Actually, I like it,' said E. 'It's really peaceful.'

Kidney hadn't noticed her. He pushed his sunglasses down to the tip of his nose and peered. He stuck out his hand.

'Nick Kidney. Who are you?'

E introduced herself. Kidney stared for a moment at her belly, then looked her in the eye.

'I loved the flayed dogs,' said E. 'They're quite witty.'

'Oh yeah,' he replied, as though he had forgotten all about the flayed dogs until E mentioned them. 'They usually go down well. Excuse me.' He began walking round the room listening to each loudspeaker in turn. After he had listened to them all he stopped walking and looked again at E.

'That took me six months,' he said, nodding at the wall-sized image. 'Every shot is different.'

'But they're all the same.'

'They all look the same, but they're different – there are eight hundred and fifty different shots of exactly the same thing.'

E looked again.

'That's not possible,' she said. 'Look at the shadows, the sky.'

'Artificial lighting. Hard to believe I know; we did it all in a warehouse in Clapton. Does that bother you?'

He glanced at her and waited. It seemed clear to E that he wanted it to bother her. That he would take that as a sign of

136

success. She walked over to the wall text: 'The Myth of Eternal Return', Nick Kidney, 1999.

'That must have been hard work,' she said flatly.

'Exhausting. You've no idea how difficult it is keeping things the same.'

The loop began again. E stared at the chalk-marked sky. Now she looked at it more closely, the blueness did appear too intense, too ideal to be true.

'Do you really like the flayed dogs?'

'Not really.' E was surprised by her own sudden glumness. Why should the news that this was an elaborate piece of trickery trouble her?

'No,' agreed Kidney casually. 'You didn't strike me as the flayed-dog type.'

The flayed-dog type, thought E. What a presumptuous twerp. Do men ever stop insisting on their own cleverness?

She watched the girl (an actress presumably) run once more over the artificial lawn. Cherry lips, blameless skin. E's spark of anger softened to sadness. Suddenly, she was on the verge of tears. She swallowed and turned her face away from Kidney. Bloody hormones.

'Are you crying?' he asked after a moment.

E shook her head. 'No, I'm not. Does your work often reduce people to tears?'

Nick Kidney stared for a second then began to laugh. The adult fingers waved once more across the bottom of the screen. The naked boy dropped his piece of cake.

That evening at the opening, E handed out hors d'oeuvres. Molly, in a highly unstable post-nursery daze, clung to the tails of E's cheesecloth maternity blouse and stumbled along behind. E knew she was taking a risk. Molly could explode at any moment, but with Morris in LA she had no choice. She hoped fervently that the hors d'oeuvres would soon be gobbled up and they could leave. Scanning the crowd of Coketown grandees, she looked in vain for the young or the hungry. Alison, enveloped in a cloud of chardonnay, ran across to embrace her.

137

'You're doing a superb job.' She patted E's tummy. 'Would Molly like some orange juice?' Molly's face turned stoney.

'Have an hors d'oeuvre, please,' said E. 'Have three. How are things going?'

'Well,' Alison took a frustratingly dainty bite, 'despite my personal opinions, I'm trying to talk things up for the sake of the gallery. But really there's only so much you can do. There are pickled penises out there.'

'I thought they were replicas.'

'Does it matter? Honestly, I fear such distinctions are lost on the Lady Mayoress. On the other hand, the artist himself is rather droll. Have you met him yet? Yes, of course you have – he mentioned your name. You must have made a good impression.'

Around the pale, spotlit galleries, the guests gathered together in small, tight-knit groups, their backs turned as though to defend themselves against the art that surrounded them. Leading trade unionists huddled beside the flayed dogs; the Vice-Chancellor's wife held court next to a mosaic made from human toenails. There was an air of wariness, hilarity and fear. Above the ambient music (chosen by Kidney, loathed by Alison) you could still hear the chant of the protestors. A rumour began circulating, passing swiftly from group to group, that the protestors had been hired by Kidney, that they were part of the show. People rather liked this rumour, as it made them feel they were involved in something clever, witty and slightly confused. After an hour or so, however, this rumour faded and died and another one took its place – that the protestors had not been hired by Kidney, but Kidney himself had started the rumour that they were. This was even more popular and was considered (by those in the know) a quite brilliant twist. To those not in the know it seemed as good an excuse as any to have another drink and to wonder out loud about the provenance of the pickled penises.

Quite soon after the spreading of the second rumour, the protestors overpowered Godfrey and burst into the gallery. They were clattery and damp. After a moment of disorientated triumph, they gathered by the stool samples and began singing a Congregationalist hymn. Opportunistically, E offered them hors d'oeuvres; after conferring suspiciously they emptied the tray. Once the hymn was over, the protestors split apart and engaged in passionate dialogue with the people in the know. A rumour began circulating that Nick Kidney was in the thick of this, that he was overpowering them with the logic of scatology and several protestors had already 'turned'.

The ambient music became louder. People began to dance. This, according to Alison, was unprecedented and probably a health and safety violation. Molly had fallen asleep and was curled in a pile of coats near the ladies'. E, who was too tired to move her, decided recklessly to have a glass of white wine. In order to avoid the increasingly bacchanalian dancing, she sought refuge in 'The Myth of Eternal Return'. Nick Kidney was already in there alone.

'I heard you were arguing with the protestors,' she said.

'I did my fifteen minutes, so as not to discourage them, but really the vim's gone out of it. They've been following me around for years; we exchange Christmas cards. Actually, it's getting slightly creepy.'

'Do they always break in?'

'Almost always. Sometimes they attack the art but that involves bail, insurance. It's a lot of paperwork, so I try to encourage them just to sing their hymn and leave it there. Thanks for offering them the hors d'oeuvres by the way, they appreciated that.'

E nodded. The football was flying over the little girl's head. There was an element of backspin she had not noticed before. The taste of the wine was astonishing, it was like drinking a short piece of poetry.

'You may be right about this one,' he said. 'It is quite peaceful, isn't it?'

'I said that before I knew each shot was different.'

'That changes your opinion?' Kidney was smoking. He turned temporarily aside so as not to exhale in E's direction.

'It makes it sadder,' she said. 'Less real.'

139

The cigarette smoke caught the light from the video projector and vague curls of bouncy castle floated momentarily in the air.

'All art is a form of mourning,' Kidney said quite casually.

'Even the penises?'

'Especially the penises.'

Nick Kidney sighed. From what E had read of him, a sigh was the last thing she expected.

'Is that your little girl,' he asked, 'curled up by the bar?'

'Yes. Is she causing problems?'

'No, it's just that several people have complimented me on how lifelike she is.'

E spluttered out some wine. Kidney grinned.

'My son Xavier lives with Gloria and Tony now,' he said. 'Did you know that?'

'Actually yes, I did.' E wasn't sure whether she was supposed to know such things. It was semi-private and she was only an administrative assistant. Kidney seemed unconcerned.

'That's why I'm here. Coketown's a hole, but it's a chance to spend time with little X.'

'*A hole!* I assume you're unacquainted with the Museum of Artificial Fabrics.'

'I've been given the official tour. Twice. Blood fortunately remains stronger than rayon.'

'I wrote an essay about you in graduate school,' E said.

'God no. That's awful.' Kidney's eyes widened with ghoulish interest. 'What did you say?'

'Oh, I don't remember – scopophilia, abjection, something like that.'

'Did you know there's a book out now by someone from Aldershot College? And I believe there's been a mini-conference. It's horrible.'

'You're a cottage industry.'

'It's beyond me. If someone wanted to write a musical about my work, do a dance, sing a hymn even, that would make sense. But how could anyone come in here and feel the urge to organise a mini-conference?'

'My partner's an academic.'

140

'So you tell me.'

E paused. She felt a twitch of defensiveness.

'Being an artist is a privilege,' she said.

'No it's not. Making money from it is, I admit, a grotesque stroke of luck, like winning the pools, but being an artist is not a privilege.'

'So what is it then, a burden?'

'No. It's just normal, it's the way people are.'

'Most people don't pickle penises.'

'I'm at one end of the artistic spectrum.'

'Maybe mini-conferences are at the other end.'

'No, no, no.' Kidney was becoming quite vehement. Behind him the girl squealed, the man sipped his bottled beer. The triangle in the right-hand corner wobbled a little.

'Mini-conferences are anti-art. It's like matter and anti-matter: the two can't co-exist.'

'You're exaggerating wildly.'

'I'm an artist.'

'Your reasoning is entirely circular.'

'So what!'

'Irrationalism is just another theory.' E was digging deep; this was surprisingly exhilarating. 'You can't escape from signification.'

Nick Kidney grabbed his crotch and threw one arm in the air like a rodeo rider.

'Signify this baby!' he yelled.

Someone peered curiously into the room, then entered and watched a couple of loops. E looked at the floor so as not to laugh.

When the person had gone, Nick Kidney grinned.

The little girl held her ribs and waved. 'Jennifer, Jennifer.' E imagined being separated from Molly, having her live with someone else. It was like glancing casually through a window and seeing a fatal accident. She suddenly felt sick.

'I can't imagine that,' she said. 'Separation.'

'No, to be honest, neither can I.'

'Why don't you come up and give a talk for us next week?' she

141

ventured. 'Orpington Primary are coming in. Alison's hopeless. You could see your son again.'

Kidney stubbed out his cigarette and stuck his tongue in his cheek.

'Isn't that a ridiculous idea?'

'Yes, I suppose it is.'

They both looked rather awkwardly ahead. The screen went black. And when the video clicked on again, Kidney was gone.

Having applied Molly's cold wraps and successfully negotiated bedtime with her imaginary henchman, Hector, E lay in her own bed and waited like a cracked dam for the long-delayed flood of sleep. Nearly ten; Morris's plane was already in the air. It frightened her to think of him so far away, dangling above a dark, foreign land. Now he was on his way back, her solitude felt worse than it had before. As the distance between them closed, his absence felt bigger and more real. She craved the old weightiness, the gloom, which pegged out their lives like a tent. From the back garden there was the whirling creak of a cat in heat. Poor thing, E thought. She had heard once that you could use a pencil for relief, the kind with a rubber, but you'd have to catch it first. 'Sex Toys for Animals', (rubber, graphite, wood), she thought, Nick Kidney, 1998.

Chapter 17

The Crocodile lay flat out on his specially engineered orthopaedic lounger and talked. His lips were glossed with spittle. His
eyes had the blank intensity of a mystic.

'Look at it this way,' he said, poking his finger upwards for
emphasis as if his auditor, Zoe Cable, were suspended from the
office ceiling rather than seated comfortably in a Mies Van der
Rohe armchair in the corner. 'If this faculty goes digital, all bets
are off. Everything happens online – teaching, marking, graduation. We can sell the buildings and move production overseas; all
we need here is a control centre, a minimal administrative core.
The cost savings are tremendous, and that's not even counting
the kudos.'

'What about the staff?' asked Zoe.

'That's the kicker. As you know, due to backward-looking
employment laws I can fire people only on the grounds of gross
misconduct or departmental closure. Although,' he added *sotto
voce*, 'as you also know, I have on occasion explored rather less
orthodox individual disembarkation strategies. Now, if the
Digital Faculty Proposal goes through, there will inevitably be
an interim period, a pause, a lacuna (as I believe it is now
fashionable to say) between the old and the new.'

'Ah,' said Zoe Cable.

'Precisely,' said the Crocodile. 'This interim period may only
be a matter of hours, but it will carry a certain legal weight. For
that brief, sad period there will be no Faculty of Arts.' The
Crocodile paused and when he spoke again his voice had a
higher, more visionary timbre. 'The weed-infested structure
which has afforded shade and protection for decades to the

143

backward and unprofitable practices of my most long-term colleagues will be swept away at a single stroke. The clear, disinfecting light of reform will shine in. It may not be pleasant.'

'Contracts will have to be renegotiated,' proffered Zoe.

'Contracts will be shredded. We will begin from scratch. Year Zero.'

'Mordred?'

'Mordred Evans,' the Crocodile whispered, 'will have to fend for himself.'

Zoe whistled. If the Crocodile had been a younger, more mobile man, she would have found him deeply attractive. Manic boldness like his was in short supply. Nevertheless, she was aware of the need to pull back, to compute the implications of this latest development for her many incongruent and over-lapping projects, most notably the Research Hub.

'The Hub would remain aloof,' she suggested.

'The Hub would be officially semi-autonomous, but in reality more autonomous than semi-. I won't touch it. Your contract of course is your own. All I ask is that you hold your nerve.'

Zoe Cable nodded. She had witnessed closing time at the Coketown Vomitorium; she had known the ladies' loos in the Kum Bar on nights when alcopops were four for a pound; she had seen slashings, glassings, bottlings. Holding her nerve would not be a problem.

The Crocodile turned his head to look at her. His eyes were moist; his moustache was, as ever, perfectly trimmed. It fringed his upper lip like a high-class draft excluder.

'Zoe,' he said, 'may I tell you something about power?'

'Are you about to become avuncular, Donald?'

'Humour me.'

She waved him on like a motorist yielding the right of way.

'Power,' he said, returning his gaze to the ceiling, 'is not proud. Power does not boast or hog the limelight, neither does it shout or cause a fuss. Power does not vary with the times – it is firm, it is constant and it lurks. You will find some men – Mordred Evans, for example, may be one – who think they have power. And indeed it may seem that they do. Such men certainly have the trappings of power; money, perhaps, or influence, or the ability to force their will upon others. They have the predicates of power so we assume they are powerful, and *they* assume they are powerful, but that, you see, is their mistake. True power is invisible. Powerful men walk among us everyday, but we do not see them at all. All we see are glasses, suits, male-pattern baldness – the true reality is hidden. Who runs this university?'

'The Vice-Chancellor?'

The Crocodile snorted. 'Dennis Sloze.'

Zoe frowned; Dennis Sloze was the dusty and timid little man who took minutes at meetings of Senate. She had never heard him speak.

'Exactly,' the Crocodile continued. 'Dennis Sloze could fire me tomorrow. How, I do not know. The procedures would remain a mystery, but I would go without a whimper because I understand how power works – that is the advantage I have.'

'Over Mordred?'

The Crocodile nodded.

'I am not myself a powerful man, but I know that power exists. I can sense its presence. I can at my best align myself with its requirements. I can serve it. The Digital Faculty was not anyone's idea. It emerged autonomously from the structures: if you read the minutes you can see it taking shape. It is rather beautiful – faculty committees, school boards, Dean's planning groups, campus-wide strategy huddles – pieces are added, patterns emerge. It fell to me to deliver, to push it through, but I am just an effect of the system, a vessel through which it will pass.'

'So you're unstoppable.'

'Let us not get carried away. We are not in the realm of metaphysics here. There may yet be blockages, bottlenecks, flaws in the system. Power finds its way without concern, unfortunately, for individuals. Our preferences, yours and mine, are not important. It takes the path of least resistance.'

'And are you meeting any resistance?'

The Crocodile fell silent for a moment.

'There is a difficulty. I may need Morris Gutman.'

It was Zoe's turn to lean back and look at the ceiling. Even in the Dean's office the cornices were clogged with dust; the cleaners really were intractable. She was trying to restrain the smirk which almost always, these days, appeared on her face whenever Morris Gutman was mentioned. He was proving to be one of her more enjoyable affairs. The potential she had glimpsed in LA was quickly, rather more quickly than she had anticipated, being fulfilled. Intellectually he was coming on in leaps and bounds, and sexually some of his suggestions were remarkable.

'Morris,' she said, 'might surprise you.'

'Has he surprised you?'

The Crocodile patted his moustache. The tips of his loafers twitched a little. Nothing, Zoe remembered, escaped the Crocodile.

'Let's just say, he's never disappointed.'

'Ah.' The Crocodile lit a panatella. The blue smoke rose and settled over the dust-caked cornices. 'Could you get the fan?' he asked.

Zoe leaned over and pressed a switch above the desk. An extractor fan began to hum loudly.

'These resistances?' Zoe asked.

'Yes. It's Bernard Littlejohn and Darian Cavendish.'

'A peculiar combination.'

'But a surprisingly effective one. Bernard, it seems, actually reads Faculty minutes. Of course, I have tried as far as I can to make them inaccessible – the locked filing cabinet, the misnumbered room – and as a secondary precaution to bury any matter of note, such as the Digital Faculty Proposal, beneath a weighty rubble of trivia: Estates and Buildings, Health and Safety, Office Supplies . . . you can imagine. My intention being, as usual, to begin consultations only after the important decisions have been made. But Bernard, it seems, is tenacious. His research skills are really quite impressive, which is unusual these days.'

'He's old-school. Where does Darian come in?'

'She has the ear of the VC, while Bernard, as you know, has the ear of no one.'

'But the VC isn't in charge.'

'No he isn't, but in this instance it might be enough. The other faculties are salivating over our virtual status – the benefits are blindingly obvious. Any sign of weakness or complication on our part and they will pounce.'

'Where does Morris come in?'

'He's our man on the inside. His history as a temporary lecturer makes him acceptable to that lot. They still see him as one of the downtrodden and disgruntled.'

'Not Darian, not after the kicking he gave her at the interview.'

The Crocodile smiled faintly at the memory.

'True, but if anyone knows the dirt on Darian it will be Bernard. If we can get to Bernard, it will all fall apart. The Digital Faculty will be ours.'

'I hate to be vulgar, Donald, but what's in this for me?'

The Crocodile nodded as though he had been expecting this. Before answering he took another draw on the now-stubby panatella.

'Geographically,' he said, 'the Digital Faculty is nowhere, which means, of course, it is everywhere. And since the Research Hub will be officially located within the Faculty,' he paused, 'I think you can imagine the rest.'

She could. Zoe Cable smiled and closed her eyes for a moment. Behind the whirr of the fan and the fumes of the Crocodile's cheap cigar, she could hear the the lapping of the kidney-shaped pool, smell the whiff of mesquite. Coketown in California. Globalisation – it truly was a beautiful thing.

147

Chapter 18

Early June: the examinations period. Around campus the students were panicking. They were discovering assignments which were long overdue. They were cursing their own laziness, blaming the malign influence of their housemates and desperately calculating the percentages that had already been irretrievably lost to them through absenteeism, incompetence and drug-induced amnesia. In the Vodafone Memorial Library, lecture notes were changing hands for ridiculous prices, pages were being slashed from books with razor blades, books were being hidden, stolen, deliberately lost. Scandalous references to Declan Monk's sexuality were being gouged into student carrels; fights were breaking out in the computer clusters; the rules against food, drink and mobile phones were being openly and recklessly flouted. The librarians stood on the sidelines like UN peacekeepers: impotent, fearful, dreaming of caravans in Normandy.

One afternoon, Morris Gutman went into the department to collect his exam scripts. The corridors of the Arts Faculty were all but deserted. Bright red 'Examination in Progress' signs were everywhere. A wild-eyed, sweating student sprinted past Morris without acknowledgement. Near the notice-boards a woman was sitting on the floor, weeping. It was like a contaminated area, the scene of some unpleasant man-made catastrophe. Inside the office the Furies were in an excellent mood. This was their favourite time of year. No one understood the examinations process like they did. They conducted its rituals and guarded its secrets like the votaries of an ancient blood religion.

'Greetings Morris,' chimed Mabel as he entered. The room was piled high with bundled examination booklets.

'I'm looking for my scripts,' he said.

'Of course you are. Let's see, "History of Critique," "Story of the Ode", "Aspects of the Augustan Age", "Misogyny and the Novel".' She pulled the requisite bundles from the pile without hesitation.

'How has it been so far?' ventured Morris.

'Madness,' she replied cheerfully, 'utter madness. But what can we expect? There's so little understanding.'

Morris looked blank.

'Of the examination process. It's been terribly devalued. In Professor Doppet's day the examination period was the consummation of the academic year.'

'The absolute pinnacle,' concurred Joan from behind a flood wall of padded envelopes.

'But now,' Mabel went on, 'with continuous assessment, take-home papers, open-book exams, multiple choice, it's a diminished thing.'

'It still seems quite intense to me,' said Morris.

Mabel was obviously cheered. 'We do our best,' she said. 'We do our best.'

'Any problems with my scripts?' asked Morris as he squeezed them into a quite sizeable cardboard box. All eyes turned to Heather.

'Candidates 01342 and 99661 failed to appear for the "History of Critique" exam,' she recited apparently from memory. '01342 discontinued studies on March the fifth following an unfortunate incident in Dalton Street car park. 99661 has no known excuse – investigations are ongoing. There was a fainting in "The Story of the Ode", it is indicated on your mark sheet. In "Misogyny and the Novel", candidate 00189 was forced to write with his left hand after supergluing together the middle and index fingers of his right hand. There is a medical note on file.'

'I bet you a pound to a penny that was self-inflicted,' said Joan.

'Of course it was,' said Mabel, 'but where's your proof?'

'Even if there is no proof, he should have marks deducted for stupidity. An exam's a test of intelligence after all.'

'But not of common sense,' corrected Mabel.

149

'Very true,' said Joan. 'And just as well for this lot. They'd all fail miserably if it was.'

'Products of the finest public schools and they can't find the Shackleton Gymnasium. We had one in here claiming it wasn't on Apollo Street.'

'Well you can imagine how surprised we were to hear that,' said Joan.

'Quite. We explained that if a building was to be demolished and rebuilt in a different and apparently hidden location, it was normal university practice to inform secretarial staff of this fact in advance. We could only apologise for what had clearly been a clerical oversight and suggest he seek redress at the office of the Dean.'

'We believe he actually went there.'

'Irony is a foreign language to them.'

'English is a foreign language to them.'

Morris Gutman regained the hallway. His cardboard box was dishearteningly heavy. Although he was now on a permanent contract, he would not be able to unload the worst of his teaching until they hired a new temporary lecturer next year. As it was, Declan Monk had offered to surreptitiously rejig the marking allocations so as to shift most of his marking burden on to Bernard Littlejohn and Nigel Qwerty – who, as officially 'research inactive', were in the academic equivalent of internal exile and would have to put up with whatever they were given – but Morris had declined the offer.

Within the department things had changed immeasurably for Morris in the months since the interview: he now had a pigeonhole rather than a shoebox, a nameplate rather than a Post-it note. The professors invited him to lunch rather than asking him to do the photocopying, and his opinion, so far as he could tell, was not entirely rejected. Yet he still felt a certain solidarity with Bernard and the rest of the lumpen academiat. Despite his growing confidence in the fictional, performative nature of self-hood, he had to admit that certain experiences cut deep. The pains of his temporary lectureship were not entirely eradicated by the pleasures (considerable and varied as they were proving to be) of permanency, and he was not yet up to shafting Bernard.

At that moment, Bernard himself came around the corner pushing a trolley-load of exam scripts.

'*The worst is not*, Morris,' he said mournfully as he drew level, '*so long as we can say this is the worst*. That's what I try to tell myself. You know what really pisses me off though?'

Morris shook his head. Bernard picked out a script and pointed to a small yellow sticker, issued by the Disability Support Office, which was attached to the front.

'Dyslexia. We had another word for it in my day: thick. You know me, Morris, I don't wish to be harsh. I love them dearly, but we're giving English degrees to people who can't read and write. Let me put it to you this way: if I were unfortunately paraplegic – wheelchair bound – I would hope not to be discriminated against. I would be vociferous in my support for ramps and so on, but I would not, and this is my point Morris, I would not expect to play inside right for Coketown United. There is a certain perversity in my opinion in pursuing a career in literary criticism when you are unable to spell Wordsworth. It is not a popular opinion, I know, but I'll leave it with you.'

'Something to ponder,' Morris said vaguely. Despite his resolve against guilt, he was feeling a little troubled by the obvious discrepancy in their marking loads. Bernard looked down at his trolley.

'No Morris,' he said, the faintest of tremors in his voice, 'in answer to your unspoken question, it is not mathematically possible for me to complete my marking within the time allocated by our esteemed chairman, His Holiness Declan 'the Mad' Monk. Or to be exact, it is possible, according to my calculation, only if there are thirty-seven hours in each day. I have asked His Holiness if this miraculous adjustment might be forthcoming and he rather surprisingly berated me as an obstructionist. Apparently, my relentless negativity is a hindrance both to myself and the Department.'

Morris shook his head in sympathy. 'I thought I had it bad,' he said.

'*You're* flavour of the month. Off to Los Angeles with Zoe Cable, very tasty. Enjoy it while it lasts, Morris. You deserve it, mate, but watch your back. Once you get past fifty round here it's *Brave New World*. Which reminds me . . .' Bernard crouched very slightly and his tone became noticeably secretive. 'There's something I wanted to ask you about. Come into my office, quick.'

Bernard's office was dark and book-clogged. There were shelves on every wall and double-rows of sun-faded books on every shelf. Above a cracked horsehair sofa there was a brown and brittled poster advertising 'The Art of the Victorian Teapot', Coketown Art Gallery, Mar–June 1979. The blackboard was covered with a hand-chalked genealogy of the offspring of Zeus.

'Their ignorance of Greco-Roman culture is mind-bending,' said Bernard, noticing Morris's interest. 'They think Nike is a shoe. Of course they refuse to read anything longer than a paragraph, so what can you expect? I tell them to read *Childe Harold* – they tell me they can't manage it, poor dears, it's too long. Too long? It's only four hundred sodding stanzas. They're too busy getting pissed and shagging each other, which is fair enough of course, but I say do it in your own time. A week before exams they're knocking at my door asking for clues. Clues? This is poetry, not hunt the bloody thimble.'

'Bernard, was there anything in particular?' Morris asked. Sitting in that office made Morris uncomfortable: it reminded him too closely of teenage visits to his grandmother in the Crystal Valley Rest Home in Ashby de la Zouch. There was that same rummage-sale smell of geraniums and incontinence, that same sickly atmosphere of bitterness and fear. 'The conversations in there,' his mother had once commented on the slow train back to Rotherham, 'are about as strained as the fruit.'

'Yes there was,' said Bernard. 'Sorry for blabbing so.' He put on his reading glasses and plucked from the slew of papers on his desk a copy of the last Faculty minutes. 'Do you happen to have read these?'

'Faculty minutes? Of course not. No one reads them. Declan specifically advised me to bin them on arrival – they're an irritating formality.'

152

Bernard's expression hardened. His face took on a look of unwonted efficiency. 'Interesting. For the last six months, they have not been distributed at all. It took me two weeks to get hold of this copy. Two weeks, I might add, in which I was subjected to a concerted campaign of misinformation, a campaign directed, I have reason to believe, from the very highest office in this Faculty. I finally had to employ my own locksmith.'

'The Crocodile?' Morris asked.

Bernard raised his hands.

'I make no accusations, but yes, it has that bastard's claw-prints all over it.' He handed him the minutes. 'Pages thirty-two to thirty-six, please read them in your own time. I have other copies. They're proposing to computerise us all. Put us on the World Wide Web. To be honest, Morris, the details escape me; for me *modum* will always be the accusative of *modus*, but I can read between the lines. It's a ploy: those of us without keyboard skills will go to the wall.'

'They'll have to consult.'

'Consultation? I've been to those meetings before. Old Donald'll smile in your face and the moment you turn around he'll have his fist halfway up your colon and he'll be working you like a glove puppet.'

'There's always retraining I suppose.'

'Yes. They had that in Red China I believe.'

'So what are you planning?'

'I've told old Darian, and as soon as the VC returns from his latest imperialistic adventure – this time it's Bahrain, I believe – she'll be in his office playing merry hell. Until then, I thought a letter from concerned Faculty members.'

'Are there any concerned Faculty members?'

'That's a problem,' Bernard agreed. 'This place is like Pentonville; people fear reprisals if they speak out. They're frightened His Holiness will come to their door late at night and render them research inactive.'

As Bernard talked, Morris flicked through the minutes. Outside the window a blanket of fog was being pierced by bright spokes of sunlight.

'Have you seen paragraph six yet?' Bernard asked. 'That's where they mention tactical restructuring prior to full digitalisation. The vile language of bureaucracy, Morris. *Clothe sin with gold*. And to think the Crocodile once wrote a half-decent article on Swinburne.'

Morris looked up at Bernard's drawn, doggish face. He was wearing a burgundy blazer and a black, open-neck shirt. He had a suntan, a thin grey beard and chest hair; there were clear remnants of the louche sexiness which twenty-five years before had made him a hot property, a lecturer of famous passion and sincerity, a bedder of progressive undergraduates, a penner of well-regarded letters to the *TLS*. When had things gone wrong for Bernard, Morris wondered? When had he stopped floating with the tides of history and started backstroking frantically against them? Should his decline be dated from the Crocodile's accession to power, or were there signs even before that? His ugly divorce from Hortense, for example, or the death of his mentor Marcus Grunwald? Not to mention the larger historical forces at play: feminism, Margaret Thatcher, the end of the working class, the decline of county cricket. Yes, as a cultural signifier Bernard was significantly overdetermined. But one thing was certain. Not eternally certain, of course, not certain in the Platonic or even Cartesian sense (cocksureness, Zoe called that), but temporarily certain, certain for a particular time and place (Coketown, 3 June 2001), certain so far as the multiplicities of history and language would allow: Bernard was teetering on the edge, and he knew it. He was staring into the void – only terror would have driven him to such precipitous action. In any less severe circumstances his courage would have failed him, Morris was sure. He would have hunkered down, drawn in his tentacles and prayed that the Crocodile found another victim. But the truth was there were very few alternative victims left to choose from. When it came to dead wood, these days Bernard's name was perilously high in the list.

'First they came for the Jews,' said Morris sombrely.

'Precisely,' said Bernard. 'Then they came for the computer illiterates. And who will be next?' He looked wildly round his

154

office as though searching for another vulnerable constituency. 'Scholars of Arthur Alderley? You never know.'

(Bernard seemed to have forgotten that Morris's research had taken a new and rather more successful direction lately. Morris chose not to remind him.)

'So you're with us?' he said.

Morris paused. There was silence. His glance quickly took in the room: Bernard's trolley, his own cardboard box, the horse-hair sofa piled with essays, the ancient kettle, the sepia-toned mugs, the pock-marked jar of Nescafé, the Remington type-writer, the endless, endless books. It was like a historical re-construction, he thought, 'Lecturer's Study, Northern England, 1950–1980'. Bernard was a historical curio, and the Crocodile was preparing to stuff and mount him (or mount and stuff him, depending on your metaphorical preference). His memory flicked back to Zoe two days before, sitting on his face in the Casa Urbano. What had she said to him then? 'Hold your nerve Morris, just hold your nerve.' He had assumed then that she was referring to country matters, but maybe not; with Zoe the line was frequently blurred.

'This foul document,' he waved the minutes in reply, 'appals me, Bernard. I'm with you all the way.'

'Terrific.' Bernard almost gasped with relief. Morris imagined he had already suffered one or two knockbacks. 'To have a younger member of staff on board will really help our case. Could you help me draft a letter?'

'Certainly, but perhaps we should meet off campus.'

'Good idea. Could you come to my home tonight? I'll cook supper, we'll have a glass of claret before we dip our pens in vitriol.'

Bernard lived alone in a rather grand Victorian semi in a side-street in Glodshaw. He had bought it for virtually nothing in 1972, a decade before the yuppies moved in. Then, the street was populated by student renters and ancient sitting tenants who cut their grass by hand and invariably owned bow-legged, yappy dogs. For a decade or more, Bernard was at the cutting edge.

155

Now, however, Glodshaw was upmarket. All the other houses on the street had been thoroughly refurbished – brickwork was cleaned and repointed, sash windows were replaced, driveways were created, paved and filled with pricey hatchbacks, children were ubiquitous. Only Bernard's house remained undisturbed. Ferns grew from the guttering, paint peeled from the doorway, there was a leggy crack up one wall and the flashing was blowing off the chimney. He came to the door wearing carpet slippers and an inadvisably tight polo-neck jumper. He was holding a glass of red wine.

'Morris!' He stepped aside and offered a little bow. The hallway had coconut matting and swirling purple wallpaper; from the kitchen he could smell moussaka, from the living room he could hear Mahler Nine. Morris shuddered. Bernard had lived alone in the house for almost thirty years; entering it was like walking into his subconscious, like seeing him naked. There was a certain kind of intimacy involved in merely crossing the threshold.

'Your timing is impeccable. The moussaka is reaching its peak. Help yourself to Brie while I fiddle with the veg.' There was a glass of wine waiting for him on the mantelpiece, next to what Morris guessed was a photo of Bernard with his father. Bernard's father looked a little like Clement Atlee. Bernard was wearing his school uniform: striped blazer, dark trousers, old but relentlessly polished shoes. They were standing by the Serpentine. Morris knew all about Bernard, at least all that was commonly known; Zoe had filled him in. Childhood in Neasden, scholarship to Mill Hill, Cambridge doctorate under Marcus Grunwald, a few years on the WEA circuit then Coketown, a poorly received monograph on the Romantic Epic, a textbook on the *Prelude*, a senior lectureship then silence. The parameters were clear enough. Now he was on the inside, however, Morris felt overwhelmed by previously unimagined detail. The wallpaper was flock, the carpet shag, the fire gas-effect. There was a sunburst mirror, pottery spaniels, a huge and alphabetically exact record collection. The room was dustless with an undertone of pipe tobacco. There was no TV and the only picture was

156

a large and, to Morris's mind, rather disheartening reproduction of Titian's *The Mocking of Christ*.

The moussaka when it arrived was, like the wine, disconcertingly good – musty and delicious. It was followed by Sainsbury's chocolate mousse and Nescafé with brandy.

'Is that you with your father on the mantelpiece?' Morris asked.

'That's right. Spring 1953, day release from Dotheboys Hall. We went to see Richardson in *Othello* and had a spaghetti bolognese supper in Soho. The old man was rather cultured for his day. Now of course he's nigh on ninety and he can't shit straight.'

'He's still alive?'

'Well, so they say. Modern medicine, if you ask me, is a conspiracy against human dignity. Tubes in every orifice – have you ever seen a bedsore up close? It's not pretty, believe me. I no longer take holy sacrament myself, but I happen to believe there is a certain sacredness to life and death. For everything there is a reason. My old man looks pickled – he has that complexion. The doctors won't listen to me of course.'

'Have you tried talking to them?'

'Well what's the point?'

'The thing to notice about Bernard,' Zoe had once said, after orgasm and before he caught the bus home, 'is his deference. Set aside the fulmination. At heart he's scared. It doesn't matter how often he goes to Glyndebourne, he'll never get over being working-class.'

'I thought class was dead,' Morris had replied drowsily.

'It survives in pockets. There are always residual elements, hangers-on.'

They returned to the living room and Bernard showed him a draft of the letter from concerned faculty.

Dear Professor McWurter,

As colleagues of long standing we seek your attention on the matter of the Digital Faculty Proposal (Faculty Minutes of 10/5/01 pp. 32–6). We, the undersigned, have served this faculty loyally for many years, and while we do not wish to appear as roadblocks, or even speedbumps, on the road of progress, we would respectfully suggest that the wholesale computerisation envisaged in this mad proposal would brutally sever this faculty and its constituent departments from the nourishing compost of its past. The legacy of Professor Doppet (founder of the English Department, twice Dean of the Faculty) is of a humanistic community of scholars, of wisdom and learning, handed down from generation to generation with tact and care. How, we trepidatiously ask, would such a vision survive the coming electronic onslaught? Books, words, poems, people: these are our stock in trade, not bytes and screens and fuzzy disks. Many students today already reach us brutalised by popular 'culture'; should we compound this horror by teaching them by television, marking them by email? It is surely our task to direct them via exhortation and personal example to the higher waters of truth, not to encourage them via labour-saving gadgetry to wallow in the salty muck of the quotidian. [*Perhaps also mention here the spectre of Internet Plagiarism – see* Daily Telegraph *Culture section 5/ 2/01.*] For another, perhaps newer, institution (the former Dukinfield Polytechnic for example), such a proposal may be appropriate, but Coketown has its traditions – chronological seriousness, independent study, scholarly accuracy. These may not be currently popular, but they are well known, and they have always stood us in good stead. We detach ourselves from them at our peril.

Yours with some urgency.

As Morris read, Bernard was nervously stuffing his pipe.

'What do you think?' he said as Morris put the letter down.

'What do you mean by "chronological seriousness"?'

'Well, in the old days, we didn't let them near the twentieth century until they were close to graduation. Most of the first year was *The Faerie Queen*.'

' "Independent study"?'

'That means we just let them get on with it. No mollycoddling with handouts or special revision sessions. Oh, and Darian made me include the stuff about scholarly accuracy – she's potty about footnotes, you should see her in examiners' meetings. She'll knock 'em down a class for incorrect use of *ibid*. Personally, I don't give a toss, but each to his own.'

'Where is Darian anyway? I thought she might be here'

Bernard swallowed the dregs of his brandy and ignited his pipe. Morris had not imagined him as a pipe smoker – a residue of his Cambridge days presumably. Morris found it strange and faintly touching that out of everything that should survive.

'Rome, I think, or Canterbury – somewhere Catholic.'

'She does that a lot, doesn't she?'

'Religiously. She loves a pilgrimage. She gets young Kapoor, her Ph.D. student, to fill in. Never pays him a farthing. She waffles on about the virtues of an apprenticeship system and he gobbles it up. Not that he needs the money of course, his uncle's the maharaja of somewhere. But come on Morris, don't be coy,' he said, gesturing towards the letter with the stem of his pipe. 'What's the verdict?'

'May I be blunt?'

Bernard seemed in two minds as how to reply to this. He finally managed: 'Of course, if you really must.'

'This is warfare, Bernard. From what I've read, from what I've heard you say, from what I know of Donald that much is clear. And in that context this letter is the equivalent of going into battle wearing red coats and whistling "The British Grenadier". *The nourishing compost of the past*. It's laughable.'

Bernard blushed and sucked rather more vigorously on his pipe.

'All right, OK, very well,' he said. 'So what are you suggesting? What counterproposal,' he repressed a belch, 'do you have?'

As he said this, Bernard's hands were noticeably shaking. Morris wondered whether he had struck too hard too soon. But that had been Zoe's advice: 'If you bark loud enough, he'll roll over. It's primitive stuff.'

159

'What weapons do you have Bernard?'

Bernard sat down on the sofa and rubbed his beard. While he was thinking he refilled their brandy glasses and turned over the Mahler.

'None,' he said eventually. 'I have no weapons at all – apart from Darian, who's loopy. I'm utterly fucked.'

'Yes and no. I agree you have no weapons. You are horribly weak, but sometimes weakness is a strength.'

'That's a very lovely thought, Morris, but try telling them that at the Job Centre.'

'I'm talking about stress, Bernard, workplace stress. It's reaching epidemic proportions.'

Bernard suddenly perked up. 'You don't need to tell me that, Morris. Old Qwerty had six months off with it last year. Muggins here picked up his teaching: three groups of "Conrad's Longer Novels" – it was torture. In the old days when your Mum died you had a morning off to do the death certificate, an afternoon off for the funeral and that was it. Now it's a bloody industry – counselling, antidepressants, stress consultants. Give them an extra essay to mark and they run off to their GP. Doctor, Doctor, I feel underappreciated. Too bloody right!'

'Qwerty got his six months off with full pay. Peter Finger got six months off with full pay, came back for three weeks, started sobbing in the middle of a lecture on George Herbert and got six months more. If you get the right GP you can string it out indefinitely. Do you see where I'm going with this?'

'I should become a professional malingerer. It does have a certain appeal, but wouldn't it have to involve therapy? If it had to involve therapy I couldn't do it.'

'At this point a carefully calibrated threat might be enough. If the Crocodile believes that pushing forward with the Digital Faculty proposal will result in a significant number of staff going on semi-permanent sick leave it will stop him in his tracks.'

'But he wants to get rid of us anyway.'

'He wants to get rid of you so he can hire a hotshot researcher and several temporary drones to do the work. If you go on sick

160

leave, he has no money to hire, and no one to do the teaching. He's buggered.'

Bernard dropped back into the sofa with a frown. He closed his eyes for several seconds then opened them and fixed Morris with a cheery, slightly intoxicated squint.

'I remember when you first arrived,' he said. 'You were too scared to use the staff toilet – daren't piss next to a senior lecturer in case they noticed something that might be detrimental to your career prospects. Now look at you. Machiavelli with a laptop.'

Morris paused. The tone was unexpected. As if, while cutting through what he thought was clay, his shovel had crunched suddenly into a layer of hard-packed gravel.

'Are you really bonking Zoe Cable like they say?'

Morris shuddered. His head suddenly ached as if he had swallowed something much too cold.

'Who says?'

'Enrique Hardcastle, student of mine who works for Sushi on Wheels. What was it the other night: Futo Maki and a six-pack of Sapporo? Does your wife know?'

'We're not married,' Morris lied.

'Sorry. Partner. That always sounds so bloody odd to me. Morris and Partner sounds like a business arrangement. But then again, in my limited experience, after the first year or two, after the initial flush and swell, that's really what it is. You wash the socks, I'll bring home the bacon – division of labour. The family is a unit of production after all, that's Engels. Would it be correct to assume that the stress idea was Zoe's?'

Morris didn't answer immediately. His mouth had dried up. He was unconsciously chewing his lip. After a while he nodded and tried a smile.

'Two things, Morris. No, three things. First, have another drink.'

He stood up and poured them both another brandy. 'Second, I'm sure she goes like a proverbial sewing machine. After seeing her in the red waders it took me almost a week to regain my equilibrium. Third, she's Lady Macbeth. Her motives are entirely ulterior. I don't know what she told you, but I'm not stupid. No, take that back. I may be stupid, but I'm not as stupid as they think I am. Sending threatening letters to the Dean? I may as well write my own P45.'

'Well,' Morris began. Bernard held up his hand like a traffic policeman. '. . . OK, perhaps it isn't a good idea.'

'I've already been here for twenty-seven years, Morris. When I arrived I was a young man: married, lusty, intellectually energetic. Now look at me. These things leave you, Morris, it's what stays that matters. I'm down to the bare bones, the core: this house, that bloody job. But that's OK, because I'm a stayer, Morris, I abide. They've been trying to force me out for a decade. Maybe they'll succeed one day. Maybe the Digital Faculty is it, but I doubt it. I survive, Morris, I'm like a crustacean, I have that barnacle quality. I cling. It's not pretty but at least I have a sense of purpose. I know who I am.'

'You're whatever's left over.'

'I'm the remainder.'

Morris lit a cigarette. Someone knew about him and Zoe; it made him tingle. He felt simultaneously proud and exposed. He was beset by memories of Zoe's flesh, its turns and bends, its angles of approach.

'How do you do it?' he said after a while. They were on their fifth or sixth brandy. The Mahler had been replaced by *Also Sprach Zarathustra*.

'Do what exactly?' The pipe was finished and Bernard had cadged one of Morris's cigarettes.

'Well, the marking for a start. Your loads are inhuman.'

'Ah yes, the marking.' Bernard's carpet-slippered feet were resting on an ancient Moroccan pouffe. His ankles were crossed, his trousers were slightly rucked up and Morris could see a white and veiny section of calf. 'They tried to break me with the marking. It almost worked. The first year after I was declared research inactive I was close to resigning. That June I had six hundred exams and almost fifty dissertations. They brought the date of the exams meeting forward on purpose, Declan was badgering me every day. Failure to complete the marking in a reasonable time is a disciplinary offence under the Crocodile's regime. The definition of reasonable, of course, being set by the Head of Department. Yes, I was close to breaking point, but then I discovered the system.'

'The system?'

'Let me show you. Stay where you are.' Bernard walked unsteadily out of the room and returned with two large black box files. He perched on the arm of Morris's chair. 'Look at that.' He handed him one of the files. It contained lists of student names and marks. 'Mabel does them for me. Every student's name, the mark they got for courses apart from mine and then the average. That's the mark I always give them, the average.'

'So you don't read the essays?'

'I haven't read an essay or exam in four years. I think my health has improved as a result. I certainly feel much more alert.'

'But you still complain about having to do it.'

'Unendingly of course. If I didn't complain, alarms would go off – I'm known for my complaints.'

'What about comments? You have to write a comment on each essay.'

'That's where the other file comes in. For each mark I have a selection of eight to ten comments – drawn of course from the days when I actually read the things. I then select from them on a random basis. Look: 66%. *You make a good effort with a challenging question. Your analysis of* . . . . *is probing and perceptive at times, but also on occasion lacks detail. And your conclusion veers between the tentative and the overegged. Please be careful with that in future but overall keep up the good work!* I also scatter a few ticks and question marks about of course. Student feedback suggests my marking is firm but fair.'

'What if they complain?'

'Well no one complains about being marked too high of course. If they want me to raise the mark I always do it, but I look pained, tell them it's a one-off and swear them to secrecy. They end up feeling special, which, it seems to me, is more or less the purpose of a university education these days.'

Morris paged woozily through the comments file.

53%. A curate's egg of an essay. Stylistically you shimmy

across the surface of this work rather than sounding its dark penetralia. Although light-footedness is sometimes charming, do try in future to be less of a ballerina and more of a bombardier – less Fred Astaire, more Red Adair, if you know what I mean.

'Does this really work?'

'Unfortunately, yes. At the beginning it felt like a reckless gamble. I just needed a short-term fix, but now I realise I could go on indefinitely.'

'So we're irrelevant?'

'Yes and no. The essays get written. Knowledge of a kind is passed on. Is a mark so important? Remember they're not students anymore, they're consumers. If we don't give them what they want they get all blubbery and run off to Student Counselling, and believe me, the last thing they want is to be confronted with the details of their own appalling ignorance. Our role is no longer to judge, sift, discriminate. Wheat and chaff? Sheep and goats? These are old-fashioned hierarchies. Suggest someone has a third-class mind and they'll have the Anti-Nazi League round picketing your lectures. We're not critics any more, Morris. We're not even teachers, we're servants, hired help. Our true purpose is to write ebullient and semi-truthful references, to ease them into the corporate world. And believe me, my references are exemplary: half a page of letterhead from me and the next thing you know, you're sitting in a warehouse conversion in Shoreditch pulling down forty grand. I say sod it, give them what they want. I'm not proud, but my conscience is clear.'

At the mention of conscience Morris shrivelled a little inside. The guilt of adultery, like its more intense pleasures, still sometimes took him unaware. There would be long stretches – hours, whole mornings even – when he would forget what he was up to, when he would assume half-consciously that this gentle welling up of pleasure, this sense of being shallow-fried in glee which he felt now almost continuously, was all OK, above board, legal. And it was only at moments like this when he caught sight, out of the corner of his eye, of the dark sternness of the law, that he remembered to feel guilty, contrite, like a louse. But strangest of all was what invariably came next, after the first bite of these feelings, the way that instead of just subsiding they changed their form, their taste. Wrongness became part of the pleasure. Guilt and contrition, just fuel to the flames. As Bernard pursued his point about the decline of the academy, Morris held tight to his threadbare armchair and waited for that dialectical kick, the moment when, after the grind of conscience, the superego flipped over into the id.

The music was building to a conclusion. Morris gave himself up for a moment to its aural gymnastics, the asynchronous throbs of fullness and depletion. Bernard noticed.

'Terrific, isn't it? Herbert von Karajan, 1959 – never been bettered if you ask me.'

Morris nodded. He could feel it happening: joy springing from pain, delight emerging from sin. Lies sprouting from truth, you could say, although of course that was not the right way to look at it at all since if so-called truth could grow out of a lie, how could it really be a lie in the first place? A lie was just a different version of truth, truth placed in a different context. Just as guilt, if you looked at it in another, a bigger, way, became a kind of freedom – an openness, a willingness to live beyond the rules. That was where he was, outside the rules, outside the lines looking back in. And so, as it turned out, was Bernard, in a sense at least – how lucky, he thought, and how unexpected.

Morris blinked. They were both badly drunk. Above the grey marble mantelpiece, the flock wallpaper was beginning to shimmy and swerve.

'Why are you telling me all this?'

Bernard thought for a moment, as if the question hadn't occurred to him before.

'Because I trust you. Because you are a person of character. I accept you are currently bonking Zoe Cable, that you've given up Arthur Alderley and, if what I hear is true, you're now doing this,' his arms flailed for a moment and he pulled a face like Malcolm Muggeridge, 'Body Studies. But all that aside, I see you as a man of clear vision and stout heart, a man who can distinguish at a glance his arse from his elbow, a man who is prepared to mucky up his hands on occasion. All in contra-distinction, of course, to those repellent and bone-idle bastards who ponce through the Department issuing orders and licking arse in the name of research. The God of research, Morris, is a false God – you know that, I know that. We may pretend otherwise, we may doff our caps on occasion, tug our forelocks if that eases things along. But deep down we know it's bollocks.'

'Literary criticism you mean?'

'Utter nonsense.'

'So what's the point?'

'We survive, Morris, we make ends meet. And in a world of unadulterated bullshit, we are at least human beings.'

'We're beacons of hope.'

'Well I wouldn't go that far. But put it this way, at least we're not Declan Monk. I'm not whispering sweet Fenian nothings in their ear while sticking my hand down their Wonderbras. You've noticed his admissions policy for the MA in Oirish Studies – chest size seems the decisive factor.'

'It's all about decency,' Morris suggested.

'The Orwellian virtues.'

Morris sat with that for a moment. Decency. It spread in front of him like the well-scrubbed deck of a battleship, clear, clean and solid. Was that it then? Decency, the simple virtue of his class which he had always fled from, always been embarrassed to admit? Had he circled round again to that? Sitting in the styleless unadornment of Bernard's sitting room, drinking Tesco brandy, listening to Richard Strauss, it seemed to work, it seemed to make a kind of sense. That when you boiled it down, when you swept away the froth, there was just this effort to be good, to be kind, to get by. From the hallway, a walnut-veneer wall clock whirred and began to slowly beat out the strokes of midnight.

Ten minutes later the minicab honked from outside. Standing in the swirling purple hallway, Morris gave Bernard a brief but unprecedented hug. Beneath the skin-tight turtleneck his back was bowed and knobbly. Morris remembered the varicose vein like a dull blue worm crawling up his calf. He thought again of his grandmother in the nursing home, slack-jawed and drooling.

166

'I'll sign that letter anyway,' he said.

'What? Oh sod that. I'll keep my head down and leave it to Darian. It's always worked before. Only three more years to my pension. I'll sell this shithole for two hundred grand and bugger off to Provence. Truffles and Côtes du Rhone.'

As Morris stumbled down the fissured and crumbling garden path, Bernard waved. As he got into the cab the front door closed with a creak and a snap. The living-room light went off. Bernard was retreating into his lair, reverting, Morris assumed, to his strange, timewarped kitchen then to his barely imaginable bedroom. Back again in the outside world, driving down Roosevelt Road past a strip of Polish restaurants and a late-night driving range, Bernard's house seemed like something from a fairytale, a house of gingerbread or straw. It was hard to believe it really existed, and that all that had been said there had actually been said. Morris reached, as if for confirmation, into his jacket pocket and pulled out a digital voice recorder. He rewound it for a couple of seconds then pressed play.

'Sticking my hand down their Wonderbras. You've noticed . . .'

The sound was good considering, and Zoe had been dead right about the longplay option.

Chapter 19

E's eyes widened as the foetus-baby's fist humped out the wall of her uterus. She made a tiny 'Eek!' but no one noticed. There was no one really to notice except the children of Orpington Primary, to whom the small vagaries of anonymous adults had long since ceased to be of interest, and of course Nick Kidney, who was so deeply immersed in explaining his toilet panorama to them that if a car bomb had gone off outside E doubted whether there would have been a noticeable pause in the gush of words.

'Yes, it's me on a toilet. Fifteen times. No, no, the same toilet fifteen times. Why are you laughing? Why is it so funny? Why are toilets funny? Because they smell? Well sometimes they do. What else? Because they are secret. I like that – toilets *are* secret. We lock ourselves in, we lock other people out. We're all alone in a tiny room – this is funny. You think my face is funny too? You mean my expression? What kind of expression do you think I have then? Happy? Sad? Scared? *Sad*? Do you all agree? Why do you think I am sad? Because I'm all alone in the toilet? Or, what did you say? Because someone has taken my picture on the toilet – so I'm not alone. Ah, interesting!'

After forty-five minutes of this manic dialogue, Nick Kidney had a tea break and the children set about drawing pictures of their own most secret places. They were wearing green sweat-shirts with 'Orpington Primary' and a picture of an oak tree on the front. Crowded on the gallery floor, scribbling, they looked like a gang of giant toads.

'What does it feel like?' Nick asked. They were sitting in the gallery bistro. In front of E was a glass of mango juice and a pile of Danish pastry. She was steeling herself against the smell of broccoli soup and tofu chilli.

'What does *what* feel like?'

He nodded towards her abdomen. 'Pregnancy. The miracle of life.' He was wearing a fisherman's smock made of camouflage fabric. Since their last meeting he had grown a fashionably sporadic beard. E pondered.

'I feel,' she said after a moment, 'life-size. Full-scale.'

'Ah reality,' said Kidney opening his eyes wide and taking a noisy slurp from his mug of tea. 'I know just what you mean. Or rather of course, I don't at all, but let's put it this way. I only understood surrealism after Xavier was born, after the actual birth. I mean, a head coming out of someone's vagina. A *purple* head. How real is that?'

'Entirely.'

'Right. The most real thing in the world is completely fucking weird. There is a lesson there.'

'I thought you were great with the children. You really got them going.'

'Kids are brutal and unrelenting. I respect them for that. They understand things we don't – physically I mean, they have several extra senses like bats or dolphins.'

'Do you really believe that?' The mango juice was sweet and fibrous, like swallowing a soft, yellow rope.

'Do I *really* believe it? What kind of question is that? I'll tell you what kind of question it is: it's an academic question – you're trying to bring me before the court of proof, rationality. You've been talking to your partner too much.'

'Morris?'

'Morris. You've been talking to him too much.'

'I do live with him.'

'Of course you do.'

A strange accusation, E thought, given that she and Morris seemed, these days, to be talking less and less. Having sex more, certainly. Late at night when he came in from working or early in the morning before even Molly started up, she would feel his eager hands, like crabs scuttling over her dormant body bringing

169

her back to semi-wakefulness. Eager was the word. *Keen*. Like a man who has rediscovered a hobby of his youth. There was a childish glee to it, like they were dressing up in funny clothes, giving up for a moment their adulthood. And afterwards not truculence – not the silences she had become used to, not that moping, clammy gruffness – but something much brisker and more curt. As though he had other tasks, not, as previously, to dwell upon or ponder, but to pursue, to carry out. These days, it seemed, he was always on the edge of leaving, even in the moment of arrival.

'You know Nick,' she said (risking something a little personal, a little close to the bone, perhaps), 'I don't think you're quite as primitive as you like to think you are.'

'How dare you. I am an *enfant terrible*. It says so here.' He waved a copy of the *Observer* magazine.

'The pickled penises are pure Cézanne.'

'That's libellous. Sod Cézanne.'

'*Sod Cézanne?* Didn't you say that once in *Artforum?*'

'That's right, winter 2000. It worked quite well.'

'But you don't believe it?'

'Don't let's start that again. Would you go out there and ask those children if they "really believe" in Winnie the Pooh? It's a meaningless question.'

'Because all truth is relative?'

'No, because all truth is imaginary. Truth is beauty, beauty truth. Can I smoke in here?'

'No, of course not. You know,' she licked a shard of icing from her thumb and thought for a second, 'I've never met anyone who could say that with a straight face.'

'Morris teaches literature doesn't he? Poetry?'

'It's not the same.'

Kidney shrugged. His mobile phone rang. It took him a few moments to locate it under the folds of camouflage material. When he answered, he didn't have a chance to say hello. The other person began talking immediately. 'Yes!' he started, then, 'No! When? Where? Why?' Then finally in an almost somnolent whisper, 'Yeah, OK, bye then.'

'My ex-wife.' He tugged morosely at a particle of beard then smiled suddenly as if struck by a cheerful thought. 'Hey, do you want to come to the Laugh Riot on Sheffield Road?'

'The Laugh Riot?'

'It's one of the new indoor play arenas for kids. There's a rash of them in London. I'm taking X for tea – it's his favourite place. Bring Molly.'

'Don't you want some time alone?'

'You're joking. Have you ever been inside one? It's like Beirut in the 80s. I need support. Bring Morris.'

'Morris has a late meeting.'

'Perfect.'

'I beg your pardon?'

'Saves you eating alone.'

Inside the Laugh Riot, bright red children roamed in loose-knit packs through a ruined landscape of vinyl and foam rubber.

'It's Claus Oldenberg meets *Blade Runner*,' yelled E above the savage roars of victory and defeat.

'Civil unrest for the under tens – it's a brilliant concept I must admit.'

Xavier was a short, intense five-year-old with a Kazmir Malevich T-shirt and a vertical shock of blue-black hair. As they queued for their colour-coded stickers, he looked on Molly with distrust.

'Does she even know what to do?' he asked Kidney.

'Yes I do,' Molly insisted, although she had never been there before and looked frankly scared by what she had seen so far.

'What to do?' said Kidney incredulously, as much, it seemed, to E as to Xavier. 'It's not like there are any rules. It's anarchy out there. It's Lord of the bloody Flies.'

Xavier looked suspiciously at E, then back at his father. 'Don't try to be clever Dad,' he warned.

There was a free table between the toilets and the pneumatic elephant.

'An hour in here,' commanded Kidney, 'then it's next door for ghastly overpriced food.'

171

Xavier rolled his eyes back then hurled himself bodily into a cage of spring-loaded toadstools. Molly stood suspiciously a yard or so from the table, watching the tides of sweaty children ebb and flow. E wished vaguely that she had had time to change – in her all-black workwear she looked like a pregnant Ninja – although what she might have changed into she didn't know: elasticated jeans, one of Morris's old sweatshirts? Perhaps it was better as it was. Kidney went for drinks. E chivvied Molly along and soon she was neck-deep in plastic balls and giggling wildly.

'Mango juice,' Kidney said, letting himself down with a gasp, 'and triple espresso. I've been up since five.'

'This place is insane,' said E. 'Look at them.'

Molly was sliding gleefully down a giant purple clown's tongue; Xavier was being dangled off the rope bridge by a gang of schoolfriends.

'It's quite unruly,' agreed Kidney.

'Isn't there an age limit? Some of these children look rather large.'

'Eight I think.'

'That girl's wearing a bra.'

Kidney looked carefully.

'I think you're right. She must be a big burger eater. McDonald's put all their cows on anabolic steroids you know.'

'Is that true?'

Kidney rather theatrically straightened his face.

'It's a plausible rumour.'

E took a sip of mango juice.

'I'm amazed there aren't more serious injuries.'

'To be honest, so am I, but children are more pliable than we sometimes imagine. They're quite hard to break.'

'You make it sound like you've tried.'

Kidney cackled and rubbed his hands witchily.

'Morris would hate this place,' E commented after a moment.

'Why?'

'Oh, the noise, the expense, the sense of imminent danger.'

'He'd be right then in a way.'

Xavier appeared from behind a shattered plastic column and

172

started hurling coloured balls at them. Nick Kidney caught the balls and threw them back. There was a brief fire-fight. The man at the table behind him had his glasses dislodged. 'Oi!' he said. 'Sorry,' shouted Kidney. Xavier made a face and disappeared. Molly ran past them wrapped in a large rubber snake and calling down curses on her enemies.

In a way, yes, thought E. He would be right. It was truly ghastly in here – windowless, stagnant, the air smelt like underwear, the noise level was actually painful and the kids were being schooled in commodified pseudo-violence. So why, E wondered, was she enjoying herself so much? Why had she been struggling ever since they sat down to keep a smirk off her face? It was Kidney of course. She was actually flirting with him, Nick Kidney, a relatively famous person. How surprising was that? It had been so long since her life had taken any unexpected turn that she had forgotten what it felt like. The sense of cheer, she realised, was crude and immediate, like eating a handful of Smarties. When he had called the week before to set up the talk her first reaction had been embarrassment. In hindsight, her offer seemed so prepos-terous, so blatant, so much the product of half a glass of Sauvignon Blanc, that her first instinct had been to furiously back-pedal – to point out, if nothing else, the incongruity of a Turner Prize nominee travelling for three hours to talk to a group of blasé seven-year-olds. But Kidney was not to be dissuaded. He pushed on, he enthused – he made it all sound quirky, interest-ing, fun. E was quite unused to enthusiasm, at least in this raw and articulate form. She found herself defenceless. As they spoke, she began to blush, burn (was it the pregnancy?), tingle. They made the arrangements, agreed expenses. E found the thought of him getting on the train, getting *off* the train, abnormally interesting. As she replaced the phone, she told Alison.

'Is he safe with children?' Alison asked. 'We are legally liable you know.'

'He has a son.'

'Oh I know. You should hear Gloria on that.'

She told Morris.

'Next week?' Morris said. He was strapping Molly into the back of the new Ford Focus. 'It's short notice. But maybe we can set up a one-off seminar, an "in conversation". Art History could chip in. There's money in the Aldershot fund.'

'He hates universities.'

'I'll talk to Zoe.'

Kidney was lolling.

'That triple espresso,' he said, 'was an insult to the people of Italy, and a slap in the face for coffee lovers everywhere. When she pulled out the foil sachet I should have called a halt right there.'

'You can't fall asleep in here,' said E. 'It's not humanly possible.'

'Actually, I can fall asleep anywhere. I get it from my grand-father who nodded off during the Verdun offensive. Or at least that was his excuse.'

A gravelly, God-like voice boomed over the fractious multi-tude: 'Children with green stickers, your fun is over. Please pester your parents to come again.'

After a small struggle, they decamped to the gaudy and only slightly quieter Chicken Cavern next door. The menu was large, chicken-shaped and monotonous.

'They seem to have a theme going here,' E said.

'Yeah, it's chicken. You know I have a theory that, in the popular imagination at least, the chicken is no longer really an animal. I'm thinking about the way it's manufactured, mar-keted, packaged – the nugget being my most powerful piece of evidence. There's no awareness of bone or blood. It now exists in that strange netherworld between fauna and flora, animal and vegetable. Its closest relative, I would argue, is the potato.'

The children were scarlet and hyperventilating. Kidney or-dered them both a giant Coke.

'Will that really help?'

'It's kill or cure. As a parent I do tend towards the reckless I know – stop me when I go too far.'

174

Kidney seemed to have found a second wind. He seemed oddly exhilarated by the Chicken Cavern. He was amused by the army of olde artefacts screwed to the walls: sewing machines, hot water bottles, golf clubs. He was intrigued by the shelves of glued-down books: a seven-volume biography of Nicolae Ceausescu, a field-guide for septic engineers. He joshed with a waiter in a foam chicken suit; he argued with Xavier about the nutritional value of ketchup; he arranged Molly's French fries into the shape of a unicorn.

'An original Nick Kidney,' he said. 'That's probably worth a bob or two.' Molly gobbled the hind leg with a grin.

It struck E that Nick Kidney was actually making an effort. She was touched and faintly alarmed by this. Alarmed because had she wanted an affair (which she obviously didn't), with the foetus-baby it was clearly unthinkable. The foetus-baby stuck out from her midriff like a buffer, a barricade, a fleshy rebuff to any untoward advances.

'It's really unthinkable sometimes,' she said out loud.

'What is?'

'The thought of a new baby. Another human being.'

'I know what you mean. I've always been fascinated by pregnancy.' (Was *that* it, E wondered? Was that what he was interested in? There was probably a name for people like that. Undoubtedly there would be specialist magazines.)

'With Xavier the scan was my favourite part. I like that it's in black and white, I hope they keep it that way. It's like signals from another planet. That grey noise, that soupy swirl, then bits emerge – the spine, the hand, the *heart*. I felt like I was seeing something I shouldn't see, like I was breaking a priestly taboo. Gloria didn't want to know anything, didn't want to look, she wanted to keep it all mysterious, but to me that's just bad faith – I told her mysteries don't need protection, it's fact that's fragile.'

'She didn't believe you?'

'She left me for a curator. A man who writes wall texts.'

'He's terribly nice.'

'Of course he is, but is niceness so important? Is niceness really

175

enough? It's necessary, I admit, it's a requirement, but let's not get caught up with niceness. If love is a whole year then niceness is about five days, ten max.'

Xavier and Molly had visited the ice-cream lagoon and were teetering back with crude, top-heavy sundaes. They were giggling and, most bizarrely, holding hands.

'Are we talking about love then?'

'What else is there?'

'To talk about?'

'In general.'

E remembered her poem. It was not actually her poem, it was Emily Dickinson's, but it was the only one she had ever memorised. And even then she had done so inadvertently. She had read it once in her first year at college and it had stuck.

> That Love is all there is,
> Is all we know of Love;
> It is enough, the freight should be
> Proportioned to the groove.

Once when she was feeling maudlin and crampy she had asked Morris to recite a poem for her and the best he could come up with was 'They fuck you up your mum and dad'. Later, to be fair, he brought to mind something by Yeats, but the moment had passed.

Outside, the car park was damp. Oversized cars hissed past them. After kissing Xavier and Nick Kidney goodbye, she strapped Molly into the Ford Focus and got into the front seat. She was having trouble adjusting to the new car. It seemed so foreign – the metallic paint, the alloy wheels, the CD player. Morris loved it. He had beaten the salesman down on the price, which had astonished her almost as much as his initial impulse to take out a loan to buy it. The engine started with a near-silent whirr. She turned on the windscreen wipers and their quiet efficiency filled her with a sudden loneliness. Although only a foot or so from her, they seemed miles away, in a different world. She could feel tears gathering under her eyelashes, dripping down her cheeks. Hormones, she thought. Molly's helium chicken balloon bobbed forwards.

'Don't lose my balloon!' she shrieked.

Sobbing, E gathered it in and clutched it to her breast like a child.

Chapter 20

It was worst immediately after orgasm. In that second or so of complete defencelessness and clarity, guilt would grip and squeeze him like a killer robot.

'Uuuuuuuur,' Morris growled out in existential agony.

'Are you OK?' asked Zoe. 'Is the piercing a problem?'

Morris shook his head. He looked down at Zoe. Her face, its childlike nakedness, pushed into him like a tin opener. He oozed sadness.

'Are you crying?'

Morris flopped over and took a deep breath. He felt like a transplanted organ that was in the process of being rejected. It was not a pleasant feeling. He decided to distract himself by kissing Zoe's breasts. They were firm, pointed and, suitably enough, non-identical. He kissed. Zoe purred. After a minute or two of that, Morris felt a little better.

'Sorry,' he said. 'I got a little overcome.'

'It's sweet. Really.'

He nodded. It was Tuesday afternoon. He was the kind of person who committed adultery on Tuesday afternoons. There were several ways to look at that, Morris supposed. He tried to focus only on the more cheerful ones.

'Fuck me,' said Zoe. 'I can see the sun.'

'No way.'

They got out of bed and ran to the picture windows. Zoe opened the blinds. She was right. Through a crack in the omnipresent cloud, the sun was visible, yellow and glorious. The first sighting of the summer, always a big day in Coketown. In Corporation Square the buses had temporarily stopped;

people were looking, pointing, stripping off their shirts. There was a smattering of applause. Inside the apartment Zoe and Morris stretched themselves and squealed like pagan devotees. Summertime at last! The jackpot of the academic year.

'Will you go away?' Zoe asked later over coffee and cigarettes.

'I expect so: Brittany, Corfu, somewhere last minute. Last year we camped in Anglesey which was horrid – I want to avoid a repeat of all that. And I've got the book of course.'

'And the baby.'

'Yes, the baby.' Morris rather wished Zoe hadn't mentioned the baby. The thought of it troubled him. It felt like a trap waiting to be sprung.

'And you?'

'Let's see. July – Cairo, Frankfurt, Vienna. August, I'm doing last-minute lobbying for the Hub plus working up here for Donald on the Digital Faculty Proposal. Then a week in Goa before it all starts off again.'

'I'm jealous.'

'Of my itinerary?'

'No.'

Zoe leaned across the teak breakfast bar and gave him a long hug. Strange, he thought as he nuzzled her ear (she smelt of wet sand and vinegar), that as well as guilt, infidelity should offer also this remarkable sense of newness, innocence, beginning again. Or really, not strange at all, because why else would he do it? What else was in it for him, for anyone, except this reminder of how sweet things once were, of what, in a sense, you were betraying? When Morris clung to her there, amidst the Danish crockery, there was a sense, a real sense – and he wished to insist on this above all – that he was also clinging to E, to the memory of E, that all this was in some way a tribute to her.

He explained his theory to Zoe.

'What do you think?' he said. 'Is it manageable? Does it convince?'

'Are you asking the right person?'

'I'm just kite-flying here. Work with me.'

Zoe thought. She tightened her kimono and pursed her lips. 'It's quite Proustian.'

'Is that good?'

'That would depend.'

'Yes, I suppose it would.'

'You're not actually thinking of trying it on E?'

'On E? God no. It just struck me. I thought it might make an article, conference paper, something like that.'

Zoe smirked. Morris remained unembarrassed, indeed these days, he always remained unembarrassed. Of all the changes effected by the untoward events, that was one of the more noticeable, as if the commission of actual crimes had relieved him at last from the shame of imaginary ones.

'How is the Digital Faculty thing going anyway?'

'In the bag apparently. Darian has already gone – Donald took Kapoor to one side and explained which side his bread was buttered on. He made a formal complaint about exploitation. QED. And with Bernard apparently it's only a matter of time.'

'Will he actually use the recording?'

'He'll make Bernard aware of its existence. The process of undermining has already begun. Actually, with Bernard it began in the early 80s, but never mind, the pressure will be increased, eventually something will give. Bernard will lose his rag, overstep a line, they'll be a complaint (real or manufactured), Donald will arrange a meeting, there will be a thick file, the suits from Personnel will be there. Donald will refer obliquely to the issue of fraudulent marking, he will drop in phrases from your conversation, hint at knowledge he should not rightly possess. The resignation will come. That's how it works.'

Morris swallowed and frowned.

'This isn't *Hard Times*, Morris. He'll cut a deal.'

'I don't think he'll crack.'

'He'll crack. The pension isn't cut and dried.'

Morris whistled and ate a piece of biscotti.

Zoe stood up and began languidly to tidy. Morris found the sight of Zoe tidying extraordinarily sexy. It was so unlike her, he thought, that to see it suggested to him an intimacy far beyond the physical.

'It's brutal.'

'Yes and no,' she said. 'It's harsh perhaps, but on the other hand let's not get carried away. This is really only a job, and not even a very good one. No lives are lost.'

'Isn't that a bit literal?'

'OK, try this one for size. It could have been you Morris, but you chose to act. Bernard and Darian chose not to. They're adults, they're professionals – that was their decision.'

'OK, fair enough. Although choice is an odd word for it.' He was thinking, of course, of the thump of Dirck van Camper against the death car, the traffic jam on Recreation Road.

'Don't backtrack Morris. You're stronger than you think. You had the balls to change.'

Morris dressed himself slowly, carefully, as if to savour the minutes before going outside, the temporary sense of himself he got from being with Zoe, the sense of his extraordinariness, his malleability. Soon, he knew, he would be back out in Corporation Square, with the diesel fumes and the clusters of dangerous-looking schoolchildren. Then he would catch the tram to the university, drive from there to pick up Molly and E, drive home, cook dinner, put Molly to bed, watch TV, sleep. As he mapped it out, the rest of the day felt in his imagination like being squeezed through a series of ever narrower pipes. When could he see Zoe again? If he had not become immune to embarrassment he might have been embarrassed by his neediness. There was the examiners' meeting all day tomorrow. That was something he supposed. But then?

'Oh, I forgot to tell you,' Zoe shouted from the glass-bricked shower alcove, as if in answer to Morris's unspoken question. 'I'm going down to London. I'm on *Going Critical* this week. Make sure you watch.'

'Are you really?' Morris was a long-time viewer of *Going Critical*. The weekly review show hosted by the porky and pusillanimous Adam d'Hote. The sensationalistic idiocy of most of the views expressed appalled and grieved him, yet he could not resist it. It was the critical equivalent of professional wrestling. The regulars, apart from the extraordinarily irritating Adam d'Hote, were the fiery and half-cut Welsh poet Geraint Davis and the ferociously cool style journalist and bestselling novelist Toby Royale. The final guest, who usually served as a sacrificial voice of moderation between the clashing contraries of Davis and Royale, varied from week to week. Sometimes it had been Deirdre Pluck. This week apparently it would be Zoe Cable.

'Yes, it's Deirdre's gout. She gave them my name.'

'I didn't know you and Deirdre got on.'

'Oh, we joust. I love that second generation stuff – it's so maternal. Floppy breasts and wholemeal bread. Will you watch?'

Zoe Cable stuck her head around the shower door in inquiry. Her face was clear and steaming wet, her eyelashes were clotted together in tiny black spokes, her beetroot hair was flat and foolish. Seeing her, Morris felt inside him a strange congeries of sympathy, protectiveness and lust. Was he falling in love? The idea struck him as both simple and appallingly inconvenient. It made him shiver.

'I always watch,' he said. 'It's a compulsion of mine.'

Chapter 21

After dinner was over and Molly was asleep, they sat next to each other on the sofa. E yawned.

'I should be going to bed,' she said. 'I feel like I'm always going to bed.'

'Yes, I suppose you do.'

E picked up the TV guide.

'Your programme's on tonight: *Going Critical* 10.30–11.00 p.m.'

'I know. Zoe Cable's a guest.'

'Zoe Cable, is she really?' E looked more closely at the guide. 'You're right, she is.'

There was a pause; the central heating roared on then almost immediately switched itself off.

'Do you think she's clever?'

'Zoe Cable? No. Yes. You don't really need to be clever for that programme, just shameless.'

'So she's shameless?'

'She's unprincipled.'

'You make it sound like a compliment.'

'It's a conscious position. That makes all the difference. It's not something she just fell into.'

'You used to loath her.'

'I did not.'

'Yes you did. You described her once as a vicious careerist with the heart of an estate agent.'

Morris burst into laughter. E stared at him.

'You have a good memory,' he said after a while.

'Certain things stick.'

E pulled her legs up on to the sofa and wrapped herself in an old brown car blanket.

'I thought you were going to bed.'

'I'll wait a while.'

They watched the news – train crash, arson, Siamese twins. As ten-thirty approached, Morris began wishing E would go upstairs. He had imagined watching Zoe on *Going Critical* as something personal, private. If TV watching could ever be private – which was in itself, he supposed, a mildly interesting question since the medium was itself so obviously public.

The phone rang. Morris, more on principle than anything else, checked his watch and frowned before answering. The voice was male, southern. He asked for E.

'Who should I say is calling?'

'Kidney.'

'He calls himself Kidney,' Morris said, holding the phone.

E straightened up, reddened slightly.

'Nick, hi,' she said. She sounded nervous. Now Morris stared. E waved him away. He looked back at the TV news – bankruptcy, asylum seekers, film premiere. Nick Kidney, of course, the artist. He and E must have hit it off the other week – didn't they go somewhere with the kids? He heard the whispery shiver of Kidney's voice. E laughed. Morris glanced at her. It was like glancing at himself, catching a sight of his own reflection in a window – that initial interest when you think it's someone else, someone else who looks likes you, and then nothing, the blank similitude of recognition. It was just E, just Morris. He could never see her with fresh eyes any more than he could see himself. Could never see her as other people, Kidney for example, saw her. That was why this was happening, he supposed – not that he disliked E, not even that he was bored, but that he couldn't *see* her any more. He envied Kidney that. Whatever his motives (and really, she was six months pregnant so how bad could they be?), at least he could see her, he could encounter her qualities and strangeness, he could be surprised by them.

E was looking through her Filofax. The news was coming to an end.

184

'I'll have to speak to Morris,' she said. 'Yes, we're going to watch *Going Critical*, one of Morris's friends is on.' Kidney said something loud and rather lengthy. E laughed again. 'Did he really? Isn't he hateful?'

Hateful, Morris thought. What a peculiar word to use.

E put down the phone. Her face was smiley and a little flushed. 'Nick,' she said. 'He's invited us to another opening in London. He said they reviewed one of his shows on *Going Critical* a year ago. Geraint Davis called him an intellectual jackanapes, and described his work as the spiritual equivalent of bowel cancer. Toby Royale loved it of course.'

'Of course.'

'Which one do you prefer, Geraint or Toby?'

'They can't be separated. Preference is meaningless. I tell my students they're perfect examples of a mutually constitutive binary. They need each other: without "Geraint", "Toby" doesn't exist, and vice versa.' He was making quote marks in the air. 'You can't have one without the other.'

E stifled a yawn.

'Like love and marriage, you mean?'

'Er, no, more like good and evil.'

From the TV came a tootle of cool jazz. The *Going Critical* logo smouldered briefly on the screen before being replaced by Adam d'Hote, who looked, Morris always thought, rather like a pink Pacman.

'Good evening everyone.' He paused. 'And welcome to *Going Critical*. Our guests this evening are, as usual, the ever-irascible Geraint Davis and the only mildly amusing Toby Royale. And, *not* as usual, from the dark satanic mills – or should that, given its reputation for drug-fuelled clubbing, be dark satanic *pills*? – of Coketown, writer, academic and sometime intellectual dominatrix, Zoe Cable.'

There was applause. The camera stopped lightly, like a skimmed stone, from Adam to Geraint, Geraint to Toby, Toby to Zoe. Zoe was wearing a boob-tube and a dog collar – she looked sardonic, bored and intellectually dangerous. Morris shifted in his seat.

185

'Does she always dress like that?' E asked.

'Like what?'

'Like it's 1982 and she's just been to the youth club disco.'

'It's deliberate.' Morris said. And then, as if to cover himself, 'I would imagine.'

First up was *Tet*, a film about the Vietnam War. There was a short clip of two soldiers shouting at each other in a foxhole. 'George Clooney and Russell Crowe enjoying a *Tet à Tet*,' joked Adam d'Hote. 'Geraint?'

Geraint Davis appeared at first not to have heard. He remained crouched and motionless in his chair for several seconds. Eventually he wobbled his jaw and slowly sat upright. He was wearing a woolly cardigan and an open-neck check shirt. His haircut, grey and frizzy, seemed to be at odds with itself.

'I find the premise of this film,' he began, 'deeply offensive, deeply offensive.' (Quick cut to Toby raising his eyebrows, Adam looking interested, Zoe looked bored, sardonic, intellectually dangerous. Back to Geraint.) 'The Vietnam War was not an American tragedy, it was a Vietnamese tragedy. One million Vietnamese died against fifty thousand Americans. But how many Vietnamese people do we see in this film? I counted them – forty-eight.'

'Oh, you did *not* count them?' mocked Toby Royale.

'Yes I did,' shouted back Geraint Davis. 'I have freeze-frame on my DVD. Forty bloody eight, I tell you. It's an obscenity!'

'I thought George Clooney gave quite a fine performance as the emotionally troubled Sergeant Troy,' said Adam soothingly.

'Not at all,' shouted back Geraint Davis. 'It's Californian navel-gazing. The self-indulgence makes me want to puke.'

'Toby?'

'This,' Toby said in his carefully crafted North London accent, 'is a movie about sin and redemption and the painful path to moral enlightenment.' (Since Toby swallowed his 't's, 'enlightenment' was not an easy word for him to pronounce – he appeared to chew it as much as say it.)

'That's poppycock,' heckled Geraint.

'I agree with you, Adam,' Toby continued. 'Clooney's central performance as Bob Troy, a man who is trying to draw himself back to human decency, is truly magnificent. This is Clooney at his very finest – he combines the louche sexiness of Montgomery Clift with the ravaged emotional intensity of Orson Welles.'

'Orson Welles?' spat Geraint. 'Welles was a genius. Clooney is a clothes horse, a mere cipher. The film is a moral atrocity.'

'Zoe?'

Zoe sprang to life. Her make-up gleamed. She seemed suddenly chirpy, fresh and extremely well caffeinated.

'Well Adam,' she confided. 'This is really a film about gay sex. It's pro-buggery and anti-war, which is in my opinion a hell of a combination.'

There were several seconds of uproar. Toby Royale laughed loudly, Geraint Davis howled in protest and Adam d'Hote made a flustered demand for clarification.

'But Zoe, there's no sex in this film at all,' he said.

'Not as such, Adam, but the central relationship between Clooney and Crowe is obviously highly eroticised. Remember the scene with the grenade launcher? The swimming pool in Saigon? It's Oscar Wilde with flamethrowers.'

'These characters are all straight, Zoe,' smiled Geraint with paternalistic moderation.

'Oh come on, Geraint. No one's *really* straight. Not even you.'

The camera switched to Geraint Davis who looked momentarily distorted, like a bad flash photograph of himself.

'God, she's rude,' said E.

'Yes, I know.' Morris was rather awkwardly developing an erection. He crossed his legs and swallowed. He was looking fascinatedly at the the soft right angle of Zoe's bare shoulder, like the bend in a pale brown pipe. He was remembering its texture, its heft in his palm as he held her.

'Do you find her attractive?' E asked. She seemed genuinely curious.

Morris swallowed again.

'The make-up, boob-tube etcetera, is all post-feminist. She's reclaiming female pleasure and autonomy.'

187

E shifted her weight and grimaced. 'Yes, I suppose some men go for that,' she said.

'You think it's a sham?'

'It's just a bit obvious. She strikes me as the type of woman who wears expensive lingerie. It's like she's scared of being too clever. She's over-compensating.'

The thought of Zoe in expensive lingerie made Morris temporarily breathless.

'Academics are never scared of being too clever,' he commented after a moment. 'That's what it's all about – who has the biggest brain.'

'It may be about relative organ size, Morris,' E said archly, 'but from what I've witnessed the brain is rarely the organ in question.'

Morris felt mildly reprimanded. Did that make sense, he wondered, or was it just an offshoot of his web of undersoil guilt? He felt, perhaps for the first time, briefly scared of E, of her powers of discovery and complication.

The next topic for discussion on *Going Critical* was Rufus Sump's latest novel, *Playing Lawn Darts With Henry Kissinger*, a dysfunctional family saga set in 1970s New Jersey.

'Toby?'

'I'm actually a huge fan of Sump. *Minnesota Cheeseshack* was, in my opinion, one of the great satires of the 90s. His engagement with the psychotic underbelly of the American boom is truly unparalleled. Mailer, Roth, Updike, Sump: these to me are *the* American post-war writers.'

'And did *Playing Lawn Darts* live up to these rather elephantine expectations?' Adam d'Hote prompted.

'Unfortunately not, Adam. I found the narrative circuitous and lacklustre. The characterisation, usually Sump's strong suit, was lackadaisical to say the least. All those brothers and sisters, you just forget who they are.'

'So, Sump on autopilot. Geraint?'

'I disagree. I thought this was absolutely terrific. Sump's previous work has in the main been execrable, childish nonsense – toilet humour for the MTV generation. *Minnesota Cheese-*

188

shack is no more great satire than *My Fair Lady* is great sociolinguistics.'

'Don't knock *My Fair Lady*,' yelled Toby

'But at last,' Geraint continued without pause, 'Sump has grown up. This is thoughtful, intricate, *moving*. For once he eschews the sensational in favour of the true. I read it all in one night, and I ended up in floods of tears.'

'I agree with Geraint,' said Adam briskly. 'I found the mother's death scene achingly real. Zoe?'

'This most important character in this novel is obviously the dog,' said Zoe.

'Dog? What dog?' Geraint Davis looked around, bewildered as though he had suddenly been dropped by parachute on to a vast and trackless moor.

'Hooydunk, the schnauzer,' said Zoe. 'He appears in chapter eighty-one. The references to Tolstoy and Kafka are obvious, but I think Sump goes one better by giving Hooydunk a kind of omniscience – the dog is the voice of God, geddit? Simple but brilliant. The margin is the centre.'

'So you liked it?'

'No, I only liked the dog. Actually, I loved that dog, but the rest is trivial and sophomoric.'

'You didn't find the death scene achingly real?'

'It's Little Nell in a duplex. Grow up, Adam.'

Adam d'Hote's face, which was permanently pink even under make-up, flushed to an orangey shade of purple.

'You think dogs are more important than real human beings?'

Morris had watched every episode of *Going Critical* and he had never before seen Adam d'Hote annoyed.

'None of it is *real*, Adam. It's all made up,' said Zoe with a grin.

'You know, Kidney never returned my messages,' said Morris.

'Yes, he's like that.' E's eyes remained fixed on the TV.

'Is he?'

'I believe so. He has a well-cultivated reputation for rudeness.'

'So I shouldn't be offended?'

'No, I think you should be. His aim is usually to offend, but then again, since that's his aim, the best way to get back at him would probably be to take it in your stride.'

Morris thought about this for a while.

'Why should I want to get back at him? Doesn't the urge to revenge suggest a certain depth of feeling, a certain back history of antagonism? Whereas Nick Kidney and I have never met. Our only link is that he failed to return my messages.'

'True, but isn't it possible that ignorance breeds intensity of feeling? That we feel strongest about those people we barely know, that we hear about or glimpse but never meet. And conversely that close and continual contact leads inevitably to a levelling down of emotion?'

'I see your point,' said Morris. 'It's very Proustian.'

They had moved on to a naturist version of *A Midsummer Night's Dream*.

'The Bard bared,' said Adam. 'But what is the point of it all? Zoe?'

'It's the id, to be monosyllabic, Adam. To me, the nudity was a treat. It's a play about sexual fantasy after all. This production goes straight to the nub and stays there. It's a little unrelenting perhaps but the unconscious can go on a bit, can't it?'

'If you go down to the woods today, you're in for a bloody big surprise, apparently. Geraint?'

'I was terribly bored. Cock and arse, cock and arse, what ever happened to the iambic pentameter? Whatever you say, Shakespeare's about language. You can show me all the pubic hair you want but if you can't speak the verse I say "piss off mate".'

'So, enunciation not depilation. Toby?'

'Let's cut to the chase, Adam. Does anyone actually like this stuff?'

'Shakespeare?'

'*Yes*, people don't really like seeing Shakespeare, it's just a way of being pompous, like opera.'

'Shakespeare's worthless. Geraint?'

'That's patent nonsense, Adam. Reverse snobbery at its worst.

190

Please don't blame Shakespeare for the rampant idiocy of contemporary culture. If people don't enjoy a good production of Shakespeare, that's their stupid fault not his.'

'Harsh words. Zoe?'

'Slap me round the head with a haddock, Adam, but I find two hours of nakedness pretty pleasurable. Libido is classless. Toby should really remove that chip from his shoulder, it's spoiling the hang of his Armani suit.'

'Nakedness is poor reward for three hours of tedious gobbledegook,' said Toby. 'Like watching porn while wearing a wetsuit. If you want sex, turn to Channel Five.'

'When I want sex, I certainly don't turn to Channel Five, Toby. Your idea of pleasure seems rather monolingual, shall we say.'

'This is all a half-veiled insult to the working classes,' bellowed Geraint.

'The working classes are dead,' said Toby. 'Get over it.'

'*I'm* not dead, you bastard.'

'Does he always get that angry?' asked E.

'No, only on special occasions. It's been a good show.'

'Zoe's held her own.'

'She's got a gimmick. That's the key. You have to have a gimmick and stick to it. Otherwise, you're just chaff in the wind.'

'Sex?'

'Exactly, she does sex. That's her niche.'

'The others weren't expecting it.'

'No, she had the element of surprise. Next time they'll be waiting for her.'

Adam d'Hote was signing off. There was another tootle of cool jazz. E yawned and began to untangle herself.

'I'm going to bed then. By the way, have you got a boner?'

Morris looked down.

'Yes, but it's just theoretical.'

Their eyes met for an implacable moment, then turned away again. Morris felt strangely non-stick.

191

'OK then, goodnight.' E staggered away. Beneath her borrowed pyjama jacket her belly was big, brown and pod-like.

'Goodnight.' Morris waved. It felt both sad and relieving, like saying goodbye to someone he had been seated next to on a long-haul flight. He switched to Channel Five.

Chapter 22

In Zoe Cable's mind, the Hub was beginning to form. It was coming together with inexorable, inevitable force, like a spiral galaxy condensing out of the chemical riot of the big bang. They had come through the first round of bidding with ease. Their only rivals now were Clapham College and the University of West Lanarkshire. The final decision would be made by a panel of four under the chairmanship of Gantry Hellespont. Zoe's conference itinerary that summer had been designed to bring her into collision with those five people as frequently and as intimately as possible.

23 June – the Cairo Conference on Urban Selves. Zoe Cable reclined in the stern of a large felucca, sharing a dizzying sheesha pipe with Angus Deedpole, Emeritus Professor of Social Engineering, University of the Wirral. They were discussing the films of Vincent Price. Deedpole was passionate about the films of Vincent Price. When he had appeared on Mastermind in 1982, Vincent Price had been his specialist subject. He had scored eleven points, passed on two and been beaten into second place by a heating engineer from Gorton.

'I just love the ending of *The Fly*,' said Zoe.

Deedpole nodded wildly in assent. 'Heelp me! Heelp me!' he cried in a weeny fly voice. 'Chilling isn't it?'

'And isn't *The Masque of the Red Death* extraordinarily prescient?' she went on. 'I mean it's the AIDS panic thirty years early.'

Deedpole sat straight up, his eyes wide with excitement. '*Exactly*,' he said. '*Exactly*. That's exactly what I've been saying. But why does no one else see it?'

'They don't see it?'

Deedpole's head shook with the sad regularity of a metronome.

'Not at all? I can't imagine why not,' said Zoe. 'I mean, isn't it obvious?'

'Isn't it though? Isn't it just.' The vehemence of Deedpole's nodding was now beginning to threaten the stability of the felucca. Their laconic steersman, Abdul Aziz, cast him a look before hawking a large goober into the Nile. 'It's right *there!*' shouted Deedpole, as though pointing to his theory on a large-scale map.

They tacked into the shadow of the Sheraton pizzeria. A dead donkey floated past with its legs in the air like an upturned coffee table.

'It's probably too audacious for the current climate,' said Zoe. 'People do get terribly hung up on details of chronology.'

'But that's just it,' agreed Deedpole, whose most recent article on HIV and *The Masque of the Red Death* had been turned down, to Zoe's knowledge, by at least three separate journals. 'It's just detail, minutiae. Why can't people see the big picture any more?'

'We need to move the profession beyond that,' agreed Zoe. 'We need a return to boldness, innovation, *size.*'

'You know I'm delighted to hear you say that, Zoe,' said Deedpole, sinking back into a pile of Bedouin cushions. 'I was beginning to feel like I was on my own.'

'Christ no, Angus. The forces of pedantry still aren't entirely in control.' Zoe offered him a concerned frown and a pat on the knee. 'And by the way, *Vagina Dentata* is always eager for original work on film. I mean, if you happen to have anything to hand.'

Frankfurt, 10 July – the Pan European Queerness Convention. Zoe Cable sat in an Ethiopian restaurant on Bleidenstrasse with Daze Krakov and Rupert Venison. They were, all three, coked up to the eyeballs.

'Listen,' said Zoe. They were drinking white wine, a bottle

194

each. They had ordered a confusing battery of dishes, none of which looked appetising, some of which appeared straightforwardly inedible. 'The Hub thing – can we just get that out of the way?'

'You wish to buy our votes,' giggled Daze.

'It's a votes-for-coke scenario,' added Rupert.

'Does that work for you?' Zoe asked. 'What have the others offered?'

Daze and Rupert compared notes.

'West Lanarkshire took me to dinner.'

'Me too.'

'It was nice.'

'Nice but, through no fault of their own, rather sausagey.'

'Yes, terribly sausagey.'

'Clapham College sent scantily clad graduate students to our room.'

'They did not.'

'No, they didn't, but I intend to suggest it. Isn't this music fantastic?'

They all listened to the music. It *was* terribly good.

Rupert semaphored to a waiter.

'*Die Musik,*' he yelled, '*was ist das?*'

The waiter knuckled his brow. Zoe pointed frantically to the loudspeaker, Daze made drumming motions. The waiter nodded, smiled broadly and returned a few moments later with a side order of what appeared to be curried goat's cheese.

Vienna, 21 July – EU-funded Summer School: The Transnational Body. Zoe sat in the Prater ferris wheel with Helmut Dawlish. Helmut, annoying at the best of times, was doing an Orson Welles impression.

'Look down there,' he said, nodding through the window. 'Would you really feel any pity if one of those *dots* stopped moving forever? If I offered you twenty thousand pounds for every dot, would you really, old man, tell me to keep my money?'

'*The Third Man*, yes.'

195

A month of oversauced food and brown-nosing had taken its toll even on Zoe, whose patience was wearing thin.

'I'm on the panel for the Hub you know,' said Helmut.

'Are you really?'

He smiled. 'I hear the Ethiopian food in Frankfurt is excellent.'

Zoe winced.

'The body truly is a fascinating subject, isn't it?' Helmut went on. 'All those *ins* and *outs*. And I realise your expertise in that area is,' he paused, 'second to none.'

Zoe was looking out of the window. Austria was so clean. Ground level was bad enough, but from here it looked absolutely, revoltingly perfect. She looked back at Helmut, whose chinos had wigwamed at the groin. She only needed a simple majority. Helmut was insurance at most.

'Give it a rest, Helmut,' she said. 'There's enough pussy at this conference to feed the five thousand. You don't need me.'

'Ah,' he sighed, 'pure Billingsgate, Zoe. Your gift for vulgarity hasn't waned. I thought perhaps a quick one for old times' sake.'

'Old times' sake?' Zoe cast her mind back. Oh Christ yes, she remembered now: Kingston Poly, 1992. 'Bloody hell, Helmut,' she said, 'I was a graduate student. There's a statute of limitations.'

Helmut placed a hand on his heart.

'Consider me truly contrite. And as for the pussy, if you have any specific names in mind please let me know.'

As they got off, Helmut did the line about cuckoo clocks then kissed Zoe on the cheek. He whispered in her ear, 'You're halfway there, but the one to watch is Hellespont – I've been hearing rumours.'

Before Zoe could press, Helmut had left in pursuit of an independent scholar from Estonia.

London, August Bank Holiday weekend – the National Funding Fair. Zoe sat in a Starbucks in Covent Garden, alone. She was worried. Gantry Hellespont was late, and she too had been hearing rumours. Rumours of politicking, of sideways moves, of guideline revision, strategy rethinks. Everything was suddenly airborne. Nothing was fixed, which was fine in principle, but for once Zoe felt behind the game, out of the loop, as if all the while she had been in Europe other forces had been at work: large, strange, dark forces which operated at a frequency she could not pick up. She felt, for one of the few times in her professional career, disorientated and out of sorts. And now this. Fifteen minutes late. Perhaps she had chosen the wrong Starbucks, there were so bloody many of them. These days they seemed to build them in clusters. Zoe stood up. She could do a brisk check of the nearest three or four and be back in less than ten minutes. Just then she noticed someone standing in the doorway: a small, bewhiskered man, wearing an aged three-piece suit, Varilux glasses and fiercely polished brogues. Noticing Zoe, he strode forward. His little heels clicked chirpingly, annoyingly, ominously on the terracotta floor tiles. Zoe sat down again.

'Mordred.'

'Zoe.' His smile seemed indirect, carefully learned, like the speech of the profoundly deaf, as if it might have been produced by some precise and skilful tightening of the sphincter rather than anything directly facial.

'So that's how it is.'

'Yes.' He perched on the edge of a chair and looked around for a waiter.

'You have to order at the counter.'

'Oh really. Would you mind? A pot of Earl Grey would be lovely.'

Zoe returned with a mug of hot water and a cranberry and blackcurrant teabag.

'It's the best they could do.'

Mordred looked faintly disgusted.

'I'm not a supporter of the teabag,' he said after a moment.

He stirred then sipped. His glasses paled in the air-conditioned shade. The eyes thus revealed were raw, pink and ferrety; they were edged with hardened crusts of pus. They had been damaged, brutalised by decades of manuscript work. Mordred

197

Evans wore them like battle scars, he used them to frighten people. 'If I can do this to myself,' they seemed to say, 'what might I do to you?'

'I'm expecting Gantry Hellespont,' said Zoe Cable, in a futile attempt to claw back the initiative.

'What *is* that person drinking?' said Mordred, nodding at the woman sitting opposite them on a lip-shaped sofa.

'I believe it's called a Frappuccino.'

'Really?' Mordred Evans' fingernails, Zoe noticed, had been recently buffed. 'Yes,' he continued. 'Professor Hellespont will not be coming. It was thought best under the circumstances that I should serve as his replacement.'

'For this particular meeting?'

'No, in general.'

'Temporarily, you mean?'

'For the foreseeable future.'

Zoe Cable said nothing. She lit a cigarette.

'I believe this is a no-smoking area,' Mordred commented.

'I believe you're right.'

Zoe continued to smoke. Mordred manifested another, smaller smile.

'Donald is a terribly talented man,' he said after a moment of silence. 'You know this, of course. He is a man of ambition and foresight. He has, we might even say, a genius for strategy. For example, the recent Digital Faculty Proposal – quite spectacular. My talents, modest as they are, lie elsewhere. I concern myself with detail, with, we might even say, minutiae. You will be aware of my survey of early English spelling.'

Zoe shook her head. Mordred's jaw tightened faintly.

'Whereas others like to travel,' the brutalised eyes lifted and lingered for a second on Zoe, 'I prefer to remain at home. I have a genius, one might say, for persistence. It is surprising how much one can learn at home. In the case of poor Professor Hellespont, for example, on closer inspection certain significant details came to light (I won't bore you with them now) which made his position as Chair of the Panel for the Body Studies Research Hub less appropriate than it had earlier appeared to be. Under the circumstances, as I say, I was deemed a suitable alternative.'

'You have no experience in the field.'

'Of Body Studies? No, indeed. But as you know, I have considerable experience of the process of competitive bidding both in the UK and the EU. It was felt that my grasp of the regulatory requirements was enough to outweigh, in this instance, my relative ignorance of disciplinary specifics.'

'You stitched him up.'

'Professor Hellespont?'

'Donald.'

Mordred made a noise somewhere between a gurgle and a whistle. For another person such a noise might have indicated a blocked airway, clogged sinuses or an attack of asthma. For Mordred Evans, Zoe Cable realised, it constituted a laugh.

'That rather depends on you.'

'What do you want?'

Mordred paused. Zoe waited.

'In three weeks' time there will be an official disciplinary hearing for Bernard Littlejohn during which charges of gross professional misconduct will be considered. Bernard's defence is that he has been the victim of falsification and intimidation due to his opposition to the Digital Faculty Proposal; Donald, as a consequence, has rather a lot at stake. Defeat could be quite damaging.'

Zoe shook her head.

'Try plan B, Mordred. There are witnesses. I don't know who's put him up to this, although I can guess, but Bernard can kiss his pimply arse goodbye.'

Mordred was utterly unmoved by her bolshiness.

'There is *one* witness, I believe – Morris Gutman. There is also a certain amount of material evidence, of course, but that can be dealt with. Aside from Gutman, there is, as I believe they say, a high degree of deniability. Bernard Littlejohn, despite appearances to the contrary, is not entirely stupid.'

Zoe stubbed out her cigarette and frowned. The teenage

199

baristas who had been looking at her uneasily returned with some relief to their gargling machinery.

'So it's Morris,' she said. 'Again.'

'Again,' Mordred agreed. 'Yes. He is proving surprisingly useful isn't he? Who would have guessed?'

Chapter 23

That summer, Morris studied pleasure. He began with Dirck van Camper's footnotes. He plumbed their depths, he examined their entrails, he squeezed them for all they were worth and then he moved on, and in, through the academic web of reference, cross-reference, refutation and disavowal. He took names, he gathered notes, he surveyed the literature, he built up a picture – a strange, unholy picture – and then he planned his riposte. His book already had a publisher, a title (*Was it Good for You? Culture, Literature and the Ethics of Pleasure*) and a deadline, but as yet no content. Did this worry him? No it did not. He had developed a trust, a faith (perhaps it was sleeping with Zoe which had done it) in his own possibilities. Ideas would occur, words would arrive, pages would be filled. He was after all the author of the well-received 'Total Mindfuck' and of 'Seven Year Scratch: Ethics and (in)Fidelity', forthcoming in Hank Bernebau's volume *Autobodies: Writing Beyond Flesh*. He knew what he was talking about. He was cutting-edge.

It was not, of course, that Morris had forgotten the dubious origins of his current success. They existed; he remembered them still with an occasional pang. He was not immune to the flailing edge of guilt, but the memories grew smaller, slighter every day. And what grew larger with every fax from his editor, with every congratulatory email, with every invitation to speak, examine, preside, was his sense that he could do it. That he could become this person, this other person, who he had never been before, who he could never have imagined being before.

He stopped wearing ties. It was a small gesture but one which E noticed.

'What on earth will my parents buy you for Christmas?' she asked.

'Socks are still an option. I'm not planning to go barefoot for another year or so at least.'

He bought himself a T-shirt with a picture of Lenin on the front.

'It's ironic,' he explained.

'It's confusing,' E replied. 'What's next? Tattoos?'

Tattoos had occurred to him, but he let it pass.

Pleasure: amorphousness was the key – fluidity – its tendency to pop up anywhere. No human practice, however dreadful, Morris discovered, was immune to pleasure. It would worm its way in, make a place for itself. Pleasure was the death of ethics, or at least of ethics as a system, of ethics as a law. It was uncontainable, intangible, omnipresent. The ethics of pleasure were, by necessity, temporary and contingent. Since pleasure, real, excessive pleasure (and real pleasure, Morris had learned, was always excessive), was not a case of either/or, was not about choices, priorities, it eradicated all that; it swept it all away in a flood of excitement, a flood of openness.

15 July. Morris sat in front of his computer (new, black, unnecessarily powerful). He had a stack of notes, a pyramid of books, an espresso machine and a carton of illegally imported Marlboro Reds. He began to write. It started slowly: he sketched out his theory; he rather pedantically positioned himself vis-à-vis the big guns (classical and modern). This took him a week. As he wrote he felt himself gradually entering another world, a world of extreme forces, a world arcing with illumination and energy. It was as if he had stuck his head into the hot centre of a thundercloud, and from that strange and elevated vantage E, Molly, everything (everything except the book, Zoe and Morris himself) seemed tiny and black – like figures on a far-flung horizon.

Chapter 1 – Freud and the Pre-History of Pleasure: a bugger to be sure but he broke the back of it in two tumultuous days: days during which he never left his study; days during which E and Molly heard as they passed the locked door – above the stuttering hum of the laser printer and the occasional whirr of the hard drive, noises both more human and more terrible – cries and sobs, gurgles of frustration, anger and joy. He emerged with a short beard, a long draft and appalling constipation. After that initial, life-threatening struggle, however, it was easy. Freud fell swiftly into place. He had a bath, ordered a prawn madras and finished it in a weekend. 'Sigmund,' he joshed in an email to Zoe, 'is my bitch.'

Chapter 2 – Masturbation and the Novel: it was workmanlike – his mind, to be honest, was on other things. Zoe was back from Vienna: two more tumultuous days. Morris began to take risks – returning home dishevelled at 7 a.m. he claimed he had fallen asleep in the Vodafone Library and been locked in. Unprecedented, actually impossible, but he offered it up nonetheless as true, plausible, real. E looked at him and laughed. He could barely see her. Molly sniffed him like a suspicious terrier.

With Zoe, he talked and talked. She seemed surprised about how much he said, about his vehemence. In her bed, in her arms, the book seemed to write itself. He tasted (literally, metaphorically, *whatever*) the intricacies of pleasure, its fragile absolution and he felt – that was his point – its goodness, its rightness and its absolute priority.

'My thesis,' he explained to Zoe, not for the first time, 'is that pleasure, bodily pleasure, properly understood, is the only possible basis for the "good life".'

Zoe was masturbating. She liked to do that sometimes, go for seconds. Morris had assured her (not that Zoe had ever asked) that it was OK with him.

'Works for me, Morris,' she groaned. Then afterwards she added. 'You mean properly *misunderstood*?'

'Exactly!' Morris made a note of it, *misunderstood*. 'Because my point is, of course, that pleasure evades conceptual understanding, it's slippery.'

They kissed. Morris felt like a planet being tugged into an

entirely different orbit, as though his switch of allegiances was neither voluntary nor accidental but rather an offshoot of the impersonal laws of physics.

'How was Vienna?' he asked.

'Clean,' Zoe said. 'Worryingly clean.'

Chapter 3 – Blood Screening: Horror Film and the Pathological Imperative: E rented a cottage in Cornwall for two weeks. Morris took his book, his notes, his computer, his newly purchased DVD collection. They had to borrow a roof-rack for Molly's clothes, toys and medical supplies.

The weather was remarkable. The sun shone, there was a light breeze, small innocuous clouds hung in the sky like cottonballs, like the frozen residue of ack-ack guns. Morris wrote. E and Molly went to the beach. Every morning they would leave, cluttered like tinkers with buckets, balls, hats and towels. Every afternoon they would return pinker, wetter, wrapped with seaweed, laughing at some coastal absurdity. He would see them coming up the path. He would pause from his labour to wave, perhaps to make a cup of tea. At this point, the issue of deception usually arose in Morris's mind. Who was fooling whom? Or alternatively, was no one being fooled? Was it all as real as it seemed? Were they really happy? Did marriage rely on infidelity? Did it feed off its own decay like a collapsing sun?

Chapter 4 – Pleasuring the Postmodern: On the Wednesday of the second week, E asked him to come with them to the beach, to have a day off work. She said this quite casually. Her tone was hard to judge, but there were undercurrents, Morris sensed, of euphemism and rancour. Although he would have preferred not to, he agreed. The next morning they walked down to the beach together. Without his computer and books Morris felt naked and weightless, as though a gust of wind might suddenly pick him off the path and carry him high and away like a lost balloon. E and Molly seemed not to notice his fears; they walked cheerily, confidently to their preferred spot – under the sheltering lee of a rust-brown boulder. Molly ran off to dig, E stripped to her swimsuit. It was already warm. The size of E's belly took Morris aback – it seemed odd and unnatural, like the nose on an AWACS aircraft.

'You're huge,' he said.

'The baby's moving. Have a feel.'

She put his hand on her belly. Under the lycra he felt something slide, like a tongue moving beneath a large cheek.

'Six months tomorrow,' E said. 'It's viable in an emergency, which is more than can be said for me.'

Morris smiled. He was checking inside, scanning himself internally for some response to what he had felt, to this child of his twisting inside his wife. There was nothing there. The sea breathed out a long, gravelly sigh; Molly was shrieking. Morris lay down, closed his eyes and thought of scopophilia.

Epilogue – Ethics in the Afternoon: it was done by mid-August. The first draft at least. It was not a great book; not even, Morris suspected, a good book, but it was a book – it had a title, a publisher and a deadline (which he had met).

Zoe finally returned from London in the midst of an unprecedented Coketown heatwave. It had not rained for a month. The River Err, usually a broad, slug-grey flood, now had the volume and the pungency of a pub urinal. Coketown Royal Infirmary was being overwhelmed with cases of dehydration, sunstroke and prickly heat. There were health warnings, hose-pipe bans. The shoddy maintenance practices of the local Water Authority became a matter of public debate.

In Corporation Square – whither Morris, armed with manuscript, hard-on and need to converse, tended at the news of Zoe's return – the pavements were lively with street musicians, stilt walkers and pink and blistery drunks. The overheated air felt dense and fat, as if breathing itself might be a form of contamination. Morris dodged past a blind accordionist, a gang of underclad scallies, a man selling hand-crafted navel rings and entered the lobby of the Casa Urbano Apartments. Inside it was air-conditioned, chilly even. Zoe buzzed him up. In the lift

205

Morris continued to sweat. He could smell himself – a high animal scent. Tucked under his elbow his manuscript felt like a weird prosthesis, a strange mutant addition like an extra arm or leg – a physical expression of his abnormal mental powers. He was clearly overexcited, het-up. When Zoe opened the door, he fell upon her instantly. The manuscript went everywhere. They rolled on its pages, they humped amid its chapters. When they were done, Zoe rolled aside and examined the sodden and wilting table of contents.

'Well, Morris,' she said, 'it's obviously a seminal work.'

The French windows were open wide. Gusts from Corporation Square fought with and were defeated by the scentless pump of the air conditioning.

'How was London?' he shouted. Zoe was in the kitchen.

'Capital.'

'Ha-ha.'

Morris lay naked on the sofa. Spots of cool dampness dappled his body. His head was empty and pure. His manuscript lay recollated on the coffee table. He felt perfect.

'What are you doing in there?'

'It's the fucking waste disposal.'

Morris was about to suggest she leave it when there came from the kitchen a sudden, ghastly grind of metal on metal and a volley of extraordinary cursing. Zoe emerged with a mangled melon baller and a look of sick fury. She flung the melon baller out of the French windows. It fell seven storeys and narrowly missed the accordionist. Morris sat up.

'Are you OK?'

Zoe lit a cigarette. 'It's the Hub.'

'The Hub's in danger?'

Zoe nodded. 'It's Mordred Evans. We're this close to being fucked.'

Morris looked down at his soft, wet genitals. They seemed at that moment rather silly.

'Go on,' he said.

'Mordred's now Chair of the Panel for the Body Studies Research Hub. Hellespont is history – don't ask me how.'

'But the Chair only has one vote.'

Zoe shook her head, sniffed. (Hay fever – virtually unknown in Coketown – was becoming an issue).

'The others will crumble. They're good people, but they have careers, families. Mordred's pitiless. In their shoes, I'd do the same.'

'So that's that.'

'No, it goes deeper. Mordred's gunning for the Digital Faculty Proposal. He wants to use Bernard's hearing to humiliate Donald and wreck the proposal.'

'But that's open and shut. I've given a statement.'

'You could change it.'

'There's a tape recording.'

'You could destroy it.'

'That's what he wants.'

'Yes.'

Morris pulled his nose, squeezed his cheeks, coughed. The dangers of betraying the Crocodile were very great and very obvious even to him.

'Will Mordred protect us?'

'He might, but we won't need it. Once we have the Hub, we're safe.'

'The Hub will save us,' Morris confirmed, as though committing it carefully to memory.

Zoe sat down beside him on the sofa. She smelt of elderberries and tarmac. Her hair had been cut into a mohican and bleached, and she was wearing a blue flannelette boiler suit.

'Look at it this way, Morris,' she said. 'We're the little people. Donald and Mordred are the big people, but the big people are out of control, they're running amok. Really, it's nuclear war out there. I mean, Christ, this Digital Faculty thing,' she shuddered her head and rolled her eyes, 'it's not even funny anymore. In circumstances such as this, we need to do what we can to save ourselves, to save what's precious to us.'

She reached over and squeezed his hand. Morris leaned his face into the hollow of her clavicle. It was like a tiny rock pool – he could still smell the salty sweat of their lovemaking.

207

They kissed. The accordionist's sad and wheezing song jerked upwards from the baking square below, like a piece of litter caught and held by the hot updraughts of diesel fumes and frying.

'I want the co-directorship,' he said.

'It's yours.'

Chapter 24

E met Stella in a tapas bar on Crotchley Street.

'Do you have anything with prunes?' she asked the waiter. 'Anything wholegrain?'

He pointed out the artichoke hearts.

'They never tell you about the haemorrhoids,' she told Stella after the waiter had shuffled off, 'nor the involuntary bowel movements. No, they keep that stuff well hid. There's a conspiracy of silence.'

'But you've been through this before.'

'I'm part of the conspiracy. It's beyond my control – the experience of childbirth floods the brain with amnesiac chemicals specifically designed to wipe out all but the most pleasant memories.'

'So these brain chemicals actually target the bad memories and wipe them out?'

'Exactly.'

'Is that true?'

E straightened her face.

'It's a plausible rumour.'

The tapas arrived. Little dishes filled the table.

'I don't care what they say, it still reminds me of leftovers,' said Stella.

'Yet another reason for not joining the Euro-zone.'

They picked.

'So how are you, anyway?'

'I'm obsessed with the baby. I really am. I feel like I'm one of those super-lorries. You know, those extra-wide vehicles which they close the motorways for, and the baby is in the cab, driving. The foetus is at the controls.'

'Is that safe?'

'I doubt it.'

'How's Morris?'

'I'm not sure.' She ate a slice of frittata. 'I think he's losing interest. I get a sense of waning enthusiasm.'

'For the pregnancy?'

'In general. He has his book of course, which I suppose is good. Last month he got locked in the Vodafone Library. He was there all night.'

'Is that possible? I thought they had emergency phones.'

'That's what he told me. Try the aubergine. How's your work anyway?'

'Calamitous. They put me on weddings and bar mitzvahs – lots of falling on the dancefloor, lots of underwear shots, kilts a frequent motif. Can we promise right here and now that if I ever show signs of wishing to dance on a table you will act?'

'Ruthlessly and without moral qualm.'

'You're a pal. Shall I order more non-alcoholic sangria?'

'No, I find it too upsetting.'

Stella nodded.

'The moral of my job,' she continued, 'is that people never learn. They continue to believe, despite all the evidence, that, for example, punchbags make good gifts for small children, that break-dancing at a wedding reception is a good idea.'

'It's touching.'

'Only the first few hundred times.'

'I have a male friend,' E said.

Stella suddenly stopped chewing, then, equally suddenly, started again.

'His name is Nick. He's an artist.'

'Nick Kidney?'

'You know him?'

'He's the *enfant terrible* of British art.'

'Oh yes,' E said, 'That.'

'So, is this an affair?'

'I'm six months pregnant. How could it be an affair?'

'Some men go for that. There are several specialist magazines.'

'You've really plumbed the depths haven't you?'

'I come from a family of newsagents. Besides, I've seen his work. The pickled penises, the toilet panorama; his interests are quite unconventional.'

'Off the record, sometimes he regrets the pickled penises. Anyway, he has a little boy.'

'A father figure then.'

'Well, it's more than Morris is.'

'I thought that Morris and Molly were like that.'

E began to eat more quickly: the chorizo sausage, the wok-turned squid.

'The passion's cooled in that area. Morris won't play her reindeer games any more, plus there's a long-running dispute over bathroom practices.'

'Sad.'

'Yes, it is.'

E began to cry.

'Hormones,' she said after a minute. 'Another thing that they mysteriously fail to mention.'

'Do you feel put upon? Let down? I get a sense of brooding resentment.'

'My immediate task is to give birth, to reach the spawning grounds. Right now it's hard to see past that. Do you have any advice?'

'You mean after months of watching people hurt themselves foolishly for the entertainment of others?'

'Exactly.'

'Always wear goggles.'

A week later, E went alone to Nick Kidney's London opening. Morris was finishing the book, his mother was over from Rotherham to watch Molly. She was not wearing goggles.

The gallery was in Spitalfields. The train was forty-five minutes late. Summer rush hour – the Central Line was a simmering chutney of pongs. In the general jostling for space and air, her condition offered E no moral advantage: it was merely a handicap, a weakness to be exploited. As they pulled out of Holborn,

211

her varicose veins began to throb, her feet felt like red-hot flippers.

'Could I possibly have a seat?' she said to a kindly looking gentleman with white hair and a blue business suit.

'Fuck off.'

E leaned against a stanchion and breathed through her mouth. Her tongue felt carpeted with yuck – there was an unavoidable taste of onions. As they finally rollicked into Liverpool Street she hurled herself backwards out of the opening doors, like a scuba diver in a hurry. The escalator was a spiritual experience. Once in the main concourse, she sat on a drilled steel bench and tried to retrieve her bearings. The station announcements wafted around her like an aural breeze. A pale yellow, swimming-pool light fell through the glass roof and softened, so it seemed to E, the faces of even the most hardened and desperate of commuters. How many years since she had been to London on her own? Five or six? Certainly before marriage. Before Molly. She had forgotten its paradoxical requirements: self-effacement, strength. Or perhaps she had never really noticed them before.

She bought an *A to Z* and a decaf latte. The gallery was a short walk away but she decided to get a cab. It struck her, as the cab progressed at sub-walking pace down Bishopsgate, that pregnancy, like drug addiction or fundamentalist religion, was really very simple. It was the things around it that were hard. All the pesky details: who to love, who to live with and why. When she paid, the driver asked if he could touch the baby for luck.

'Would that be my luck or yours?'

It was an installation piece called 'The Compulsion to be Dry'. Inside the gallery it was drizzling. Kidney had set up an elaborate sprinkler system: pipes and nozzles completely covered the ceiling. The floor had been tarmacked, there were drains. On entering, E was offered a plastic poncho and a glass of champagne. Certain people, obviously in the know, had worn their own more tasteful waterproofs; others had already taken off most of their clothes. The atmosphere was festive, the drizzle was pleasantly warm. E wandered into a back room. She saw Nick Kidney holding court beneath a mocked-up bus shelter – he was dressed like a trawlerman. E waved. Kidney came across. They kissed.

'It's Coketown,' she said.

'Of course it is. But no one else has cottoned on. They're so fucking provincial down here. Do you want to see my workings?'

He unlocked a door into a cupboard-sized room full of plastic pipes and pumping gear. There was a control panel attached to the wall.

'It's on two at the moment,' he said. 'It goes up to ten. Ten is when I want people to leave. Ten is torrential: it threatens the water supply, it breaks bylaws. And I can do wind. Do you want to see?'

He turned the dial. A faint breeze arose from nowhere in particular. The drizzle curved slightly.

'We've had technical problems with the wind, so I won't push my luck.'

He turned down the wind and closed the door.

'What do you think?'

E, who without thinking had drunk most of the champagne, opened her mouth and then closed it again.

'A traditional answer is "utterly marvellous",' prompted Kidney. '"Quite superb" will do at a stretch.'

'I don't know what to say.'

'It's about emotion,' he said.

'Yes, I thought it might be.'

'The irritating constancy of emotion. The way it's always there whether you want it to be or not.'

Although the room was becoming crowded, the drizzle, like shivery curtains, drew them into a kind of privacy.

'The inconvenience of it all,' she said.

'Right.'

The afternoon sun was slanting in through the picture window, there were brief rainbows by the buffet table. Someone nearby began to tap dance in the puddles. Several people were trying and failing to light cigarettes.

'I think it's remarkable,' said E.

'OK,' said Kidney. 'OK, that's good, because I made it for you.'

'You did not.'

'Yes I did. It's dedicated to you – look at the artist's statement.'

He turned to point to the relevant wall, and they both realised that a rather dense and disorientating mist had formed around them.

'Interesting,' mused Kidney, 'but quite unplanned. Perhaps I should try more wind. I'll be back in a minute.'

It was two hours before E saw him again. By then everyone was drunk, the critics had left, the food had heroically been served and E had read the artist's statement more than once.

> *I try to draw our attention to the things we don't see, things that we overlook and underlook. The things that we fear to look at, or the things that we know only too well. To me, this is the purpose of all art – to return us to reality. This particular piece is dedicated to Eugenia – who is quite impossible to overlook.*

'Impossible to overlook,' she thought. It made her sound like a scenic valley, or rather *not* like a scenic valley. And how did he know her name was Eugenia? No one called her that. She went outside. There were a lot of other people out there already, cheerful and attractively wet. They looked like the victims of a well-organised, upmarket shipwreck.

'Look at you,' said a man drunk enough not to care who she was. 'The poncho actually fits.'

'If you say it suits me, I'll cry.'

'My dear,' he touched her on the arm and paused, 'you'd look good in a paper bag.'

'Thanks for the tip.'

'Oooh, hoo, hoo, *the tip*, I like it.' He reeled away, giggling. Kidney popped up. He looked the worse for wear.

'How did you know my name was Eugenia?' she asked

He looked initially confused.

214

'Oh that. It was Gloria. We do occasionally talk, information is exchanged. E seemed too . . .'

'Too short?'

'Too short, yes.'

He looked at his diver's watch.

'It's time for the monsoon,' he said. 'I'm beginning to get wrinkly and I heard several people inside mention trench foot. Will you come for dinner? It's all arranged. Good. Back in a minute – I mean it this time.'

He went back inside. A minute later there were screams followed by a rapid evacuation.

'My initial plan included hail,' confided Kidney over dinner, 'but the refrigeration costs are berserk.'

'Hammy,' he called down the table to Gert Hamster, his dealer. 'Tell her about the refrigeration costs.'

'Five figures,' Hammy shouted back. 'It's not worth talking about.'

'The hail would have been nice though.' Kidney's eyes glazed slightly as he thought of the hail. 'Would have made a nice touch.'

'What will the critics say?' asked E.

'They'll play with words – a damp squib, sodden but not surprising. They'll footle. That's their calling. I despise them all.'

'All? Really?'

'No, one or two are all right. One or two you can go for a drink with. Where are you staying tonight?'

'At a friend's. She's on holiday, but I've got a key. Finsbury Park.'

Kidney nodded, then sat suddenly straight as if he had remembered something.

'You must be exhausted though,' he said. 'You must be utterly knackered. Why don't you stay with me? It's only round the corner. Ten minutes. I've got mountains of room.'

'Mountains,' confirmed Ghee, a strangely beautiful woman sitting diagonally opposite. Kidney glared at her, then glanced quickly back at E.

215

E was not tired at all, or perhaps she was, but the tiredness was trapped below so many other, better feelings that its tedious and plaintive cries could not be heard. The dinner had been great. Kidney's friends were boozy and unconfined. They had cryptic nicknames for the waiters and told detailed and salacious anecdotes about people E had read about in the newspapers. When the discussion turned to pregnancy, they made it seem arty and exciting, as if giving birth was a project, a piece of work. And that was really, she thought, as it should be – children *were* works of art. They modified the world and made it more real. They were not, as Morris seemed so often to imply, an annoyance, a task, a burden, a thing to be got through or seen off. What an arsehole he could be sometimes, what a prick. The job which was supposed to change everything had really changed nothing, she realised – he still lived in a weird half-gravity of his own devising. The tenor had changed perhaps, a switch from moroseness to half-cocked levity. But he was no weightier, no more real than before. Bangor, she thought, that bastard Underseel; would it ever end?

E looked across at Kidney. He was wearing a white T-shirt and yellow sou'wester, he had a cigarette in the corner of his mouth and his eyes were hooded against the smoke. His forehead was ridged and shiny in the restaurant's warmth like the bed of a stream. He was smiling.

'You're right,' she said. 'I'm shattered.'

Nick Kidney lived in a surprisingly ordinary house off Brick Lane.

'I'm shocked,' said E. 'I was expecting a penthouse or at least a loft.'

'I don't like lifts that talk.'

'Have you tried hypnosis?'

'It's not a fear, it's a quirk. I'm against them. "*Doors opening.*"' He mimicked a talking lift. 'What's that about?'

'Fantasies of domination and servility I imagine.'

'Exactly. It's like sex tourism.'

'But only in the vaguest, most abstract way.'

216

'That's good enough for me. Shall I brew up? Isn't that what they say in Coketown, "brew up"?'

They were in the kitchen, which was made entirely of stainless steel. Kidney was pointing to the space-age teapot.

'That's what they say. I'm not really tired, you know.'

Kidney turned to look at her. It was a real look, the kind of look E had forgotten about, the kind of look that you could have hung your washing on. Stripped of his thick rubber jacket, Kidney had sinewy, rustic forearms and little bony knobs on his shoulders; you could see them under his T-shirt. Here in his own kitchen his body seemed dense and forthright. She had said it without thinking. She had stepped over something, she knew. A line or a cliff?

He walked across the kitchen towards her. The comical trawlerman boots squeaked a little on the industrial steel flooring. E's hair, frizzed and thinned out by pregnancy, was wrapped in a plum-coloured chiffon scarf which had once belonged to her Aunt Judy. She felt suddenly certain that the scarf had been a terrible mistake – that it made her look ill rather than interesting. Kidney, without apparently noticing the scarf at all, leaned across her belly and kissed her.

Bristle, tongue, nose.

So that's what it feels like, she thought. That's what it feels like to be kissed by someone who isn't Morris.

They moved slowly and imprecisely apart. Kidney's eyes, she noticed, were rimmed with red. His breath smelled dusty and charred.

'I'm actually speechless.' He seemed genuinely surprised.

'Well, let's see,' said E. ' "I've wanted to do that for a long time" is an old favourite or, barring that, a simple "Cor" might do.'

'Phwoar?'

'*Cor.* There's a subtle but important difference.'

The kettle clicked off.

'Saved by the boil,' said E.

Kidney warmed the pot, then looked for teabags. The only other man she had ever met who warmed the pot was Morris. He

217

did it assiduously, four swirls then out. He also used loose leaf tea and a cosy. It had been the first thing she noticed about him – before they had started going out, when he was just a name, an odd but oddly sexy face on the edge of her grad-student circle. She had always loved the way he made tea, the casual carefulness of it, the assumption that that was simply the way it was done. So sure, so easy, as if Rotherham was *it*.

Kidney took a tea cosy out of the drawer. It was black and made by the ICA.

'Is that a tea cosy?'

'Of course.'

He came back at her. They kissed again. E thought of Morris at the kitchen sink, swirling, warming, measuring out the tea. Kidney's tongue was granulated and gentle. She wished the idea of Morris would go away, for a while at least – for an evening. She tried to concentrate instead on the kissing. She pressed against his teeth. She thought of Morris measuring the milk, giving the pot a stir, pouring. Kidney sidled around her bump to change the angle of approach. He started doing something lovely with her hair. It was nice. She wanted more of it. Kidney felt like a path she could run down, a grassy, sloping path with gentle, lolling turns. She thought of them all: Morris, Molly and her sitting at the kitchen table on Sunday morning, drinking tea, eating Hobnobs, surrounded by mess and crumble. It was raining, the radio was on, Molly was cranky, Morris was silent. It was all crap except the tea. The tea was always right – hot not burning, strong but never stewed, sour, sharp, profound, perfect.

Kidney stopped kissing and looked at her carefully. He angled his head. It was the kind of look she imagined he might give to a piece that was not quite coming together, that was evading him – sad, fierce and puzzled. With some embarrassment, E realised that she was panting.

'Is it the baby then?' he said after a while.

'Actually it's the husband.'

'Is it *really*?'

'I know,' said E. 'Who would have guessed?'

* * *

218

Next morning, E's train slid past the East Coketown redevelopment zone. They were removing the scaffolding from the Matterhorn leisure complex. Its steel cladding barked back the brightness of the unseasonable sun. It glared like a ziggurat on the plains of scrubby grass and hardcore. Passengers pointed and raised their eyebrows. On the left were the boarded up and valueless terraces of Rumpswick, a last stronghold of negative equity, a place where the remaining residents hunkered before their huge TVs and dreamed of EU funding.

E was in a non-smoking window seat in carriage G. Opposite her was a man in a brown stocking cap with an Adam Ant-style band of acne across his nose and a liking for novelty ring tones. E was working on her birth plan: things to demand; things to refuse; things to take and leave; dos and don'ts; nevers and maybes. It was becoming long and complex – there were arrows, subdivisions, appendices – but she was enjoying it anyway. Life, she felt that morning, that sunny Coketown morning, was pointing forwards for once. Knowing she would not sleep with Kidney had given her a sudden, unexpected strength. If necessary, if she had to, she could carry them all – Morris, Molly, the baby. She would strap them to her aching back and lug them forwards. She would make them happy whether they liked it or not.

Coketown was dusty and hot. Hotter than E could ever remember it being. Hotter even than when she had left the day before. Above the streets there was haze and wobble, while below in the culverts and storm drains there was only dryness and peace. These alien conditions had produced in the normally temperate Coketown population a tendency towards acts of unusual beneficence or spite. E was shepherded to the front of the taxi rank and whisked away by a foul-mouthed Moldovan in a permanent state of road-rage. The journey was so quick it was half the normal fare. On arrival, the driver kissed her hand, apologised for his foul language and refused a tip. The house seemed smaller, more precious than she had remembered, and for once there was no smell of mould. The garden was a palette of yellow and brown. Oh, what will become of the slugs, she

219

wondered? Would they have a bolt hole, a secret place of dampness and slime wherein to regroup, to save themselves, until normal conditions returned? She hoped not. Her baby would be born in the year of the heatwave then, after a summer of extremes: the summer when the River Err coagulated; the summer when mineral water was more expensive than beer. That was how the child would have its beginning.

Morris was at work, she remembered. It was the day of the trial, disciplinary hearing, whatever it was. Molly and Morris's mum were undoubtedly at the park, which boasted a large and lavatorial lido. She opened windows and tidied. She felt suddenly, uncharacteristically minded to wash the floor.

She found the mop and while she was looking for a bucket she noticed there was a message on the machine. The tape whirred back to its beginning. There was a beep and then an old, slurred, but shouty male voice.

'This is for Mrs Gutman. Your husband, partner, whatever he is, is fucking Zoe Cable.' There was a long gap. In the background there were boings and whirrs as if the man was standing next to a fruit machine. 'Also, he's a maleficent rogue with the probity of a bucket of shit.'

There was another beep and then another less catastrophic message from her Uncle Tim.

After a minute or two, E found the bucket. She filled it with warm water and soap and began to mop the kitchen floor. She did it thoroughly and carefully. She moved the kitchen chairs and table, she even pulled out the gas cooker and confronted the knobbly weave of grease and dirt which lay beneath.

After she had washed it once she rinsed, and after she had rinsed, noticing certain patches of dried-in filth, certain cracks where decades of dirt had hardened and cauterised, she got down on her hands and knees and scrubbed. She was dismayed to find, however, that these areas would not come clean. The muck seemed to have become ingrained, a part of the very flooring that was designed to ward it off. She became irritated by this, then annoyed and then finally enraged. She began, in her frustration, to stab at the reluctant lino with a paring knife and then to pull it off in uneven chunks. She found that she enjoyed doing this, that it gave her more pleasure than cleaning ever had. When her mother-in-law and Molly returned home from the park an hour or so later they discovered E carrying out the kitchen floor in bin bags.

Chapter 25

The disciplinary hearing was to be held in Cormorant Hall, Committee Room L. Cormorant Hall, which was at the epicentre of the Coketown University Administrative Pentagon, was accessible only via annex A of the Cripponden Building, and thence through a cobbled, subterranean walkway and up along a shoeworn flight of pink marble stairs, the balustrade of which was inset with the porky visages of the seven founders of the original Coketown College.

Morris rather wished he had brought a map. Either that or listened more carefully to the perky woman from Personnel who had offered him directions over the phone. The corridors of Cormorant Hall were long and inscrutable. The brass-knobbed doors which led off them were poorly signed and offered little or no hint of what they concealed. Seeking assistance, Morris opened one. It was a cupboard. Another revealed a language lab full of men in uniform chanting useful Russian phrases, a third opened into an office with a single metal desk. Behind the desk was a spruced-up woman in a houndstooth cardigan, who appeared to be expecting him.

'I'm looking for Committee Room L,' he said.

'Of course Dr Gutman.' She stood up.

'Right out of here, through the double doors, up the staircase on the right.' She was gesturing as she spoke in the drilled but ironic manner of an air stewardess going through the safety procedure. 'Left, then left again, through the double doors. Follow the left fork. Double-back and Committee Room L is on your right. I'm sure they're expecting you.'

Morris thanked her. He turned right, went through the double doors and was climbing the stairs when he ran into Zoe Cable. She was wearing a shredded peasant blouse and oil-streaked Levis.

'I'm not here,' she said.

'Officially, you mean?'

'Yes, but unofficially it's good to see you. Do you need to review?'

'I doubt it. My role is to deny everything.'

'That's it. We're going negative.'

Morris slipped a finger inside one of the rips in her peasant blouse and fondled her midriff. Feelings of lust and need slid forwards and crashed against his ribcage like foot passengers on a cross-channel ferry.

'You should go the back way,' Zoe advised. 'You don't want to run into Bernard or the Crocodile at this stage. It might throw you off your game.'

Morris nuzzled her neck. Zoe leaned her head back and ummed and ahhed a little.

'There's a back way?' he said.

'Of course. Down the stairs, turn right, through the double doors. Through the swing door marked "strictly no admittance" over the metal gantry, up the fire escape and in through the first window – there's a stained-glass architrave of the founders distributing knowledge to the benighted African. You can't miss it. Committee Room L is two doors down on the left. You should hurry.'

They kissed. After Morris had recovered from his disorientation, he descended the stairs. He turned right and went through the double doors. He was just about to push open the door marked 'strictly no admittance' when it swung open from the other side and the Crocodile burst through.

'Morris!' he said, beaming. 'You know the back way.'

Morris gulped. The Crocodile squeezed his upper arm and nodded.

'I know,' he said. 'I know it's a big day. Bigger than we thought – Bernard's nominated Mordred Evans as his advocate.' The Crocodile's grip tightened, his nostrils flared.

'Is that good?' asked Morris vaguely.

'Oh yeah,' said the Crocodile, dropping into a tone of cool certainty. 'It's good. Let me put it this way, Morris: we can work, we can plan, we can scheme even (although I dislike that word intensely), but our greatest joys come always from above. I'm not a religious man Morris, as you know, but today is a gift in my opinion. *Mordred*. Who would have imagined?' He bit his lip and nodded again. His nose was rather close to Morris's. 'This is how it ends.'

'I'll do my best,' said Morris.

'Your *best*?'

The Crocodile looked at him. There was long and uncomfortable eye contact. The Crocodile's gaze had the intensity of a CAT scan. As it continued without pause or explanation Morris felt irrationally certain that he could see what Morris was up to. That through those black, magnetic eyes, Morris's treachery would stand out clear and red as a haematoma. Morris stopped breathing, then braced himself.

'You should understand, there will come a point in there today,' said the Crocodile eventually, 'when things become quite unpleasant. If when that point arrives, Morris, you begin to feel qualms, if you are touched by the chill hand of doubt, do me a favour – look around the room and ask yourself one simple question: who is the biggest bastard here?'

There was another weighty pause. Morris felt like a weld about to crack. From behind the swing door came the hum of large machinery.

'That's right,' the Crocodile winked. 'It's me.'

Morris's legs wobbled as he crossed the iron gantry. His stomach was being gently stroked by nausea. The thought of crumbling appealed to him strongly, but there was, he realised, no place left to crumble. The only way out was forward – through the Crocodile, through the Digital Faculty Proposal, through Mordred even, to Zoe and the Hub. It was, he sadly realised, now much too late for fear. The LA Body Conference, the Dalton Street car park, the job interview – those had been the places for fear, not Committee Room L. Committee Room L, wherever the hell it was, (the iron gantry seemed unusually long and bendy), was the place for tight-bollocked, groin-led courage. The place to fuck or be fucked.

He found the fire escape, ascended a flight of rusted, clangy steps and climbed back in to Cormorant Hall through an already open sash window. A man from Personnel was waiting for him.

'Dr Gutman,' he smiled and offered his hand. 'I think they're ready to begin.'

Committee Room L was fluorescently lit, wood-panelled and unpleasantly hot. It smelt of radiators and old floor polish. In the centre of the room was a large, U-shaped table. At the far side, raised on a shallow, carpeted stage, was a long desk with six throne-like chairs. Looming over the desk was an allegorical painting of the founders offering the oil lamp of wisdom to the cringing and grimy apprentices of Olde Coketown whilst skewering the windy serpent of trade unionism with their free hands.

Seated at the desk were Brendan Bombay, the well-groomed Head of Personnel, his assistant and ex-lover, Roy Dervish, and the three tribunal members. Slightly to one side, half-hidden in the shadows of a fire hose, there was a small, dingy and unassuming man whom Morris immediately recognised as Dennis Sloze.

At the far side of the U-shaped table, sitting together, were Mordred Evans, Bernard and a hairy and unconvincing union rep named Yacob Macomb. Mordred's glasses were pale brown, his suit was several shades of green. He sat silently, looking straight ahead with the fierce stiffness of the newly dead. Bernard had a black eye, the rest of his face was drained and chalky. He seemed to have dressed in instalments, there being no identifiable relationship between tie, shirt and jacket. Morris could smell beer from twenty-five feet. Bernard's condition (re sobriety or drunkenness) was clearly an issue for Yacob Macomb, who was whispering energetically in his ear and plying him with instant coffee.

Directly opposite the group, on the other side of the table, was an empty orthopaedic chair (obviously the Crocodile's) and, next to it, Doris Pamplona, the Faculty Secretary and designated minute-taker.

225

Morris was shown to his seat on a side bench. Brendan Bombay smiled emptily at him. Bernard sneered and made a wanking gesture before being seized by Yacob Macomb.

'We're just waiting for the Dean,' explained Brendan Bombay. Morris nodded. The Crocodile was obviously taking his time, ratcheting up the tension. Hardly necessary, thought Morris, since Bernard was already a lump and Mordred Evans looked about as easy to faze as a breeze-block. After about five more minutes, the Crocodile came in and sat down without explanation or apology.

The hearing began. Brendan Bombay began to talk; Doris Pamplona began to write. The air was dense with fear and expectation. Morris doodled, made notes to himself ('deny everything'), concentrated on breathing regularly. Fat photocopies of University ordinances and regulations were handed out. Bombay reviewed them, pointing out recent amendments, pertinent sections, areas for possible discussion. His tone was flat but cheerful. Mordred Evans raised his skeletal hand and pointed out passionlessly that Brendan Bombay was in error when he suggested that paragraph four of Regulation XVIII was a recent amendment – it was actually a revival of a regulation which had been temporarily suspended since 1979. Roy Dervish confirmed this. Brendan Bombay apologised to the tribunal. Mordred Evans accepted his apology, the transparent purpose of this exchange being to remind all concerned that if this case came down to University regulations, Mordred Evans would piss all over them. The Crocodile looked amused. He whispered something to Doris Pamplona, who giggled.

They continued. Bombay outlined the charges against Bernard – gross professional misconduct in relation to his statutory duties of examination and assessment. As he listened, Bernard's face seemed to fade beyond paleness to a grotesque, glutinous translucency. He was blinking uncontrollably. Bombay reviewed the material evidence, which struck Morris as surprisingly skimpy. A review of the past several years of Bernard's exams and essays had, it appeared, revealed his tendency to repeat the same comments verbatim from time to time, but little else. Rigorous

226

triple marking had indeed not shown any statistically significant discrepancies between the marks Bernard gave his students without ever reading their work and the marks their work apparently deserved.

Bombay asked Mordred Evans whether he would like to comment on these findings. Mordred swivelled to face the tribunal. His left ear, Morris noticed, was as hairy as a coconut.

'We believe these findings speak very clearly for themselves,' Mordred said, 'but since Dr Littlejohn's explanation of the very minor peculiarities of his assessment practices, the . . .' Mordred paused as if these peculiarities were indeed so very minor they had actually slipped his mind, '. . . occasional repetition of comments on assessed essays, is that they were the unfortunate but inevitable response to the intolerable marking burden placed upon him firstly by Professor McWurter, while Head of Department, and then by his carefully groomed successor, Professor Declan Monk, we wish to remind the tribunal that when the investigating officers came to gather the scripts and essays from the last five years of Dr Littlejohn's teaching, in order to transfer them from the department's storage facility to the investigator's base room, the sheer bulk of paper was found to be so massive that I believe the services of a fork-lift truck were required to effect the transfer. Was that not so, Mr Bombay?'

Brendan Bombay confirmed that this had indeed been the case. The eyebrows of the tribunal were collectively raised. There was a certain amount of jotting. Bernard nodded and whispered rather loudly: 'Too fucking right.' The Crocodile's look of amusement stiffened slightly.

Brendan Bombay moved on to Morris's evidence and to the damning statement he had given to the investigating officers, a précis of which had been distributed to all parties well in advance.

'Professor Evans,' he said, 'I believe you wish now to call Dr Gutman as a witness?'

'Indeed.'

Morris walked to a large chair, placed in between the wings of the U-shaped table, and sat down.

'Let us not dawdle, Dr Gutman,' said Mordred briskly. 'You made this statement two weeks ago, I believe.'

'Yes.'

'My question is simple. Do you stand by this statement today?'

In the pause before he replied, Morris could hear the quiet squeak of Doris Pamplona's fibre-tip.

'No, I do not,' he said.

The Crocodile stood up. His orthopaedic chair flew backwards and bumped against the wall.

'Mr Chairman,' he began.

'Professor McWurter, please.' It was Brendan Bombay. 'You have no authority to cross examine here.'

'So you wish to retract your statement?' Mordred continued.

'We were very drunk,' said Morris. 'My first statement may have contained inaccuracies.'

'So you wish to withdraw it?'

'Yes. I feel that in the circumstances I cannot be certain of anything.'

No one moved. Morris could hear the Crocodile breathing – the air whistled through his moustache like wind through the blades of a combine harvester. The tribunal collectively frowned. Dennis Sloze audibly sucked his teeth.

'And what of the voice recording you apparently made of that evening's conversation?'

'Unfortunately erased,' said Morris. 'The buttons on those things are really fiddly.'

'Oh I'm sure they are,' agreed Mordred. He seemed to be enjoying the consternation. Morris was trying not to look at the Crocodile, but the thought of his flesh-wrapped and reddening face made him shiver. He fancied once or twice he could smell him, hot and visceral like a plate of giblets.

Brendan Bombay was clearly confused.

'May I clarify, Dr Gutman,' he said. 'You wish to withdraw your previous statement. And due to alcoholic befuddlement you wish to offer the tribunal no alternative version of that evening's conversation?'

'That's correct. I can't be certain of what was said.'

228

'You're sure?'

'Of my uncertainty? Yes, absolutely.'

The tribunal collectively leaned back in their chairs and looked quizzically at Morris. The Crocodile made a loud and frightening 'bah'. Morris smiled and fixed his gaze unflinchingly on a shiny red mole just above Roy Dervish's right eyebrow.

'You're aware that this is quite irregular?' Brendan Bombay continued.

'I thought it preferable to risk some personal embarrassment rather than be party to an injustice.'

'Very noble, I'm sure,' said Mordred.

Given the circumstances, Morris thought, the tone was rather sardonic. Morris turned to look at him. Mordred's large brown lenses gave back in miniaturised form the parallel lines of fluorescent tubing.

'I thought it a price worth paying,' he said tartly. He didn't much wish to provoke Mordred, but he thought it only fair to remind him of exactly what was going on here. Almost immediately, however, Morris realised that this had not been a good idea. Mordred's already stiff and lifeless face stiffened further and died a little more. He looked down for a second at his notes, removed his glasses and looked up again.

The tribunal emitted a collective gasp. Doris Pamplona dropped her pen. Mordred's eyes were swollen clots of pus and blood. They looked like badly fried eggs, like oysters that had turned. As they stared at him unflinchingly, Morris had a sudden appalling vision of his own death, the decomposition of his flesh, the disappearance of his mind, the nullification of all that he cared about and loved.

'So why did you lie to the investigating officers?' Mordred asked.

'Lie?' Morris's mouth hung open for a second. He was transfixed by the two weeping slits like elephantine urethras inset into Mordred's face.

'It wasn't a lie,' he managed after a while. 'It was a confusion.'

'A *confusion*?' Mordred echoed. 'It's a quite long and detailed confusion, isn't it? Seven pages in the original.' He replaced his glasses. Morris blinked and began breathing more regularly.

'Um yes, I suppose it is,' was all he could manage.

'Yes, I suppose it is,' echoed Mordred again, but more unpleasantly. 'Isn't it more likely,' he continued, 'that rather than this statement,' he waved it, 'being a product of confusion it is actually a deliberate and malicious fabrication, constructed by yourself and unnamed others to blacken the name of Dr Littlejohn?'

Morris realised with horror that he himself was being doublecrossed. That Mordred, having got the (false) retraction was now going on the attack, using Morris to get at the Crocodile, lumping them both together in a conspiracy to deceive. He should have seen it coming. It was fucking obvious. He was screwed. If he tried to retract his retraction he would be admitting to at least one large and obvious lie; if he turned against Mordred no one would believe him and even if they did he would have to bring Zoe into it.

'That's ridiculous,' he said.

'Ridiculous? Tell me, Dr Gutman. After a night on the tiles, of which I'm sure you have had more than your fair share, do you often find yourself struck by the uncontrollable urge to make defamatory statements about a colleague. Do you make a habit of it?'

'Of course not.'

'Of course not. So this is a one-off?'

Morris didn't respond.

'I was asked for information,' he said eventually.

'By Professor McWurter, I presume?' said Mordred.

'If I am myself the subject of an accusation,' said Morris after another pause, 'I would like the chance to respond formally and through the proper channels.'

'I'm sure you will be given that chance, Dr Gutman. For now, I agree that enough is certainly enough.'

After giving them a moment to digest these sudden events, Mordred turned ponderously to the tribunal.

'With no witnesses and no significant material evidence, I see no reason for this case to continue, gentlemen,' he said. 'You may be curious, as indeed I am, as to why and how it was brought in the first place, but that, I suspect, is a matter for others to investigate. I would only urge that such an investigation be rapid and unflinching.'

Brendan Bombay began to confer excitedly with Roy Dervish. The tribunal talked heatedly among themselves. During this temporary lull, Dennis Sloze got to his feet, padded over to Brendan Bombay and handed him a carefully folded note. He then turned and left the room without glancing to either side. Brendan Bombay read the note then carefully refolded it. He rose to make an announcement.

'I believe it would be best,' he said, 'to close the hearing at this point in order to allow the tribunal to consider the rather startling evidence offered by Dr Gutman. I can assure Professor Evans,' he leered fawningly at Mordred, 'that the possibility that these accusations were maliciously motivated will form part of those deliberations. Participants will be informed of the tribunal's decision in writing within seven days. Good afternoon.'

The Crocodile was staring at his shoes and sucking his lips so hard that his moustache had all but disappeared. Above the metallic blue of his afternoon stubble his cheeks were blanched entirely white, save for two small dots of throbbing redness, one on each cheek, like dollish caricatures of health.

Whatever the Crocodile was thinking, and his thoughts were undoubtedly both deep and violent, Morris knew it presaged no good for him. No good at all. Mordred's investigation would come to nothing, he suspected – there was no real evidence to link him with the Crocodile – but it was designed to maim, not to kill. The Digital Faculty Proposal was gone already; for the Crocodile it was now a question of damage limitation. And when it came to finding a patsy, a man to take the bullet, a body to throw on to the flames, Morris knew very well whose body would be uppermost in Donald's mind. Why had he ever put his trust in Mordred? He had been a fool to imagine that that bloodless carapace would give a toss.

Morris sank back into his chair, closed his eyes and tried to dispel the memory of those eyeballs like old and raggedy vaginas cut into Mordred's face. When he opened his eyes again the room was empty. He was staring up at the allegorical painting which loomed like a Renaissance altarpiece above the tribunal's empty chairs. The seven founders dressed in Grecian robes were proferring the oil lamp of wisdom to the benighted operatives of Coketown. The latter seemed in the main rather ungrateful for the offer. Some were clearly turning away, dazzled by its brightness, others were being deliberately pulled off into the outer darkness by a red-faced publican, a sinister-looking trade unionist and an obviously syphilitic whore. A number of the other operatives were simply asleep. There was only one of their number, a sallow-faced young man whose kneeling form occupied the painting's middle ground, who seemed to be actively interested in the oil lamp of wisdom. He was indeed stretching for it yearningly, his eyes slurred by tears of joyful anticipation, his fingertips forever poised, it appeared, an inch or so from its adamantine base. The title of the painting, spelled out in gothic script on the brass plate affixed to the dense gilt hedgerow of the frame was *The Worthy Poor*. The sallow-faced young man reminded Morris of a skinny cat leaping up amusingly for a toy kept forever beyond his reach. Hopeless. Had Zoe known what Mordred was planning? Perhaps she had. Perhaps she had thought he could handle it, talk his way out. Perhaps she hadn't really cared. She'd got the result after all. The Hub was hers.

His mobile rang. It was Zoe.

'How did it go?' she asked, her voice a trembling mezzanine of anticipation.

'Case dismissed.'

She whooped. Morris held the phone away from his ear.

'You sound different,' she said.

'I haven't said anything.'

'Something's wrong.'

'I've looked into Mordred Evan's eyes. That has an effect on a person.'

'I should have warned you about that. Mordred doesn't believe in antibiotics – he's hardcore even for a medievalist.'

'I saw things, Zoe. I had a flash.'

'Things?'

'Rottenness, decay, failure, death.'

'Are you OK?'

'Hardly. Mordred just accused me of lying and conspiracy.'

'Shit. He told me he wouldn't do that.'

'You discussed it with him?'

'He's very unpredictable, Morris. When it comes to the history of spelling he's a legend but he has the social skills of a nine-year-old. Did you say something to annoy him?'

'No, I did not. The man's a fucking lunatic. He doesn't believe in antibiotics? Isn't that a clue?'

'Listen sweetie, the Hub's safe. That's what counts.'

'The Hub's safe, but my balls are dangling over the Magimix. I need help.'

'I know what you mean, but politically, the Hub has to remain aloof.'

'Aloof?'

'Think medium-term, Morris. If you survive this, the co-directorship will still be there.'

'If? You can't cut me loose, Zoe. I know too much.'

There was a pause in which Morris involuntarily recalled every inch of Zoe Cable's body, from her purple toenails to the tip of her bleached mohican, giving special attention to certain areas in between. He began to deeply regret what he had just said.

'To be honest, Morris,' Zoe said, 'I doubt whether threats are the way to go on this one.'

Morris said nothing. Looking down, he noticed that his legs were sticking straight out in front of him. His heels had risen several inches from the parquet floor.

'Listen,' said Zoe, 'I can guess it was rough in there Morris, but it's over now. Get a cab to my place. We'll get pissed.'

'No, I have to go home.'

Morris rather portentously pressed 'end'. It took him forty-five minutes to leave the building. When he finally emerged into the main quadrangle the sun was angling in through the Western

233

Gate, gilding the thinly gravelled car park and the cast-iron planting pots. Seeing his shiny Ford Focus, he felt both comforted and accused. How hard would Mordred push, he wondered, and how hard would the Crocodile push back? He was now the meat paste in their thick and unpleasant sandwich. All he could do was wait, hope and keep his consistency. He should talk to the union, but then again, what could he tell them? The truth was appalling. Perhaps he could claim alcoholism, that he was an incorrigible drunk, prone to malicious fantasising. That would get him six months in rehab, light duties for a semester and thereafter a murderous teaching load, no hope of promotion and, in twenty years' time, enforced early retirement, a bunch of flowers and a kick up the arse. It was an option; he had seen it done.

Before starting the car, he glanced at himself in the rear-view mirror. His eyes were bloodshot, he looked sweaty and sick. He also noticed a strange taste in his mouth – a bitter, cloying egginess – which he recognised but couldn't name. He thought for a second. Then he remembered it was the taste of humiliation. Eighteen unsuccessful job interviews – how could he ever have forgotten? Yes, he had been humiliated in there. Mordred had dressed him down, peeled him like a piece of fruit. And today was only the beginning. He was now Mordred and Donald's plaything. He was the new ball in their vindictive game of tennis. And Zoe, it seemed, was content to spectate, to watch him being batted back and forth, all for the sake of her precious bloody Hub.

Perhaps there was another way out, if he could only think of it, some triple-cross, some procedural loophole. But his confidence in his own fledgling ability to scheme had been so badly damaged by the afternoon's events that the thought of further machination only scared him. He needed refuge, safety, a place to catch his breath. He thought suddenly, hungrily – in a way he had not done for months – of E and Molly.

When he arrived home, Morris was surprised not to see his mother's car in the drive. Hadn't she said she was staying two nights? He walked in. Molly was sitting on the sofa in the living room, intently watching a Channel Five documentary on teenage Satanism.

E was standing in the kitchen doorway.

'Is this programme suitable?' he called out.

'I doubt it.'

He came out into the hallway and looked at her. She was poised like a gymnast about to hurl herself at the asymmetric bars. Then he looked past her.

'Where's the kitchen floor?'

'It's in the wheely bin.'

'Where's my mother.'

'Rotherham.'

'Is there something wrong?'

E walked back into the kitchen and pressed play on the answering machine. Morris followed her. He recognised Bernard's voice before he realised what was being said.

When it was over, E looked up at him.

'Well?' she said.

'That's Bernard Littlejohn. I just sacrificed my career to save his arse.'

'With hindsight,' E said, 'probably the wrong choice. Is he telling the truth?'

'Bernard?'

'Yes, Bernard.'

'Yes.'

Yes, he had said it. Yes, he had given himself up to the truth. It felt, for that first half-second, soft and forgiving, clean like a hotel bed – a place where he could stay, could become human again. Then E stuck the vegetable peeler up his nose.

'It's unforgivable,' she said. 'I'm pregnant, you bastard.' Her protuberent belly, like a vast third breast, was pressing into his groin. Morris was wondering how the kitchen floor fitted into all of this.

'OK,' he said. 'OK. Ethically, I'm nowhere. But look at it this way . . .' He paused. 'Relationships develop, change, there are periods of alteration, backsliding. The ideal of constancy is after all purely theoretical, it has no actual equivalent in nature.'

235

'You're pathetic.'

'Perhaps so, but hear me out. Yes, I was unfaithful, but is infidelity really so different from faithfulness? Think about it. They contain many of the same elements. We share ninety-five per cent of our genes with the banana. Perhaps it is time to think beyond these hackneyed oppositions.'

E started crying. She took the vegetable peeler out of his nose.

'Where do you get that crap from?' she asked.

Morris looked at her. His wife. Her face was knobbly and purple, like a punnet of plums. He felt something happening in his chest, something painful and archaic. He tried to touch her, but she pushed him away.

The Crocodile's revenge was swift and thorough. After a dinnerless evening of serial recrimination, a deeply uncomfortable night on the tartan sofa and a dull, lonely morning watching cartoons with Molly and listening with his whole body for even the slightest sign of a lessening of connubial tension, Morris received a phone call from Doris Pamplona.

'The Dean would like to see you as soon as possible, Morris,' she said.

'It's Saturday morning.'

'The Dean would like to see you as soon as possible,' she repeated more slowly.

Morris got into the car without shaving or showering. His shaggy, pungent body struck him immediately as an affront, an insult even to the dustless vinyl swoops of its recently manufactured interior. He loved the Ford Focus; the hire-purchase payments were £250 per month. On the way to campus, he drove significantly below the speed limit; he was overtaken by a learner driver and a triumphant cyclist. Turning around occurred to him, as did sabotaging his car or getting deliberately lost, but it seemed better in the end to get it over with, to know the worst. The sun was still shining, the privet hedges were dusty, the lawns were brown, plants drooped from hanging baskets like ragged and untended dreadlocks. Perhaps he could get away with a formal warning, thought Morris, buoyed up perhaps by

236

the signs of the marvellous, unfailing summer. An off-the-record bollocking, a pledge to scupper his career whenever and wherever possible – that would be par for this particular course, but publicly, perhaps, a warning would suffice. Wouldn't the Crocodile want to steer clear of disciplinary tribunals for a while at least? Wouldn't it be better for him really to stick Morris in some corner office and forget about him for thirty years or so? There were only two other cars in the car park: Crocodile's Mercedes and Doris Pamplona's Spitfire. Morris had always wondered about that Spitfire. The campus was, of course, deserted. As Morris pushed open the mammoth bronze doors of the Arts Faculty, he experienced a strange surge of holiday euphoria. He felt briefly, very briefly, like a schoolboy who had lingered after school and now had the run of the place. He knocked on Doris Pamplona's door. She looked at him with gentle contempt. Morris normally found her manner irritating and inappropriate, but now it struck him as about right.

'Go straight in,' she said. 'They're expecting you.'

They? Morris was surprised that the Crocodile would want a witness. And who could it be? Zoe perhaps? The thought that they might still be in this together perked him up. Surely Zoe could soften this somehow? She had the Hub as leverage. Yes, he thought, as he slowly crossed the ten yards from Doris Pamplona's office to Donald's, it was definitely a good thing Zoe would be there. She owed him – not only for yesterday's ambush, but also for the imminent collapse of his marriage.

He knocked and entered. It was not Zoe; it was Dirck van Camper. He was in a wheelchair, one of those up-to-date ones with composite wheels. His glasses were the same, but he had grown out his hair in a strange, indiscriminate style. It sat like a large, vague furball on top of his long, expressionless face. The Crocodile, whose own face suggested he had recently enjoyed a very pleasant brunch, gestured towards an empty chair. Morris sat.

'Morning Dirck,' Morris said. 'You look well.'

Dirck snorted. The Crocodile grinned. He reached into his desk drawer and brought out a copy of 'Total Mindfuck'.

'Yes, Morris,' he said. 'Dirck is well. So well, in fact, that he has been able to return to his studies at the University of Amsterdam. Imagine his surprise when a month or so ago, whilst searching the MLA database for recent work on embodiment, he came across a piece by his old tutor Morris Gutman.' The Crocodile held up the copy of 'Total Mindfuck'. 'Imagine his even greater surprise when he discovered it was identical, word for word, to an essay he submitted for your "History of Critique" class in the spring.'

Morris's whole face had gone numb. It was as if his nerves had retracted, U-turned back into his head, leaving the flesh of his face stranded and helpless. He swallowed loudly. He was having flashbacks to the car park, the blood pool, the Do It to Julia fans.

'Isn't it possible . . .' He breathed heavily once or twice. He wasn't sure whether he was really going to say this, but then again he wasn't sure it was possible to make things any worse than they were. He looked at the Crocodile. The Crocodile seemed quite eager to hear what he had to say. 'Isn't it possible,' he went on, 'that Dirck copied my article? What evidence have you got that he wrote this essay first?'

'We have statements, Morris. Certified, *unretracted* statements from several friends of Dirck, including one Professor at the University of Amsterdam to whom he sent a copy of his essay in March. I'm amazed you thought you could get away with it.'

'You knew a month ago?'

'Three weeks. I suppose I should have threatened you earlier, but you live and learn. This is for you.'

He pushed a sheet of paper across the desk. It was a letter of resignation. The Crocodile offered him a pen. Morris signed.

'Oh, by the way, I've also informed your publisher, who seems to be having second thoughts about your book, and the *Guardian* education section is running a piece on plagiarism next week, citing you as a prime example.'

'Won't publicity damage the Faculty?' said Morris vaguely.

He was beginning to have problems with his peripheral vision: windows and walls seemed to be leaning in towards him.

'Perhaps, but I thought it a price well worth paying. You can keep the pen.' It was a Bic. 'Think of it as your leaving present.'

Part Three

Chapter 26

Morris realised with regret that he was awake again. Another day. The pleasant whirliness of his dream-thoughts had curdled, stiffened into something that was identifiably if unfortunately him. He got up, dispensed his morning bowl of generic corn-flakes, opened the mini-fridge and sniffed the milk with suspicion. From next door he could hear the usual Slavic yammerings. Why did Kosovars, he wondered, have so much to talk about? The batteries in his transistor radio had been dead for several days so, for amusement, Morris looked out of the window as the kettle boiled. The view was of the communal car park, the four-lane Isaiah Berlin Parkway and, beyond that, behind a thick hedge and a newly erected council sign – *Coketown Education: Excellence Whatever the Cost* – the Albert Schweitzer Primary School.

He had a shower, dried himself and put on his uniform. Morris was now a guard for Alpaca Security Services. He wore a beige shirt with brown epaulettes, brown trousers with a beige stripe and a hexagonal brown cap with a shiny black peak and a spurious gold badge. He worked in the wine and spirits section of Sir Savalot, the flagship store of the Rumpswick Shopping Precinct.

Yes, it was a step down. There was no point in pretending otherwise. No point in pretending even that it was only temporary, since any such state of temporariness would have required Morris to have a plan or at least a notion of an alternative future, and Morris had neither of those. His vision, indeed, as he paced solemnly everyday from the New World whites to the cut-price mini-lagers, was entirely rearward. All he could see was the uniformly depressing vista of the recent past: his career, terminated a month before in circumstances, according to the *Guardian* education section, of 'unexampled ignominy'; his affair with Zoe Cable ended with similar rapidity once his plagiarism was made public; his marriage to E was currently under suspension pending a post-partum review, the results of which Morris anticipated with gloom. Such catastrophic and simultaneous failure was surely unusual, Morris thought. He was the victim of, if nothing else, improbability. Improbability and poor design. His life had split apart in mid-air like an ageing Tupolov, and all Morris could think to do now was to sift the wreckage looking for clues, momentoes, a little hope. That, anyway, was how he passed the long days at Sir Savalot. Between shooing off the homeless and offering directions to the condiments aisle, he stood to lopsided attention behind his mirrored aviator shades, replaying again and again in his mind the long moments before the crash.

Morris polished his shoes with yesterday's underwear, checked the sell-by date on his flat-pack sandwiches, donned his pac-a-mac (the record-breaking summer was at an end) and set off for work. If he was honest with himself, he would admit that his choice of accommodation, like his choice of job, was mainly a gesture. When he had announced to E that he had found a place for ten pounds a week, that his neighbours would be asylum seekers and that he would be working as a supermarket security guard, he had expected some expression of sympathy or contrition, some suggestion that perhaps he had gone too far. He had been offered none of these. Instead, E's aggressive display of insouciance had made Morris so angry that he had taken the bedsit and the Sir Savalot job to spite her.

As he locked his front door Morris waved to the Al Houja family, who were standing at the end of the corridor. The looks of shock and terror they gave back made him wonder whether the common wave might have an altogether different and more obstetrical meaning within the culture of the Maghreb. He descended the sewage-tainted staircase with a sense that yet

244

more weight had been added to his bulging panniers of gloom. It was seven-thirty. The Isaiah Berlin Parkway was snarled with wet and honking traffic. Morris took a deep breath and entered the subway, emerging on the other side of the road blue-faced and rather more worldly than before. He passed the Albert Schweitzer Primary School then turned right into the unkempt pedestrianisation of the Brueghel Maisonettes – roaming German Shepherds, children on mountain bikes, blue-green graffiti rising up the walls like elephant grass. He crossed a ravaged play area and a residents' car park dotted with pools of window glass. Ten minutes later he ducked under the half-open shutters of Sir Savalot.

Darren, his co-worker, Darren of the virulent aftershave and the lewd Tweetie Pie tattoo, was standing next to a bin of cut-price Pot Noodle, talking to check-out girl Rasha Jenkins. Morris took up his usual position between the eggnog and the cherry schnapps. It was five to eight. Rasha regretfully detached herself from Darren and remounted the check-out stool. Morris adopted a pose of semi-aggressive vigilance, donned his aviator glasses, closed his eyes and began to think.

He thought of E, always of E. Her pink face, glowing with pregnancy, drifted past him like a lost balloon. Perhaps this really was for the best. He had done all he could. He had. He had apologised solidly for a whole week. He had sought neither to defend nor justify his actions. When E had characterised his adultery as a desperate act born of pathetic insecurity, he had agreed that there were issues he needed to deal with. When she had thrown things at him, small electrical items mainly, he had ducked then picked up the pieces. When, temporarily defeated by the energies of her own anger, she had asked for a hug, he had given it. And when she returned again an hour or so later to the attack, he had resisted mentioning the hug. It had been, indeed, as though the hug had never occurred. He had cleaned the house while E locked herself in the bathroom and spoke endlessly to Stella on the cordless. He looked after Molly; he did long-forgotten jobs. His penitence had been exemplary, unexceptionable, but he had performed it with the expectation that it would eventually end, that one day E's fury would abate, that her bitterness would sweeten, her verbal assaults become less frenzied and less frequent. After a good week of it, however, he realised that events were moving in the opposite direction.

Sunday morning. He rose from the tartan sofa with the usual accumulation of spinal numbness and muscular strain, collected the already howling Molly, fed her on Weetabix and precisely heated milk, anointed her eczema, dressed her after lengthy negotiations, tricked her into mounting the pushchair and then pushed her, screaming but strapped in, to the park. Before leaving he did the dishes and left a selection of bran cereal, a sliced kiwi and a large glass of cran-orange on the table for E. He hoped that they had reached a point where such open displays of affection and effort might provoke in E some recripocal softening. He was hoping, in truth, for a pang. After a week of cringing he felt that he was due a pang. When he returned from the park, however, he found E still in her pyjamas, lying on the tartan sofa watching pubescent TV and eating Tweenie yoghurt. His high-fibre breakfast was untouched on the kitchen table. Morris was not cheered by this sight, but he still thought it possible that a pang might have occurred in his absence.

'We've been to the park,' he explained.

'You were supposed to go swimming.'

'What do you mean?'

'Molly has her swimming lesson on a Sunday morning.'

'Swimming lesson?'

'Yes Morris.' She turned to him. '*Swim-ming les-son*. Surely that's not too complicated for a hot young lecturer like yourself?'

Morris said nothing. Molly, who had woken up from a brief but entirely revivifying nap, launched a panting, Houdini-like assault on her pushchair harness. E stood up without looking at Morris, clicked the harness open, carried Molly back to the sofa and gave her a chocolate biscuit.

'That's a special treat,' she explained to Molly, 'because you missed swimming today. And I know how much you love swimming.'

'Swiiimmmiiing!' Molly looked suddenly and utterly bereft. Tears rolled instantly off the chubby overhang of her cheeks and dropped on to the dark wavelets of her chocolate digestive. E plied her with another.

'If,' she went on, addressing Morris but still not looking at him, 'instead of shagging your colleagues and writing your piss-poor books, you'd paid the slightest attention to your daughter, you would know she has been having swimming lessons every Sunday for the last two months.'

Morris had given up on the pang. The pang, he realised, was still a long, long way away. He reached rather wearily down into himself for another apology.

'I'm really . . .'

'Yes?' snapped E.

'Really . . .' Instead of grabbing the usual apology Morris realised that he had come up with something quite different, something much darker and angrier, a sticky black mass that suddenly wanted out.

'Really tired of your incessant victimhood.'

E finally looked at him. More than that, she stood up and stared at him, her eyes bulging like water balloons.

'You don't tell me how to feel,' she hissed.

'There's enough pain to go around, you know. You don't have to hoard it. You don't have to hug it like a fucking security blanket.'

Morris paused. The image of the blanket had suddenly triggered a whole range of associations in his mind. He felt that he was having a breakthrough moment.

'That's it. That's it!' he continued. 'You're clinging to this as a form of comfort. It gives you an identity, "the betrayed wife". For you it's perfect. For once you can feel good about feeling bad because you have someone else to blame entirely – me. Everything that's wrong is my fault. It's so simple. Morris is the root of all evil. I think you're enjoying this. Why else would you cling on to it? Because it gives you something you can't get anywhere else

247

– an explanation. An explanation for everything that's gone wrong, *ever*. I'm like Hitler for you, I'm like Saddam. It's fundamentalism. You're an emotional fundamentalist.'

'Have you finished now?' E shouted back. 'Have you finished now? Because I'll tell you, you're a complete fucking lunatic. Did you know that? Did you . . .'

'No I have not finished. I HAVE NOT FINISHED!' Morris was shouting as loud as he could. He had not done that, not tried to do it, since he was a child. He couldn't believe the sensation. How big it made him feel. Molly's mouth hung open, a small red pocket, full of yellow crumbs. 'I have something else to say. What about *my* pain? I've lost my fucking job. What about that? Does that even appear on your horizon? I doubt it, because you're too busy cuddling up with your betrayal. "Oh my poor betrayal, my little betrayal", like it's a fucking guinea pig. Like it's the end of the fucking world.'

E stepped back. She was frowning and looking amazed. Molly was clinging to her leg.

'You're not making sense anymore Morris. I think you should leave.'

'*You* think I should leave? *You* think I should fucking leave?'

That was when he left. After slamming everything that was slammable he stormed out. He got into the Ford Focus and drove like a fool, a complete fool, setting off three speed cameras on the Coketown flyover alone, until he found a pub that was obviously open. He entered the Mountebank Arms glassy-eyed with a desire for oblivion, like a Lothario of the void. He ordered and drank in quick succession three pints of Superbrew, finishing the third with a long, tumultuous and symphonic burp, a burp which might have served, in its lengthy, self-regarding ugliness, as a tragic summation of his life so far.

From Morris's left came the soft, wet crash of wine bottle on concrete. He opened his eyes. The aisle was already filled with the dense, clingy aroma of ripe cherries and fried halibut. Someone had dropped a bottle of the East Texan Shiraz – reduced to

£3.99 and recently recommended in the 'Guzzle It Up' column of the *Telegraph*. Morris walked across. A grey-haired man in a bottle-green blouson jacket and grey trousers was standing by the red puddle, staring at his hands.

'May I help you sir?' Morris was wondering whether this was a genuine accident or the result of an attempted robbery. The blouson jacket looked easily baggy enough for half a dozen bottles.

The man turned. It was Bernard. Morris stepped backwards and emitted a harsh guttural eek similar to the sound of a drawer jamming.

'I do apologise, sir,' Bernard said, not seeming to notice the noise. 'I can only claim temporary insanity. The thought of East Texan Shiraz at under a fiver has obviously loosened my cogs.'

Morris removed his aviator shades. Bernard's thin lips all of a sudden became the shade and shape of a loose elastic band.

'Morris,' he exhaled.

'Bernard.'

There was a pause. Bernard noticed the uniform.

'Have you joined the army?'

'I'm a security guard.'

'Oh.' Bernard thought. 'Here?'

'Yes, here.'

'Right . . . very nice.' Morris looked at him. 'No, I suppose not. Um, you won't be charging me for . . .' He waved his fingers at the red puddle. 'Will you?'

Morris shook his head. Half the bottle was still intact – the neck and a jagged two prong crown. Morris looked at it. Bernard saw him looking. His eyes widened with alarm.

'OK Morris,' he said. 'The phone call was unforgivable. But I was in a state of near hysteria, and all the indications were that you had shat on me from a very great height.'

'I saved your pimply arse.'

'In the event yes, you did. And my gratitude for that is unbounded. But how could I know in advance? That taffy bastard treated me like his punkah wallah. We're both victims of a rotten system, Morris. We're cannon fodder. They sit in their offices with their strategic bloody reviews in one hand and their carbuncular dicks in the other, and we're the sods who go over the top.'

'Not me, Bernard. I work for Alpaca Security.'

'Alpaca is it?' Bernard noticed the patch above Morris's breast pocket. 'Strange, not really an animal noted for its ferocity.'

'Actually the owner's Peruvian, but as I was saying you've got a career.'

'I'm taking early retirement.'

'What?'

'Think about it, Morris. OK, after the investigation the Croc couldn't touch me, but he doesn't need to. All he has to do is check I do my marking, or get the Mad Monk to check for him. No one can complain about that. But without my system it's undoable, I'm finished.'

'Can't you modify the system?'

'There are new procedures: blind triple-marking, carbonised multiliths. They'll drop them after I'm gone, but there's no point in fighting it.'

'What about Mordred?'

'On sabbatical in Finland with an unlisted email. He doesn't give a fuck. We're prawns in their cocktail.'

Morris looked down at the broken bottle then back again at Bernard. Could he really have aged so visibly in a month? His skin looked like a part-defrosted chop and his body sagged all over as though his clothes were lead-lined.

Darren turned sharply into the wine and spirits aisle.

'All right, Morris.'

'All right, Darren.'

He looked at the red puddle.

'I generally find it tastes better in a glass, sir.' (He always said that).

He sniffed.

'East Texan Shiraz. Quite a snip at £3.99. You're right to come in early, sir. After that write-up in the *Telegraph* they'll be none left by teatime. Need a clean-up, Morris?'

'Please, Darren.'

Darren sloped off to make a staff announcement. Bernard, as though spurred on by Darren's enthusiasm, put four fresh bottles in his trolley, then after a moment added two more.

'£3.99 really is remarkable,' he said.

Morris nodded. The veins in Bernard's nose looked like a clutch of tiny bloodworms.

'Listen, let me buy you a drink,' Bernard said with renewed jollity. 'The Cro-Magnon Arms isn't far. They still do a serviceable pint of Postlethwaite.'

'I don't get a break until twelve.'

Bernard looked at his watch and whistled.

'Let's say twelve then.'

The Cro-Magnon Arms was a hostelry of many rooms, each of which smelt faintly like a fish tank. After a brief search, Morris found Bernard sitting in the snug with half a pint of Post-lethwaite and a copy of *The Ecclesiastical History of Bedford-shire*.

'Morris!' Bernard raised a finger and Morris waited an awk-ward and unbelieving few seconds for him to finish his para-graph and replace his leather bookmark.

'You know, Morris,' he said, closing the book with a dusty phut, 'as I get older I find myself increasingly drawn to the literature of dullness.' He waved *The Ecclesiastical History of Bedfordshire*. 'Now why should that be?'

Morris shrugged.

'Preparation perhaps. I imagine eternity is terribly tedious.'

Bernard guffawed.

'Cheeky git.' He stood up. 'Pint of Postlethwaite? I'll get a couple of pasties while I'm up.'

Morris lit a cigarette. He felt inexplicably nervous, as if this meeting with Bernard were some kind of date, as if it contained the possibility of yet more failure. He took off his brown hexagonal hat and placed it next to the ashtray.

Bernard came back holding the drinks and shaking his head.

251

'I've known that landlord for years,' he said. 'Terence. He's a funny old bugger, he really is.'

They sipped. Bernard inhaled suddenly and with evident discomfort, as though breathing were new to him. Morris waved away his cigarette smoke. He was experiencing uncomfortable memories of the last time they drank together.

'Want to frisk me?' he joked.

Bernard grimaced.

'Come on Morris,' he said.

Morris blushed.

After another weighty pause Bernard spoke again.

'What's all this about then?'

'What?'

'This?' He gestured at the uniform as if it were an offensive and deliberately inexplicable work of art.

'Bernard,' Morris said, 'I'm a convicted plagiarist. You may have read about me in the *Guardian*.'

'Bullshit. That's all stuff and nonsense. Whatsisname, Dirck van Camper. He's a bloody quisling. He's got his tongue so far up the Crocodile's arse it's a form of colonic bloody irrigation. I don't believe a word of it.'

Morris felt a sudden crushing sense of love for Bernard and this irrational, misguided show of faith.

'What can I do though?'

'If the union weren't so fucking useless they'd have got you off already. That Yacob Macomb, he looks like a syphilitic Art Garfunkel and he's got about the same amount of gumption. They're quick enough to chase you for your dues but when it comes to the crunch it's union officials and children first. It's a bloody scandal.' He bit into his pasty. 'Have you tried talking to them?'

'The union?'

'Yes.'

'No.'

'I don't blame you, they're bloody useless.'

Morris looked out of the leaded window. There was a ten-foot with wheely bins. He only had half an hour for lunch and drinking on duty was a dismissible offence.

252

'It's over with Zoe,' he said.

'Hate to say I told you so.' Bernard pushed the other pasty across to Morris. He took a bite – its vague, wet meatiness struck him as strangely delicious.

'So this security job, is it all right? Do you actually like it?'

The question, which Morris had never dared ask himself before, was like a plumb line dropped into his inner emptiness. It fell and fell and fell then thumped to a stop.

'It's a living death,' he said. 'You wouldn't believe the people.'

'They're proles. I hate to say it, Morris. It's not PC, but face the facts. Their idea of culture is some fat tart banging out "Nessun Dorma" on karaoke night. That may be where we come from Morris, you and I, but we've grown. We've tasted the ambrosia of knowledge. There's no going back. This job, this uniform, this is not you. I know that. You're a scholar, an intellect. I've read your work on Alderley.' (Morris seriously doubted that, but he let it pass.) 'Magnificent! Old-fashioned of course, but all the better for that I say. Your time will come again. This plagiarism nonsense will blow over.'

'Do you really think so?'

'Of course it will. My time is gone.' Morris opened his mouth to object, but Bernard swept on. 'But you are young. Play the long game Morris, the long game. That's my advice to you.' He took a long swig of Postlethwaite. 'Another pint?'

'I'll get them.'

As Morris walked to the bar he felt a strange, dizzying surge of hope. Perhaps Bernard was right. Perhaps things weren't quite as desperate and final as he had imagined. 'The long game.' He liked the sound of that.

'You need to position yourself,' Bernard continued after Morris had returned with the drinks. 'Bide your time. These things are cyclical. The Crocodile won't last forever. Zoe Cable will burn out. I've seen it before. Couple of years' time he'll have a bypass and retire to Guernsey; she'll come down with neur-asthenia and turn to organic gardening. I've seen it before, Morris, believe me.'

'The long game.'

'The long game.'

Morris looked at his watch. It was twelve thirty-five.

'I've got to be getting back.' He stood up. Bernard waved him back down.

'Listen,' he said. 'I've got an old mate, Rupert Tong, runs Trident Education. Have you heard of them?'

Morris shook his head.

'I've worked for them for years, on and off. Rupert and I go back to the old, extramural days. It's lectures for A Level students mainly – *Lord of the Flies, The Handmaid's Tale*, whatever Shakespeare they're doing that year. Then occasional Adult Ed. trips – Stratford, the West End. I've even done the odd bus tour – Brontë country with eminent Victorianist Dr Bernard Littlejohn, an afternoon's nattering, a hundred quid plus tips. I just do it for pocket money, but there have been people who've lived off it. You can do three or four lectures a week if you're prepared to travel. Plus expenses. The money's not bad.'

'Would he take me even after the *Guardian* article?'

'Christ, Rupert hates the *Guardian*. The *Racing Post* and the *Telegraph* crossword are as far as he gets. Anyway, I'll put in a word for you. He's always on the lookout. Here's his telephone number.'

Bernard took out his fountain pen, pulled the facing off a beermat and wrote the number with a flourish.

Morris looked at it carefully. He found the thought that someone might actually want him, for whatever reason, rather moving. He looked again at his watch.

'I'm late and I'm pissed.' He said it as much to himself as to Bernard. 'I could lose my job again.'

Bernard leaned back and looked quizzically into his glass.

'Far be it from me to sway you Morris,' he said, 'but I will merely point out that a) it is my round and b) that uniform makes you look like Flash fucking Gordon.'

The offices of Trident Education were above a ladies' hair-dressers in Glodshaw. As Morris climbed the narrow, blue-carpeted staircase he felt full of nervousness. Another bloody interview. He had imagined that the one advantage of being fired and disgraced was that he would never have to do this again. Yet here he was. It was hardly Coketown University, he reasoned, hardly even the Eccles Institute, but then again neither was it Alpaca Security Services, where the interview had consisted of checking for a criminal record and ensuring he had a full set of teeth. Morris knocked on the door.

'Enter.'

Rupert Tong had floppy white hair and was dressed in a baggy teal sweatshirt, black exercise trousers and flip-flops. He was pedalling an antiquated exercise bike, which was squeezed into a corner between two paper-strewn desks.

'Do excuse me,' he panted. 'I've been put on a most rigorous exercise programme by my GP. My arteries apparently resemble the inside of an electric kettle. Ten more minutes of this madness I'm afraid. Do sit down. There's a chair under there somewhere.'

Morris put some box files on the floor and sat. Rupert continued to pedal.

'Are you able to talk?' Morris asked.

'Oh God yes. I'm always able to talk. I'll still be talking when they box me up and put me in the ground. Now, let me remember what old Bernard said about you.' He clenched his damp, pink face for a second in an effort at recollection. Morris held his breath. Bernard had promised to talk him up, but you never knew with Bernard; he could easily have let something slip.

'No good,' said Rupert after a moment. 'My memory's completely shot. I blame the male menopause. Although, of course, they'll all tell you it doesn't exist. But anyway, I know he raved, positively raved. And Bernard rarely raves you know. He can be rather dour, Bernard, rather . . .' Rupert paused for a moment as if selecting precisely the right adjective from a rank of worthy candidates. His feet continued their slow rotations.

'Gloomy,' he finally said.

Morris nodded eagerly. 'Well he has had a hard time with the Department lately.'

'God yes, he told me about that, harrowing, absolutely harrowing. Some of the stories he tells.' Rupert shook his head. 'It seems to me, Morris,' he said, 'that something has gone rather terribly wrong, that the true meaning of a literary education has been forgotten. It's been Balkanised – queer this, women's that. I taught Declan Monk at Cambridge, but *now*,' Rupert rolled his eyes, 'it sounds like he's completely bonkers.'

In response to this unnerving speech Morris offered a selection of pleasing but non-committal facial gestures. Rupert continued to talk.

'Bernard tells me you've had a run-in with that lot too.' Morris flinched. 'Well as far as I'm concerned that's a badge of honour. You'll find the work we do here quite traditional – character analysis, plot summary, patterns of symbolism, that kind of thing. It's not nuclear physics, but it changes lives. You should see the letters I get. I keep a file. It's the Adult Ed. people especially. They've been working in a works canteen all their lives and someone talks them through *Jude the Obscure*. Pow! Pow! Pow!' Rupert made little explosions in the air with his hands. 'They're never the same.'

'I'm very interested,' said Morris. 'Bernard spoke very highly of your programme. Would you like to see my CV?' He reached across and handed it to Rupert.

Rupert's reading glasses were on a cord around his neck. He put them on and peered. After a minute or so he unexpectedly stopped pedalling. Morris steeled himself. This was it. What would it be this time he wondered? Overqualified? Underqualified? Too many holes in his career? Too few? Previously he had been shot down from so many angles he had no idea which direction this particular bullet would come from.

Rupert continued to peer.

'This,' he said after a long moment, 'is remarkable, quite remarkable. Not only Coketown, but the Eccles Institute, the University of Ipswich, the College of West Mercia! I'd go so far as to say that for someone of your age your wealth of experience is unparalleled. Not to mention your Ph.D. with Conrad Underseel, author of that wonderful Alderley biography. You're abso-

256

lutely perfect for us.' Rupert took off his reading glasses and beamed.

Morris beamed back. Despite the doubtful provenance of Rupert's lavishness (how terribly little he really knew) it made him feel instantly bigger and more powerful.

'How much work would you be interested in?' Rupert asked. 'I assume you have other commitments.' The pedalling had recommenced.

'Well, not so many at the moment,' Morris admitted. 'I can probably take as much work as you've got.'

'Ah!' Rupert called out in joy. 'Even better. I'll tell you we have a pretty full schedule this year and one of our regulars has dropped out with angina. How are you on Gerard Manley Hopkins?'

'I could brush up.'

'Course you could. "Soft sift in an hourglass". It's a piece of cake. Our usual fee is a hundred pounds per session plus expenses. You can make a decent living if you like.'

I'm in, thought Morris, as easy as that. He could make four or five hundred pounds a week. More than he'd ever made at Coketown. It wouldn't be much work either. He'd spend his days on the train, reading. He might begin to write again: more essays on Alderley, a textbook perhaps. He could get a reasonable flat, patch things up with E. Maybe the worst really was over. Bernard had saved him. Quid pro quo.

'When could I start?' he said.

'Well, let's see.' Rupert's egg timer went off. He dismounted stiffly and looked down at the saddle with a frown of comic contempt. 'It may be good for my arteries,' he winked, 'but it's doing bugger all for my piles'. He hobbled over to one of the desks and consulted a file. '26 November.'

'26 November? That's two months.'

Rupert looked up at the sheepdog wall calendar. 'Yes, you're right,' he said. About two months.'

'I was hoping it would be sooner.' Morris's university wages had stopped abruptly upon his resignation, and for the last

257

month he had been surviving on four pounds fifty an hour from Alpaca Security plus his father's old building society account, willed to him six years before and superstitiously untouched since then. He could still write cheques on the joint account of course, but he knew that E's maternity pay would barely cover their bills and expenses. He reassured himself that once he started lecturing for Rupert, things would be fine. But still, two months was a long time.

'Summer's our slow patch of course,' Rupert explained. 'That won't be a problem will it?'

'No, not at all.' Morris didn't want to risk any kind of derailment. 'I'll be glad of the break.'

On the bus home he thought about the next two months. The idea of another temporary job appalled him, but could he really manage on the building society account? There was £250 in there. After rent he would have £17 a week. It would be tough, brutal even, but the thought rather excited him. He would have to cut his life down to the bare bones: tinned food, plastic bread, candles even. It might be invigorating, purifying. It would prove, at least, that he could survive alone on his inner resources, that he didn't need anything else.

That evening he ate plain spaghetti and spent three hours writing out a minutely calibrated budget. Around eleven-thirty one of the Afghans threw a gas cooker off the fourth-floor balcony. It hit the communal car park with a pandemonic bang. After a few moments of shocked silence a roar of East European invective rose around him from every side. Doors slammed, there was scuffling in the corridor, children howled, a fire engine arrived with sirens. (The gas cooker had not been disconnected before being hurled.) Amidst this tumult Morris sat silently on his foldaway chair and looked with a startling sense of inner peace at the rows of precisely pencilled numbers. This, he thought, might just be the making of me.

For the first week Morris came in under budget every day. He had bread and long-life orange juice for breakfast, nothing for lunch and something boiled for tea. He spent the days in the local branch library, carrying out a careful rereading of the collected poems of Gerard Manley Hopkins. In the evenings he felt empty, mildly bored but quite tranquil. He slept deeply and dreamt of desert islands, empty planets, mountain peaks. By the weekend he had accumulated a surplus of £2.50. He put the three coins on his small kitchen table and looked at them. He picked them up, polished them thoughtfully with the edge of his T-shirt, then put them back. They were a vindication, he thought, proof that he could manage. He stored them in an old jam jar on the shelf above his bed.

The next week, although officially he stuck to the same budget, unofficially, surreptitiously, in a secret plan fully revealed to no one (not even paradoxically himself), Morris aimed to beat his previous record, to smash it. Instead of the off-peak student haircut he had budgeted for, he shaved his head with a Bic razor. He washed his clothes in the shower, he substituted tap water for the orange juice. By Friday night he had £5 on the table and a line-by-line mastery of *The Wreck of the Deutschland*.

On the third Monday of his new regime, feeling light-headed from lack of food and unable to concentrate properly on 'The Windhover' (just what the fuck, he thought irritably, is a *sillion*?), Morris left the library earlier than normal and walked briskly home. In the communal car park, near the rough-edged crater left by the gas cooker, there was a rusty skip, part-filled with crumbled plasterboard and broken council-issue furniture. As he passed, Morris noticed in one corner, under the remnants of a pine-look video cabinet, an old and greasy portable television. He reached in immediately without shame or hesitation and started tugging. After a minute or so the television came away with a creak and bang and a smell of rubbish and cement. Once upstairs he plugged it in. It fuzzed. He rotated the aerial, fiddled with the knobs on the back and, after a long *woooow*, the snow solidified into a picture – *The Weakest Link* in black and white.

'What is the highest mountain in Africa?'
'Kilimanjaro.'
'Correct. What is the meaning of hirsute?'
Morris stared. His heart was racing. It felt like he was watch-

ing signals from an alien world, a world of chirpiness and plenty. He switched the television off and boiled some rice with a chicken stock-cube. When the rice was ready he sat on the bed, the steaming bowl hotting up his knees, and looked at his new acquisition. Had it been a mistake to pick it up, he wondered? Might it sully the purity of his whole budgetary project? Perhaps he should return it to the skip, or give it to the Al Houjas. On the other hand, he had pulled it from a skip, an asylum-seekers skip at that. This was not luxury. After a day of 'hurling and gliding smooth on the bow bend', an hour or so of free entertainment was hardly a matter for guilt.

That evening Zoe Cable appeared in Morris's bedsit. He came across her by accident. Tiring of the show-jumping from Hickstead, yet with more than an hour to go before his prearranged phone call to Molly, he twisted the channel changer and there she was. Her hair was dark brown, she was wearing black-framed glasses and an off-the-shoulder trench coat. Morris clutched his knees and stared. It was a half-hour discussion show, chaired by Adam d'Hote, on the shortlist for the Schumacher Prize.

Zoe dominated the discussion. Her comments were consistently witty and delicious. Her performance was even better than it had been three months before on *Going Critical*. She was developing a TV manner, Morris could tell, easing into the medium. There was no hesitation now, but neither was there an unruly urge to make her point. She was domineering without being shouty. Their break-up, he also noticed, had clearly not affected her at all. There was in her appearance and manner no hint of personal trauma or emotional unsteadiness. No facial tics, no lines or bags, her fingernails were lengthy and unbitten. She looked as replete and knowing as always. Her career was bounding ever onwards – Channel 4, the BBC. There would soon, he could tell, be weekly columns, features, interviews. And what did he have? Trident Education. Morris felt sick with envy and self-contempt.

When the discussion was over he switched off the television and looked about his room. It was smelly and derelict. This was where they had brought him: Zoe, the Crocodile, E. This was their fault. The thought occurred to him that hurling a gas cooker off the balcony was not such a bad idea after all. But why stop there? He would happily toss away everything he had: the mini-fridge, the bag of dirty clothes, the alarm clock, the television, the books. Destroy them all. His eyes fell on his carefully pencilled budget.

Tuesday dinner: day-old barm cake, half a can of Sir Savalot cola, chips and scraps. 70p.

Seventy pence for dinner. He thought of sticking a corkscrew into his upper arm and twisting, twisting, twisting. Where would Zoe be now, he wondered? In a taxi going to Heathrow? Or perhaps she had more Hub business to conduct – unwinding at the Sheraton, chumming it up with Adam d'Hote. As he sat there on the single bed with greying sheets he could smell her: lavender and petrol. He could taste the salty folds of her breast, the glycerine slickness of her lip gloss. It was time to call Molly. The queue at the communal pay phone was even worse than usual: men with thick black bristles and phone cards, peasant women with scarves and plastic shoes. The thought of waiting made his anger nearly uncontainable. He walked furiously past the queue down the stairs and out of the building. He did not stop walking until he reached the Chaudhary Brothers Grocery and Off-Licence, where he wordlessly purchased a four-pack of Superbrew and a quarter bottle of Wee Hamish. By the time he got through to Molly he was terribly drunk.

'Have you seen the Queen?' he shouted. (They were staying in London with E's parents). 'Have you seen Prince Philip?'

Molly didn't say anything, but he could hear her breathing. She would be shaking her head, he knew, or nodding. That was what Molly did on the phone, shake or nod. It was not an ideal form of communication. He thought bitterly of E watching at the other end, rolling her eyes, laughing.

'Have you been to the zoo?' he yelled. 'Have you seen the elephants?'

Her breath was a gentle push and pull, a see-saw of air.

261

'I love you,' he said. 'Don't forget that. I'll see you very, very soon. I love you.'

His money ran out. There was a clunk of change being taken and then a long ridiculous beep. Morris looked at the phone for a moment – it was gnarled and worn with use – then replaced the handset. As he walked back to his bedsit past the long staring line of refugees, tears were dripping from his chin.

A week later Morris was leaning against the Chaudhary Brothers' newly installed ATM, trying to remember his PIN number. He had a cigarette in one hand and half a can of Superbrew in the other. He was squinting suspiciously at the prompt. Was it 0925 or 0926? His father's building society account was empty. He had spent it all on Superbrew, top-shelf pornography and takeaway food. Now he was trying to rifle what he could from the joint account which he had promised E he would never, ever touch. 0 . . . 9 . . . 2 . . . He gritted his teeth . . . 5. Yes! *Cash Without Receipt*. He pressed the £100 button. *Insufficient funds*. He checked the balance. There was only £42.63 in the account. He took out £40 of it. As he did so he noticed an unwelcome crackle of cognitive activity above his left eye. Despite all his efforts at befuddlement a message was coming through. Something about the £40 and E and Molly, something about solitude, divorce and brutal loneliness. Morris took this as a firm signal that he needed to drink more. He bought more Superbrew, a litre of Wee Hamish and a hundred cigarettes. As he walked back to his bedsit it began to rain. He was wearing a T-shirt, the trousers from his interview suit and a pair of plimsolls. That morning he had tripped in the shower and blackened his eye. At the same time his scalp was covered in nicks and gouges from an unwise attempt to reshave it the previous night. As the rain stiffened, diluted blood dripped from his head wounds into his good eye. Morris opened the Wee Hamish and took a drink – the gag reflex, the burn and then the long slide of pleasure. That was how it always was. That was how it should be.

The bedsit still smelt from when he had set the curtains on fire.

As he walked to the bed there was the rustle of old kebab wrappers and the chink of empty Wee Hamish bottles. His gas cooker was topped with a black, volcanic-looking beret of tar and grease, which Morris, though he couldn't exactly remember, imagined had something to do with an earlier effort to make pancakes. Sticking out of the green-rimmed toilet was a half-melted wok.

Morris turned on the television and started to drink. *Camcorder Calamity* was on. As he watched, Morris was attacked by thoughts and memories. He tried to fend them off – Wee Hamish with a Superbrew chaser was like being hit on the head with a rubber mallet. He dealt himself blow after boinging blow. But that evening the ideas seemed especially resilient. They came back at him in waves. They attacked from behind, from the side. They slipped through his defences. He felt besieged, infiltrated. What had he done? What had he been doing? Had he really failed so utterly? Had he really lost so much? He thought of Dirck van Camper, that second of resistance as Morris reversed. He thought of Zoe Cable coming into his room at the LA Body Conference, grabbing his dick, latching on like a breastfeeding baby. He thought of his father's corpse being carried from the house, bagged up like a new suit. He thought of E, the flailing foetus-baby roiling her skin. He thought of Molly making faces, pulling out her lips, showing off the pink of her eyelids. Was it all lost? Had he squandered everything – job, marriage, even his father's building society account? He drank a quarter of the bottle in one go and came up panting. The news came on.

Rain blew through Morris's open window, soaking the charred curtains, causing the kebab wrappers on the floor to wilt and release their pong of papery grease. Morris blinked and lit a cigarette. Vision was becoming a problem. All he could find to eat in the mini-fridge was a tub of margarine. He ate it with a knife. Sections of his book came back to him. He dug out the manuscript and read from Chapter Three.

The ethics of vampirism may be most teasingly reimagined
if we realise that the undead are also in a vital post-
Nietzschean sense the ungood. It is only via such a
redescription that the full, scandalous, sacramental impli-
cations of the vampiric bite can be thought dialectically as
both true and false and so simultaneously retained and
reneged.

The news ended. Morris ran out of whisky. He tottered into the
bathroom and threw up into the wok. He wiped his mouth on
the wet kebab wrappers and fell back on to the bed. He was
sweating. There was a sharp, itchy rawness in his lungs which he
could only compare to a pulmonary version of athlete's foot. His
mucus was bright green and gelatinous. Unmarked images were
swooping through his mind: Bernard on an exercise bike, Molly
with the weeping eyes of Mordred Evans. He couldn't be sure
but he thought he saw Zoe Cable on television again. He
dropped to his knees and peered into its hideous black and
white face. Was it the right day for *Going Critical*? He had no
idea. Wasn't it her though? She was wearing a leather bikini top
and a jacket that was stitched together from the hides of ancient
Barbie Dolls. He leaned towards the screen and kissed her. Her
lips were dusty and cold. Morris's eyebrows (the only hair left on
his head) stood on end. He closed his eyes and entered the
churning netherworld of drunken sleep.

On the television screen, visible above the blood-streaked
dome of Morris's skull, Zoe Cable addressed the camera with
a twinkle.

'Well, on that pusillanimous note we have to finish for this
week. Next week, in a programming decision little short of
treasonous, *Going Critical* will be replaced by coverage of World
Championship darts, but I assure you we will be back the
following week, when our guests will discuss among other things
the new Dragoslav Rankovic film, *The House at Hough End*,
based on a little-known novel by obscure Edwardian novelist
Arthur Alderley. We'll see you all then.'

The tootle of cool jazz was drowned out by Morris's high,

264

mucal snoring. As the night deepened the rain became heavier. It formed a puddle on the layers of kebab wrappers and began splashing against the TV screen, dripping through its plastic cooling slots. Just past midnight there was a fizzle, a strong smell of burning and the screen collapsed to blackness.

Chapter 27

E pushed another pillow under her ankles in an attempt to mitigate the throbbing from her varicose veins. She had avoided them with Molly, but this time they seemed to have arisen almost overnight. Her calves looked like they had been carved from blocks of Stilton. From downstairs she could hear Molly bossing her grandfather about.

'Stop it! Naughty Grandad.'

E's father was chuckling and making plaintive noises of complaint. Inside E's womb the foetus-baby was jigging like a breakdancer. She couldn't get comfortable. Every position came with its own battery of aches and pains. Once again the afternoon nap, which she looked forward to, which, indeed, she craved more than any peculiar or exotic food, was evading her. Why couldn't she sleep when sleep was all she wanted, when she was draped all day with tiredness, varnished by it? It was Morris, of course, she knew. Morris had stolen her sleep. These days it was always Morris. In his absence he was omnipresent, a lingering, clamouring ghost.

She gave up trying to fall asleep. Externally this made no difference. She continued to lie motionless on her parents' spare bed, her limbs, back and breasts curved around her huge belly, hugging it, holding it, like the brim on a bowler hat. Internally, however, it was a relief, a relief to stop chasing this soft, evasive cloud. At last she could relax. Something inside her cracked gently and her tiredness began to seep out of her, leaving behind a peaceful, neutral numbness. She coughed, wriggled a little, then dozed off.

She was woken by someone touching her face. It was a

tentative, quizzical touch like the touch of a blind person, like a dog's first sniff. Morris, she thought. It was Morris, still half-asleep, feeling his way back to wakefulness; warmed up, she imagined, softened by a half-erotic dream. The fingers came and went; she turned slightly to allow them fuller access to her neck. They wisped against her throat and ear. Ummm. They took hold of her nostril and yanked. She opened her eyes.

'Molly, no!' she yelled.

Molly looked shocked, and then with a movement as slow and inevitable as a Central American mudslide she gathered herself to howl.

The noise of her daughter's crying filled E as fully as a moment before she had been filled by the soft emptiness of sleep. She grabbed Molly and hugged her. They rocked woefully back and forth.

It was almost four o'clock. E's mother padded upstairs to offer tea and to prise Molly away with offers of lollipops. E pivoted herself into an upright position, selected one from her depressing range of smocks and made her way downstairs to face another evening.

As she entered the living room her father was standing beside his armchair, holding a small notebook and a pencil. He looked like an over-eager cub reporter.

'There are messages,' he announced.

E yawned and slumped on to the sofa. She still wasn't sure how to respond to her parents' obvious excitement at her return – that she was here, with them, indefinitely, that in her time of need she had actually come back.

'Fire away,' she said. They had an answering machine, but it was never needed. Her father carried his cordless in a calfskin holster: people rarely made it beyond the second ring.

'Morris,' he said. 'He sounded drunk again.'

'I wish you wouldn't say that. What proof do you have?'

'He slurred his words.'

'Some people slur their words, father. That's how some people speak.'

'That's how *drunk* people speak, Eugenia.'

267

'Not only drunk people.'

'Are you suggesting that Morris has aphasia? He mispronounced anathema. He said *athanema*. I heard it distinctly, *athanema*.'

What was she supposed to do now, she wondered, defend him? And what kind of conversation could they possibly have been having which required the use of the word 'anathema' anyway?

'What did he say?'

'Well it was rather hard to follow.' E clenched her jaw. Her father noticed and quickly carried on. 'But it was something to do with money. He seemed to want to apologise for taking money out of your joint account.'

E sat up. 'He promised he wouldn't do that.'

'Yes, well, he said it was an accident.'

'How can you accidentally draw money from a bank account?'

'Quite.' Her father's face remained carefully blank. E pursed her lips. What was going on? Was Morris really trying to hurt her again? Had they reached a point where pain was their only means of communication? She felt, as she felt at least twenty times a day, newly and suddenly bereft.

'He wants you to call him back.'

'I can't call him back,' she said, exasperated. 'I always get the same person, Mahmood.'

'Mahmood, yes, I mentioned him. I don't think it sank in. As I say . . .'

'Yes, I know.' What was Morris doing? It seemed like he was in the midst of a nervous collapse: these idiotic phone calls, the job at Sir Savalot. She braced herself against the wave of sympathy produced by the thought of Morris losing his mind alone in a bedsit in Rumpswick. It crashed over her and spread with a sizzle. Still standing, she breathed deeply and tasted again the familiar blend of anger and protectiveness which had sustained her for the last month. She leaned back on the Dralon cushions.

'Was that the only message?'

'Oh *no*.' Her father seemed mildly offended by the suggestion. He turned a page in his notebook. 'A friend. Nick . . .'

'Nick Kidney?'

'That's the one. Heard you were in town and wondered if you'd like to meet for tea.'

'How did he hear I was in town? How did he get this number?'

'Good lord, how do I know? He didn't say. He sounded rather pleasant though. Have you known him long?'

'Four months. He's an artist.'

'Well there you go. You two must have a lot in common.'

The thought of her father approving of Nick Kidney was ludicrous. Should she mention the pickled penises? It would be a low blow, but she was certainly tempted. Kidney must have got her parents' number from Alison via Gloria, she realised. So he would certainly have heard about Morris. What was sparking his interest now, she wondered? Sympathy or ghoulishness? Not sex surely. She would require a quite elaborate hoisting mechanism even to make the attempt.

'Here's his number.' Her father removed a page from his notebook and gave it to her.

The evening meal was beef stew with seaweed.

'Is this *seaweed*?' her father asked incredulously.

'Kelp. It's a nutritional marvel,' his wife explained. 'You've got twenty-five milligrams of magnesium on your fork right now.'

E's mother was taking the pregnancy very seriously. She had even bought a book, *Eat Yourself Happy*.

'The stew's fantastically rich in iron,' she confided to E. 'I don't think we need to worry about anaemia any more.' She said it, E thought, with the chilling smugness of a hitman after a successful job.

'What's this, Grandma?' Molly waved an oddly involuted piece of meat at them.

'That's a ventricle, sweetheart.'

'A *ventricle*?' E and her father said it together.

Her mother was initially jolted by their reaction, but recuperated quickly.

269

'Of course,' she said. 'Beef heart is an outstanding source of protein. Indeed, organ meat in general has a lot of nutritional advantages.'

E's father shrugged and tucked in.

'I'm sure you're right,' he said. 'Bit on the chewy side though.'

E's mother rolled her eyes forbearingly.

'If you like,' she said to E, 'we could drive to the Mothercare outlet store tomorrow to look at prams. It's next to the Chicken Cavern. We could go there for lunch. Molly would like it – they have a lovely soft play area.'

'Soft play area!' cried Molly still brandishing the ventricle.

'I don't think I can eat this,' said E.

'Are you feeling nauseous? That can be a sign of B6 deficiency.'

'It's not that. It's just the thought of organ meat. I was practically a vegetarian before the pregnancy.'

'I know, and we're so glad you gave it up. It's flirting with disaster if you ask me.'

'We're built to eat meat,' her father opined. 'It's not always pleasant, I admit it, but it's a fact. There was no nut roast in palaeolithic times.'

E ground her teeth.

'How do you know that?' she asked without thinking.

'What?' Her father hammed a look of mortification. 'Archaeological evidence. That's how. There's no archaeological evidence of nut roasts. None.'

'But how do *you* know that?' She was acting like a teenager. It always happened. Their dining room functioned as a kind of time machine.

'Well it's obvious,' he said dismissively.

'Not to me it isn't.'

Her mother grinned and helped Molly with a piece of seaweed.

'I really can't eat this,' E said.

A line of concern appeared on her mother's forehead.

'It's not all heart,' she said. 'There's some liver in there too.'

E put her hand to her mouth. She felt a rolling flush of nausea.

Her mother and father put down their knives and forks and leaned towards her.

'Do you need a glass of water?'

'Perhaps you should go and lie down for a while?'

'Are you ill?'

E shook her head. 'No thanks, the prune juice is fine. I'll just eat the seaweed. I'm sorry.'

'No, I'm sorry,' said her mother. 'I obviously didn't think.'

They ate for a while in silence.

Molly looked puzzled.

'Quiet,' she said.

They grinned at her in unison.

'Wasn't Morris a vegan at one point?' her father asked eventually, sucking at a piece of seaweed that had become stuck in his teeth.

'Yes that's right,' said E's mother. 'Remember when we went to Bangor that time? He wouldn't eat an ice cream, and he insisted on reading every label. It took me the whole afternoon to do a shop.'

'That was just a phase,' E said. 'Morris likes to test himself sometimes. At least he used to.'

'Oh good *God*!' said her father, obviously shocked by a sudden burst of memory. 'We had to have soy milk in our tea.' He pulled a comical face. Molly giggled.

'That can't be good for you,' he continued after a while. 'Apart from anything else, where's your protein?'

'It's a fad, like Eugenia said,' her mother agreed. 'Rather a foolish one if you ask me, but I imagine most people grow out of it. Morris was just a late developer.'

'I didn't say it was a fad,' said E. She had found Morris's two months of veganism a severe irritation, but she wasn't about to admit that now. 'There are good ethical and political reasons for being vegan.'

'But it weakens you,' her father said. 'It must weaken you. Those people you see on the protests for instance. They're always so pale.'

'Which protests?'

'The road protests.' E's father gestured in an easterly direction. 'They were up in the trees for three months trying to stop that bypass at Newbury.'

E rolled her eyes.

'I must say,' her father went on, 'I always thought Morris looked rather pale himself. I know, sedentary occupation and all, but some days he'd look positively gaunt. I used to wonder whether there wasn't something wrong with him.'

'Something *wrong* with him?' said E, raising her voice despite her best intentions. 'So why did you never say anything? Why did you keep this penetrating diagnosis to yourself?'

'Your Dad and I discussed it,' said E's mother, who had lied so often to save her husband's dignity that she no longer noticed she was doing it. 'But at the time we felt that it was inappropriate to say anything. With hindsight, of course, there obviously was something wrong with him. How else can you explain . . .' She didn't finish.

'There is nothing *wrong* with Morris,' E shouted.

Molly stopped chewing her seaweed. Her parents stared at her with puzzled concern. E realised what she was saying – surely there *was* something wrong with Morris, wasn't there? Whether physical or mental. Otherwise why should he, as her mother had suggested, do what he had done? Why would he threaten (because that was how she thought of it, as a threat) the life of the baby?

'I think I need a rest,' she said.

'Yes, of course you do.' Her mother sprang to her feet and started frenziedly clearing the table. Her father sat entirely immobile and then, as Molly watched, began to wiggle his ears.

Back in the spare room, E telephoned Nick Kidney.

'Kidney,' he said.

'It's E. You heard about it then.'

'Morris? Gloria told me he was shagging some woman off the telly.'

'Zoe Cable.'

'Bad timing.'

272

'I'd say so.'

She was thinking about his kitchen, their kiss. Trying not to regret what had happened (or not happened). She didn't need any more mess. Any more complication and she would howl.

'Actually, your dad sounds all right,' he said.

'He's awful.'

'Is he really?'

'Will you please invite me out for a drink?'

'So you're drinking now?'

'No, not really. Lunch then.'

'Tomorrow?'

'Is tomorrow the earliest you can do?'

'For lunch? Tomorrow's the earliest anyone can do.'

'Yes, I suppose it is.' She said it gloomily with the sense that now even the calendar was conspiring against her. 'I'm feeling a bit unhinged. We just had beef heart for dinner, with kelp.'

'Beef heart and kelp? Jesus, there's enough iron in there to build a battleship.'

'I believe that was the idea. My mother's bought a book, *Eat Yourself Happy*. Don't laugh.'

Kidney laughed. Behind him she could hear music, and a clickety-clackety sound of plates? Chairs?

'Am I being too pushy?' she said, 'about the drink?'

There was a pause as if he was actually thinking about it.

'No, not at all,' he said eventually. 'It didn't sound pushy to me. And believe me I know pushy.'

'Thanks.'

Had she ever felt so simultaneously hard and soft, E wondered? Some parts of her were iron-plated, while others . . . She felt if anyone touched her there she would simply pop like a balloon and fart away pathetically into the middle-distance.

'Come to the studio,' he suggested. 'We can order in.'

What sounded like an air-raid warning whirled up the stairs from the dining room.

'I'd better go,' she said. 'Sounds like Molly's involved in a dispute over pudding.'

'Let me guess: prunes? Figs? Something purgative?'

E listened for a moment to the cadence of Molly's heaving wail.

'Sounds like prunes to me,' she said. 'Prunes are non-negotiable for Molly. Prunes are the deal-breaker.'

The wail turned into a staccato bray, like the noise of a winded mule. E got the address of Kidney's studio and then rushed down the stairs backwards, arriving in time to see Molly's bowl of inky and testicular prunes replaced by a large, pre-packaged chocolate sundae. Molly beamed, tears dripping from her fire-engine cheeks like rain after a storm. E's parents glanced up at her guiltily.

'She's been *so* well behaved,' her mother explained. 'And she ate almost all the kelp.'

'Anyway, there's nothing wrong with refined, white sugar,' her father insisted. (E noticed he also had a sundae). 'It's a myth. You know the real cause of tooth decay? Excess fluoridation. We saw a programme about it.'

E ate the prunes.

'Great prunes,' she said unexpectedly.

Her mother glowed.

'They're nature's Prozac. That's what it says in my book.'

Nick Kidney's studio was on the top floor of an old wireworks. As she caught the lift up E was hit by a burst of pre-emptive disappointment. Why was she coming here like this? What could she possibly get from Nick Kidney at this point, right now, that she actually needed? What *did* she actually need? Everything and nothing. That was one consequence of the hard-soft thing. If she needed anything she needed everything – and in the face of that vast, undifferentiated yearning Nick Kidney seemed so detailed and specific, so inevitably slight, that she couldn't imagine that all this, whatever all this was, was possibly going to work.

It was a long, very long, whitewashed room, roofed with safety glass and veined with pipes, pulleys, rails and other industrial impedimentia. Nick Kidney was sitting on an old corduroy sofa, sketching. He stood up and hugged her with his forearms – his hands were black with charcoal. His beard was longer but no more uniform, she noticed; his face looked as tufty as a sand dune. He was wearing paint-marked jeans and a grey vest – his arms and neck and face were muddy brown, the rest of his torso was white. She could see the spiky fringe of his armpit hair, the porky arc of a nipple. She forgot her disappointment.

Splashed open on the sofa were expensive-looking books of Renaissance art. Taped to a nearby wall were several very large, rough drawings of the crucifixion.

'What *are* you doing?' she asked.

'Practising.'

'You practise?'

'Don't tell anyone.'

'What about "sod Cézanne"?'

' "Sod Cézanne" was just a metaphor. People are always so fucking literal. It's seen as a virtue to mean what you say. If you ask me, anyone can mean what they say. You don't need any talent for that.'

Kidney had gone back to his sketch. E was wandering through a maze of stacked canvases, oil drums and cast-off latex body parts.

'I'm not sure you need very much talent to lie either,' she said.

Nick Kidney stopped sketching and looked at her.

'You're thinking of Morris of course,' he said. 'That's different. Morris lied for a reason. At least I imagine he did.'

'What reason though?' she said. 'What possible reason could he have?'

Nick Kidney put down his sketch pad, leaned back, lit a cigarette and handed her a sheaf of take-out menus.

E read them carelessly.

'Isn't it obvious?' Kidney said.

'Obvious?' she paused. 'You mean sex? You think sex is the reason? You think it's really as simple as that? Because if it is I'm more pissed off than I thought I was. I mean *sex*? It's so bloody trivial. It's so minor.'

'Oh I agree,' said Kidney. 'By the way, the pad thai is delicious.' He pointed with a blackened finger. 'Sex is a red herring. The idea that men are driven by their dicks is a myth.

275

And by that I mean a bad myth and not a good one. Do you know what really gets men going? What really pushes their buttons? Shall I tell you? What are you having by the way?'

'Baked potato with cheddar.'

Nick Kidney looked dismayed.

'I thought you were eating yourself happy. That's the culinary equivalent of a call to the Samaritans.'

'Go on.'

'OK, you want to know the secret of the male psyche. This is your second secret and you've only been here ten minutes. Shall I tell you?'

'I wish you would.'

'It's fear.'

'Fear?'

'Yes.'

'Fear of what?'

'Ah well, there it gets more complicated. There you take your pick: failure, success, intimacy, loneliness, death, life – should I go on?'

'Fear?' She thought about it. 'No, fear doesn't make me feel any better. We all have fear.'

'Course we do. Course we do. Existence is terrifying. I mean look, just look.' He scrambled around on the coffee table and came up with a paint-splattered Al Jarreau CD. 'Look at this. *This* could easily outlive me. *Al Jarreau, Live in London* – I find that petrifying.'

'Are you trying to make me feel sorry for him?'

'For Morris? Of course not. Morris is clearly a fuckwit, I mean just look.' He held out his hands towards E as if presenting her to a large studio audience. 'Come on. But to go back to my original point. Lying for a reason as Morris did, the reason in his case, being to escape from fear . . .'

'In your opinion.'

'In my opinion, it's really no better than telling the truth, no better and no worse. They're essentially the same. What I'm talking about is the creative lie, the lie for the sake of art. The leap beyond reality into the unknown.'

276

'That's just cod-existentialism,' she said. 'Nietzsche, Heidegger, Kierkegaard.'

'Don't give it names.' Kidney cried. 'Please, this is not about names. Look, look.' He pointed to her bulge like a sailor sighting land. 'That's real. This,' he waggled his sketchbook, 'is real. Crap perhaps,' he tossed it aside, 'but real.'

E felt herself. She hefted up her bulge and felt it lighten. Like pulling herself up by her own bootstraps.

'What ever happened with you and Gloria?' she asked.

'Me and Gloria?'

'Yes.'

'It was the drug phase. She left me while I was busy taking drugs. I mean, it was several months before I realised she wasn't there anymore.'

'It seems like everyone has a drug phase these days. It makes me wonder whether I missed out.'

'You never had a drug phase?'

'I had a Bacardi and Coke phase – better for your synapses but worse for your teeth.'

'How about Morris?'

'Morris had a vegan phase.'

'Now that's a cry for help, if you ask me. Where's your protein?'

'Do you regret it?'

'The drugs? Not really. The drugs are just a thing. You do it, you stop doing it. People exaggerate the drugs.'

'I meant the divorce.'

'Yeah, that I regret. Not that I ever want to live with Gloria again. It's more the principle. I was brought up Catholic. Marriage is a sacrament.'

'You still believe that?'

'Why the fuck not? What else is there?'

'I think you've said that before.'

'You'll find I have a quite limited set of ideas. I repeat myself a lot, I'm afraid. It's beginning to attract critical attention.'

They phoned for food. It arrived: baked potato, pad thai, carrot juice, beer. They ate on the sofa, listening to Al Jarreau.

The baked potato proved to be perfect – its temperature and consistency, its degree of buttery saturation.

'This is the perfect baked potato,' said E.

'Is it really?' Nick Kidney leaned over for a taste. Their shoulders rubbed. E felt a stomachy shudder break over her uterus like a wave over a seaside boulder. 'You lucky sod,' he said. 'For me this is one pad thai too far.' He untangled one elasticky noodle and scowled. 'I thought it might be. Don't you hate that feeling?'

'You might never be able to eat pad thai again.'

'It could be years.'

'Decades.'

'Familiarity breeds disgust.'

They looked at each other. E took another yellowy, wet-dry bite. She was trying to ration herself, to hold herself back from gobbling.

When the food was over E leaned back and closed her eyes. It was warm in there and chemically fragrant, like a greenhouse; she was tippling on the edge of sleep. Kidney had gone back to his sketching. She could hear the soft shushing of his charcoal pencil. All that stopped her nodding off was a familiar spike of worry that jabbed at her like a loose spring. After ten minutes of unsuccessfully pretending it wasn't there she sat up and opened her eyes.

'But what about Morris?' she said. 'I can't do this on my own. My labour was thirty-two hours last time. There were pools of blood, I mean literally *pools*, you could have paddled in the buggers.' Feeling tears coming, she crossed her arms and tried to suck them back in.

'Stay with me.' He said it casually as though giving refuge to pregnant acquaintances were an everyday thing. 'Why not? It's only, what? A month or so? You can switch to Barts. I'm not doing anything. The rain thing's opening in Frankfurt next week but I'll be there and back in a day. What do you say?' He leaned across the back of the sofa and looked at her with comic eagerness like a dog hoping to finagle a walk.

'That's really a ridiculous idea.' Was Kidney trying to turn this grotesque situation into an opportunity for fun?

'I know,' he said, 'but look at it this way: I have several spare rooms, I have a cleaner and I'm not your mother.'

E was noticeably swayed by these arguments, especially the last one. Kidney was certainly not her mother, yet there was something, as she had noticed before, inextinguishably if incongruently parental about him. Even if everyone else sank, she thought, Nick Kidney would somehow float. He had that buoyant, polystyrene quality; he was, despite appearances, quite clingable. And given current circumstances, she felt more than ready to cling.

'Do you really have a cleaner?'

'Course I do. After the drugs phase, the cleaner phase. That's how it works.'

It was early evening by the time she left. They had talked it all through. Molly would stay in X's room, her parents would babysit now and then, Kidney would cook (no kelp). They would have separate rooms. It was set. That morning there had been nothing, she thought, and now there was this. This nervousness. It had all been so easy. She was used to Morris's habit of making things, anything, hard, of digging down for difficulties and holding on to them whatever the cost. As she walked down Petticoat Lane looking for a taxi, her bulge felt like the prow of an ice-breaker crunching its way casually through what had recently seemed so solid, so capable of squeezing her to death.

Chapter 28

Zoe Cable was becoming a celebrity. She could feel it happening to her gradually, day by day. She felt ever-bigger, ever-weirder. It was like body-building except quicker and less ludicrous. Now people looked at her oddly in the street. They seemed surprised when she spoke or moved. She had been touched by television. Twice weekly it laid its fat pontifical hand on her head. Adam d'Hote was out for six months with a brutal case of the shingles, and Zoe was the stand-in host of *Going Critical*. The studio rumour, started by Zoe herself but now gathering steam, was that Adam would not be back, ever, that shingles was the thin end of the medical wedge, that he had finally gin-and-tonicked himself into the ground.

Zoe now understood how it would be. The Hub was small, but television was big. Television was vast and ineffable and all she had done so far, the purpose of her career to date, was just to bring her to this point, to offer her this vantage. Like Moses on Mount Pisgah she could see the promised land and it was wide-screen and multi-channel. Unlike him, however, she was determined that she would live there herself. She had already passed the daily running of the Hub (and indeed much of the strategic thinking) over to Dirck van Camper. He was the obvious replacement for Morris, plus his appointment had been an easy way of resoftening Donald after the Mordred double-cross. Not that she needed Donald so much any more, but as a long-term enemy he would undoubtedly have been a pain in the arse. Now, with his wheelchair, Dirck was of course big on Disability Studies: it was all supercrips and ableism; he had already spent half the budget on ramps. So be it. Zoe was working on several pilots. She spent her days conferencing with production companies, her evenings, aside from Tuesday and Thursday, beering it up with the creatives. She had a scheme in every pipeline. She was Joan Bakewell with balls.

Did she ever think of Morris? Hardly at all. After their last phone call – on the day of the hearing – she had realised he was badly damaged. And the more she learned about the events in Committee Room L the worse it sounded. He had been half-devoured by Mordred Evans. There was no way she could let him near the Hub after that: he was lamed, weakened. Failure had entered his bloodstream. It was only a matter of time, she knew, before he was cut down entirely. Not that she had been expecting the manner of his departure, not at all. Indeed, when she had first heard about the plagiarism, her interest in Morris had for a brief while been rekindled. That he was not the author of 'Total Mindfuck', which she genuinely admired, was bad, but that he was prepared to quite shamelessly pass himself off as the author of 'Total Mindfuck' and to build a whole new career upon that supposed authorship was really, she felt, rather good. It indicated a certain depth of desperation and will, a willingness – which she couldn't help but respond to – to set aside the claims not only of ethics but of probability. There *was* a darkness in Morris, she had been right about that, but it evidently had a deeper, thicker tone than even she had guessed. This cost her a moment of regret for the way she had cut him loose professionally and amorously (could the two ever really be distinguished?) – and, when it came to regret, a moment for Zoe Cable was an unusually long time. It occurred to her that if she ever again had the opportunity to help Morris Gutman, in a small, non-committal sort of way, she would perhaps take it.

In the event even Zoe Cable, with her talent for prophecy, was a little surprised at how soon and how unignorably such an opportunity arose. That the latest film from Yugoslav wunderkind Dragoslav Rankovic was to be a literary adaptation had been a rumour doing the rounds for some time. Since Rankovic, however, shot all his films on a closed-sound stage in Smederevo using technicians drawn entirely from his own extended family,

281

Zoe had had to wait until the script meeting on the Monday morning of her third week hosting *Going Critical* to learn that Rankovic had chosen, with spectacular peculiarity, to attempt a filmic version of Alderley's little-known and less-loved *The House at Hough End*.

'That's berserk,' she said when asked for her opinion of its suitability for the show. 'Why did he choose Alderley?'

Pam the producer knocked her reading glasses from her hairline to her nose and rifled through her notes.

'It's odd I know,' she said, 'but believe it or not Alderley is huge in the former Yugoslavia. They read him in the schools. Apparently there's a statue in Belgrade, or there was before all that bombing.' She moved her glasses up again. 'But listen, the news is that the film is absolutely masterly. I think we have to do it.'

'There's talk of an Alderley revival,' chimed in Bathsheba, the assistant producer.

'I imagine there is,' said Pam. 'Reprints, tie-ins. He *was* English wasn't he?'

'Whitstable,' said Zoe.

'Well there you go, I can feel an episode of *Arena* coming on. But for now, do we need a boffin? I'm thinking background, no one's heard of this bloke.'

'Do you want the boffin on the panel or just for a snippet?'

'I was thinking snippet, but since Geraint's buggering off to his hermitage for three weeks we could do a twofer. Do you have anyone in mind? I've got one name already.' She looked through her notes again. 'Conrad Underseel.'

Zoe put out feelers, but it proved harder than she had expected to locate Morris. She had not realised how few friends he had, how slender and breakable were his links to the world. She thought of his mother in . . . Doncaster? Sheffield? But directory enquiries revealed an unsurmountable glut of South Yorkshire Gutmans. She had Mabel call his wife, but there was no reply and the answerphone was switched off. His mobile was dead; his Coketown email account had been immediately cancelled. She found her way eventually to Bernard, who was clearing out his

282

office. He was coated in dust. The drawers of his filing cabinet gaped open, their yellowy contents spilling out like the half-chewed breakfast of a toothless OAP.

'Ah,' said Zoe, 'the place where memos go to die.'

Bernard didn't smile.

'It's like being made to dig your own grave,' he said. 'The final fucking indignity.' He stopped sorting and looked at her. 'What brings you to the outer rim anyway? You're not after my office are you?'

She looked around, there was a smell of decaying paperbacks and pigeonshit. The windows looked permanently breathed on.

'Why should I want your office? It's minging.'

'I don't know. To house another of the transportationally challenged? Van Camper's filling every cranny with Tiny Tims. They can hardly muster a full set of limbs between them. It's one leg good, two legs bad out there. They were picketing the front steps the other day – the actual steps.'

'Do you imagine that retirement will mellow you at all, Bernard?'

'Do not go gentle into that good night, Ms Cable. I'll tell you, a gallon of four-star and a packet of Swan Vestas and this place is a smoldering ruin. And I'm *that* close.'

'I'm looking for Morris.'

Bernard started sorting again – WEA pamphlets on Samuel Johnson; Health and Safety Regulations from 1973.

'Morris is all right,' he said.

'You've seen him then? I need his address.'

'You're surely joking.'

Zoe looked at Bernard. He was wearing a cap-sleeved T-shirt and bum-hugging shorts. He had arms like an old woman. She found him amusing but not that amusing.

'Listen Bernard. I slept with him. You told his wife. I'd say that makes us about neck and neck. Now I'm sure you two are lovely together but I'm offering him six hundred quid for a two-minute interview. And if the rumours I hear are true that's a little more than he makes at Sir Savalot.'

'You know about Sir Savalot?'

283

'A box of Ferrero Rocher and Mabel babbles like a coke fiend. I thought you'd know that by now.'

Bernard winced.

'Have you got that address?'

After a minute or two of dusty searching Bernard found his university pocket diary and passed it over to Zoe. She began keying the address into her Palm Pilot.

While she keyed, Bernard pondered.

'Is this interview for the television?' he asked.

Zoe nodded.

'How is Adam d'Hote anyway?'

'They say his liver looks like a spam fritter. I'm viewing flats in Chiswick next week.'

Below Bernard's bum-hugging shorts his pimply hams tightened involuntarily. He looked for a moment pale and friable, as though confected from dust and scraps of ancient paper.

'Did you know we were at Downing together?' he asked. 'He was a year below.'

'Hmm, strange he never mentioned you.' Zoe dropped the Palm Pilot into the depths of her purple Gucci bag. 'I look at it this way, Bernard,' she said with a wink. 'There is a tide in the affairs of man. And surf is definitely up.'

Zoe stood in the communal car park next to the gas-cooker crater – which now, filled with grey rainwater, looked like a brutalist water feature – and looked up at the blasted façade of Hattersley Court. It was, she thought, truly grim. Not that grimness bothered her per se; indeed, certain sorts of grimness she liked a lot (the whole inebriation project testified to that), but Rumpswick, Jesus, it was the most sexless place she had ever seen – it was as though the lust had been sucked out of it with a pump. What was Morris doing here? She felt vaguely annoyed with him for taking failure so literally.

The buzzer was broken but the front door was swinging open anyway. There were children eating dirt and chasing each other with broken toys. The hairy smell of mould, like a large and continuous fart, assaulted her. She wondered for a second whether all this was an elaborate joke by Bernard, but quickly decided he wasn't clever enough for that. She put on her mirrored goggles and lit a cigarette. The walls of the stairwell, gouged and graffitied in languages Zoe didn't recognise, resembled the Rosetta Stone. From the first-floor landing came the sound of Demis Roussos and the smell of boiled beetroot. She shook an empty Pot Noodle carton from the heel of her yakskin boot. Flat nineteen. Morris had better be bloody grateful, she thought. If she had known it was going to be this much trouble she would have stuck with Underseel. She knocked, waited and knocked again. The door opened and she saw half of Morris's face – it looked ghastly. The door closed again.

'If it helps, Morris,' she shouted at the peephole, 'this is business. *Going Critical* needs an interview on Alderley. It's six hundred quid.'

The Al Houja family drifted past. They were all wearing identical trainers.

Morris opened the door again. The second half of his face unfortunately matched the first.

'Have you had a stroke or something? And where's your hair?'

'No one,' he said, 'has *ever* needed an interview on Arthur Alderley. Have you come here only to mock?'

There were smells coming from the bedsit which Zoe preferred not to identify. She looked Morris up and down. He was shoeless, his charcoal suit trousers were torn at the knee, and his white T-shirt was so comprehensively stained that she thought for a moment that it had been tie-dyed. Glancing past him she took in a slice of the bedsit: the floor was cobbled with empty whisky bottles; the bed was a foul swirl of soiled sheets and dried-up food; the kitchenette looked like something salvaged from a wreck. Zoe wasn't sure whether she wanted to go in; she was actually experiencing revulsion.

'Haven't you heard?' she said, trying not to breathe through her nose. 'Dragoslav Rankovic has filmed *The House at Hough End*. There's going to be an Alderley revival. I'm serious.'

Morris stood back and put his hand on his forehead. It was as though he were trying to remember how to think.

285

'That's right,' he said after a while. 'He's big in Yugoslavia. I believe there's a statue in Belgrade.'

'There used to be. They bombed it.'

He nodded as if he may already have known that. He stood for a while in the middle of the bottles and wrappers, just breathing.

Zoe took a small step forward. She noticed the wok in the toilet bowl, the state of the shower. She was used to abjection, it was her stock-in-trade, but this was severe even for her.

'If you're not up for it that's OK, Morris. There's always Underseel.'

'Underseel? That bastard.' Morris snarled. His teeth, Zoe noticed, were the colour of antique pine. She lit another cigarette. She noticed the curtains.

'What is this, Morris?' she said finally. 'A book project? A feature? *Down and Out in Rumpswick? My Life as an Asylum Seeker*? Because that's the only way I can see this making sense.'

He looked blank and slightly fearful.

'I guess not,' she said. She could hear the growl of the Isaiah Berlin Parkway, the rotund whitterings of Demis Roussos.

'I saw you on the TV.' Morris nodded towards the defunct set. Zoe felt an incongruous tingle of pride. 'What did you do to d'Hote?'

'Do to him?'

'I was wondering how you got rid of him. What particular method you used?' As he said it Morris stumbled slightly; there was a second of raucous clinking.

Zoe crossed her arms.

'Don't get shirty with me Morris. All this,' she nodded at the bedsit, 'is you, not me. You made your choices.'

'*Choices?!*' Morris moved suddenly towards her with a fierce, red-faced scowl. His eyes, even the blackened one, bulged like boiled eggs. Zoe thought it possible he would hit her. She had never been hit before, not deliberately. She felt a sudden irrational desire to cuddle her own face, to care for it the way you might care for an abandoned hedgehog or a baby bird. She braced herself. Morris sniffed. He sniffed again.

'What's that?' he said.

'What's what?'

'The smell.'

'Oh that. It's er . . . cumin and formaldehyde. It's new.'

Morris nodded. His face had paled to the colour of an old banana. He dropped on to the bed.

'Could you buy me a drink?' he said.

Zoe's throat was still stiff. She swallowed and shook her head.

'I need to get the train.' She rummaged in the purple bag. 'Here's fifty quid.'

Morris took it with a nod.

'When's the interview then?'

Zoe had forgotten about the interview.

'Next Thursday,' she said. 'We'll pay your expenses. Here's the number to call.' She looked at him again. 'You'll need a shirt. Whatever you're doing with your hair please stop it, and I'll warn make-up about the eye.'

Morris looked up. He was, she thought, the embodiment of failure, and not the glorious, reckless, sexy sort of failure she had been hoping for, but rather the dull, grinding, hopeless and embarrassing Rumpswick kind of failure. The Demis Roussos and boiled beetroot kind of failure. Morris, she realised with a start, was probably the most English person she had ever met.

'Will I see you on Thursday?' he asked.

'Thursday?' She was already thinking how this could be avoided. 'Oh I should think so.'

'We could have that drink.' He smiled. She saw the teeth again.

'A drink. Yes,' she said, 'that's what we could have.' Zoe looked at her egg-shaped digital sportswatch. 'I have to dash.'

Morris was still looking at the fifty-pound note. He stood up suddenly as if hoping for a hug.

A hug? Christ no. The thought that parts of him had actually been inside her was already causing Zoe some dismay.

'Listen Morris,' she was backing rapidly away. 'Buy that new shirt and don't get pissed.'

Morris nodded eagerly.

'Of course,' he said. 'Sorry about this mess by the way. I had

287

people over for drinks last night, and one thing just led to another.'

Zoe nodded and waved. She was dialling for a taxi.

'And you're right about the feature,' he shouted after her, the words echoing around the lavatorial stairwell. '*My Life as an Asylum Seeker* – it's *The Road to Wigan Pier* meets *Seven Years in Tibet*. I'm hoping for the cover of the *Sunday Times* magazine.'

Chapter 29

Zoe's fifty-pound note was Morris's return ticket to the land of Wee Hamish, a land from which he had already endured two days of tormented exile. As soon as she had gone he started searching frantically for his shoes. After five brutally frustrating minutes, he remembered that two days earlier he had thrown them at a honking minicab parked in the communal car park.

Unheedful of the stew of contaminants which paved the stairwell, he dashed down to look for them. For several minutes he jogged and hopped around the perimeter of the communal car park like a down-at-heel morris man.

'Where the fuck *are* you?' He screamed at the missing shoes. He then stopped and stared at the foul coagulating brew which now filled the gas-cooker crater. Without hesitation, with a kind of Arthurian bravery, he dropped to his knees and plunged his arm in up to the elbow. He came up with a shoe. It was laceless and covered with slug-grey silt. He slipped it on to his foot. It was chilly and slick, like the anus of an ancient cold-blooded beastie. After a further period of noxious dredging, Morris gave up on the other shoe and decided to hop. It was less than a mile and the pavements, well, they were covered in broken glass, syringes and dogshit, but there would surely be the odd spot where he could stop to rest. He hopped across the Isaiah Berlin Parkway with some alacrity. With the fifty-pound note in his pocket he felt suddenly buoyant, capable of tremendous feats. As he passed the Albert Schweitzer Primary School his hops became long and confident, like the hops of a triple jumper, like the boings of a disabled-but-still-up-for-it kangaroo. He could all but taste the Wee Hamish now, the memory of its long, thoracic burn filled him with cheer. He hopped past the Rumpswick Scout Hut, the disused Max Beckman carpet showroom, the prefabricated Church of the Ever-Rising Jesus. The Chaudhary Brothers' off-licence was just round the next corner. His right thigh was dense with pain and he was experiencing hot, needle-like jabbings in his knee, but Morris was confident that he could make it. He was a winner. As he took the final bend, however, the sole of his laceless, still-wet shoe caught on the edge of an uneven slab. The shoe came off and Morris, who was still full-throttle in his quest for inebriation, stumbled badly. His unshod foot came down hard on a spike of red translucent plastic – the remnant of a recent nearby car crash. Morris, yelping, tumbled forwards and leftwards, his shoulder, elbow and finally forehead cracked into the dog-toothed edge of a low-lying concrete wall.

Morris was half-concussed and bleeding from several places when Mahmood Chaudhary came out to see what was going on. He looked at Morris's foot and winced.

'You've got a big bit of brakelight in your foot, mate,' he said. 'You want to get that seen to.'

Morris nodded. He pulled the fifty-pound note from his pocket. 'Bottle of Wee Hamish please.'

Mahmood looked at the note then gave it back.

'We don't take fifties, mate. Never have.'

'What?' Morris was not sure why he was having this conversation while lying on the pavement, but he pressed on. 'What do you mean?'

'Too many forgeries. It's not worth it.' Mahmood walked around to get a better view of Morris's shoulder. 'That's a possible dislocation,' he said.

Sheets of dizziness like panes of double-glazing were beginning to separate Morris from the world around him.

Aziz Chaudhary came out for a look too. He was eating an orange.

'Brakelight in his foot and possible dislocated shoulder,' said Mahmood. 'Better phone an ambulance.' Aziz nodded and shuffled back inside. Morris smelt orange, saw slippers. As he

290

waited for the ambulance a crowd of feral youths gathered and stared. He could see the spokes of their mountain bikes, the iridescent flanks of their training shoes. His foot felt not so much painful as plaintive. Aziz Chaudhary returned with a pack of cut-price toilet rolls and tried to staunch the flow of blood. Mahmood was smoking. Morris tried to return his fractured and dissolving mind to the pressing matter of the Wee Hamish. On the one hand, he thought muddily, Zoe Cable's fifty-pound note (crisp, perfumed); on the other, the phlegmatic and risk-averse Chaudhary Brothers. It was a question merely, merely – he felt for a moment that he was bobbing on an ocean of nausea with only *merely*, the word *merely* like a piece of broken spar to keep him afloat. Merely (he felt better now) of getting from A to B. A to B? He wondered what that meant exactly. Urrr. He could smell the sharp tobacco breath of one of the feral youths who was leering into his face.

'I think he's in a fucking coma,' said the youth.

Nonsense, Morris thought, coma indeed. It was merely a question of getting from A to . . . Suddenly the pavement at Morris's feet hinged, his head dropped away and he pivoted bodily into black unconsciousness.

He came to on a trolley in A&E. His pain was comprehensive – he felt like he had been given pain implants, pain patches. A nurse arrived and asked him a lot of questions.

'Are you a nurse or a bloody market researcher?' Morris asked grumpily.

'I'm a nurse.'

'I'm in significant pain.'

She raised her eyebrows, ticked a couple of boxes and gave him two large painkillers. The painkillers were rather good. They had a similar effect to the Wee Hamish but without the disadvantageous taste. A doctor stitched up his foot and eyebrow and relocated his shoulder. The nurse gave him a plate of macaroni cheese and an old copy of the *Daily Mirror*. From outside his cubicle he heard snatches of consultation, diagnosis, condolence. Wails of injury and suffering broke against his floral curtains. He snoozed like a transatlantic yachtsman – anxious but semi-secure – and at some unknown and lugubrious hour they moved him to a ward.

He was woken the next morning by Dr Nono.

'Good morning Mr Gutman,' she said briskly. 'I have questions for you.'

Morris sat straight up; he was amazed by the size and shape of the ward, but most of all by its cleanliness. Dr Nono had black curly hair, olive skin, glasses. She was obviously Greek? Turkish? Italian? Something anyway. And she was terrifically clean too, even cleaner than the ward. Her cheeks shone.

'How exactly did you injure yourself?' she asked suspiciously.

'Well,' Morris thought, 'I was walking and then I fell.'

'Is there a longer version?'

'No that's it.'

Dr Nono looked openly unconvinced.

'Were you under the influence of drugs or alcohol at the time?'

'Oh no,' Morris shook his head. He felt anxious to please Dr Nono, to be on her side.

'But you weren't wearing shoes.' She said it with a sigh like a bored QC, like she had seen it all before.

'Only one,' he admitted.

Dr Nono nodded. Her nod managed to express quite clearly the conclusion that Morris was another self-deluding drunk. Morris noticed this with concern – was he being pushed so quickly away from this new world of cleanliness and light, back into grubbiness and dirt, back to Rumpswick? Back to *himself*?

Dr Nono felt his head. She smelt of wool and talcum powder. She peered into his eyes, took his pulse.

'Headaches, dizziness, insomnia?' she said.

'No.'

'OK,' she turned over the form and noticed a gap. 'What do you do for a living?'

'I'm a lecturer,' said Morris without thinking.

Dr Nono looked at him over her glasses.

'Really?' she said.

'I teach at the university. In the English Department.'

Dr Nono looked quite confused. Morris felt an urge to help her out. Dr Nono, he thought, does not deserve confusion.

'I'm currently doing research on asylum seekers. That's what took me to Rumpswick. It's more journalism than literary criticism, really, but I like to do a little of both.'

'Aren't you teaching at the moment?'

'I'm on sabbatical.'

Dr Nono actually smiled.

'Amazing,' she said. 'So you're writing a book?'

Morris felt quite elated by the success of his lies. 'Well, I hope to work it up into a book eventually,' he said. 'For now I'm just gathering material.'

'It's quite a topic,' she said.

'Yes it is.'

'Well we can discharge you later today. I'll give you a prescription for painkillers and dressings. And we'll set up an appointment to have the stitches out. I'm sure you're keen to get back to your research. I look forward to reading the book when it comes out.'

'I'm on television next week,' said Morris, more to delay her departure, to milk her approval, than anything else.

'Is that so?'

'Yes, in terms of the appointment I mean. I'm away on Thursday. It's *Going Critical*.'

'Uh,' Dr Nono's mouth opened, she looked for a moment quite girlish. 'I love that programme. They're so *clever*. Don't worry about the appointment. I'll sort it out. What will you talk about?'

Morris hesitated a beat, unwilling to lose his so recent gains.

'Arthur Alderley,' he said with some reluctance.

Dr Nono frowned in recollection.

'Mmm. I just read about him in the paper, I think. Isn't there a film out?'

'Yes there is.' There were few astonishments as great in Morris's experience as finding a normal person with a knowledge of Arthur Alderley.

'It sounded fascinating,' Dr Nono continued, unaware of the

293

effects on Morris of her casual enthusiasm. 'I don't read as much as I should, but if I ever got the time. What's the title again? *The House at Hough End*?'

'That's it.'

She wrote the title on her pad. 'I'll try to get a copy.'

'I'll send you one.'

'I beg your pardon.'

'I have lots of copies at home.' (He did.) 'I'll send you one.'

'Well thank you very much.'

There was a moment of conversational stalemate. Morris felt like a man who had been half-pulled from quicksand. He was much better off than he had been, but there was still a danger of being sucked back in. He needed something more.

'The interview was quite last-minute,' he said. 'Zoe Cable just came to see me yesterday.'

'Zoe Cable? Oh I think she's terrific. I liked Adam d'Hote, but Zoe Cable is just so . . . so vibrant.'

Morris agreed. 'Vibrant,' he said. 'And funny.'

'Funny, yes. Do you know her very well?'

'Zoe? Oh yes, I've known her for years. We're like this.'

'Great,' said Dr Nono.

'Great,' said Morris.

'I'll be seeing you when you come back in then.'

'Thank you,' said Morris. (I'm on dry land, he thought. I'm back.)

Dr Nono flicked the curtain aside and turned to leave. She was putting final touches to the form.

'Oh,' she said. 'So is it Mr Gutman or Dr?'

'Dr.'

Morris didn't return to the bedsit. He bought a T-shirt and a pair of flip-flops from the hospital shop and took a taxi back to the house. He was expecting E to be there but she wasn't. He knew she couldn't bear her parents for more than two weeks. Had it been two weeks yet? He didn't know.

Morris checked the cupboard under the sink for Wee Hamish. He made do instead with a bottle of the marginally more

294

expensive but significantly less incendiary Glen MacRuffin. As he wandered through the dusty house the only sounds were the chink of ice (ice!) in his whisky glass and the soft splat-splat of his flip-flops. E had evidently tidied up before she left – the rooms presented themselves with a chilly orderliness as though arranged, he thought, according to a particularly officious school of feng shui.

He taped a Sainsbury's carrier bag to his foot and had a bath. He dipped his head below the surface. His eyebrow smarted; the sour taste of follicles and Lifebuoy reminded him of childhood. He thought of Zoe. She had come back to him, wasn't it as simple as that? The slightly-too-warm water gripped his skin like a surgical stocking. He felt, as always, the dark lure of cavil and complication. He resisted it. He fought it off. He took a large glug of the Glen MacRuffin. She had come back to him. And now the Arthur Alderley revival. It was eerie, if you thought about it, that at his lowest (he recognised that for a day or two there he had been quite low) he should be plucked up like this, rediscovered, set to work once again. He remembered Bernard's promise in the Cro-Magnon Arms that the plagiarism would blow over – the 'long game'. Who would have imagined, though, that the long game would be quite so short?

The following Thursday early in the morning Morris sat in the first-class carriage of the Coketown-to-London Express. He was wearing a jacket and tie, a new blue shirt and a floppy mop-top wig purchased from Shrewsbury and Son on Dunkirk Street. He was still unsure about the wig – he had ummed and aahhed about it for a week, but had decided in the end that there was no other course available. His face was bad enough – it still resembled a topographical map of the Grampians – but his skull! Several of the razor cuts had, despite his best efforts, become infected. They were hot and oozing and around them the hair was returning only in uneven patches. In TV terms it was just unthinkable, plus the mop-top had the advantage, if he arranged the fringe just right, of more or less covering the stitches in his eye. Perhaps they could shoot him from the side anyway.

He opened his briefcase. The train lurched into motion. He began to reread the letter that Bathsheba Ffytche had sent him the day before. According to the letter his interview would form part of a five-minute introduction to the panel discussion of *The House at Hough End*. They would interview Morris for an hour or so in the morning then edit it down and add a voiceover and some graphics. Bathsheba had wished to confirm that Morris was fine with this.

Morris was perfectly fine with this. There was, however, another part of Bathsheba's letter that Morris was not at all fine with, and which he was now rereading with care. It was the casual final paragraph in which she invited Morris to join the panellists for a drink in the green room before the show that evening:

Zoe will be there, of course, along with our regular panellists, Toby Royale and Deirdre Pluck, and our special guest whom I am sure you already know from your academic studies, Professor Conrad Underseel.

The bastard Underseel! Over the previous few days, most of which he had passed on the tartan sofa deep in thought, Morris had decided that what had seemed like abandonment on Zoe's part was actually only a tactical withdrawal. She had needed time, he reasoned – time to secure the Hub, time to make peace with the Crocodile – and now those things were achieved she could reel Morris back in. It would have been reassuring to have known her tactics in advance, but comfort had never been one of Zoe's strengths and, besides, the lack of reassurance was more than made up for by the perks attached to this reunion – the professional rejuvenation, the six hundred pounds, the night (surely not alone) in the luxurious Balmoral Hotel. This suddenly announced involvement of the bastard Underseel, however, had given Morris pause, had cost him several hours of bitter second-guessing. He sensed a plot. He couldn't immediately guess the purpose or mechanics of such a plot, but that, as recent history amply demonstrated, certainly did not prove that no such plot existed.

As the train whizzed through the West Midlands Morris thought hard. Through his window great flat clouds gathered and divided like tectonic plates, fields of aggressively clipped sheep flew past. He turned the alternatives over in his mind. What possible mutual benefit could there be for Zoe and the Bastard in Morris's humiliation? (For if there was a plot he was horribly certain that his humiliation would be the pay-off.) He could think of none. Then, in a sickening reversal of his earlier complacencies, it occurred to him that this might be Zoe's way of ending it forever, of signaling her utter disdain for him and all he stood for. Morris's head dropped into his hands; his fingers encountered the strange, alien tonsure and he felt a strong urge to smash himself into unconsciousness with the fold-up tray-table. It was, he realised, terribly plausible; Zoe was like that. But then again, he remembered, many things were plausible, there were always a multitude of alternatives to fit the facts. It was only power, will, which made one true and the others false. He urgently needed a better, more cheerful option – one that he could believe in, one that he could bring into being.

They passed a dismal scrapyard, the back of a new greenfield estate. Morris ground his teeth. He was thinking with all his might. Beneath the mop-top wig, his head was a bloated whirligig of thoughts and possibilities. Just past Nuneaton it came to him: it was a test of strength. Underseel and the Bangor calamity were the twin roots of Morris's failure and now Zoe was giving him the chance to confront them, to vanquish them, to begin again. That was it. It was obvious. He would prove himself through a long-delayed victory over the bastard Underseel. He would show Zoe who he was, what he was truly capable of. He breathed again. When the trolley came round he ordered a miniature of Wee Hamish and a bag of BBQ Mini Cheddars. He removed from his briefcase a first edition of *The House at Hough End* and began to read it for the twenty-ninth time.

Chapter 30

Zoe Cable was not plotting for or against Morris Gutman. In fact, she had spent most of the previous week trying, not always successfully, to forget all about Morris Gutman and his odoriferous bedsit. She had a row of significant meetings coming up about *Legless in Gaza*, her proposed mini-series on art and inebriation, and the last thing she wanted was the memory of Morris's catatonically gloomy life tugging at her chi. Yes, Morris had got to her, Rumpswick had got to her, a little at least. They had shown her her own edges, the distant line where what she was (which was a lot) ended and something else began. Ordinarily Zoe liked edges, limits. She saw them as a challenge – something to leave behind, something to blur. Indeed she had blurred her own so many times that she thought it likely that they would never come properly into focus again. But Rumpswick was different. She had a feeling that if she leapt over those edges – the edges denoted by Morris's unholy lifestyle – she would land not, as usual, in a realm of heightened and expanded pleasure and possibility, but rather in a land of soul-sucking emptiness. It was not a place of death (death she liked) but of nullity. And Zoe didn't do nullity. Nullity was her parents, nullity was Epsom, nullity was her years of crippling shyness. She didn't go there any more.

When Thursday arrived she determined to see as little of Morris as possible. The meetings had gone well: they started recording the pilot in a fortnight. Morris was behind her. He had always been behind her of course, but now he was so far behind her he was out of sight. They had agreed that Bathsheba would do the interview and that Zoe would be unreachable all afternoon. There would be the green room of course, but that would be absolutely it, and with Conrad Underseel there (Zoe vaguely remembered some aggro between the two of them) Morris, with luck, wouldn't show his face anyway.

Mid-morning, she was sitting in Pam's office discussing strategies for *Legless in Gaza* when Bathsheba knocked and rapidly entered.

'Zoe,' she said. 'Have you *seen* him?'

'Morris, you mean? Is it the black eye? I thought that would be manageable with make-up.'

'There are *two* black eyes. There are also stitches and some kind of wig.'

Zoe closed her eyes. She felt (irrationally, since she had herself invited him) that she was being stalked by Morris.

'Tell Josh in make-up to lay it on thick,' said Pam dismissively. 'We'll fiddle with the lighting. It'll be fine.'

'I really think you should see him,' said Bathsheba.

The phone trilled. Pam picked it up. After a moment she placed her ring-laden hand over the mouthpiece.

'Zoe, could you be a love?' She wrinkled her nose endearingly. 'I've got a Dimbleby on line two.'

Zoe stamped down the corridor.

'You really don't think this is doable?' she said.

'I think he might need prosthetics.'

'Prosthetics?'

'An eyebrow and a nose. It's not normal but that's all I can think of.'

'Bloody hell.'

She knocked on the door of Morris's dressing room and went in. Morris was sitting on the sofa; he looked like someone who had become confused about the date of Hallowe'en.

Seeing Zoe, he stood up with a barmy grin.

'Morris,' she said. 'What the fuck is *this*?'

'This?' he pointed to his face. She noticed he was hobbling and that his left shoe had been slit open from tongue to tip. 'Another accident I'm afraid. I did leave messages.'

Zoe had deliberately not listened to them.

'Is that a wig?'

'This? Yes it is. Ludicrous I know but I've had some complications with my scalp. I should really be on antibiotics, but you know what it's like getting an appointment with a GP. It's just a stop-gap. I'd happily wear a different one, or indeed nothing at all.'

He began to unpeel a sideburn.

'That really, really won't be necessary,' said Bathsheba pre-emptively.

Zoe was speechless. Was this a deliberate attempt to embarrass her? She swiftly decided it was. It seemed Morris was more gutsy but significantly less sensible than she had once imagined.

'We'll have to cancel the interview,' she said magisterially. 'The state of your face just makes it impossible to continue.'

'No, no, no,' said Morris. He limped forward rapidly and placed his hand on Zoe's elbow. 'I'm absolutely ready to do the interview. I'm prepared. The face is unfortunate, I admit, but Bath . . . er.'

'Sheba.'

'Bathsheba mentioned prosthetics. We could do prosthetics or even a stand-in. Why not? I have something important to say.'

Zoe hardened herself. Yes, she had made a rather large mistake, but no, there would be no more repercussions.

'We'll still pay you,' she said.

'That's not it.'

'It *is* it.'

'No it isn't.'

Bathsheba stepped in. They had been standing too close, and the hand on the elbow had been a giveaway. Any idiot could have guessed that they had once slept together. Zoe stepped back.

'Why don't we just go to make-up?' Bathsheba said steadily. 'See what Josh has to say.'

*   *   *

300

Conrad Underseel was the most pompous man that Zoe Cable had ever met. They were introduced in the green room later in the day by an eye-rolling Bathsheba.

'Professor Underseel,' Zoe said, shaking his hand. 'I got quite a kick out of *Arthur Alderley: Portrait of a Confused Young Man*.'

'And your name is?' said Underseel.

'Zoe Cable,' repeated Bathsheba.

'Ah. And you are the producer?' He was still gripping her hand.

'No. I'm the presenter. Have you not watched the show lately?'

'I live, I'm afraid, without the benefit of a television set. I don't approve, you see.'

'Of television?'

'That's right.' He finally released her hand. 'Judging from my undergraduates its effects on the brain are quite . . . catastrophic.'

He said the last word as if it was a punchline, as if he expected a burst of applause.

'Yet you've decided to join us anyway,' Zoe said. 'How lovely.'

'Occasionally it is necessary to sup with the devil.' He grinned as if this too were a winning remark. Bathsheba's mouth dropped open. 'I'd like to be clear, Ms Cable,' continued Underseel without pause. 'My purpose in appearing on your programme is not to promote Arthur Alderley but rather to protect him.'

'They say the Alderley revival is already underway,' said Bathsheba, who had quietly regathered herself.

'Yes, that is my fear, and I would like to do what I can to stop it. In my experience popularity is universally corrosive.'

'You'd rather no one read Alderley then?'

Underseel offered a pained smile.

'The horrors of misinterpretation are hardly to be exaggerated, Ms Cable. If there is a paperback, God alone knows the kind of people who might get their hands on it.'

301

Underseel was wearing a beige safari suit and a purple paisley cravat. He seemed to have brushed his eyebrows especially for the occasion.

'So the purpose of scholarship, as you see it, Conrad, is to stop people reading books?'

'Certain people, Ms Cable, certain books. I believe in vocational training, you see, and so very few people,' he leaned forward and brushed Zoe's arm with his fingertips as if to honorarily include her in this privileged number, 'have the vocation of scholarship.'

'Have you watched the film?' asked Bathsheba.

'Ah, the film, yes.' Underseel turned aside and cast a disinterested glance at the buffet table. 'But I would prefer to reserve my comments on *that*, until the programme begins. I believe we have an hour or more.'

Bathsheba nodded. 'Please help yourself to refreshments. There's wine.'

'Wine, ah.' Underseel's cakey eyes twinkled as he scanned the room with sudden vim. Bathsheba indicated the ad hoc bar and Underseel, who seemed to have forgotten Zoe Cable completely, toddled over and began reading labels.

'He's a total wanker,' said Bathsheba when Underseel was more or less out of earshot. 'Why does Arthur Alderley attract such freaks?'

'Pam's gone too far this time,' said Zoe. 'I'm all for eccentricity, but this guy's Mussolini in a toupee.'

'You should have seen the interview,' said Bathsheba.

'The interview?'

'Morris Gutman.'

'Oh.' Zoe had the uncomfortable feeling that Bathsheba, who had previously been satisfyingly awed by Zoe's combination of coolness and learning, was now rather milking her privileged if vague knowledge of Zoe and Morris's previous intimacies.

'Josh patched up his face and they buggered about with the lighting; to be honest I think it looks like *Nosferatu*, but Pam says it's OK.'

'She does?'

'Yes, but then I think she's looking ahead now anyway. This Dimbleby thing's in the pipeline for her.'

'I didn't know that.'

'Oh yeah. But anyway, you should have heard Gutman go on. I asked him why Arthur Alderley might appeal to a contemporary readership, and his answer lasted twenty minutes. No one could understand a word of it. At one point he started madly quoting Firenze Beach, from memory. Pam's salvaged something in the end, but Jesus.' She shook her head.

Zoe swallowed and lit a cigarette.

'Sorry Zoe,' said Bathsheba with a quite obvious and quite maddening tone of pity. 'I don't mean to be rude. I know he's a friend of yours.'

'That's OK,' said Zoe. 'Do you happen to know if he's coming?'

'Here? Oh yes. He's very keen to meet everyone. He asked me for directions several times.'

'You stressed that Underseel would be here?'

'That only seemed to make him keener.'

Toby Royale entered breezily, trailing a make-up girl and laughing into a mobile phone.

'Oh God,' said Conrad Underseel, who was sampling an Australian red, 'a mobile telephone. How ghastly.'

Toby Royale looked at him.

'Toby Royale,' he said, sticking out his hand.

'Conrad Underseel. Are you a stagehand?'

'I'm a panellist.'

'Ah. You see I don't watch.'

'Television? Neither do I mate. I'm on so much it's hardly worth it.' Toby laughed.

'Judging by my undergraduates,' Underseel continued imperviously, 'its effects are quite . . . catastrophic.'

Bathsheba had left to hustle up Deirdre Pluck, who was compulsively late; Zoe was eating an egg roll and concentrating on her seventh chakra. She could already feel an orb of warm white light emanating from her loins, growing, flattening until it

303

encircled her like a neon hula-hoop. She had had more than enough of this. It was time to crush a few fingers.

Toby sidled over. 'We've got a right one there,' he said, nodding at the still-glugging Underseel.

'I say we gang up on him,' said Zoe. 'Do him in.'

Toby wobbled his jaw mischievously. 'Fine by me, but Deirdre won't go for it. You know her, she's all donkey sanctuaries and open dialogue.'

'She will when she hears him speak,' said Zoe. 'He may dress like Alan Whicker but he talks like Enoch Powell.'

'Sweet.'

Bathsheba returned with Deirdre Pluck, who seemed as always to be looking for her reading glasses. She noticed Zoe and Toby. 'Oh God,' she said after the hugs. 'Slim pickings this week, isn't it? I mean the Alderley film's bad enough – there are no strong women in it *at all.*'

'Isn't there a chambermaid?' said Toby. Deirdre poked him.

'The opera I could just about manage. But, Zoe, why do we have to do computer games? *Can't* you speak to Pam about it? At my age the thumbs just aren't there. It's embarrassing.'

'I did mention it,' said Zoe, untruthfully, 'but I think her mind's elsewhere.'

'The Dimbleby thing you mean? Yes I heard about that.'

Zoe frowned despite herself. Deidre peered about. 'Gosh, is that Conrad Underseel?' she said. 'I haven't seen him for *years.*' Deidre wafted across. There was a flurry of greeting.

Toby winked and chuckled. Zoe cornered Bathsheba near the melon chunks.

'Where's Morris?' she said.

'Gutman? He's on his way. Did you and he have a thing?'

Zoe moved half a step closer to Bathsheba. Bathsheba's denim-skirted bottom grazed the crudités.

'Time, Bathsheba,' Zoe said in a fierce whisper, 'is a great destroyer. And contrary to misogynistic rumour, male beauty is not impervious to its ravages. Orson Welles, Marlon Brando, Muhammed Ali – you've seen the pictures?'

304

'Does he have Parkinson's?'

'Morris? No, but there's a continuum. It's grim I know, pathetic perhaps, *funny* even.' Here she paused to allow Bathsheba to writhe a little. 'But I try to think of what he was, not what he is.'

Chapter 31

All afternoon, Morris had been sitting in the BBC bar sipping Wee Hamish and meditating on the splendidness of his interview. He had given Alderley a theoretical makeover, he had brought him up to date, he had spruced him up as he had never been spruced up before. Zoe was bound, he thought, to love it. It was, after all, aimed directly at her. And, almost as importantly, Conrad Underseel would hate it. He would see it, Morris hoped and expected, as a personal insult, a slight which would have to be revenged. As he limped down the corridor to the green room, the prostheses, which he rather liked, still glued like translucent leeches to his face, Morris felt gladiatorial. The bastard Underseel and his recherché neo-humanism were going down at last.

As he firmly pushed open the door to the green room, however, and immediately and without fair warning saw Underseel pouring a goblet of red wine and whooping it up with Deirdre Pluck, Morris was struck by a violent combination of awe and dread. He felt all of a sudden tiny and unmanned, as if his puberty had been rudely ripped from him. While Underseel, in contrast, whom he had not seen or spoken to (except in recurrent nightmares) for six years, loomed – in his beige safari suit, his purple cravat, his triangular toupee – utterly unaffected by the passage of time, as large and immovable as the pyramids of Giza. Morris felt a strong urge to run, or at least hop, away and never return. He gripped the anodised aluminium doorknob as though it were an amulet against his fear. He saw Zoe. She was dressed in black silk pyjamas embroidered with images of Muffin the Mule. Her hair had been goaded into a bleach-tipped aileron. Morris sniffed – dandelion and swarfega. She was looking at him. It was a look, he decided, of trepidatious anticipation. She surely knew what was about (if he could only release his grip on the doorknob) to occur. He thought of the harsh slenderness of her hips, the sacred point where her tattoo of Jacques Derrida met the valley of her bottom. By a gargantuan effort of will, Morris pulled himself into the room. He limped across the carpet as though it were the bed of a deep, malicious ocean.

'Professor Underseel.' He offered his hand. Underseel looked at him, opened his mouth, closed it, and looked at him again.

'Is it . . . Morris Gutman?' he said eventually.

'Yes it is.' Morris stuck out his hand still further. Underseel shook it.

'Have you had reconstructive surgery Morris?'

'No, it's the make-up from my earlier interview. You've heard about my earlier interview I presume.'

Morris imagined that everyone was looking at him now, that the whole room, indeed the whole television centre, was hanging on his words.

'Have you met Deirdre Pluck?'

Deirdre Pluck unsqueamishly kissed him.

Morris swallowed.

'Morris is a student of mine,' Underseel explained. 'I might say former student except I prefer not to think of the apprenticeship of a scholar as bounded by the brief period of Ph.D. Three years really.' He was talking to Deirdre Pluck now. 'It's hardly enough for a decent annotated bibliography.'

Deirdre chuckled. 'Oh Conrad,' she said. 'You're such a terrible old fart. You always were, even when you were twenty-five.'

Underseel faked astonishment. Morris got a strong and horrible sense that he and Deirdre Pluck might once have had a thing.

'Now Morris,' Deirdre went on, 'you're not still working on dull old Alderley too are you?'

Morris sensed an opening. 'No,' he said, 'my interests are a great deal broader now. I recently finished a book on physicality and ethics.' Deirdre raised her eyebrows encouragingly. 'But I still dabble in Alderley occasionally, more for amusement than anything. Hence my earlier interview.'

'There you go Conrad,' said Deirdre coyly. 'Someone seems to have escaped your reactionary clutches. Physicality and ethics sounds fascinating. Do you know Firenze Beach?'

'Yes,' purred Underseel cheerily. 'I obviously gave Morris rather too long a rein.' Was it the wine, Morris wondered, or the presence of Deirdre Pluck that was producing this unwelcome mellowness? He glanced at Zoe, who seemed not to be watching at all.

'Firenze Beach? Yes I do,' he said. 'Indeed, in my earlier interview, I applied her work on dismay to Helga in *The House at Hough End*.'

'Really?' said Deirdre. 'Helga. Do you find that works?'

'It may, it may not,' said Morris, staring fixedly at Underseel. 'But then really, in the end, who cares? It's all just words isn't it?'

'Words?' said Underseel.

'Signifiers,' said Morris. 'Meaning is just a side-effect of power after all, don't you think?' He was looking now at Deirdre, but he was still concentrating entirely on Underseel.

'Well Firenze, who I love dearly, does go a little far for me,' said Deirdre. 'I'm antique enough to believe in truth and falsity, emancipation and oppression.'

'Useful fictions, I admit,' Morris replied. 'But it's important not to confuse the heuristic with an absolute, don't you think? It may be helpful to describe some things as true and others as false, so long as we don't start believing they really are.'

'Well of course I'm against dogmatism,' said Deirdre. 'Who isn't?' They both glanced momentarily at Underseel. 'But it's the baby and the bath water again isn't it? If you insist, as Firenze does, that everything is just language, even the body, and language is just an effect of power, then what do you have left to build on, to inspire?'

'Moments of transgression,' said Morris. 'Aporias, lacunae.'

'No one ever started a revolution with an aporia, Morris, my love, you need ideals.'

'Well,' interrupted Underseel loudly. 'Enough of this sophomoric chit-chat. This Tasmanian red is surprisingly palatable. Should I pour you a glass, Morris?'

'Yes please,' said Morris, who was already noticing the painful if familiar signs of the Wee Hamish departing his system. 'But I would like to say, *Conrad* . . .' Morris swallowed. Underseel reddened violently; this use of his first name by a student of whatever age or status was, they both knew, entirely unprecedented. It was for Underseel the procedural equivalent of a goosing. 'There is nothing sophomoric about the issues Deirdre and I were discussing. These questions, *Conrad*, are central to contemporary literary studies.'

'I am sad to see,' said Underseel, 'that, judging by your enthusiasm for the half-baked blatherings of Ms Beach, since leaving Bangor you have fallen among theorists. I must say that the tendency of such people to parade their own educational and mental limitations would be merely vulgar if it did not also, through the sheer volume of its platitudinous bellowing, threaten to distract attention from work of real value. When you studied with me I believe I made it clear that the road of scholarship is narrow, winding and, above all, long. If you have chosen, as it seems you have, to ride instead the tawdry escalator of literary fashion, then you have squandered not only your own, admittedly rather small, talents, but also, much more importantly, my own precious time and energy. I should evidently have chosen better.'

Deirdre Pluck raised her eyebrows in alarm and then attempted a diffusing wink. Morris adjusted his wig and ran his tongue slowly along the uneven line of his front teeth.

'Yes, Professor Underseel,' he said after a moment. 'I remember your homilies on scholarship very well. In the years since we met, they have stuck in my mind and I've always used them as a sort of yardstick.' Underseel's face softened slightly in anticipation of a climb-down. Morris glanced over at Zoe, who was still pretending not to look at him. 'Yes indeed, whenever in life I am confronted by a particularly tedious bore, I bring them immediately to mind and I can console myself with the fact that whatever this person is saying, whatever hellacious depth of self-serving vacuity he or she is currently sounding, it is at least not as bad, not nearly as bad, as one of Professor Underseel's disquisitions on scholarship.'

Deirdre Pluck gasped. Underseel's nostrils flared like loon pants. His face was pale on the surface with dark, subcutaneous streaks of fury. It looked like a well-used whiteboard.

'When Morris first arrived at Bangor,' Underseel had turned suddenly to Deirdre and was addressing her with intense and unswerving casualness, 'I thought that, although rather primitive, he might be polished up. I see now that I was quite wrong about that. Such base material cannot be improved. There are certain ingrained crudities that we simply cannot reach. And perhaps, on consideration, it is really kinder not to try. The results after all,' he nodded at Morris, 'can really be such a horrible botch.'

Morris noted with alarm that Zoe was about to leave the room. She was chatting with Pam and heading definitely doorwards.

'Zoe!' he shouted out. 'Zoe!' Everyone in the room except Zoe looked at him.

'Zoe,' he said again. She turned.

'Yes Morris.'

He reached out and pulled her over.

'I'd like your opinion about something,' he said. 'You see, I was just explaining to Professor Underseel, Conrad, here, that I find his views on scholarship, well, actually on more or less everything, both idiotic and repellent. That indeed, as an academic, a Ph.D. supervisor and a human being he represents for me the very acme of contemptibility. And *he* was explaining to Deirdre that he regards me and people like me (I'm not quite sure what he means by that, but I imagine Rotherham comes into it somewhere), anyway, me and people like me, as both unworthy and incapable of education. And I was wondering, erm, where you stood on that?'

'On what?' said Zoe.

'On the question of me and Underseel?'

Zoe looked at him. It was not the kind of look Morris had

310

been hoping for. If he was going out on a limb, he might have described it as cool, but really, more conservatively, it was a sneer.

'*Going Critical* is a programme which thrives on robust differences of opinion,' said Zoe. 'We're certainly pleased to have both of you here today. Now, if you'll excuse me.'

'Hold on a second,' said Morris. He wasn't about to let her go. He wasn't about to abandon his train-bred paradigm, he was convinced he could still make it work. He could still squeeze it into the slot marked truth.

'Have a drink. Underseel's been banging the gong for the Tasmanian red.' He forced a glass into her hand. Zoe immediately leaned past him and put it back on the bar.

'No thanks, I'm rather busy. Don't you have a train to catch Morris?'

Morris was stunned by her disingenuous.

'I'm at the Balmoral,' he said with a nudge.

'Are you really?' Zoe said emptily. 'I had no idea we were so generous with expenses.'

'Have you seen my earlier interview?' he asked.

'No, but I've heard about it.'

'Then I'm sure you've heard it's a powerful brew. I recommend you show it to him,' he nodded at Underseel, 'as soon as possible. That is, if you really do enjoy a robust difference of opinion.'

'No, what I heard Morris,' said Zoe with sudden vehemence, 'was that your answers were unintelligible, and that you looked like Klaus Kinski on a bad day.'

All around him, in octophonic surround sound, Morris heard the sudden, shattering clink of a breaking paradigm. *Klaus Kinski?*

Underseel stepped forward with a forbearing grin.

'Ms Cable,' he said. 'Since Mr Gutman is obviously incapable of apologising for himself, I will apologise for him. I might charitably assign the extraordinary lack of discretion and judgement that he is displaying to the effects of alcohol on a personality which is at best wobbly.'

311

'Wobbly? What the fuck are you talking about?' said Morris.

'Yeah whatever,' said Zoe.

'I would, however, very much wish to emphasise,' Underseel continued without pause, 'that his views and behaviour are by no means representative of mainstream Alderley scholarship. Indeed the majority of Alderley scholars would find them quite atrocious.'

'I thought you *were* the majority of Alderley scholars,' said Zoe.

'I am yes, so I know whereof I speak.'

Zoe Cable rolled her eyes.

She rolled her eyes, Morris thought, the way a teenager might roll her eyes at a hopeless but well-meaning parent. But Underseel was not a hopeless but well-meaning parent – he was a source of evil, a spring of darkness. Six years ago he had shattered Morris's life, poleaxed his career, and now, *right now*, he was doing it again. He was humiliating him in front of Zoe Cable. Zoe Cable who was herself, he now realised, a bastard too, but at least a thrillingly humpable bastard, a bastard who he yearned for with every fibre of his painfully sobering body.

Zoe was turning away; Underseel was lolloping over to Toby Royale; Deirdre Pluck was investigating the sushi. It was over for them, he realised. *He* was over. All they would remember of him, if they remembered anything, was the slight embarrassment, a small, hardly noticeable hillock in the gorgeous flatness of their lives. Morris felt himself receding rapidly. He would spend the night alone; he would return to Coketown; he would never appear on television again; he would eke out a living giving paltry lectures for Trident Education; he would drink himself first into chronic illness, then into an early and under-resourced retirement, then eventually, after years of miserable coping, he would die. Alone. That was it. That was all of it. And there was nothing he could do.

A sudden thought occurred to Underseel. He turned round slowly and walked back over to Morris.

'I just remembered where I recently read your name,' he said.

'The *Times Higher Education Supplement* had a very interesting piece on plagiarism. I think, in the light of your conviction, it would be only proper for the university to carefully review your Ph.D. for evidence of malfeasance. If there are any irregularities, you would of course be stripped of your doctorate.' He grinned.

Morris leaned back on his heels and stared for a second at the grey polystyrene ceiling panels. He then, ignoring the scream of pain from his wounded left foot, swayed forward on to his toes, bent his knees, and with a sudden upwards and outwards motion, broke Conrad Underseel's nose with one well-aimed thump of his wig-cushioned forehead.

Underseel went down like a leaky dirigible. There was a hubbub. Deirdre Pluck shrieked and dropped her sushi. Toby called for ice. Bathsheba gathered towels. There was much toing and froing. The stricken Underseel moaned like a child with toothache. Blood was oozing from his sausage fingers, quite a lot of blood. It was dripping on to the purple cravat and beige safari suit, it was spotting the pale grey carpet.

Morris was panting, the room was bobbing up and down in time with his gasps. The skin has a memory, he thought. He could still feel on his forehead the precise and gentle give of Underseel's nose. Zoe was looking at him now. She seemed frightened; he reached out to reassure her.

'Don't touch me, you fucking animal,' she said.

Pam phoned for security.

'It was a moment of madness,' Morris explained. He was lying. It wasn't. It was a moment of rare coherence, a moment when for once everything had pointed in the same direction: heart, body, mind. Hatred could do that, he supposed. Hatred was a superb organiser.

Zoe was still standing there. Her head was not so much shaking as shuddering. Was she angry?

'I know what you are trying to do to me, Morris,' she said, 'but you'll fail. You're not big enough. You're not even half big enough.'

'I was trying to bring something into being,' Morris explained. 'To go beyond the binaries.'

313

'Which binaries would those be exactly? Sane and lunatic? Because I'll tell you, if that's the case you've gone straight to lunatic. You know there's an important difference between deconstruction and just fucking things up.'

'I thought you liked lunatic,' Morris said. 'I thought lunatic was what you went for.'

'No Morris, I go for transgressive, I go for alarming, I don't go for demented. Demented is where I draw the line.'

'But lines are made to be broken, Zoe.'

Morris was wondering whether there was still a chance for him and Zoe, the two of them, whether if they could get beyond these immediate difficulties – the head-butt, the anger, the imminent arrival of security – they might rediscover something truer and deeper between them.

'Fuck off, Morris.'

Perhaps not. This was really it then. *It*. Although *it* didn't sound quite right. *It* was too substantial. If *it* was a thing, a weight, a presence, what had occurred, was still occurring, was really *its* long, slow withdrawal, the accelerating failure of *it*. He was entering – he could sense it in the throbbing of his sutures – an *it*less phase, a phase of pure and ferocious absence. He wondered how long he had before the scorching adrenalin rush of the head-butt wore off and the dull brutal pain of fucking things up entirely with Zoe kicked in. An hour? Less? However long or short, it was important, vitally important, he knew, to fill every minute of it with Wee Hamish.

Chapter 32

E and Kidney were watching television. They were slouched on his snaky purple sofa. He was rubbing her feet. E liked Kidney to rub her feet; indeed E liked Kidney to rub almost any part of her: neck, shoulders, back, calves, knees – you name it, it was pleasant. No, it was more than pleasant, it was exciting. Initially, when the rubbing first commenced, she had been surprised to find herself still capable of excitement. She had thought it had been washed out of her by the rigmarole of adultery and separation, but no, there it was, that energising inner tickle.

'Mmm,' she sighed and shifted her position. 'When are you going out?' she asked. Kidney always went out.

He looked at his watch. It was as big as a hamburger and digital.

'Midnight. I'll have a couple of beers at the Pantagruel.'

'Is that fun? Beers at the Pantagruel?'

'Not really, but it's what I do. Other men have allotments.'

'Other men have girlfriends.'

He continued rubbing.

'I wouldn't want the howls of pleasure to disturb your sleep.'

'Are there *always* howls?' she asked.

'Oh, always.'

'It sounds rather violent.'

'Hey lady, I pickle penises for a living, what do you expect?'

'I thought your penis-pickling days were behind you.'

'They are but I can't entirely shake them off. In the eyes of the public it's definitive. I'll always be the pickled-penis guy.'

'I imagine that has some disadvantages. With the ladies I mean.'

Kidney shrugged.

'This is London. There are pros and cons.'

'Can you do something with my knee? I've been experiencing shooting pains.'

E hitched up her cheesecloth smock; Kidney shuffled closer and started rubbing.

'What about Ghee?' she said. 'Ghee is stunning.'

'Ghee is a former Miss Calcutta. She's so physically beautiful it's not even funny.'

'You make it sound like a problem.'

'It's a distraction. I mean it's not normal, really, it's freakish. She has no bad angle, I've looked for one. It isn't there. It's like fucking an alien.'

'So you've tried?'

Kidney coughed. The light was poor, but E thought she saw the rather endearing signs of reddening.

'Ghee has a thing for artists.'

'She's a collector.'

'You could say that.'

'I don't blame her.'

'What do you mean?'

'Artists. I've met your friends. They're exciting.'

'It's a job.'

'No it's not. You know it isn't.'

'No, you're right, it isn't.'

Kidney's fingers were short and spatulate. They gripped and squeezed her knees like twin anemomes trying to attach themselves to a slippery rock. His thumbs described soft, soothing semicircles on her lower thighs.

'Artists are sexy,' she continued. 'I know it's a generalisation.'

'That's OK,' he said. 'I like generalisations. In fact, I like everything about them.'

'I know you do,' she said. 'I know . . .'

Something was happening to E's lungs. Already shunted up by her ever-expanding uterus, they seemed now to have shrunk even further. Her breaths were coming shallow and sharp like the puffing of a small locomotive. A certain weight within her, a

316

dark mass she had assumed was unshiftable was, she realised, beginning to shift. She thought strangely of men pulling lorries along with their teeth; you just had to get them going, break the force of gravity. After that, after that – she felt a spasm of relaxation – things became easier.

'What about the ugly artists?' said Kidney.

'There are no ugly artists,' said E, trying to recompose herself. 'I've never met an ugly artist.'

'Christ, I'll have to introduce you to some. There's a whole colony out in Clerkenwell. They're hideous.'

'What about their work?'

'Exquisite. It's a Dorian Grey sort of thing. Is that OK for you?'

E blinked. His fingers, she felt certain, were now roaming more widely, more freely than she had ever expected . . . Imagined . . . Hoped for . . . ?

'That's fine,' she said. She heard herself swallow – it sounded frail and a little pathetic. She hoped Kidney hadn't heard.

The pretence of the knees was over now. If pretence was the right word. If that's what it had been. Had it? Hadn't it? She pulled the smock up further. She couldn't see what was going on. Kidney had disappeared like a moon behind the stretch-marked planet of her bulge. All she could do was feel. Feel the removal of, oh God, her vast Mothercare maternity briefs. ('Brief,' as her mother had put it, 'they are not'.) If Kidney's ardour could survive the tortuous trek past her swollen ankles, varicose veins, painful knees and now vast flapping granny pants, he richly deserved, she felt, whatever he could get.

Oh. It was happening already. It was happening *right now*. She further opened her knees, adjusted herself. She wanted to be helpful, wanted this to work.

After a number of quite blissful minutes, Kidney's head popped up.

'Is this going to work?' he said.

'Emotionally or logistically?'

He shrugged.

'Yes and yes,' she said. 'Hold on a second.' She pulled off her

317

smock and unhooked her bra. Her breasts, oh God they were huge, but not, she felt sure, in a good way. Perhaps it was best, she thought, not to actually think of this as sex, but rather as something similar, a cover version of sex.

'Um,' she looked around as if selecting a place to pitch a tent. Kidney followed her gaze.

'Can I help at all?'

'No. I mean yes, of course you can. I just have to find a good spot.'

She found one, but it involved some rearranging of the furniture. 'Sorry to be so workmanlike,' she said.

Kidney stripped off: the iridescent Bermuda shorts, the 'Free Nelson Mandela' T-shirt, the hamburger watch. His ardour had clearly survived.

His body, she noted fondly, as he shuffled into place, was as tufty as his face. He looked, overall, like a badly mown lawn.

The only light in the living room was from the muted TV. It flickered like the surface of a stream over the sofa cushions, over Molly's scattered, half-clothed dolls. E could still smell dinner – cumin, Marmite, frizzled sausage.

The phone rang. They ignored it. Cars went past. E forgot for a moment who she was. She was just a body with another body inside her, and then another body inside her. It was both complicated and simple. Too complicated, too simple. She stopped trying to think.

There was a thump as Kidney keeled over on to the carpet.

'Blimey,' he said.

E flopped beside him. There was that smell.

'You forgot to howl,' she grinned.

'No, *you* forgot to howl.'

She kissed his neck, his clavicle, she had always liked that bit. It was semi-public. Semi-public was nice. She felt full of smiles. She giggled for no reason.

'The baby's moving.'

Kidney watched it move.

'It's like a shark,' he said. 'Like a submarine. That moment before they break the surface.'

318

'That's right,' she said.

He found a blanket and a beer. E took a sip. She turned up the volume on the television. It was *Going Critical*. She started to turn it off then decided not to.

'That's her,' she said. 'Zoe Cable.'

'Mmm,' Kidney looked. 'Should I make denigrating comments about her appearance?'

'I think that would be helpful.'

'So what's the deal with that hair?' he said. 'It should be bolted to the back of a Ford Fiesta, not attached to someone's head. Does she moonlight in a Flock of Seagulls tribute band? And the Muffin the Mule thing doesn't work, it's too studied. She's trying much too hard, the whole persona reeks of urgency and effort. To me she looks strained, terribly strained.'

'And utterly false,' suggested E.

'And utterly false, yes,' agreed Kidney. 'And she's much too thin.'

'Whoa!' said E.

'*Gaunt*, I mean,' Kidney corrected himself. 'Gaunt and un-healthy.'

'She actually does look a bit gaunt,' said E. 'I wonder if something's wrong.'

'What could be wrong?'

E shrugged. She cuddled up to Kidney. His body felt new and unexpected, like something she had just taken out of its box.

'That bloke next to her doesn't look too chipper either,' said Kidney. 'Look at his eyes.'

E looked.

'Bloody hell,' she straightened up. 'It's Conrad Underseel.'

'Who?'

'Conrad Underseel. Morris's Ph.D. supervisor. He's really dreadful. He topped my most-hated list for three years in a row.'

'You have a most-hated list?'

'Beware – it's constantly updated.'

'Does he always look as bad as that?'

'Actually no. He's terribly puffy isn't he? I wonder if he's on steroids.'

'Next on the menu,' said Zoe Cable, 'is the much-awaited new film by Yugoslav wunderkind Dragoslav Rankovic. Since the success of the neosymbolist allegory, *The River and the Mountain*, Rankovic has become, one might say, the Britney Spears of the East European arthouse cinema.'

'Except without the lip gloss,' heckled Toby Royale.

Zoe Cable grinned and carried on. Underseel, E noticed, looked like a mole-faced monument to misery.

'The subject of his latest film has been a closely guarded secret. It was only revealed two weeks ago that Rankovic has, with characteristic wit and audacity, chosen to make a costume drama based on *The House at Hough End*, a little-known work by the obscure Edwardian novelist Arthur Alderley. Alderley, who was English, wrote twenty-seven novels and innumerable essays, stories and letters. While he enjoyed modest success in his own lifetime, upon his death his reputation, in this country at least, dropped out of the sky like a low-cost airliner.' Underseel coughed loudly. Zoe continued. 'So why has he now been plucked from the landfill of history by Dragoslav Rankovic? Why is there talk of an Alderley revival? Who exactly *was* Arthur Alderley?' She swivelled to face the large video screen behind her. Kidney's television filled with a montage of sepia head-shots.

'This is incredible,' shouted E. 'There's going to be an Arthur Alderley revival. Arthur Alderley – that's Morris's thing.'

'Why are you getting angry?'

'Because this is Morris's *thing*. On television. He's been working on it for years and people have laughed at him, mocked him. People like Zoe Cable. And now look: Conrad Underseel's on *Going Critical*; Rankovic has made a film. This is it. This is what he's been waiting for. It's just incredible.'

She dropped back into the sofa and shook her head. She thought of Morris Gutman, convicted plagiarist, in his Rumpswick bedsit losing his mind. She thought of him patrolling the liquor aisle at Sir Savalot. He was, she thought, whichever way you cut it, a deeply unlucky man.

'He should be on there,' she said, pointing disdainfully at the television. 'It should be him, not Underseel.'

As she said it, a padded, shadowy version of Morris appeared on the screen in front of them.

'Fuck me, that's him,' she said.

'No it isn't,' said Kidney, who had seen pictures.

'Yes it is. It is. They've done something strange to him – the lighting, the hair – but it's definitely him, look.'

The words popped up in the corner of the screen – *Dr Morris Gutman, Alderley Scholar.*

'He looks a bit like Klaus Kinski,' said Kidney.

'It's useful to think of Arthur Alderley,' Morris was saying, 'as ideologically and personally polysexual. In imagining his heroines, the tomboyish Helga Cabbage for example, Alderley is engaging in an obvious if highly convoluted textual cross-dressing. He's a woman trapped inside a man who is projecting himself on to a man trapped inside a woman.'

They cut to a sepia clip from *The House at Hough End*: Helga Cabbage dressed in jodhpurs standing on a ha-ha, explaining to the local tenants her radical plans to turn the house at Hough End into a syndicalist co-operative. The dialogue was in Serbo-Croat with English subtitles.

'Is it meant to be black-and-white?' said Kidney.

'What?' E was still reeling from the sight of Morris – he looked like an *after* picture, but after what?

'*Moj čin nije čin velikodušnosti, već nadoknade,*' said Helga. '*Kolege, ja ne mogu izbrisati zločine moje porodice ali se mogu odreći, i to i činim, svog prezimena. Više se neću zvati Cabbage!*'

Morris came back.

'Any Alderley revival,' he opined, 'will surely be founded on a wider appreciation of the radical vagueness of his major period. In his late novels, his life-long wish to be all things to all men is transformed from a fractured monument to failed liberalism into a *cri de coeur* for pan-sexual utopianism. Hence the final orgiastic croquet game in *The House at Hough End*.'

A cut to the Rankovic version of the croquet game – a mallet's eye view which struck E as anything but orgiastic. There was a final platitudinous voiceover then back to Zoe.

'I think he's ill,' she said.

321

'Why do you say that?'

'His face,' she said, 'in particular his nose. He's definitely ill.'

They looked at each other. E felt for Kidney's hand. Their nakedness struck her suddenly as peculiar and dream-like. Kidney sighed, finished the beer, kissed her. She tasted carbonation then tongue.

'You're upset,' he explained. 'You've been thrown by the sudden quasi-ghostly appearance of your husband on television with a new haircut and a striking resemblance to Klaus Kinski, only a matter of minutes after the rather spectacular conclusion to what could, in strictly legal though definitely not moral terms, be described (but I would never ever do it myself, no fucking way) as an act of infidelity.'

E nodded and sighed.

'It's understandable,' he said.

She smiled, and touched his cheek, twisted a tuft of facial hair.

'I think I should talk to him,' she said. She couldn't help it. The sight of Morris had shaken her. He had looked like a maltreated hostage; she had half expected him to hold up a copy of today's *Beirut Times*. The things he was saying, perhaps they made sense in themselves, but they seemed in their self-conscious cleverness so much at odds with his bodily weirdness – that *couldn't* be his own hair – that she couldn't help thinking something had gone badly wrong for him. That this brief TV debut, this small foothold in the putative Alderley revival, had been purchased at a severe cost.

E gradually stood up.

'Haven't you tried phoning him before?'

'I think I should try again.'

Kidney nodded and began to re-dress. E pulled her smock back on. In the TV light her belly gleamed like a well-polished bowling ball.

Hobbling towards the kitchen phone, she felt a line of warm wetness roll down her inner thigh. Kidney, she thought, smiling. 'Big Cum' indeed. She turned into the downstairs toilet, tore off a handful of gingham-print toilet paper and sat down. As she did so, the line of wetness widened into a stream then became

322

suddenly, undeniably, a gush. There was a sweet, sperm-like smell and a quarter-pint of amniotic fluid splashed into the stainless-steel bowl.

E took several long, deep breathes. Tears filled her eyes.

'OK,' she said. 'All right. Here we go again.'

Part Four

Chapter 33

Morris opened his eyes and saw himself from above. He was lying asleep on a narrow, pine-effect bed. The room was small. Around its edges were a toilet, a basin, a desk and a chair. There was a smell of floorwax and, from beyond the uPVC window, a faint wail of wind. Morris hovered near the ceiling in puzzlement. Below, his body sniffled, farted, resettled. Where was he? He reviewed the room for clues. It was too small for a hotel but too big for a hospital. On the desk was a transistor radio and a packet of soluble asprin. The furniture was new but institutional. Had he gone back to college? Was he on a youth-hostelling holiday? On the wall beside the door he noticed a framed list of fire instructions. He zoomed in to look more closely: there were dos and don'ts, a diagram of the fire exits and gathering points; it was signed Herbert Splang, Governor, Flat Hill Open Prison, Lincolnshire.

Whooooooosh. Morris roared back into his body with the force and sound of an aircraft lavatory. He sat up straight and blinked. Now he remembered. Three months in jail – Underseel had been unrelenting – one night down, ninety-one to go. He felt a clench of terror and then, remembering what he had just seen, a swathe of salving numbness. He was just meat and bone. He was a body on a bed, in a room, in a prison. That was how it would have to be, he realised. That was how he would survive.

'This place is like a lay-by,' he said to the prison psychologist who wore jumpers and smelled like a dentist. 'I mean, it's neither here nor there.'

'So what *is* real, Morris?'

Morris looked at him. They were sitting in a circular consultation room with floor-to-ceiling windows and smoky glass brickwork. The Flat Hill open prison was very well-designed. It had won an award.

'Perhaps you're right,' he said.

'Perhaps I'm not.'

Morris decided he didn't like the psychologist – he didn't like his jumpers, he didn't like the way he smelled.

'You think I'm not clever enough to understand you,' said the psychologist. 'Don't you?'

'That would be absurd. I'm sure you're very well-qualified.'

'Are you worried about hurting my feelings?'

Morris looked out of the windows. The grounds were landscaped. There was a low brick wall and beyond that dark, chocolatey farmland. Flat clouds nudged across the sky like ice floes. The cylindrical room was murky and cool. He wished the psychologist would turn the lights on, ask another question, *do* something.

'So you're suggesting this is it?' he said.

'For a while, yes.'

'And then?'

'Something else I suppose.'

Morris looked again at the psychologist. His green eyes were twinkly but motionless – he had the inert readiness of a machine on standby. He was here, Morris realised with a shock, by choice.

'I'm sorry,' Morris said, 'but that really doesn't work for me at all.'

He travelled down to London on day release. E met him in the tea house in Regent's Park. Molly wouldn't talk to him at first, she swivelled away and sucked her orange juice at an angle.

E blushed.

'Don't worry,' she said. 'She's just overwhelmed.'

Morris was more worried about E's embarrassment, which made him feel uncomfortably separate and new. He peered into the pram. Hedda's face looked like something that had been carved into the handle of a walking stick and rubbed away over years. He had seen her once before, in the hospital. He had been staying in a bail hostel in East Acton and had just been to visit his solicitor. On that occasion, lying in the transparent Perspex crib, she had struck him – in comparison to the technicolor virulence of his woes – as pale and nothingy.

'Can I pick her up?' he asked.

'You're the father.' The tone was factual.

He picked her up. She was weightless, lighter than air. If he let go, he thought, she would bob upwards and away on the steamy vortices of frying and frothing.

'She's tiny,' he said. 'You forget.'

E smiled tightly. 'I know. You do.'

'She makes Molly seem so big.'

'I *am* big!' Molly shouted without turning around.

Morris ordered a bacon sandwich.

'How's the food?' E asked.

'In jail, you mean? Well it's free, that's the best way to look at it.'

Hedda started squawking. Her body tightened like a muscle; she turned bright red and began to vibrate, as though battery-powered.

E took her off him, hitched up her shirt and began to breastfeed. There was a small struggle and then rhythmic slurping.

'I am sorry about what happened, Morris. Underseel's just astonishing.'

'It's not so bad.' Morris bit into his bacon sandwich. Molly, he noticed, was trying to sneak a look at him over her shoulder.

'Do you have time to write?'

'Yes,' he said. (He had not read or written a thing.) 'Yes I do.'

E looked down and readjusted her shirt. Morris could still see a triangle of areola. He winked at Molly, and Molly covered her face with her hands.

E looked up suddenly, her cheeks were reddened and her eyes actually wet.

'Oh God, Morris,' she said. 'It must be really awful. I can't believe you're in jail.'

'It's not so bad,' he repeated.

'But you're locked up.'

'Yes, there's that. There is that.' He winked again at Molly. Molly giggled. E was looking at him expectantly, there was a crease between her eyes, she seemed deeply, off-puttingly concerned.

Morris steadied himself, picked a crumb of soft-hard bacon fat from his plate.

'I miss you,' he said. 'All of you.'

She leaned back. The crease disappeared; she seemed mildly unimpressed. Morris realised belatedly that he had made a mistake – jail was his trump card, he should have stuck with that. E didn't know anything about jail, but she knew all about marriage, their marriage anyway.

'Doesn't it *bother* you?' she said. 'Being in jail? It doesn't seem to bother you very much.'

'It bothers me,' he said with a sense of back-pedalling. 'It bothers me quite a lot. But it's just . . .'

'Just what?'

He shook his head. He didn't know what to say. 'Just that now everything, even this, feels so carpeted, so lagged, so rubberised.'

'I would have thought you liked that,' E said. She seemed annoyed. Morris realised that if he had come (as he may have come, he wasn't sure) with a plan of winning back E, it wasn't going well.

'Why would I like it?'

'You don't have to *do* anything. You don't have to deal with anyone. Isn't that what you really want?'

Morris wondered whether she was right. 'No,' he said.

'Pudding!' shouted Molly. 'Ice cream!'

Morris looked at her, the pastel planes of her half-sized head. Seeing her was like being sutured, the same strange sense of internal tugging. He picked up a menu and ordered the chocolate bombe.

After dessert they walked over to the playground. Molly ran on ahead. In the pram, Hedda squealed like a bicycle brake.

'Are you still staying with Kidney?' he asked.

'We're living together.'

'Living?'

'We're involved, Morris.'

'Involved?'

Morris could feel something move, break inside, like an old mercury filling giving way.

'Do you still hear from Zoe?'

'Zoe and I were never *involved*,' he said. 'Never attached. It was more . . .'

'Accidental? Yes, I remember you saying that.'

'Distant,' he said.

'Well, I'm sorry for you then,' E said. Molly waved from the top of the climbing frame and they both smiled suddenly and waved back. 'Sorry that you would want to exchange our marriage for something like that.'

Morris turned to look at her. He felt like he was a child and she was a grown-up bigger, sterner, more knowing than he. It occurred to Morris that he had never taken the serious parts of life very seriously at all, and now he was paying for it.

'That's not quite fair. It's the opposite of what I meant,' he said.

'But it's exactly what I meant.'

'You're just being clever.'

'I thought you liked that.'

When the afternoon was over they walked back with him to the Tube. Morris felt unexpectedly, dreadfully tired, as though the day had been a sucking swamp through which he had had to trudge. After a joyous hour, Molly had slumped into a trough of anger when she had learned he was leaving. She coiled around Morris's leg and bored her head rather uncomfortably into his groin. E hugged him. Her smell – coffee, breast milk, gum – gave him vertigo. He had to blink.

'When will you visit again?' she asked.

'When I'm released. A month or so.'

'Released,' she shook her head and laughed. 'Bloody hell, Morris.'

331

He laughed too, and it seemed for a moment that all of it, *all* of it, might just be a joke between them.

'Call us first, won't you?' she said.

'Of course. Yes.'

She nodded and rubbed his cheek-bone with her thumb as if wiping away a tear. With difficulty, Morris unclamped Molly from his leg. Her wails filled the ticket hall. As he descended the escalator, towards the Bakerloo line, he felt as though he were fleeing the scene of yet another crime.

Back at Flat Hill Open Prison, Morris polished floors. The polisher wowed and span in front of him like a UFO. Behind him the pink composite flooring switched suddenly from matt to gloss. People tap-danced round him, winked. He was offered gardening but he turned it down – he liked to polish, polishing was his thing.

'What will you do next?' asked his psychologist.

Morris looked at him.

'It's not a trick question.'

'I like to polish,' he said.

'I've noticed.'

'But realistically, I'll teach. There's an offer on the table.'

'What about your marriage?'

'There's Nick Kidney.'

'The pickled-penis guy?'

'Exactly. They're involved, the two of them. That was the term she used.'

'Involved?'

'Exactly.'

'What about the children, Molly and . . . ?'

'Hedda. Yes, my visitation rights are open-ended. I have to call in advance, make an appointment, but apart from that.'

The psychologist nodded eagerly. He was wearing an Arran sweater with little white knobs hanging off it like woolly goo-seberries.

'And how is baby Hedda?'

'Well,' Morris crossed his legs. 'She has that retarded look, she drools, she squints, she whinnies.' He flailed his arms briefly.

'There's no motor control. At this point it's all hypothetical isn't it? She's something waiting to happen.'

'How exciting.'

Morris didn't feel excited. He felt dull and frightened. In his recent dreams, Hedda had come to him as an angry purple piglet.

'Yes,' he said. 'I suppose it is.'

It was summer once again when Morris was released. The air was warm and soft with occasional currents of coolness. The wet, green fields seemed unnaturally clean and broad. The wheels of the euphemistically named Transpennine Express made a slithery shush, the carriage smelled dusty and domestic. It was like coming back from a long trip abroad – the shock of recognition followed by the reassuring cuddle of the everyday. The world is all before me, he thought, looking out of the window at the half-built valleys, the weirs and war memorials, or perhaps it's all behind me.

Morris had never smelled anything like his bedsit. It was as though, left alone, the smell had evolved an intelligence, a personality, an attitude. It nudged and heckled him, it sat down next to him and farted like a tramp. Cleaning it was like conducting a post mortem – curiosity blended with violation and death.

He bought bin bags, bleach, Brillo pads and rubber gloves from the Chaudhary brothers. They asked him about his foot.

'You look good,' they said. 'You look fat.'

After a week, Bernard came round.

'I heard you were out,' he said.

'No one knows.'

'Well then, maybe I'm here on the off chance. Fancy a pint?'

'You've still got a job with old Tong,' Bernard explained a little later. They were in the snug of the Cro-Magnon Arms. 'If you want it.'

'Doesn't he know?'

'I explained it was a *crime passionnel*. A moment of madness.'

'It was the sanest thing I ever did.'

333

'Well, that's just between you and me then.'

Bernard was ageing unevenly – part of him was still boyish, while other areas looked already dead. His lips were full and rosy, but the skin round his eyes looked stiff and greenish.

'How's retirement?' Morris asked.

'Much like jail, I would imagine – tedious beyond belief. I am all for the examined life, Morris, but Christ, week after week of stewing in your own bloody juice. It's like sucking at the same dried-up tit, it really is.'

'Jail's not so bad.'

'Well, I imagine not. Open prison! It's like Pontins by all accounts – satellite TV, counselling, en-suite toilets, gym – all at the taxpayer's expense. And I have to beg for a bus pass. It's bloody scandalous.' Looking up he saw Morris and stopped himself. 'Not in your case, of course. You should never have been in there in the first place. That was a miscarriage of justice, if ever I saw one. Nutting Underseel – you deserve a Chair, not three months in clink.'

'It was open and shut, Bernard; there were twenty-three eye witnesses.'

'Of course there were, but I'm talking intention, provocation, *history*. There's no sense of history these days, Morris. If it happened more than a fortnight ago it's not worth knowing. The reasons for your attack on Underseel were historical, but did they listen to that?'

'I tried to explain the reference issue of course, but the jury . . .'

'Well that's your problem, the jury system. Twelve thick bastards and true. They're raised on *Eastenders* and egg and chips. Why should they understand? Bring back the property restriction, I say. Jury of your peers, my arse. I won't be judged by someone who lives in a council flat. Present company excluded, of course.'

Bernard had become red-faced and shouty. Morris had the impression that he had not spoken to anyone for a long time. As for himself, he was surprised to notice that the dull, nerveless, upholstered feeling which he had assumed was exclusive to prison was still with him. His experience of the Cro-Magnon

Arms, of Bernard, was muffled, neutralised as though he were covered in a layer of hard, dead skin, as though reality, the world, had become hobbled and sleepy.

'Anyway, I am doing some work for Rupert too. It's a piece of piss and I need the money to supplement that poxy pension scheme. I'm sure the Crocodile screwed me with that – I don't know how but I'm sure that bastard had a hand in it. Plus my ISAs are a laughing stock. Are you OK Morris? You look a bit vague.'

Morris smiled and burped. After three dry months, the first pint of Postlethwaite had gone immediately to his head.

'It's good to see you again, mate,' Bernard said. Morris blinked. He had, even through his befuddlement, a strong sense that in his absence his friendship with Bernard had grown into something rather larger than it was.

'OK,' he said after a pause.

This seemed, surprisingly, to be quite enough for Bernard who stood up with a grin, and went to buy a round.

Morris lit a cigarette. He had not had a drink since the day of the Underseel attack when, in the five minutes between the nutting and the arrival of security, he had sucked down a bottle and a half of the Tasmanian red. At Shepherd's Bush police station, he remembered, they had relieved him of his belt and shoelaces, given him a hairy brown blanket and a cup of machine-made coffee and put him in a holding cell to sleep it off. Morris had drunk the coffee, thrown up on the blanket and slept fitfully until 3 a.m. when he was woken for questioning.

'So, Morris, you agree that your assault on Professor Underseel was unprovoked?'

'I said it was irrational. That's not quite the same thing.'

The constable tightened his jaw and wobbled his ballpoint.

'OK, let's try again. Why did you nut him, Morris?'

'In a word?'

'Please.'

'*Scholarship.*'

Released into the grey, windless roar of Uxbridge Road six

hours later, Morris had experienced a second of liberation and lightness before reality kicked in. Magistrate's court the next day, then a trial. The nutting of Underseel was one of the few truly exuberant, truly real acts of his life, but now he would pay for it. He was in the system, and the system, like a monstrous dough-faced baker, would pat him and prick him and mark him with an *F*: *F* for fucked, utterly, utterly fucked. If only, Morris had thought, he could bury himself somewhere hilly and remote, if only he could dig a deep, dark pit, fall into it and sleep.

Back at the Balmoral Hotel, he had been presented with a bill he could not possibly pay and a note informing him that his daughter, Hedda Melinda Gutman, had been born at 2.48 a.m.

Bernard came back with drinks. 'You look flushed,' he said.

Morris tried to shake it off. The memory was like a needle pushed through his upholstery and into his core. He had a flash of utter worthlessness.

'I've made some terrible mistakes,' he said.

'Oh we all have, Christ.' Bernard shook his head. 'If I had to do it again I'd be a stockbroker. You can stick the life of the mind up your jacksie. It's too late now though, I've got a dick like cannelloni, but you could play ping-pong with my prostate. Old age is a terrible thing, you know. The days last for ever, but the months fly past.'

'I worry sometimes that I've done it all to myself, that it's my fault.'

'That's nonsense. You're a man of principle. That's our problem, we're both men of principle, but evidently it's the arse-lickers who inherit the earth. Zoe Cable, Dirck van Camper, Nick Kidney, they're all empty vessels, they're all pigs' bladders. I've got no money, my house is falling down, there's nothing to look forward to, but I can hold my head up. I can look those wankers in the eye.'

At these heroic and ungainly words, Morris felt an answering chill of righteousness shudder across his arms and neck. Perhaps Bernard was right, there was only anger and pride and beyond that, nothing at all.

'They're not interested in your shame, Morris,' Bernard went on. 'Do you think E really cares whether you're sorry or not? Really?'

Morris's body felt like a poorly pitched tent – baggy in places, painfully tight in others.

'I'll tell you: she doesn't. You're doing that to yourself. Just *forget* it.'

'And then what?'

Bernard shrugged. His eyes looked suddenly murky and half-dissolved, like something you might come upon unexpectedly in a bowl of hotel soup.

'I'm buggered if I know: Mahler, foie gras? It's matches struck in the fucking darkness Morris. I've never been one for hope.'

Rising from the carpets of the Cro-Magnon, Morris could smell the dusty, stubbed-out, ale soak of decay. The fruit machine in the corner pinged then rattled. The room, the windows, the world beyond them seemed to him to have the false depth of poorly painted scenery. He could see through it; he knew what it was, and it wasn't much.

Morris moved into Bernard's lopsided house on Dauphin Street.

'Why pay rent?' Bernard reasoned. 'The house of the lord has many rooms – several of which contain double beds and hand basins.'

They split the bills and shared the cooking. When Tong phoned they took turns to lecture. On Saturday mornings they shopped together at Sir Savalot – Morris pushed the trolley, Bernard ticked off the items on their list: ratatouille, Ribena, tinned peas, oxtail, lamb neck. In the evenings they drank Peruvian claret and railed. The arrangement pleased Morris. Since his release he'd lost all curiosity, all will to be anything he already wasn't, so Bernard, whose capacity for hope had years ago collapsed in upon itself like an ageing sun, and who was as a consequence quite brutally and unremittingly himself, felt suitable. There was a comfort, Morris found, in Bernard's bitterness, a centripetal promise that things were already so bad that realistically there was nothing further to worry about. If Bernard

337

was failing, fading, so (his logic continually went) were everything and everyone else, Morris included. If only they knew it.
Literature was dead, morality was crocked, they were all just
soap suds swirling on the lip of a vast inhuman plug hole. And in
the face of this grim metaphysics the efforts they made together
of eating, shopping, lecturing even, were, they both silently yet
certainly believed, a kind of heroism – an endeavour for which
they deserved, but would never get, tremendous unbridled
applause.

One chill September morning Morris raised himself from his
soft, almost springless mattress, drew water from the spluttering
tap and shaved and dressed himself in preparation for catching
the early train to Cirencester: a sixth-form conference on *King
Lear*. They had tossed for it and Morris had lost. Bernard was
already up; he was wearing a plush-velvet dressing gown and
espadrilles. It had taken a while for Morris to get used to this
sight – the stringy, hairless stretch of Bernard's skin across his
collar bones, the venous bobby socks of flesh between robe and
espadrille – but now he was immune to it.

'What have they given you?' Bernard asked. He was poaching
an egg.

Morris looked again at the letter.

' "Tragedy – Its Meaning." '

' "Tragedy – Its Meaning?" ' Bernard spooned out the ragged
white sphere and plopped it on to his toast.

'Yes.'

'What a load of bollocks. I mean, what's the point?'

'They're seventeen,' agreed Morris. 'I'm talking to them about
death, and they're sitting there squeezing their blackheads and
getting spontaneous hard-ons.'

'Is it at the college?' Bernard asked.

'Cirencester College.'

'That's a shithole.'

It was. The lecture theatre was littered and dusty, the central
heating banged, the fluorescent lights flickered and fizzed. He
was introduced as Professor Morris Gutman of Coketown
University. He spoke for fifty minutes on hubris. At the begin-

ning the audience seemed unsettled: they shuffled and coughed, they winked and giggled, sent text messages and swapped pens. He looked up at them. The brightness of their blazer badges, the unfocused eagerness of their eyes, struck him as forming a grotesque contrast to the truths he was giving them – the truths of failure, morbidity and death. The pause lasted rather longer than he meant it to; they were looking back at *him* now, all of them. They looked eager, he thought, inquisitive, alive, like hatchlings waiting to be fed. He continued: the Aristotelian categories, the Faustian pact. After twenty minutes they stopped talking and shuffling; after forty, they stopped writing and just stared: stares of empty amazement as if he had touched something raw and yet unformed. He ended the lecture with Lear's words on the death of Cordelia: '*Never, never, never, never.*'

He stepped down from the podium in silence; the only noise as he left the hall was the slight crinkle of crisp packets under foot.

Afterwards, as Morris stood in line at the coffee urn, he overheard one of the teachers describing his lecture as the dullest thing she had ever heard in her life. Another teacher nodded in agreement.

'I know,' she whispered back. 'Wasn't it painful? I thought he was going to dry up completely at one point. Talk about "Tragedy – Its Meaning". I was expecting an analysis not a bloody demonstration.'

They laughed. Morris filled his cup, took his complimentary bourbon biscuit from the open tin and went outside for a cigarette. It made no difference. Shame was with him all the time now, like a plastic hip or a pacemaker; he didn't feel it anymore but he knew it was there. And in a strange way it kept him going; buried within him the deadness reminded him of who he was, who he wasn't.

It was past seven by the time Morris got back to Glodshaw. The evening had turned windy and crepuscular, and the autumnal air was heavy with the smell of decomposition and cut-price fireworks. He crossed Dauphin Street amidst a roiling flak of unswept leaves. Bernard's house was warm with the aroma of boil-in-the-bag coq au vin and the soft warblings of Dame Kiri Te Kanawa. As he dropped his briefcase in the hallway and hung up his rain-streaked mackintosh, Morris was already thinking with some excitement of the opportunities for bitching that his day would afford: Professor Gutman of Coketown University, Bernard would love that.

'Littlejohn!' he yelled. 'You idle bugger. Where's my aperitif?'

Instead of the usual snuffle of invective from the kitchen there was silence. Then, after a moment, the living room door squeaked open and Bernard's bog-brush face peered out. It was wearing, absurdly Morris thought, a look of mild disapproval.

'*Morris*,' he whispered. 'We have a guest.'

'What? Why on earth are you whispering?' Morris looked impatiently past Bernard's shoulder and was taken aback to see, seated near the gas fire, lightless and multiplanar like a peculiar postmodern extension to Bernard's beige settee, an actual nun. She was fronted by an empty sherry glass and an untouched plate of gingernuts. The issue of fancy dress occurred immediately to Morris but he dismissed it – there were too many woolly layers, too many dangly gee-gaws and specialised buttonholes. Plus the smell – communal, pre-war, faintly soapless – it couldn't be faked. Was she here for money then, Morris wondered? Did nuns do that sort of thing? And if they did, why had Bernard not given her the same unceremonious heave-ho he gave all other attempts to tickle his untickleable conscience?

The nun turned to look at Morris. It was Darian Cavendish.

'Jesus Christ, it's Darian!' he said.

Darian winced at the blasphemy. Bernard, who Morris quickly realised was hardly less flummoxed than he was himself, began to blather an apology. Darian stopped him with a shake of her black origamic head. She offered Morris a spooky smile. Her squared-off, isolated face and her dark, bodiless body struck him as having the clumsy and nauseating quality of a very early form of special effects.

'Is this . . . are you . . .' he paused, 'quite serious?'

340

Darian looked at him emptily. She looked as uncomfortable in a nun's outfit, he thought, as she had in every other outfit he had seen her in. But now perhaps that was the point.

'I was never a great practical joker, Morris. I think Bernard can attest to that.'

'Oh absolutely,' Bernard agreed. 'I mean absolutely *not*.'

'So yes, Morris, I am quite serious. It was not a snap decision. I have been in contact with the Sisters for some years. My resignation . . .' she paused for several uncomfortable moments to rearrange the folds of her habit, and when she began again her voice was a notch higher, '. . . my *so-called* resignation from the university only hastened a process that was already, you see, well underway.'

'I see.' Confronted by this sour and unexpected apparition, Morris felt suddenly and ravenously hungry. Faced with the possibility of having to make conversation with a newly con-secrated Darian Cavendish, he discovered that all he really wanted to do was eat – to chomp through breast and wing, to fill his mouth with wine-soaked baby carrots, to gorge on the semi-liquid ooze of Sir Savalot croquettes. His hunger, as he leaned on the jamb, unwilling to commit himself to the living room unless absolutely forced to do so, had the frenzied thrill of lust.

'Will you be joining us for dinner, Darian?' he asked.

'Oh no.' Darian seemed faintly shocked by the suggestion. Morris wondered if there was some kind of curfew involved.

'Darian has something for you,' offered Bernard.

'For me?' Morris remembered the job interview, the Nietzsche jibe. Was this payback time? Or, more terribly, was it possible that Darian now regarded them all – Bernard, herself and Morris – as linked, bonded by their sufferings (however arrived at, however escaped from) between the salient and ever-dripping jaws of the Crocodile? Was it possible that this was a social call?

Bernard proposed a top-up. Morris pursued him into the kitchen.

'What is this?' he hissed. 'Is she really a nun? Don't they have a probationary period? How's the coq au vin?'

'She was fast-tracked, Morris. They're a dwindling band. Think about it – shame's gone. Commit a mortal sin these days and all you get is a cuddle and twelve months' counselling. And without shame what have they got left? A bride of Christ? You think the kids are going to go for that? I mean, look at the outfit. I'm all for tradition, but she looks like she's been mummified by Moss Bros.'

'Bernard,' Morris urged. 'What *are* you on about?'

'They need the numbers, Morris. Plus they got their hands on her bungalow, which, given the property boom in Gooseberry Hill, must have been worth a packet. Oh she's a nun all right – and she probably gets the corner cell and extra salt on her gruel.'

'So why is she here?'

Bernard shrugged and raised the clanging lid on the coq au vin. They both peered in.

'It's part-irradiated in the factory,' Bernard said. 'It won't come to any harm.' He looked back at Morris. 'She says she has some information you might be able to use.' Bernard opened the oven and glanced at the croquettes. 'That's all I know,' he closed it again, 'and all I need to know.'

Morris carried the two brimming sherry flutes back into the living room. Darian took hers and sucked off the meniscus with a slurp.

'Thanks ever so,' she said.

Morris still found it hard to look at her.

'You think I'm a fool,' she said.

Morris hesitated.

'That's fine. You don't need to be polite. I'm rather beyond politeness now.'

'Yes, I suppose you are.' Morris wondered whether that didn't also mean she was beyond revenge.

Darian took another sip.

'You may be right, of course,' she went on, 'but foolishness is not the worst of sins. There are others, as we both know, far more corrosive, far more cancerous. Lust, for instance.'

Morris swallowed.

342

'Lust for power – that monstrous gargoylism of vanity and pride. You know of course of whom I speak.'

'I can't help you,' Morris said.

'Help me?'

'With the Crocodile. I can't go back there.' As he said it, Morris's eyes prickled. He felt like a small child who was being asked to go back into the deep end.

Silently, one of Darian's pale, clawish hands disappeared into the worsted waves of her habit and emerged with a long white envelope.

'I don't come here with a request, Morris, I come with a gift.'

'A gift?'

'You are acquainted with the theology of grace, I presume. It is normal to think of God's grace as unbidden and undeserved, but in my opinion we pay too little attention to its inconvenience. It really can be terribly inconvenient. Look at me: I had a rather lovely bungalow in Gooseberry Hill; now I share a loft room at our convent in Porksby. And you, Morris, well *you* were looking forward to your dinner this evening, coq au vin, I believe. You certainly weren't planning on talking to me, or hearing my particular, peculiar story, or receiving,' she glanced at the envelope, 'my particular, peculiar gift. Yet here I am.'

'Here you are,' echoed Morris, wishing that Bernard had chosen the schooners rather than these dinky flutes, and at the same time wondering why the thin layer of fear produced by the first sight of Darian's envelope was now warming, bubbling, into something closer to excitement.

'Allow me to explain myself,' Darian continued. 'My room-mate at the convent is Sister Unke from Utrecht. Unke has now retired due to ill-health but for many years she was a nurse at the University of Utrecht Medical Centre. Her specialism was physical rehabilitation. She worked with accident victims of various kinds – quadriplegics, paraplegics, stroke patients and so on.'

Morris nodded. The white envelope, sealed but outwardly unmarked, seemed to him to throb with the very possibilities – of action, of justice, of righteous retribution – which Bernard's

343

nihilistic lifestyle had been built to deny. Its appearance on his coffee table seemed thrillingly impolite.

'Sister Unke took her degree in physiotherapy. She is an excellent masseuse.' (An unwelcome image flashed into Morris's mind. He blinked it away.) 'But she also believes, as we all do, in the power of prayer, and at the hospital she would always pray for her patients. Of course it rarely worked.'

Morris raised his eyebrows. Darian noticed.

'It is one of the fallacies of secularism, Morris, to equate faith with stupidity, even with a kind of blindness, whereas the opposite is closer to the truth. It is the faithless, in my experience, who turn away from death, from suffering, who give themselves over instead to foolish fantasies of immortality, painlessness, *speed*. We tend to the sick, Morris. We bury the dead. Prayer isn't like writing a prescription. It's a way of giving up control again and again. A way of reminding ourselves that anything can happen.'

Outside, a late bus barked, a rogue firework cut a swizzling purple corkscrew above the leafless branches of Bernard's magnolia tree. Darian grinned.

'*Sometimes* people heal, Morris. Sometimes the dead rise up, the lame throw away their crutches, the speechless find their tongue. I've seen it happen. Sister Unke saw it happen many times. Many times, yes, but there is one occasion which is of particular interest to us. He was a young Dutchman who had been paralysed from the waist down in an accident. He was very bright, he came from a well-known family, but nothing could be done. Unke's job was just to teach him the exercises, keep his spirits up. But being Unke, she also prayed. She prayed unceasingly. One day the young man moved his toe. The next day he moved another toe, then his foot. Within three months he could stand with a stick. Within six months he was walking again. It was beyond medical explanation. There was no precedent. It was a miracle.'

'Are you serious?'

'You have asked me that once already, Morris. You may prefer a different word, I realise, a different paradigm. But I

344

speak of a mystery for which the appropriate language was given to us quite some time ago.'

'Who was this person?'

'Can't you guess?'

(He could guess.)

'It can't be true.'

Darian raised her eyebrows. The skin of her forehead rippled over her wimple like a pie crust.

'I didn't expect an act of faith, Morris,' she said tartly. 'I came with evidence.'

'An affidavit?'

'Two. Plus the medical records.'

'Is that legal?'

Darian closed her eyes slowly and then opened them again.

'Sister Unke is very old. There is the possibility of several miracles. One needs to build a case.'

'You're going to canonise her?'

'Please don't be crude, Morris. These things are the work of decades. For today our interests are less elevated.'

'You're saying Dirck van Camper is pretending to be disabled, that really he can walk? It's preposterous.'

'It is blasphemous, Morris. That is my,' she paused, '*angle*, if you will. It is a denial of God. It is an act of monstrous crudity and ingratitude.'

Morris's world was undergoing a kaleidoscopic rearrangement – shards of colour and light, hectic geometries of chaos and form, shaped and dissolved before his eyes. The envelope was dynamite. If even half of it were true he had Dirck van Camper by the balls.

'Theoretically it's superb, of course,' he said after a minute of frantic thought. 'You have to give it to him. He's dissolving the binaries – healthly/crippled, sick/well. It's dialogic.'

'Yes.' Darian's face looked as though she had bitten hard into a lemon. 'Sister Unke said there was some such nonsense talked when she confronted him over his refusal to abandon the wheelchair, over his insistence that the rehabilitation be curtailed. She didn't understand a word of it, of course, but I imagined that it

345

had something to do with whatever passing fad Mr van Camper has lashed himself to. What is it now? Disability Studies?'

Morris nodded. Looking into Darian's nervous, ferrety eyes, he had a sudden and frightening sense of her capabilities, of the vast and inhuman scope of her moral imagination.

'As I said,' Darian tapped her waxy fingertips on the white envelope, 'it is a gift. How you use it is entirely up to you.'

'Isn't that rather reckless?'

Darian drained the last of her sherry and squinted at him.

'I've just become a nun, Morris,' she snapped. 'Does that strike you as the act of a sensible person?'

Chapter 34

Adam d'Hote had come back. Zoe couldn't believe it. His torso, by all accounts, still looked like it had been run over by a gang of mountain bikers; his face had the colour and firmness of a two-week-old melon. The man was obviously sick, but he was back. Zoe was demoted to the list (it actually existed, she had seen it) of occasional panellists. What was more, she felt painfully, maddeningly certain that d'Hote's Lazarus-like rise had been prompted by his overhearing the Zoe-fuelled rumours of his ultimate demise. How exactly the strains of this rather well-orchestrated piece of misinformation had reached d'Hote's bedside Zoe didn't know, but she was prepared to make a guess: Bathsheba Ffytche. Pam had decamped to the Dimblebys and Bathsheba had made her play – she was acting producer, she had the sickly and manipulable d'Hote in her pocket and she was playing up the Underseel fiasco for all it was worth. Zoe doubted there was a cameraman, an editor, a tea boy at the BBC, who didn't now know that Zoe Cable and the insane Underseel assailant had once been lovers.

The flat in Chiswick was off. She was back in Coketown. *Legless in Gaza* was still a possibility, yes, but without her profile as presenter for *Going Critical* the lager louts at XSTV were noticeably less 'turned on' by the concept. And to add to the final gravitational tug of this tide of unforeseen reversal, in her nine months' absence Dirck van Camper had taken firm control of the Hub. She still got a salary but almost nothing else: he had fiddled with job descriptions, changed accounting practices, brought in his own (one hundred per cent disabled) secretarial staff. She had seen the memos. His work, she had to admit, was superb. Organisationally the Hub was now glass-smooth; it offered her no niche, no cranny, nowhere even to start. She was shut out, it seemed, from her own creation, which had been transformed under the four-wheeled steward-ship of Dirck van Camper into the behemoth of disability studies. In the great atlas of crippledom there was no country, no province even, in which Dirck did not have his special, well-trained and fiercely loyal envoy. He was the Metternich, Zoe thought, of bodily dysfunction.

Zoe did a lot of Qi Dong, a lot of Jujitsu. She visited Mr Chan.

'So what's up, Mr Chan?' she said. 'Why's life giving me the finger?'

Mr Chan, who was from Ormskirk, was not a good listener. He was, in his opinion, paid to pierce.

'There is neither good luck nor bad luck,' he said wearily, 'only Tao.'

'Come again?'

'You heard.'

'That's what it says on that calendar.'

'So it does.'

Zoe thought about this. She thought about the great rondello of Tao, the crashing electric ocean of Is. She decided that Mr Chan was, as usual, right. There was no wrong step, only limited vision. Wrong and right were just terms, words; she knew that. It was a question, as always, of shifting the paradigm, shaking the kaleidoscope – waiting for a different pattern to emerge, for blowback to become opportunity, for churn to become chance. She still remembered the kidney-shaped pool; she could still smell the mesquite. For a solid week she rolfed, she visualised, she balanced her chakras. She waited for insight to arise, for the tedious murk of the necessary to settle and the glowing loophole of the just barely possible to appear. On the Monday she paid a visit to Dirck van Camper.

'Zoe!' Dirck said, as though he had not been expecting her, as though he had not planned meticulously for this day. 'Welcome!'

He reversed away from his wrap-around smart desk. 'How are you? I hope you are enjoying yourself.'

'Doing what exactly, Dirck?'

Dirck van Camper wobbled his head and looked uncertainly in the air.

'Ah, whatever.'

'There have been a lot of changes,' Zoe said. 'Nine months away and I hardly recognise the old place.'

'The ramps, you mean, the automatic doors, the hearing loops. These are small things.'

'Yes they are small things. I was thinking more of the alteration in my job description, the changes in committee structure, the rewriting of several key funding proposals.'

'All passed by the Centre,' said Dirck. 'And of course approved by Donald.'

'What the fuck does Donald have to do with this? Faculty has no power over the Hub.'

Dirck smiled. 'That's what we call "old thinking", Zoe,' he said. 'These days there is a fruitful symbiosis between the two of us.'

'Donald will eat you up,' she said.

Dirck van Camper tossed back his head and chuckled.

'Zoe, you really are rather melodramatic. Donald and I are great friends. My stepmother is coming over next week; the Faculty and the Hub are jointly sponsoring her seminar on body dismorphia. Donald is very excited. You really should attend.'

'I don't think so, Dirck.' She dropped her grey Borbonese rucksack on the floor and sat down. She crossed her legs. She was wearing a suede prairie skirt, dayglo clogs and a singlet crocheted out of fusewire.

'What is that smell?' said Dirck.

'Pineapple and naphthalene. By the way, I've always wanted to ask: what exactly is wrong with you, Dirck?'

'Wrong?'

She nodded at his legs.

'Ah Zoe. There is nothing *wrong* with me. You should know

that. I have changed, I have become different, the unfortunate incident was in that sense,' he paused as if for thought, although Zoe was certain he had delivered this nugget innumerable times before, '*en*abling not *dis*abling. It opened me up to perspectives, to understanding, I would never otherwise have known.'

'I see,' said Zoe. 'But still, it must make you very angry.'

'Why so?'

'To think that someone, some unknown person, has robbed you of your faculties. Oh I know, I've heard the enabled/disabled stuff a million times, but let's face facts Dirck: you're on wheels; you wear nappies. There's an element of humiliation.'

Dirck clenched his jaw.

'I choose to live without the coercive fantasy of bodily perfection. All that fascist normativity,' he took a deep calming breath, 'is behind me now. And by the way, I don't wear nappies.'

'Oh, of course,' said Zoe backing off slightly. 'I imagine it would be behind you. Still, you must be curious.'

'Curious?'

'To know who did it. Who exactly made you different. Because although you talk about choice, it wasn't really your choice, was it Dirck? It was someone else's. The person in the red car.'

'Who said it was red?'

'Oh, you didn't know? I thought you might have noticed the colour as you went down. As it reversed over you. I supposed you might have caught a glimpse.'

Dirck sucked in his already sunken cheeks. His eyes tightened.

'Are you offering information, Zoe?'

'Well that would depend, wouldn't it, Dirck? In my opinion certain pieces of sensitive knowledge should be shared only by colleagues of equal professional standing.'

'But you are of course much more senior than myself, Zoe.'

'Nominally, yes. But as we both know the directorship has now been reduced to a sinecure and all power lies with the assistant director, yourself. I am proposing a certain redistribution.'

'A return to the *status quo ante*. And in return you have a name?'

'I do.'

Zoe swallowed. She took out a cigarette. Dirck van Camper saw it, winced and shook his head.

'It would have to be a rather special name wouldn't it?' he said. 'To be worth such a price.'

'It's the name of the person who put you in that wheelchair.'

He smiled.

'Let me guess.'

'I don't think you could.'

'Let me try.'

Zoe nodded. 'If you like.'

Dirck half-closed his eyes, pirouetted a few times and hummed to himself.

'Let's see,' he said. 'How about,' he stopped spinning and looked straight at Zoe, 'Morris Gutman.'

Zoe croaked and dropped her unlit cigarette.

Dirck guffawed.

'Ha! Is that the best you can do Zoe? Morris Gutman, bloody hell.'

'I heard him confess.'

'Maybe you did, maybe you didn't. But from what I hear about it, Morris would confess to whatever you told him to. The Underseel incident made the *Guardian*, you know.'

'Yes I saw that.'

Dirck offered an avuncular smile.

'Really Zoe, I think you need to reassess, take some time off.'

Dirck turned back to his smart desk and resumed his typing.

Zoe looked at him: he was wearing a double-breasted Mao jacket and rimless glasses; below the gleam of his bald pate was a faint horseshoe of head stubble. He was waiting, she imagined, for her to plead, to blink, to cut a deal, to accede in some as yet as unspecified way to this cremation of her own career. Above Dirck's head there was a framed poster from the Seventh Annual Disability Studies Convention in Geneva. Was it possible, Zoe

351

wondered, that she had been wrong all the time, *always*? That it would end not with the kidney-shaped pool, not with the mesquite barbecue, but here, amid the teak-walled hyper-accessibility of Dirck van Camper's office? Was it really likely that instead of enjoying Californian underemployment, she would spend the next two decades *teaching*? Wiping educational arse in a provincial factory farm? Was it possible that they had really won – Dirck, the Crocodile, Adam d'Hote – that these men had actually, *actually* beaten her?

On leaving Dirck van Camper's office Zoe took a black cab directly to the Kum Bar. She was the only customer there. It was three hours before Happy Hour. The tattooed, metal-bound barstaff, with their cut-marks and coldsores, bruises and wax burns, looked at her as though *she* was strange. She *was* strange, she realised, strange and absurd and faintly ludicrous. To have ever imagined that she could win on her own, that her will, even *her* will, with its dark, blood-fed virulence, would be enough. Oh the vanity of it! What had Donald once told her about power? *True power is invisible. Powerful men walk among us everyday, but we do not see them at all. All we see are glasses, suits, male-pattern baldness.* After her near-death experience she had come to think of power as dark, brooding, glamorous. Wrong. Power was Dennis Sloze; power was Dirck van fucking Camper. It inhered not in the flows but in the systems, not in the flux but in the form.

What could she do next? She couldn't imagine. She didn't want to. She just wanted to stay where she was, sloshing in the depths of her own stupidity, drowning in the pitch-black barrel of her own benightedness. She was drinking the nastiest cocktails she could think of – gin and Coke, Scotch with grapefruit juice. She was drinking for the hangover, drinking for the retch and burn. A boy with hedgehog hair and a purple trench-coat sat down beside her.

'What's that smell?' he asked.

She told him.

'Cool!' He peered into the remnants of her drinks and sniffed. 'Have you been making those up yourself?'

She nodded.

'Owww kaaay.' The boy licked his lips. 'I may have something for you.'

'I really doubt that.'

'Hear me out.' He reached into his trench coat and removed a transparent plastic folder with zip-up pockets. Each pocket contained a nucleus of brightly-coloured pills.

Zoe rolled her eyes.

'It's new,' he said.

She laughed. '*New*, right. New so you smoke it instead of snort it? New so you stick it up your arse not in your arm? There is no new. New is old.'

The boy sighed and shook his head. 'Normally I would share your cynicism,' he said. 'The world of narcotics is indeed a hive of bullshit. But that's the nature of the consciousness-altering industries. Our customers need constant escalation, and if it isn't there we have to pretend it is.'

'But now?' said Zoe.

'But now it is here. May I direct your attention to this beauty in the corner.' One pocket contained a single triangular pill the colour of tomato ketchup. 'They call it Snail. It's locally made – an offshoot of the biological weapons programme over at Wetterton. It'll rip out your synapses and turn them into a papier-mâché effigy of Mao Tse Tung.'

'Hallucinations?'

'Severe.'

'I want something that will hurt and scare me,' said Zoe. 'I want something that'll teach me a lesson. I don't want happy-clappy, I don't even want mildly terrifying; I want apocalyptic, I want to feel my soul sucked out through my fucking nostrils.'

The boy raised his hooped eyebrows, pursed his studded lips and grinned. 'Girlfriend,' he said, 'I think you've just met Mr Right.'

The Snail did the trick. After twenty minutes Zoe was staring at the lush green surface of her wheatgrass and schnapps cock-tail, convinced that it was sending her messages – that the glints and twists of light, the tiny but perfect pricks of shadow were forming words, symbols, runes; that they were speaking to her in long elegiac, riffs about failure and loss and despair, about the abstract universality of error and the terrible specificities of pain. After forty minutes the drink rose out of the glass in a slick green column and wrapped itself around her neck like a chilly boa constrictor. It then wrapped itself around her head and arms, her legs and torso, her feet and hands and face until she was mummified by its ghastly green rope. Then it started to squeeze, to fill her mouth and arse and vagina, to buffet and flay her from inside and out, until at last she felt her soul sucked out through her nostrils and saw it lying on the table in front of her, quivering, vulgar, murky, like a large plate of phlegm.

After an hour she was back in the Kum Bar. Her cocktail was untouched. The boy with hedgehog hair was chatting to a barman and sipping crème de menthe.

'An hour!' she said. 'Sixty quid and it only lasts an hour?'

'They're working on that,' he said. 'This is only mark one.'

'It's built-in obsolescence,' she yelled. 'You're a fucking disgrace.'

'Wow, watch what you're saying. These are craftsmen. This is not buying a chemistry set and flogging bad E to teenyboppers. This is good gear. These are gastrodrugs. Now tell me I'm wrong.'

He looked her straight in the face. The silver studs on his upper lip looked like the residue of a permanent, mythic sneeze.

'OK,' she said. 'How much for three?'

By the end of the evening, according to the hedgehog boy, Zoe had taken more Snail than anyone else on earth *ever*. Her body, he claimed, now had the status of a chemical experiment and should be treated accordingly.

'What does that mean?'

'Carefully observed.' He grinned, winked and stuck his tongue in his cheek.

'Forget it,' she said to the hedgehog boy.

'Call me a cab,' she said to the barman.

The thought of being touched by anything human bored her immeasurably. She wondered whether the Snail had ruined sex for her forever. Perhaps it had. If so, she wasn't sure it was such a bad bargain. Sex, after all, had misled her badly. It had told her it was everything; it had promised that if she clung to its flanks, if she gave herself to its tides, it could raise her up, it could cast her to the very heights. That had been a lie.

Zoe was in a cab going home. No other living being had ever come down off four consecutive hits of Snail. She wondered what it would be like; she wondered whether it was even survivable. Outside the Casa Urbano she saw beggars, hordes of them – a dwarfish army of beggars waving their polystyrene cups, patting their noisome dogs, chanting in Wagnerian chorus: *Spare change please, mate.* After a moment the army shrank, steadied, coalesced into the form of only one beggar: Trevor, whom she knew quite well, and his dog Dirty Harry. She found the sight of Trevor and Dirty Harry, however, more terrifying in its straightness, its accuracy, its crude and unbudging sense of realism than any hallucinatory begging army ever could have been. Zoe's world, she realised, had been horribly disenchanted, not only by the retreating Snail (which was certainly bad enough) but also more basically and brutally by the failure of her vision: by the draining of the kidney-shaped pool; by the recession of the ontic tides; by the sudden flattening of the electric ocean of Is. Never had she felt such a sense of nullity, never had she imagined that the world could present itself to her as so utterly little, so terribly poor. As she stood in the lift watching the carpet's paisley pattern wind and unroll around her feet, she had no idea what to do next. As she clicked off the digital door lock and stepped into the apartment, it struck her that in some blunt and basic way this was the end.

Seated at the head of her bed in a cross-legged position was the angel of death. He was superhumanly large, with vast, rather camp, black wings, but was otherwise dressed quite normally. He also possessed, quite surprisingly, the face of Morris Gutman.

'Death,' she said.

'What?'

'Death,' she said again.

355

'Are you OK?' said the angel of death. 'Look, I'm sorry, I let myself in. I realise that was probably a bit much. Are you really OK? You look . . .'

Zoe stared at the angel of death. She was not frightened of him, whatever he portended. Since that day, eighteen years ago, when she had felt him scurrying inside her – the black hamster death – he had been the source of all her power. Had he come to claim her at last?

'Why are you here?' she asked.

'I have the dirt on van Camper.'

Zoe wobbled – the cocktails, the Snail and now *this*!

'There is no dirt on van Camper,' she quibbled. 'I've checked.'

In answer the angel of death produced an envelope. It was long and white. He got off the bed and walked towards her. As he walked, his wings disappeared, he shrank to a more human size, but his face remained that of Morris Gutman. Another layer of Snail exited Zoe's brain.

'Morris,' she realised. 'What are *you* doing here?'

'I just tried to explain,' he shouted back. 'I let myself in. I have something.'

She looked at the envelope. It was still there. It seemed solid, actual. She reached out to touch it. It was.

Morris told her the story.

'It's just too fantastic,' she said. 'It can't be true.'

He showed her the affidavits, the medical report. As Zoe read them she began to weep. It was so beautiful, so shapely. Dirck van Camper was a fraud, a *fraud*! As an idea it went far beyond revenge: it had the pure, unearthly elegance of a spiral galaxy or a single snowflake. It was proof, if she still needed it, if she really had forgotten, of the great, dark forces beyond her control, proof that despite all her fears (how foolish they now seemed) the flux was still alive, still throbbing. Big, fat tears sprouted from Zoe's eyes and splotted against Sister Unke's laser-printed words. Morris gently eased the documents from her shaking hands and put them safely to one side. With a long, post-Snail sigh, she sank into his fleece-clad arms, into the still-identifiable scent of Bernard's coq au vin. From far away she

356

could hear the merry sounds of jacuzzal bubbling, the booming slosh and hiss of tidal waters rising once again. She could already smell the mesquite.

'Dennis Sloze,' she mumbled triumphantly, 'can kiss my bloody arse.'

Chapter 35

Morris Gutman sat in Dirck van Camper's grandiloquent ante-chamber and waited. He had been waiting there for two hours already with nothing to read but back issues of *Disability Today*, and nothing to look at except the humming back and forth of Dirck's new secretary, Marge. Marge, Morris had concluded after only a few minutes, was probably the most thoroughly disabled person he had ever seen. She had motor neuron disease, cerebral palsy and, for some other reason Morris couldn't guess at, had tiny, child-sized arms and legs. She spoke through a computer and typed with her mouth. Marge, Morris thought, was obviously Dirck's beard. After the pre-emptive horrors of Marge the idea of quibbling over someone's disabled status struck even Morris, with the envelope in his pocket and with his will screwed to the sticking place, as in horribly bad taste.

'Professor van Camper will see you now.' Marge's voice came disconcertingly from a speaker high on the wall behind her.

Morris stood up. He took a deep breath and recalled Zoe's pep talk from the night before: *Your purpose in going in there, Morris, is to maim, destroy and terrorise. What you possess, from Dirck's point of view, is a catastrophe in a business envelope, it's five A4 sheets of mayhem. You need to let him know that his empire is in your hands now, that he is dangling over the flames of personal and professional humiliation and that you, Morris, are a vengeful fucking god.*

Dirck van Camper was typing. He didn't turn to acknowledge Morris, indeed the only sign that he was aware that Morris had entered the room was a slightly increased expression of sourness around his bloodless lips.

'So they let you out already?' he said.

Morris glanced around the room: the glass-topped conference table, the yak-suede sofa, the wall-mounted plasma screen, the cut calla lilies, the framed posters from the Seventh Annual Disability Studies Convention (keynote speakers: Firenze Beach, Dirck van Camper), the filigree bowl of paw-paw fruit. He remembered his rotting room in Bernard's house, he remembered Cirencester, he remembered Rumpswick; he remembered, above all, Flat Hill Open Prison. He felt rather happy with what he was about to do.

'Yes,' he said, seating himself without permission on the yak-suede sofa, 'and here I am again.'

'Again, yes.' Dirck swivelled. 'Isn't the wish to return to the scene of one's crime a little cliché, Morris? I would have thought so.' He looked at his watch. 'But anyway, I have only five minutes before my next meeting, so perhaps we could expedite this. What on earth do you imagine I can do for you?'

'I'd like a job, Dirck,' Morris said. 'In fact, I'd like your job, which is what Zoe promised me before the . . . incidents.'

Dirck looked back at him in silence for several seconds. He then shook his head slightly, took a business card from the holder on the desk in front of him and wrote something on the back of it.

'Please call this number, Morris. She is a friend of mine; her name is Dr Bland. She is not cheap, I realise, but I believe there is a sliding scale and the first consultation is free.'

He wheeled himself the six feet across to the sofa and held out the card. It was, Morris realised, in Dirck's mind a magnanimous gesture. He ignored the card.

'Perhaps you think it would be inappropriate, Dirck,' he said, 'for someone like me,' he twiddled his hands and feet, 'someone with moveable parts, to take over the Hub as it is currently constituted?'

Dirck's face clenched.

'You are not taking over the Hub, Morris. That is a fantasy. And I warn you, if you become offensive I will call security.'

'I see what you're saying, Dirck,' Morris continued. 'I mean, it

359

might look a bit off for someone like me – fully functioning and all – to take over this big Disability Studies operation. But I thought if it was a problem, if it looked really bad, maybe I could just fake it?'

'*What?*'

'Fake it. You know, I'd get myself a wheelchair like yours, say I'd had a nasty accident a while back, couldn't walk but otherwise OK. It wouldn't have to be too extreme, just enough to be part of the team, to be *included*. That way I could keep the grants rolling, keep the invitations coming in. Plus, if you think about it, it's theoretically superb – I'd be stepping beyond the binaries, wouldn't I? Dirck?'

Dirck hadn't moved.

'You,' he said, 'are a sick individual. I would like you to leave.'

'Sorry Dirck, but I thought that was the point. This whole enabled/disabled thing is a fiction, right? We're *all* disabled in some sense, aren't we? Isn't that what you said in your book? That once you set aside the Platonic paradigm of bodily completion (which is fascistic after all), you realise that we are all missing something, we're all flawed in some way – tonsils, appendix, asthma, arthritis, you name it. It's just that for people like you and me, Dirck, this universal disability thing is a little more metaphorical than for someone like, say, Marge.'

Dirck tossed the business card in the direction of the sofa and turned back towards the smart desk.

'I think I will call security now,' he said.

'I know what happened, Dirck,' Morris called out. 'I know about Sister Unke.'

'Sister Unke?'

'You must remember Sister Unke. Utrecht University Hospital? She prayed for you ceaselessly, I'm told.'

Dirck had his back to Morris, his hand was halfway to the phone.

'Sister Unke is dead by now, I think.'

'Surprisingly not, Dirck. She has moved to a convent in Porksby, which, I admit, is quite close to being dead, but literally, she's still breathing, still talking, talking quite a lot actually.

They're upset about what you did, Dirck. They think it's blasphemous.'

A small spot of redness blinked open at the apex of Dirck's shaved skull. As Morris watched, it spread down and across like the flesh of a cracked egg until the whole of his head shone hard and half-purple. Morris felt a sudden thrill of vindication and certainty.

Dirck inhaled violently; the redness faded as quickly as it had arisen. He turned round.

'I have no idea what you are blabbing about Morris.'

Morris removed the envelope from his jacket pocket and laid it on his thigh. It felt like he was unzipping a monster schlong and placing it crudely, unignorably on display.

'I have proof Dirck,' he said. 'Affidavits. You're so fucked it isn't even funny.'

'This is all nonsense, Morris. I don't know what imbecilities you have transcribed from the mouth of that foolish old woman, but I can assure you they are of no relevance to my position here at the Hub. That you, apparently, imagine they are testifies only to the tenuousness of your grip on the real world. I have friends, contacts, colleagues. You, Morris, as if I need to remind you, have nothing.'

Morris nodded.

'Zoe said you would say that. The initial denial is exactly what we expected.'

At this mention of Zoe, Dirck flinched. His nostrils ballooned.

'We don't expect you to cave, Dirck,' Morris went on. 'That will come later. What you need to realise now is that your balls are in our hands, and we are prepared to squeeze as hard and as often as is necessary. That is the message I am passing on.'

'Both of you are utterly disgusting.'

'Oh come on, Dirck, give up the high ground. It really doesn't suit you. Between you and me, the wheelchair stuff is wonderful, very creative. We're prepared to let you keep it going, but you need to make a deal. I know you're thinking you can blag it, freeze us out, smear us. If it were just me of course that would be easy, but Zoe changes things. She's still a player. We have two affidavits and a certified copy of your medical record. I'll be back in a week.'

He stood up. As he did so he worried for a moment that his head might bang on the ceiling rose, so vast and unending did he feel. He had flattened Dirck van Camper. It didn't matter what Dirck said now, what he pretended, Morris remembered the blinking Belisha beacon of his skull. It had been as good as a confession. Sister Darian was kosher.

Once outside, he phoned Zoe.

'We've got him,' he said. 'He's ours.'

Zoe whooped.

'You, Morris,' she said, 'are a vengeful fucking god.'

'He denied it all of course.'

'Of course he did.'

'He took the high ground.'

'Except there is no high ground here. Morally we're way below sea level. He needs to realise that. Did you mention my name?'

'He nearly barfed.'

Zoe giggled. 'Come in Mr van Camper, your time is up.'

'What will he do now?' asked Morris.

'His first thought will be the Crocodile, but then he'll realise of course that that would be suicide. He can't turn to the Disability Studies community, they'll rip him to shreds. We're all he has.'

'I gave him a week.'

'He'll phone me tomorrow. We need to finalise our demands. Come over. We'll have dinner and so on. I just discovered this extraordinary new gastrodrug.'

'Snail, yes you told me about that.'

'Did I? Short-term memory wipe-out, I'd better write that one down. They've asked me for feedback. I'm their pilot scheme.'

'Do you really want me to come over?'

'Of course. Why not?'

Morris looked up at the screed of traffic on Sheffield Road: the airbrushed buses, the bilious minicabs, the black-market mountain bikes and filth-slicked motorcycle couriers. Above them all the pumice-stone sky was cross-hatched with early evening rain.

Morris could feel its coldness speckling his lips. Could he really leap over so much so easily? Could they really continue ('dinner and so on') as if none of that had ever happened?

'I was thinking of Underseel,' he said.

There was a gap.

'That was yonks ago, Morris. This is a new day. You're the angel of death, remember.'

The angel of death, right. Morris turned up his coat collar against the drizzle and set off walking against the beige-grey tide of grumpy-looking students. It was the ease of it which shocked him, that so much could be retrieved with so very little trouble. Five sheets of A4, half an hour of vicious threatening and he was back. Morris paused for a cigarette beneath the pressed concrete awning of the university shopping precinct. Was it a form of survivor's guilt, he wondered, settling on a bench, this sense that now he had made it, now he was once more safe he shouldn't be, that it was all somehow wrong? *Wrong*? What kind of an idea was that? As if being jailed, as if losing his wife and job and family were somehow *right*.

A tall, bearded man of middle years with NHS specs and a page-boy haircut sat down next to him on the bench and smiled.

'I know you,' he said.

'I really doubt that.' The man smelt overpoweringly of patchouli.

'No, I have a very good memory. Some have called it photographic.'

'That must be quite a pain.'

'Ah, you're suggesting that a certain element of the unknown, or at least the unremembered, is vital to keeping things interesting?'

Morris, although surprised by the stringency of this response, didn't answer.

'Well, that's what the future is for in my opinion,' said the man. 'You're Morris Gutman.'

Morris turned to look at him. He was wearing winkle pickers and skinny black jeans. When he smiled his enormous eyebrows almost merged with his hairline.

363

'We met at a party in Bangor in 1992. We were drinking Hofmeister, you were debating the merits of veganism and you had a girlfriend: E-something.'

Morris remembered, 'You're Victor Morley-Brown.'

They shook hands. There was half a minute of weird silence.

'Have you heard about the Alderley revival?' Morris asked.

'Oh that. Yes. I sold all my Alderley stuff, years ago unfortunately, it might be worth a bob or two now. I'm more into sci-fi now.'

'Sci-fi? Underseel told me that you were still active, an independent scholar.'

'Conrad's a compulsive liar – I'm sure you've realised that yourself – as well as being generally bonkers. I only really did the Ph.D. to pass the time. I was living in Beaumaris with a law professor. It was all rather intense and academic, a lot of cocaine, a lot of lipstick, a lot of live jazz, but we split up just before my viva. I thought about applying for lecturing jobs, but Conrad gave me a long absurd speech about scholarship so I said bollocks to all that and went down to London.'

'You gave it up,' said Morris as much to himself as to Victor.

'I joined a band, I started a youth theatre company, I imported Levis, I sub-edited, I plumbed, I packed cucumber, I drove a bus.'

'Underseel told me you were at Safeway.'

'That was very temporary.'

'You gave it up?' Morris said again.

'It was a phase really, a particular time. Judith had this astonishing cottage overlooking the Menai Straits. On a fine day you can see Snowdon from the bedroom window. 'See Snowdon and come,' she'd say. It was that kind of relationship, there were a lot of allusions. And I was quite keen on the late novels – you know, *The Scent of Horseradish*, *A Flag for Veronica* – I thought I could really do something with them. In the end the dissertation was a bit of a bodge.'

'Yes, I read it,' said Morris.

'Did you really?' Victor laughed. 'There should be a prize for that. Anyway, yeah, I pretty much lost interest, but old Conrad convinced himself that it was the seed of something major. That's what he said, *the seed of something major*, another ten years of research and it might be publishable. Ten years, yeah right.'

'What do you do now?'

'Herbal highs and drug paraphernalia. I have a stall.'

'Do they work?'

'The herbal highs? They're like paddling-pool drugs. You get your feet wet, but there's no danger of drowning.'

He began to roll a cigarette.

'What have you been up to?'

Morris thought about it.

'I married E,' he said.

'Mmm. Good choice.' The end of his cigarette flared briefly. He waved the pouch at Morris. Morris took it. 'She was very attractive, very sharp, I remember that. She had sort of Madonna thing going, didn't she?'

'Briefly, yes.'

'Kids?'

'Molly and Hedda.'

'Fantastic. I'm kidless myself – that's my one regret.'

'Really?'

'Oh yeah. I envy you that.' Morris glanced across at him. There was a pebbledash of acne scars across his neck. A curlicue of wax lay athwart the fuzzy bunker of his outer ear. He seemed actually sad. 'I mean, what else is there,' he said, 'really?'

Morris nodded. He remembered Molly in her cot at night, so quiet and motionless it was like she had been cast in Latex: her knuckled, hairless head, her short, overstuffed arms raised in surrender. To know she was still alive he had had to lean down and place his ear against her mouth to hear the hot give and take of her micro-breathing. And once he had not heard anything, nothing at all, and it had taken him a deep, ghastly second to remember he was wearing earplugs because of the party next door. Just a second, but it had occurred to him in that bottomless moment of silence that there were certain things too terrible to live through, certain events he would not wish to survive.

Twenty minutes later, as he said goodbye to Victor Morley-Brown, Morris felt the long white envelope rub up against his chest like a holstered weapon. How odd it felt to him now in the quotidian afterglow of their unexpected meeting. What would Victor have said, he wondered, if he had told him the whole story: the plagiarism, the adultery, the separation, the assault, the imprisonment and now, at last, the brutal bullying revenge? Would he have taken even that in his stride? It pleased and comforted Morris, as he left the sheltering wing of the precinct and returned to the flashing wetness of the Sheffield Road, to think that he might have, to think that Victor's heroic casualness might be capacious enough to include even him.

As Morris reached the bus stop, raindrops rattled across the pavement in front of him like seed. They herded down through the early orange lamplight like sad, slow sparks. While he waited, with the wetness sponging up his socks, he thought of Zoe Cable, high in the Casa Urbano, scheming and setting traps, of Dirck van Camper at his wrap-around smart desk erecting barricades, preparing rebuttals. It was what they lived for, he knew that: outsmarting other people, being clever, cleverer, clever*est*. He closed his eyes and lost himself, by way of contrast, in the warm memory of Victor Morley-Brown and his life of cheerful underachievement. Morris had finally had, he realised with some amazement, more than enough of cleverness. He removed the long white envelope from his jacket pocket, knelt down at the kerbside and posted it, without hesitation, through the curved metal ribs of a drain.

Epilogue

'Do you remember your Madonna phase?' he said to E. They had finished dinner. Molly was in her aardvark pyjamas; Hedda was gooing and laaing in Morris's arms. The darkness of Kidney's living room was gilded and softened by ponds of pale uplighting.

'It was hardly a phase.'

'Oh I don't know. The crucifixes, the corsets – I'd say it was a phase.'

'I suppose so.' E was on her knees, tidying Lego. 'You liked it.'

'I liked its parodic quality.'

'You liked the corsets.'

'I did,' he admitted. 'I liked the corsets.'

He told her about Victor.

'He gave up!' she said.

'He grew out of it. Not that he grew into anything else. He seemed younger now than then. I hardly remembered him, but he remembered you.'

'I was obviously memorable. Did you say Judith Carmel? I knew Judith Carmel, she was a friend of Graeme and Bert – she went to their parties. She had the most fantastic house.'

'You knew everyone. You were in.'

'It was Bangor, for Christsake. It was too small for anyone to be out. Everyone was in.'

'I wasn't.'

'No that's true, you weren't.' She smiled. 'I had to bring you in. Under the cover of darkness on occasion.'

Half-asleep, Molly stumbled headfirst into the sideboard.

'There, there,' said E, pulling her up, kissing her ear. Then more briskly, 'Well I suppose those days are behind us anyway.'

'The corset days you mean?'

'No, the corset days may well be ahead of us. I mean, look at me.'

Morris looked at E's body. Everything was bigger, more dangly. In her jeans and sweater she was thick and wifely, but it just gave him a keener sense of loss. Should he tell her that?

'I was thinking more of the other stuff,' she continued.

'The fun stuff?'

'No. Well, yes, maybe the fun stuff.' She swallowed and rubbed her neck, her face seemed to harden and recede. Molly was tugging Hedda's feet.

'Sweet Hedda,' she hissed creepily, tightening her grip. Morris could hear her tiny teeth grinding.

'Molly, stop that please.' E clattered the last lumps of Lego into the box.

Molly tugged harder; Hedda turned red and squealed. Morris stood up and tried pulling Hedda away from her sister, but Molly hung on for a second then bounced off the armchair and on to the floor, screaming.

'Bath time!' E shouted.

Morris lowered Hedda into the kitchen sink. E was upstairs with Molly. After the bath, they would swap places. He would brush Molly's teeth and tell her stories. E would feed Hedda and put her down. That was the bedtime ritual. She had explained it all over dinner. On this occasion he was playing Nick Kidney, who was in New York for three days, or perhaps more precisely, he was playing Nick Kidney playing him. He was, he thought, a father twice removed, a copy of a copy.

Hedda stiffened and splashed. She opened her mouth and winked as though she had just cracked a good joke. She was a chubby child: her thighs were like lumps of Battenberg; her pale sinless flesh flared fattily above ankle and wrist. She started to pee; it rose out of her like the arc of a drinking fountain. Morris picked her up and wrapped her in a pale yellow towel. The pale yellow towel had been Molly's, he recognised it. There were things like that throughout Kidney's house: toys, rugs, a vase. It made him feel oddly at home there. He put Hedda down on the kitchen island; she pawed the air and strained like an overturned tortoise. Morris rubbed her with skin cream, then put the nappy on and then the sleeper. The thought of Kidney doing this every night filled him with rage. He could feel his face heat up, redden. Tears sprang to his eyes. Hedda's eyes widened, she smiled. Morris picked her up. She was heavy now, not like that first time when it had seemed she might easily fly away, like she was immune from gravity. She had real heft to her now. She was weighty. Morris noticed a clot of breast milk like a smear of cottage cheese on his shoulder. He could hear Molly calling from upstairs: 'Milk please Daddy.' Kidney's stainless-steel fridge was crudely edged with foam rubber. So were all his other appliances – Molly was just the right height for kitchen disaster. He poured the milk and went upstairs.

Molly was in her bedroom, looking at herself in the mirror. She had a Barbie bed, an ironic dressing table, space hoppers, tricycles, shelves of toys he had never seen. Morris felt like a burglar.

'Am I lovely?' she asked him.

Morris's face felt numb, nerveless. She *was* lovely he realised, horribly lovely, much too lovely to bear.

'Just joking,' she said with a big fake grin. She lifted up her arms and span lopsidedly on one foot. Hedda shuffled against his neck, burped. He thought for a moment that everything in this house was a source of pain.

E came in. She smiled. It was a half-smile, a smile that threatened to snap shut if he reached too far into it.

'Changeover time.' She reached for Hedda. Molly rushed at his thigh and clung. For a moment he had both of them pressed against him clinging. He felt big and perfect. He passed Hedda over to E. She started rooting madly. Morris noticed the milk patch on E's blouse; he worked to suppress his memory of her breasts, but even the suppression seemed exciting, breast-shaped. He picked up Molly with a grunt. Looking at E, he raised his eyebrows and puffed.

'I know,' she said. 'It's incredible. Remember when we washed her in the sink?'

'In the sink?' said Molly. '*No.*'

Now she smelt like a person, Morris noticed, not like a child. She had the fusty bedtime smell of a fully-fledged human being.

He brushed Molly's teeth. They were like tiny railway arches. Someone had taught her how to spit.

The problem is timing, Morris thought. The problem is having one thing but never having the other. He thought of Dirck rising from his wheelchair, healed against his will by the power of prayer: Dirck the destroyer, Dirck the redeemer. What did Morris expect? What did he really want?

He carried Molly back into her bedroom and tucked her into the Barbie bed.

'Tell me a story,' she pleaded.

'One day . . .' he was lying on the floor beside the bed, his head resting on a beanbag.

He told her a story about bears, about the difference between bears and people. Bears don't eat cornflakes, he argued, bears don't wear clothes. Molly looked sceptical: she had always been a doubter. He could see, in the luminous yellow whisper of the night-light, that groove between her eyebrows. He closed his eyes. Don't doubt me, he thought, not now.

'Isn't that right,' he said, 'about bears and people?'

She looked surprised.

'Of course it is,' she said, 'of course it's right.'

She believed him after all! They were in accord about bears and humans, about their differences. He and his daughter saw eye to eye on that at least. He lolled back into the beanbag as if that were the only truth that mattered at all: the one about bears and humans, clothes and cornflakes.

'It's perfectly true,' he said out loud.

'What? What did you say?' Molly was falling asleep. He opened his eyes and saw that hers were drooping. She looked like a doll laid flat, her eyelashes stiff and sharp.

'You can imagine the rest.'

Did he say that or think it? He could hear the ticking of the

Mickey Mouse clock, the see-saw of her breath, or was it his breath? Morris couldn't tell.

Hedda's eyes rolled back into her head, her lips lolled off E's nipple and her tiny mouth fell open, pink and cushioned like the box for a wedding ring. E could feel sleep tugging her sideways, coaxing her in. She shook her head and blinked it away. If she fell asleep now, she would lose her only child-free hours of the day. Where was Nick? She remembered now – New York. It was Morris in the other room. Christ. The crippling strangeness gripped and squeezed her. What had she done? What was she doing? She stood up. Hedda mewed, crackled then relaxed. She lowered her into the cot and wound the musical mobile. Hedda was so much easier than Molly had been. As a baby, Molly would roar and rage against sleep. Every night with her was an epic, tear-filled battle that she always lost but never seemed to learn from. She was like Morris in that way – the inarticulacy of her rage, the pointless persistence of it.

E refastened her industrial-strength bra and tucked in her breast pads. She walked across the landing to Molly's door and listened. Too late for a goodnight kiss; all she could hear was breathing. She tiptoed in. There they were, the two of them, asleep. The night-light fanned on to the wall above Morris's head like a Byzantine halo. Molly's vanilla face was cupped like an orb in her Tweeny pillow. He seemed happier now, she thought. She had noticed that in only a day and a half. Was he seeing someone? She felt a flash of jealousy and sadness. But no, it was probably just the job. Being finally out of all that. Not that working for the Chaudhary Brothers sounded like the greatest option. Wasn't there some happier middle ground? But Morris had never been good with middle ground. She stepped closer. God, they looked alike. Now more than ever – that nose, the slight backward bulge of the head. Morris snuffled and snored, stopped breathing then started again more smoothly. She should really wake him up – they had things to talk about. But she didn't.

Her love for Morris was still there, she realised. It was like an outfit hanging in her wardrobe which she didn't wear anymore, but couldn't throw away. Every now and then, when she was looking for something else, getting ready for her day, she would notice it again. Now as he lay there, silent, perfect, like a swollen echo of Molly, she thought it possible she could try it on again, it might still suit her. She took a blanket from the rocking chair and laid it over Morris so just his head was showing. He smelt of something, of what? Of Morris. She groaned at this evidence of his absoluteness.

The problem is time, E thought. The problem is having one thing but never quite having the other. She thought of Morris working in the corner shop; Morris the teamaker; Morris the fool. What did he expect, she wondered? What did he ever really want?

The Mickey Mouse clock ticked. Morris opened an eye and saw her there.

'Oh God,' he said. 'Is it really late? Have I slept for hours?'

A NOTE ON THE AUTHOR

Ian McGuire currently teaches American Literature at the University of Manchester. This is his first novel. He lives in Manchester with his wife and two children.

A NOTE ON THE TYPE

The text of this book is set in Linotype Sabon, named after the type founder, Jacques Sabon. It was designed by Jan Tschichold and jointly developed by Linotype, Monotype and Stempel, in response to a need for a typeface to be available in identical form for mechanical hot metal composition and hand composition using foundry type.

Tschichold based his design for Sabon roman on a font engraved by Garamond, and Sabon italic on a font by Granjon. It was first used in 1966 and has proved an enduring modern classic.